The Stockport Girls

Lilly Robbins grew up in Scotland, and has lived in London, Stockport, and Ireland. Whilst living and teaching in Stockport – her husband's hometown – she became fascinated by its World War Two history and the link between Stockport and Guernsey. Her later research focussed on the Italian Prisoner of War Camp located in Stockport, and the hat-making industry in the area – both of which inspired The Stockport Girls. *The Stockport Girls* is Lilly Robbins's second book after *The Nightingales in Mersey Square*.

Lilly also writes under the name of Geraldine O'Neill and has published:

Tara Flynn
Aisling Gayle
Tara's Fortune
The Grace Girls
The Flowers of Ballygrace
Tara's Destiny
Leaving Clare
Music From Home
Sarah Love
Summer's End
The House on Silver Street
A Letter from America
Music Across The Mersey
A Liverpool Secret

The Stockport Girls

LILLY ROBBINS

ORION

An Orion paperback

First published in Great Britain in 2022 by Orion Fiction
This paperback edition published in 2022 by Orion Fiction,
an imprint of The Orion Publishing Group Ltd
Carmelite House, 50 Victoria Embankment,
London EC4Y 0DZ

An Hachette UK company

1 3 5 7 9 10 8 6 4 2

A CIP catalogue record for this book is
available from the British Library.

ISBN (Mass Market Paperback) 978 1 4091 9204 6
ISBN (eBook) 978 1 4091 9205 3

Typeset at The Spartan Press Ltd,
Lymington, Hants

Printed and bound in Great Britain by Clays Ltd,
Elcograf S.p.A.

www.orionbooks.co.uk

The Stockport Girls is dedicated to my dear friend, Bernie O'Sullivan, and to the memory of her lovely husband, Brian Brady, who is missed so much.

Chapter One

Sophie lifted the hem of the dress, then stepped back to study herself in the wardrobe mirror. 'Oh, Mummy... it's absolutely perfect.'

Dorothy Morley stared at her blonde-haired daughter for a few moments. 'She's made a good job of it.'

Sophie looked back at her mother, willing her to say something nice, something complimentary. Tell her that she looked a picture in her lace wedding dress, that she was the most beautiful bride she had ever seen. The sort of things she imagined a mother would say to her daughter – her only child – when she was getting married.

Usually, Sophie and her mother loved to chat about fashions and hairstyles. Dorothy was a fine-looking, slim, blonde woman in her mid-forties who still turned heads. Sophie was a younger version of her with curly blonde hair.

Sophie ran her hand over the small silk petals on the opposite sleeve. 'The pearls and the little white flowers really lift it, don't they? They took Edna hours to sew on, but they really brighten it up. I was worried when the only dress I loved was more of a cream colour, but she knew exactly what to do to fix it.' She nodded her head. 'The whole effect is pure white now. I wouldn't want anybody thinking that we were rushing it because I was expecting.'

Dorothy's perfectly groomed eyebrows shot up. 'There's nobody stupid enough to think that. How could you be expecting when you've only known him a few weeks?'

'Oh, Mummy, don't start that again. It's long enough to know that we love each other, and that's all that matters.'

'*Love*? But you've only met each other a handful of times. You hardly know anything about him.' Dorothy moved forward so their faces were only inches apart. 'All you know is that you want to jump into bed with a handsome lad in a uniform you've only just met, and, like a lot of young girls, you think this damned war and a marriage licence gives you the right to do it straight away.'

Sophie sucked her breath in. 'It's nothing to do with Tony's being handsome or anything like that. I've never met a lad I got on so well with – a lad I can talk to properly and one who treats me like a lady. And at least I'm doing the decent thing. There are girls my age who are living away from home now and they see whoever they like and do whatever they want.'

'You don't need to tell me. I hear stories every day about how women have become loose since the war started. Going around, throwing themselves at any available men and to hell with the consequences.'

'Well, you should be pleased I'm not like that.'

Dorothy gave a huge, frustrated sigh. 'I just think that getting married this quick is sheer madness.'

'Mum ... the wedding is booked, the church and the Bluebell Hotel and everything. Tony and I are getting married next week, and I just want you to be happy for me.'

'You're caught up in all the glamour and excitement of a wedding, and he'll soon be gone again to London or Birmingham or wherever, and you'll be left here, obligated to him. You won't be able to lead a normal life like your single friends. You'll be sitting waiting for him – terrified you're going to get bad news all the time – and wondering what on earth possessed you.'

Sophie closed her eyes and shook her head. 'Can you not just be pleased for me? I know it's quick, but we really love each other. As you said, Tony will be gone back to London again soon and God knows when we will see each other again.' She held her hands out. 'Life can change overnight – when you know something is right, you have to take your chance at happiness. Look what happened to Dad . . . how quickly everything changed . . .'

Sophie's father, George Morley, had died the previous year, after complications from an operation. He had contracted polio as a young boy, and been left with a deformed and painful leg. He wore a calliper and specially made footwear, but he was a quiet, stoical man who rarely complained and just got on with things. He had developed circulatory problems in his leg, and after an emergency operation the wound became badly infected and he was readmitted to hospital. Dorothy and Alice had only been home a few hours when they received a phone call to say that George had developed septicaemia, and by the time they drove back to the hospital he had died.

Dorothy looked at her with tear-filled eyes. 'Do you think I've forgotten one minute of what happened to your father?'

'Of course not. I didn't mean to say . . .'

'The same way you didn't mean to tell this Tony about the factory?'

Sophie closed her eyes. 'That's really what's behind all this, isn't it? You think that Tony is some kind of manipulative man who only wants me because we own a factory?'

'It was the one thing I warned you about after your father died. Not to tell any lad about the factory until we were absolutely sure that he had the right feelings for you. I hoped you had more sense and would have waited until you knew for certain that he was marrying you for yourself.'

'I am certain that he's marrying me because he loves me.'

'It's a big coincidence that you tell him about the factory, and a few nights later he proposes.'

'He would have found out anyway. I couldn't keep pretending I was just an office girl.'

'You could have waited to see if he proposed without knowing about it. You'd have been sure then that he loved you.'

3

Dorothy gave a huge sigh. 'He'll think he's fallen on his feet, marrying into a family who own a factory and with no man about. A ready-made business for him to step into.'

'He doesn't need the factory. Tony has a good job as a telephone engineer, and it's important enough that he's sent to London and all over the country to maintain and repair the major telephone exchanges.' She sighed. 'Can you not accept the fact that someone might actually love me, just for myself?'

'I just want a man who would take you if you never had a penny to your name. Like your father took me.' Dorothy's face suddenly crumpled, and she searched in her cardigan sleeve for her hanky.

Sophie was taken aback to see her mother visibly upset.

'You just think I'm some old fuddy-duddy who doesn't understand all about being madly in love ... well, you're wrong. I was young once and I know what it's like to meet someone who sweeps you off your feet, and makes you think you will never meet anyone like them again.' She took a deep, shuddering breath. 'I know what it's like to make mistakes, too, and that's why I'm trying to save you from doing that.'

'But you and Daddy were happy ...'

'Oh, we were, compared to most people, we certainly were,' Dorothy said. 'And thank God I grew up in time to know the difference between a man who was good and dependable, and one who just floats along.' She looked at Sophie. 'A lot of young men these days are only good for a bit of fun – dancing and drinking, and making you feel like you're Betty Grable – but they don't always make good husbands.'

'I'm grown up enough to know the difference. Underneath his cheery nature, Tony is quiet and thoughtful.'

'It will be a long road on your own after you get married. I just don't want you regretting things.'

'I won't ... and I'm one hundred per cent sure of his feelings for me, and I know it has nothing to do with the factory.'

There was a silence now as Dorothy's face gradually softened.

'Well, since you're so determined about him, I suppose there's nothing more I can say or do.'

'You could say something nice...'

Dorothy took a few steps back to stare at her daughter. 'You make a beautiful bride,' she said. 'As nice as any I've ever seen in the magazines.'

Tears of gratitude welled up in Sophie's eyes. That was as much as she could hope for.

As she turned away now, Sophie wished for the thousandth time that her father was still alive and there for her big day. He would have understood about Tony. He was kind and easy and would have softened things between herself and her mother. But he was gone, and nothing would ever change that.

Chapter Two

Alice wrapped the carefully weighed six ounces of cheese in a square of greaseproof paper and then cut a length of brown twine and tied it up.

'Doesn't go far, does it?' Sally Parker said, putting her ration book down on the counter. 'A few sandwiches and a bit of topping on a shepherd's pie is all you get out of it. We could do with a lump of cheese double that size every day to feed our four. Thank God Jim gets fed in the railway canteen or we'd never manage.'

Alice shrugged sympathetically and handed the little parcel over. 'I find grating helps it to go a little further.' She lifted the ration book. 'Did you need anything else?'

'Plenty, but I have neither the coupons nor the money to pay for them.' Sally smiled wryly and put the cheese on top of the potatoes and onions already in her bag. She took her purse out and counted the coins to pay for them.

Alice put the money in the till and handed back the change. She then bent down to a box of vegetables and lifted out three carrots and a slightly wilted bunch of parsley. 'If these are any good to you, you're welcome to them.'

'Ah, thanks, love,' Sally said. 'That will help stretch the mince.'

Alice followed her out. 'At least it's a nice evening,' she said, coming to stand on the step at the open door. She lifted her face to the sun, its rays catching the fair streaks through her shoulder-length, light brown hair, which she had tied back for work.

'Any word from your Greg yet?' asked Sally.

'He's still at the training camp down south for a few more weeks, but they're giving him home leave before he's posted abroad. He's due home next Thursday, so he might know where he's going after that.'

'He's a brave man, isn't he? Volunteering to go out abroad again after being injured at Dunkirk.' She shook her head. 'I remember how bad he was when he came home, he could hardly walk.'

'His back is much better now, especially since he was down at the training camp. They have physical instructors there who gave him physiotherapy and exercises which have helped. He's on desk duty, and it will be the same when he goes abroad.'

'He's in one of the Army Intelligence Units, isn't he?'

'I don't really know much about it ...' Alice felt uncomfortable discussing Greg's army business, although she knew Sally was unlikely to be a German spy. *Loose lips sink ships*, and other familiar phrases had been drummed into everyone early in the war, and she thought it was better to be vague.

'You can tell by the way Greg talks, that it's an important job.'

'All the soldiers are doing their best for the country,' Alice said, 'whatever they're trained to work in.'

'Very true,' Sally agreed. 'Greg's mother was very proud of his work. She worshipped the ground he walked on, typical with an only child.'

Alice's face became solemn now. 'She was a lovely mother-in-law. It's still hard coming into the shop in the morning and her not being here.'

'That's life, isn't it? And it's more unpredictable than ever with the war on. We just have to get through every day until it's all over. I bet you're looking forward to seeing Greg again?'

'I am, especially as it's my old schoolfriend's wedding next Saturday. With Greg being posted abroad soon, he's due home leave before he goes.'

'A wedding is always lovely, isn't it? I can't remember the last time I had the occasion to get dressed up.' Sally looked down at her bulging stomach. 'Just as well, none of my dresses or costumes would zip up on me now. Havin' four kids in under six years hasn't done my figure much good.'

'You always look well,' Alice said kindly. 'And your hair is always lovely. I don't know how you have the time to curl it with all those little ones to run after.'

Sally's eyes glowed at the compliment. 'Me and my sisters always did each other's hair at home. After all these years, I could put curlers in blindfold.' They chatted for a few minutes then she said, 'I better get moving or they will be killin' each other back home.'

Alice stood for a while, her arms crossed, leaning against the door jamb, her gaze fixed over the terraced houses of Edgeley and further on to the railway viaduct of Stockport. The sound of two chattering women coming down Aberdeen Street towards the shop jolted her. She turned back inside and started tidying around the counter, and then a short while later she moved to wipe down the shelves and refill the display box of potatoes.

Her mind was filled with Greg's return, trying not to anticipate how things would work out. So much had happened since he was last home on leave. The biggest change was that instead of being a primary school teacher, Alice was now running the Fairclough's family shop. Prior to being called up, Greg and his widowed mother, Betty, had managed the corner shop together.

Alice had met the confident, twenty-three-year-old Greg at a dance when she was eighteen and studying at teacher-training college in Manchester. He was bright and confident, and full of plans for the future. Being with him made Alice feel more confident about herself, too. They got engaged after four months and married only weeks before war was declared. Alice had moved into the house attached to the shop with Greg and his mother, until the country was more settled, and then they would buy their own house.

When Greg had been posted out to France, Betty had taken over the shop, with Alice helping out on Thursday and Friday after college, and all day Saturday. The two women got on very well, and Alice found her mother-in-law to be a warmer, more easy-going person than her own mother. She found working in the shop light and easy, and a balance to her studies, and the wages helped her to be financially independent until she was qualified.

Alice was grateful that they were staying with Betty when Greg was returned from Dunkirk with injuries to his back. After having survived the brutal military campaign in France, Greg was on the beach at Dunkirk waiting to be rescued when he was thrown in the air by an explosion, which effectively finished off his active career in the army.

Returned home, he had a back operation that took months to recover from. As soon as he was up and moving again, Greg found himself bored, and, without telling Alice or Betty, he volunteered his services to the military training centres. Useful work was found for him training new recruits and helping with the piles of administrative work that grew bigger every day.

When Alice qualified, she found a teaching post in a local school, which was near enough to allow her to continue working in the shop. She enjoyed the shop work and got on well with the local customers. She also liked Maeve, from County Offaly in Ireland who worked a few afternoons, and the young local lad, Freddy Thompson, who came before school to help Betty lift the boxes and crates displayed outside. He came again after school, to brush and wash the pavement outside and assist with any odd jobs that needed doing.

Freddy, thirteen, was one of a large family from the bottom end of Edgeley, and the few shillings he got helped his mother out. His father was a heavy drinker at times, and spent money needed at home, so Betty made sure the boy had a bowl of porridge before school and shoved a sandwich in his pocket for the lunch break.

It was Freddy who found Betty, and it was Freddy who came running from the corner shop all the way up to the school in Shaw Heath to tell Alice the news about her mother-in-law. She was still in her classroom, after the children had gone, at her desk marking books when the feet came running along the corridor. Freddy threw the door open and, red-faced and panting, said, 'Mrs Fairclough wasn't well and went to have a lie down,' he said. 'Maeve asked me to run upstairs and see how she was, and I couldn't wake her. Maeve phoned an ambulance, and she's been taken down to Stockport Infirmary.'

When Alice and Freddy ran back down Shaw Heath and then Greek Street to the hospital, they discovered that Betty had suffered a heart attack at home, and then a bigger one in the ambulance. The doctors told Alice that her mother-in-law was already dead on admission to casualty. Still in shock, Alice then had the complicated task of making contact with the training unit where Greg was currently assigned, in order to break the bad news.

Greg arrived home two days before the funeral, his face strained and solemn, devastated by his mother's loss. Normally sure of himself, he was almost silent with grief until the funeral was over. A few pints of beer and several glasses of whisky helped him thank all the mourners who attended the reception in the Bluebell Hotel after Betty was laid to rest. He made sure his mother had as good a send-off as wartime allowed. The local butchers, greengrocers and bakers from Edgeley, who stocked his shop, ensured the mourners enjoyed a hot roast beef meal or cold cuts and salad. Afterwards, they had dishes of trifle or sponge cake dotted with raisins and accompanied by custard, then the waitresses came around with trays of glasses filled with sherry, whisky or brandy. Later, they walked the short distance from the Bluebell Hotel back to Aberdeen Street, Alice holding her husband's arm to stop him weaving towards the edge of the kerb.

When they came back to an empty house and darkened shop, Greg suddenly turned to Alice and said in a whisky-thickened voice, 'What's going to happen here now? We won't have my mother behind the counter. She's gone forever, and I've no idea when I'll be back...'

He had voiced the thoughts in Alice's mind when she was

making funeral arrangements with the undertaker, organising hymns and readings with the vicar, and sorting flowers. 'You've enough to think of without worrying about anything else.'

'We'll have to look for somebody who knows how to manage a shop.' He pushed his hand through his army-cut hair. 'We'll have to start interviewing and then training them to take over. God knows who we'll find that we can trust.'

Alice saw a rare look of uncertainty – almost defeat – on his face, and she felt a wave of pity for him.

'We'll have to put a notice in tomorrow's *Manchester Evening News*,' he said. 'And maybe one in the shop window. What do you think?'

To Alice, the answer was suddenly obvious. 'I'll take your mother's place.' She had seen the startled look on his face. 'I know everything that has to be done here. I'll hand in my notice at school tomorrow. They'll understand.'

'You can't give up your professional teaching job to work in a shop... it wouldn't be the same for you.' He shook his head. 'You studied hard for your qualifications, and you love the kids.'

'It's your family's shop,' she said. 'Your grandfather and your father and mother worked in it. It wouldn't be the same being run by strangers. And anyway, I'm here after school every day and at the weekends. I enjoy it. I can always go back to school when the war is over.'

There was a silence then Greg looked at her. 'Are you sure?'

She saw a huge wave of relief wash over him. 'The shop is needed here more than ever. We've long queues every morning waiting with their ration books and...' She shrugged. 'If we take on a complete stranger, I'd feel we were letting your mother down.'

Greg drew her into his arms and held her tightly. 'You're the best,' he said. 'There are times when I think you're too good for me...'

Alice had felt his breath on her face and neck, then, as he pressed against her, she had frozen. Her instincts were to pull away, but she caught herself and forced herself to relax and move closer to him. Gone were the days when she couldn't wait for him to touch and kiss her, but she knew that whatever she felt towards Greg now, she was married to him for life. The only thing that would make things easier would be the baby she had longed for.

If that happened, when Greg came home for good, things would be different. Things would fall back into place again. He would have the responsibility of being a father, and they would settle down to normal family life in time. He wouldn't have his mother there to make excuses or to cover up for him when he didn't come home when he should. In time, Alice had thought, she might also recover the feelings she once had for him.

It was now almost a year since Betty had died, and she had waved Greg off on the platform at Stockport Station. During the few days they spent together after the funeral, Alice had pushed all negative thoughts about Greg out of her mind and had comforted him in his grief.

Since the shop was closed for a few days in respect to Betty, Alice had lingered in bed with him in the mornings. Their physical closeness had helped thaw the cold spots in her heart, but in the weeks that passed after Greg's departure, the feelings began to melt away again. The baby she had hoped and planned for had not materialised.

Chapter Three

Footsteps sounded outside the empty classroom door, and when a light tap came on the pane of glass, Emily Browne lifted her head from the books she was marking. She smiled as her Guernsey colleague, Louis, came in, carrying his briefcase. 'Any luck in finding a place?'

'Not yet,' he said. 'There's a nice family in Davenport who offered to squeeze them in, but they already have two older Guernsey boys staying there, along with three of their own. I think it might be too much for the family, and I also think Philip especially would be better off in a quieter house. He's a serious child, very sensitive, and mixes better with adults than other children.'

'Is his twin sister the same?' She tucked a strand of her dark, wavy hair behind her ear.

'Gabriela is a lot more confident mixing with other people,' he said, 'but she's delicate in her own way, and gets upset about missing her family.'

Emily touched her pen to her teeth. 'It would be easier if it was only one child...'

'Yes, and of course we don't want to separate a brother and sister, especially twins. It is hard enough for them to be away from their parents all this time.' Louis shrugged. 'They were so settled, and it was such bad luck that Mrs Ponsonby became ill, and then moved to Manchester to live with her daughter. She was a lovely lady, and has looked after them for the last four years like a grandmother. Her moving away is yet another loss in their young lives.'

'Are they staying with the vicar's family again tonight?'

He nodded.

'Her next baby is due any day, so that can't be very convenient for them either.'

'I feel so sorry for them being moved from pillar to post. If we could just find them a family, or someone capable like Mrs Ponsonby, to keep them until the war is over. It might be only one more year.'

Emily sucked her breath in, thinking. 'I'll ask around,' she said, 'but most families who could help already have Guernsey children.' A thought crossed her mind. 'I'm seeing some friends tonight. It's a sort of "hen party", a women-only night out for an old schoolfriend who's getting married.'

'I've seen a few wedding parties wandering through Stockport town at the weekends,' Louis smiled. 'We have those parties back in Guernsey, too. I remember my sister's; they all ended up the worst for wear with wine.'

'They often end up like that,' Emily said, laughing. 'Although we won't be wandering through the town or anything. It's just sandwiches and a few drinks in the function room of the Bluebell Hotel.'

'I pass there on my way home from Stockport,' he told her. 'I walk up through the station and the hotel is in front of me.'

'Of course, your digs are only five minutes away from there, up in Shaw Heath,' Emily said, smiling.

'Well, I hope you enjoy your ladies' night.'

A thought suddenly struck her as he moved towards the door. 'Louis,' she said, lifting her little black book, 'if you give me the vicar's phone number, I'll ring him if I hear of anyone who might be able to help out.'

Emily cycled down towards the row of shops at Heaton Chapel, her long hair held back from her eyes by a tortoiseshell clasp. She dismounted the bike and pushed it along the road until she came to Barlow's grocery shop, which had a section for gifts and cards. She pulled the bike up onto the pavement and leaned it against the wall of the shop.

Inside, she went over to the display of birthday and special occasion cards. They had half a dozen wedding cards, so she spent a few minutes looking through them and reading the sentiments inside. She eventually decided on one that showed a couple standing beside a three-tiered wedding cake, which she felt had just the right words for Sophie. She moved towards the magazine stand, when it occurred to her that a picture of a large, decorative wedding cake might be a bit insensitive. Given the war restrictions on flour and sugar and all the other ingredients, most brides were lucky to have a one-tier wedding cake. The card might remind her of the big fancy wedding she would have had in normal times.

Emily turned back to the cards to choose another one, and found herself in the path of a young, dark-haired man in a brown working uniform, carrying an open box with a news-paper on top. He stepped to the side of the aisle to avoid her, and, unwittingly, she moved in the same direction so that they suddenly collided. He quickly moved back and then stumbled over a sack of potatoes, sending his box flying across the shop floor. Emily froze, a hand over her mouth, as the newspaper and the contents of the box rose in the air, and then clattered down onto the stone floor.

'God! I'm so sorry...' Emily gasped. 'I didn't see you. I hope you're not hurt?'

He smiled and held up both hands. 'No, no... I am OK, thank you.' He shrugged. 'It was an accident... me, too.'

Her gaze moved down to the scattering of carved wooden crosses and angels, and strings of wooden rosary beads, and her heart sank. Of all the things she could be responsible for breaking, these precious, holy objects had to be the worst. 'I'm really sorry...' She was almost afraid to look up at this polite man, who she had vaguely registered as being a foreigner. 'I hope nothing is broken...'

'No worry, signorina... miss,' he said, stooping to pick up the biggest cross. 'If it is broken, I can fix.' He placed it in the box and then moved quickly to pick up several smaller crosses and a dozen or so rosary beads. When they were all safely back in the box, he looked at her. 'I think all are OK, thank you.'

Emily felt a sense of relief wash over her, and when she looked up at him properly, she was startled to see how handsome his tanned face was, and how friendly and warm his dark brown eyes were. He was as good-looking as any film star she had seen. He smiled, and she felt an embarrassed heat rise to her face, as if he had known what she was thinking.

There was a noise behind the counter and when she looked over, she saw Mr Barlow, the heavily set shopkeeper, in his tan shop coat. He had come through from the house and was carrying a mug of tea. He looked over at Emily. 'Can I get you anything, love?'

'I'm just looking at the cards,' she said. 'I won't be a minute.'

'Take as long as you like, love.' He paused, then he put his mug down and bent to look under the counter. 'I think we have a magazine here for you. It's the *People's Friend* you get weekly, isn't it?'

'Yes,' she said, 'it's for my mother – Mrs Browne.'

'That's right,' he said, bringing the magazine up. He checked the name written on the corner. 'Don't you collect another one?'

'*Vogue*,' she told him. 'But that's monthly, and I got it from Mrs Barlow last week.'

'I don't know one ladies' magazine from another, me,' he said. 'Our Audrey deals with all of them.' He handed her the magazine.

'Thanks,' she said, putting it in her bag. She paused for a moment, slightly awkward. 'My mother sorts the paper bill at the end of the week.'

'Your family's name is good here,' he said, smiling benignly.

Emily turned back to the display area. 'I'll just get the card now.'

Mr Barlow looked over at the young man Emily had bumped into. 'All OK there, Marco?' he asked, taking a drink of his tea.

'Yes, yes, Mr Barlow. All OK. I bring more items for holy shop.'

The shopkeeper beamed at him. 'Good lad, I've got a few more orders for you since last week. My friend knows a lad who has a religious stall at one of the Manchester markets, and he likes your work.' He gestured towards the back of the shop. 'Come on in. I've just made a pot of tea, and there's a Chorley cake waiting for you.'

'Very kind of you, Mr Barlow.'

'It weren't me, lad,' he laughed. 'It was our Audrey who put the cake by for you and warned me not to touch it.' He patted his rounded stomach. 'She's limiting the sweet treats for me at the minute. Says I have to cut back, so she only gave me one instead of two or three.'

'She is very good wife,' Marco told him. 'She is looking after you.'

'So she says,' the shopkeeper said, shrugging. 'So she says. Anyroad, come into the back when you're ready.' He went off through the glass-panelled door.

Emily noticed how friendly and relaxed Mr Barlow was towards the young foreigner, and it confirmed her own instincts that he was good and decent.

Marco looked back at her now. 'Very nice to meet you.'

She smiled, not quite sure what to say, then she gestured towards the box. 'I'm glad they are all OK. I would have felt terrible if I had broken such lovely, holy things.'

'You know them?' he asked.

'Of course,' she said, smiling back. 'I'm a Catholic, and we all have rosary beads.'

'I am Catholic, too, from Italy.' His face became serious. 'But of course, now . . .' He gestured towards his work uniform. 'I am from camp – the Mellands camp.'

Emily caught her breath. He was a prisoner of war in the internment camp a few miles away. She then noticed the yellow circle on the leg of his brown trousers, which marked the Italian prisoners out. She could see he was watching for her reaction.

'I've heard of the camp...' She was unsure what to say to him now. He was not at all how she imagined any of the prisoners to be. She had seen them in the Pathé newsreels in the cinema, when they were marching along with Mussolini in their army uniforms. Later she had seen them looking battle-worn and bedraggled when they had surrendered, and afterwards seen newsreels which showed some of the Italian men working in farmers' fields, wearing the prisoners' uniform. But she had never imagined them as individual people like the young man in front of her.

Many people, including her father, were highly suspicious when they heard that some of Mussolini's supporters were living so close to them in a prisoner of war camp, although it was reported that a number of the Italians had been forced to join his army. She knew many local people were even more unhappy when they heard some inmates were allowed out to work or to do voluntary labour at the weekends. Emily herself had never heard of the Italian prisoners doing anything wrong. In fact, some of her teaching colleagues had recently been talking about how two of the camp inmates had volunteered to help at a local farm, when the husband was ill and his wife was struggling on her own.

'The camp is not so bad,' he said, sensing her discomfort. 'We are lucky – we are alive... we are fed and treated OK. Some local people like Mr Barlow, very good. They know many Italian men not want join army. Not want fight...' His gaze held hers for a few moments and then he smiled again. 'We pray God this war... will soon be gone...'

Emily smiled back at him. 'Yes, hopefully it will all be over soon.'

'Thank you.' He turned away and walked towards the counter to place the box on it.

Emily had gone back over to the card display, when she heard the footsteps behind her. When she turned, he was there again, holding out a pair of wooden rosary beads.

'A little gift for you.'

Emily looked down at the beads and then shook her head. 'That's very kind of you, but I couldn't . . .' She lowered her voice. 'You're making them to sell.' She imagined now what her parents or her friends would say if she told them she had taken a gift from a stranger she had met in a shop. Whatever they said would be magnified ten times when they discovered he was one of the Italian prisoners.

'Mr Barlow has friend who buys anything I make.' He shrugged, still holding the beads out. 'I make things very quickly; it keeps me busy at night in camp. I am very happy if you will have the rosary beads. If you please, say prayers for my family back in Italy – especially my mother.'

She looked down at his rough, work-worn hands, then silently reached to take the beads from him. 'Thank you,' she said. 'That is kind of you, and I'll use them when I am saying my prayers.' She put them in her coat pocket.

'Thank you,' he said quietly. 'I must go now.' He turned towards the counter then stopped. 'I come to shop on Monday and maybe Thursday – at this time – when I finish working in the gardens at camp. And you? Do you come to the shop?'

Emily hesitated. For all he seemed nice, she knew she couldn't give this Italian prisoner any information about herself. She shouldn't even be talking to him, and yet, something was tugging at her conscience, to treat him as she would any nice person. She looked around the shop to see if there was anyone who might know her and overhear. 'I come here on my way home from school some days . . .'

His brow creased. 'School?'

'I'm a teacher.'

His brown eyes opened wide in amazement. 'And I am a teacher, too.'

Emily was surprised, she directed her gaze to the box he was holding. 'Woodwork?'

He laughed. 'No, no, that's just . . . hobby? I am teacher. I instruct students in . . .' He halted, embarrassed now, struggling for the correct words. 'Forgive my English. I am teacher in a college in Lucca. I teach...'

'Where is Lucca?' Emily interrupted, seizing on what she thought was a simpler subject to explain.

'Lucca is... close to Florence.'

'Ah, Florence,' she said, nodding. She had seen pictures of the famous city, and knew how beautiful it was, and there was a part of her intrigued to know more. 'You must miss it – home. Your life back in Italy.'

'Of course, but some very kind people here.' He shrugged. 'I must go, Mr Barlow waiting.' He took a few steps backwards. 'Maybe I see you again here... a Monday or Thursday at this time?'

Emily suddenly realised that she had given him the wrong impression. That she had momentarily been diverted by his good looks and friendly manner, and a sense of guilt that she might have damaged the lovely items he had made. By chatting to him, and treating him like a local lad, she had given the impression that they could somehow be friends. She could just imagine her father's reaction to her taking a gift from an Italian prisoner, who he fully believed were enemies of Britain. There was no way she could explain it that would be reasonable in his eyes.

She could tell this Marco – as Mr Barlow had called him – liked her. Had they met under different circumstances – in a different world – they might well have been friends. She would have loved to hear about Florence, and places like Rome and Naples, and asked him about the food and music. The reality was, they were in Stockport in England, and she had a brother who had been killed by the Nazis. The Nazis, who Marco's country had supported and fought alongside, under that other awful dictator – Mussolini.

No matter how nice or kind this Italian fellow was – or how innocent he himself was of any war crimes – she could not entertain the idea that they might become friends of any description. It was different for Mr Barlow and his wife – they had a business arrangement, and were benefiting from his craftmanship as he was benefitting by having an outlet to sell his work. Her hand felt for the beads in her pocket now. 'I don't know when I will be here,' she said quietly, 'but thank you for the beads again.'

He smiled and said, 'You are welcome,' but she saw the disappointment in his eyes.

As she cycled home, she wondered at her foolishness in accepting the gift from him. Refusing the rosary beads would have made her feel almost sacrilegious. She could never use them, she realised. The large, wooden beads were too distinctive – too foreign – and would immediately draw attention. Even in her depressed, distracted state, her mother would notice how different they were from the usual pearl or imitation gemstones, and would wonder where they had come from.

Chapter Four

Dorothy's car pulled up outside the shop. 'Are you sure you don't want me to run you both over to the hotel?'

Sophie opened the car door. 'No, thanks, it's dry out tonight and it's only a five-minute walk over to the Bluebell.'

She had already worked out that if she accepted her mother's offer of picking Alice up and driving them to the hotel, she and her close friend would have no time to talk privately together before the party began. When they got into the hotel, the staff would be there sorting drinks and the other girls would start to arrive and they would have no chance to be alone. Getting dropped off at Alice's house an hour before was the only way they would have a chance to chat.

Sophie turned back to her mother now. 'Thanks again for the lift, Mum. Don't wait up for me, I'll get a taxi home later and I'll see you in the morning.'

'I don't mind coming back for you,' her mother said. 'I probably won't sleep until you come home. You just have to phone when you're ready.'

'No, honestly. I might go back to Alice's for a while, and I don't want to feel I'm keeping you up. An early night will do you good.' She closed the car door behind her, then, ignoring her mother's disappointed face, she smiled and gave a little wave. Without looking back, she walked smartly over to the shop door and pressed the bell.

As she waited for her friend to answer, she could see out of the corner of her eye that her mother was making no effort to move the car. She was just ready to ring again when Alice – wearing a floral dress and with her hair newly waved – opened the door wide.

She gave a welcoming smile and said, 'Is that your mother in the car?'

'Yes,' Sophie said, stepping inside. 'Don't give her any encouragement or we'll never get rid of her.'

Alice noticed Dorothy turning on the car engine again. She gave her a big wave and then closed the door behind them. 'I feel rude not asking her in.'

'Well, you needn't.'

'How are things?' Alice gave her a quizzical look.

'I need a break away from Mummy. The wedding has her up to high doh. I don't know what she would have been like if it was a really big one, like yours. In some ways, the war has done me a favour.'

'That was because Betty had to invite lots of the local business people and her best customers.' Alice gave Sophie's shoulder a sympathetic squeeze. 'Go through to the sitting room.' As she followed Sophie down the narrow hallway, she thought how lovely her friend looked – her curly blonde hair, her tall, slim figure. 'Your outfit is beautiful,' Alice said. 'You always look fabulous, but tonight you are even more fabulous than usual.'

'Oh, thank you!' Sophie said. 'You look lovely, too, and your hair is gorgeous with those waves.' She gave a low sigh. 'I'm such a nervous wreck about Saturday ... checking my dress is OK, and that everything is all organised.'

'Everything will be fine,' Alice said reassuringly. 'You'll be like something out of a fashion magazine.' She touched her hands together. 'Now, can I get you a tea or maybe a drink?'

'A drink. Definitely a drink! I need to be relaxed before we go out tonight.'

'I was going to have tea, but I'll go mad and join you. I have sherry or gin or brandy.'

'I would love a gin with orange – if you have it?'

'I do indeed, one of the little perks of having a shop. Although there's not too many these days with rationing.' She went over to the walnut cabinet in the chimney recess and opened the glass display doors, taking out two of Betty's crystal tumblers. She set them down on a side table then went to the lower part of the cupboard and retrieved a bottle of gin and a bottle of Club Orange. She poured two capfuls of gin in each glass and topped them up with orange.

'How are you managing things here on your own?' Sophie asked. 'Do you miss school?'

'Sometimes, but I'm actually happier in the shop than I would have imagined. I have young Freddy Thompson helping in the mornings and evenings, and Maeve works in the shop at the busier times. All in all, I can't complain. There are people far worse off.' She came over to Sophie and handed her a glass.

'Oh, thanks,' Sophie said, taking a big gulp. 'I suppose you miss Greg a lot?'

Alice lifted her own drink. 'Yes,' she said. 'It's strange not having him and Betty around, but what can I do?'

In truth, she missed Betty more than Greg, but she had never uttered a word of that to anyone else. What would they think if she did? Who could begin to understand her feelings? Her own parents over in Altrincham, and her sisters and brothers who lived around Stockport and Manchester, would not have any sympathy if she told them how she felt.

She was the youngest in the family – the only one who had been given a scholarship to the girls' school, where she had met Sophie and Emily, before going on to teacher-training college. She was regarded as being more cosseted, as the others had had to leave school early and go out to work after their father died. It was their financial contribution to the household that had enabled her to go to teacher-training college. After she met Greg, who had been to university, and whose family owned a thriving corner shop, she was regarded as the favoured one in the family. The one who had had the easiest time of it. Except it wasn't easy.

'Do you ever get lonely at night?' Sophie asked. 'With Betty gone and Greg away.'

'Sometimes,' Alice admitted. 'From a Thursday to Saturday, time usually flies because we're open until eight o'clock, but the other evenings are slow enough unless I'm over visiting my mother or some of the family,' she smiled. 'Or at the Plaza with you and Emily.'

Alice sat down in the armchair opposite her friend. 'I was considering getting a little dog,' she said. 'I've been asked to take a pup, and I thought it would be company for the winter coming in.'

'A dog? Oh, you lucky thing,' Sophie said. 'I've always wanted one, but my mother won't hear of it. As soon as Tony and I have our own place, I'd love a little Pekinese that I can brush and put a bow in its hair – or maybe a poodle. A white poodle. What breed were you thinking of?'

'I'm not sure what breed they are,' Alice said. 'Freddy's father has a dog – and it had four pups a few weeks ago, and he said if they don't get rid of them, he's going to drown them.'

'That's awful,' Sophie said.

'From what Freddy and his mother say, he's a devil when he takes too much drink.'

'That sort of man won't have a decent dog,' Sophie said. 'It will probably be a horrible mongrel.'

'Freddy has brought her here to the shop a few times, and she's a lovely, quiet little dog.'

'But wouldn't you prefer a little Yorkie or a Pekinese? You can get fancy little tartan coats for them.'

'I haven't made my mind up yet,' Alice said. 'It might be hard work training a pup. I'll wait and see ...'

'I want to ask you something,' Sophie suddenly said. 'With you being married already ...'

Alice's heart gave a small lurch.

'I'm really nervous about the honeymoon. It's not that I don't want to ... you know, and I'm absolutely mad about Tony. The thing is, we've spent hardly any time on our own, and I'm just a bit worried about what exactly I should do.' She took a gulp of her drink. 'I've heard that it can hurt ... and Mummy's little private talk last night didn't exactly help. She says it hurts the first time, and whether you enjoy it or not, it's something all women have to get used to if you want a good marriage. It makes it sound awful.'

Alice took a sip of the gin and orange. 'You'll be fine,' she said. 'It's only natural to feel like that; I was the same before my first time with Greg,' she smiled. 'The first time is really not that bad if you go slowly, and after that it becomes natural.'

'That's what I'm hoping,' Sophie said, 'but I can't even imagine it.'

'There wouldn't be all these people in the world if it was so difficult. When you're on your own with Tony, you'll find that it all just progresses naturally, and each time it gets better.'

'Honestly?'

'Honestly.' Alice could say that truthfully. 'When you're in love, you become so carried away, that you hardly even think about what's happening. Just tell Tony you're a bit nervous, and he'll understand and be gentle with you.'

'I was worried he might think I was being childish, especially when you hear how some girls are carrying on with American soldiers and everything.'

'He's marrying *you*,' Alice said, 'and he's not going to compare you to those kinds of girls, or expect you to be experienced with other men. I'm sure most girls are nervous the first time, but they just don't talk about it.'

Sophie suddenly smiled. 'Well, I'm glad I asked you. I feel much better about it all now.' She looked around her. 'You have the room looking really lovely.' She patted the arm of the chair she was sitting on. 'I really like the style of the sofa and chairs. You've made quite a few changes since Greg was last here, haven't you? He'll get a bit of a surprise when he comes home.'

'It desperately needed doing,' Alice told her. 'Betty kept saying she was going to buy some new pieces of furniture and get the place papered and painted, but she never got around to it. I had planned to help her during last summer school holidays, but of course…' She shrugged now, her eyes suddenly filling with tears at the thought of her lovely mother-in-law.

'It's still hard for you,' Sophie said. 'I know you were very close.'

'I never imagined how much I would miss her. We were closer in some ways than I am to my own mother.' She halted. 'I wondered about changing things, but then I thought of all the times that Betty said it would be great to do the place up and give Greg a big surprise when he came home.

'I mentioned it to him in a letter a while back. I told him I gave young Freddy's family anything I had to get rid of, and he was happy about that because his mother was very fond of Freddy, and he would have done anything for her.'

Sophie finished the last of her gin and orange. 'Does Greg's back affect him much?'

'It's improved a lot this last year, but he has to be careful with it. He's not supposed to lift anything heavy.'

Sophie looked at her. 'Does it affect him when you're… you know.'

Alice was startled at the question.

'Oh, sorry,' Sophie said. 'I shouldn't have asked such a private thing.' She shook her head. 'I'm obsessed worrying about me and Tony.'

'It's OK, I don't mind.' Alice paused. 'At times I think it's a bit uncomfortable, but not enough to put him off.' She gave a little embarrassed smile. 'He just has to be careful about the position.'

Sophie started to giggle. 'Oh God, Alice – I think the gin has gone to my head!'

Alice laughed, then lifted her glass and finished her drink. 'I think it might have gone to mine, too!' Sophie and Tony, she knew, would be fine. She had only met Tony a few times, but she liked him, and something told her he was intrinsically decent – that he would be a good husband. Whether she and Greg would ever be fine again was something she did not know. Whether that feeling of absolute love and trust would ever return again.

Alice checked her watch. 'We had best make a move in case some of the other girls arrive early. Emily asked us to be there before her, so she doesn't have to walk into the hotel on her own.'

'How is she? It's weeks since I've seen her.'

'Busy with her schoolwork and organising her Girl Guides.'

'Still no man in her life?'

'Not that I know of.'

'She's so lovely-looking and very clever.' Sophie halted. 'I would only say this to you, but I worry that Emily is a bit too serious at times, and she's never going to meet anyone if she doesn't go to more dances. She spends most of her time out of school reading or in the library planning class projects.'

'It's not exactly an easy time to meet anyone with a war going on.'

'She could wear more glamorous dresses and make a bit more effort with her make-up.'

Alice laughed now. 'You've said that for years. Since we were all in school together.'

'And it's not made a bloody bit of difference,' Sophie said, laughing. 'She's absolutely gorgeous, but she'll only make an effort when she's going somewhere special like tonight. She needs to make an effort *every* day, not just for special occasions. My mother always told me that people judge you on how you look all the time.'

'I'm glad you agree with your mother on something.'

'Another thing about Emily – being too clever can have its disadvantages. Men like to feel they're the ones who are looked up to.'

'From what you've told me, Tony is absolutely mad about you, and lets you make all the decisions. You said he treats you like a princess, the way your dad used to.'

'He does,' Sophie agreed. 'But I'm not as intellectual as you and Emily. More ordinary or light-headed, as my mother often says.'

'You're the owner of a factory,' Alice reminded her. 'And

28

you're better off financially than me or Emily. We're the ordinary ones, teaching. Or in my case now – working in a corner shop.'

'I know, I know,' Sophie said. 'But I'm not as interested in history and museums and Vikings.'

'*Vikings*?' Alice laughed. 'How often do we talk about Vikings? That's just school projects.'

'I like fashion and make-up, going to the cinema and reading about film stars in magazines.'

'I like all those things, too,' Alice said, 'and Emily buys fashion magazines.'

'I'm not even that great at work,' Sophie said. 'Really, it's my mother and the manager who run the factory. I don't mind choosing the material for the hats and the trimmings, but when it comes to the machinery and the orders and balance sheets, I don't understand half of it.'

'I was like that with the shop at first,' Alice confessed, 'but you pick things up. Learn what you need to know.'

'That just proves how clever you are.'

'It's just being adaptable, and if you were put in the same position, you would learn quick enough.'

'I still think you and Emily are cleverer than me.'

'And we are less glamorous than you,' Alice laughed. 'The world would be very boring if we were all the same.'

Sophie's face brightened. 'I never thought of it like that. And I suppose we look for different things in men to suit the differences in us?'

'I suppose so.' Alice suddenly wondered – with all she knew now – whether she would have chosen Greg or whether she would have run in the opposite direction.

Chapter Five

Emily was standing outside the door of the hotel, wondering if her friends had arrived before her. She'd spent ages getting ready, not sure what to wear as it wasn't a dance or a formal event, and had eventually settled for a floral sleeveless dress with a full skirt. She glanced through the glass part of the door, and was relieved when she saw Alice coming down the tiled corridor towards her.

'That was good timing,' Alice said, grinning. 'I've been watching from the function room window upstairs, and when I saw you come up Station Approach, I came running down.'

Emily gave her a hug. 'I'm always self-conscious going into a bar or lounge on my own in case someone thinks I'm looking for a man or that I've been stood up.'

'Me, too,' Alice agreed. She stepped back to study her friend. 'You look really glamorous tonight – your dress and your hair are gorgeous.'

'You look lovely, too.' Emily leaned in conspiratorially. 'We have to make a big effort for Sophie, she'll be dressed up to the nines as usual. I'm lucky if I have time to put on a bit of lipstick and powder before rushing out to school.'

'I'm sure Sophie wouldn't be impressed with my beauty routine for the shop. All I do is wash my face and rub on some Pond's Cold Cream, before slipping into a lovely brown shop coat, or a glamorous waxed apron if I'm handling meat or cheese.'

They fell against each other giggling as they always did when they were at school together.

'Is she already here?' Emily asked.

'She's upstairs in the function room with some of the girls from the hat factory. More are due anytime now.'

Emily slipped her arm through her friend's as they walked along the corridor towards the wide staircase, listening as Alice explained about Sophie coming round to her house earlier in the evening before they set off. 'She was a bit anxious about the wedding when she arrived, but she seems to have relaxed now.'

'It's bound to be nerve-wracking,' Emily said. 'Especially when it's all had to be arranged so quickly.'

'She'll be fine,' Alice said. 'How are you? How is school going?'

'We're doing a project on the Normans this term, so the kids are collecting egg boxes and milk bottle tops and silver paper to make shields and swords and God knows what.'

'You're brilliant at art,' Alice said. 'Let me know when you've finished the display and I'll take a trip out to the school some afternoon to see it.'

'The class would love that.'

When they reached the function room, Sophie came rushing towards them and gave Emily a big hug. She then linked both their arms and propelled them inside. 'There are some girls you haven't met, and I want to introduce my two gorgeous best friends to them.'

Alice and Emily were then taken around the group of girls, with Sophie explaining how they had met at school and been best friends ever since. They had just sat down when a waitress arrived with drinks for them.

The other girls arrived in ones and twos and gradually the small function room filled with loud chatter and laughter. The manager and a waiter set up the record player and soon music was playing above the happy babble of noise. Within minutes, some of the girls were up, jiving and swinging around the floor. Sophie went around dancing with all the girls in turn, moving on with each new tune, enjoying every minute of her pre-wedding party.

Alice and Emily came back towards their table, laughing and breathless after energetic dancing to Bing Crosby's 'Swinging on a Star'.

'I haven't had so much fun in ages,' Alice said, flopping down in her chair.

'And we'll all be dancing again at the wedding in a few days' time,' Emily laughed.

Sophie beamed around the group of girls, her eyes slightly glassy from the gin and orange. 'I've had a wonderful night, and I'm grateful to have such brilliant friends. Thanks for all the lovely cards and presents and the good advice.' She held her glass out to Alice in a salute. 'And after talking to my old married schoolfriend, let's just say, I feel much happier about my honeymoon night!'

The group of girls all whooped with laughter and Alice felt her face flush as they looked towards her expectantly. She shrugged and gave an embarrassed grin.

Sophie held her hand up. 'I won't talk about personal things publicly, but what Alice said made all the difference.' She giggled now. 'And I'm going out tomorrow to buy some fancy pieces for our first night together!'

All the other girls cheered again, and Alice laughed along with them. Whilst a little mortified, she was happy that Sophie was more relaxed about the wedding. She was also glad that Sophie hadn't mentioned her mother so far, and hoped it was a good sign for the wedding.

Two waitresses came upstairs carrying trays of sandwiches, which they set down on the tables between the girls, and then went back down to the kitchen for teapots and cups and saucers. Emily moved to sit in the chair beside Alice.

'I've just heard you're thinking of getting a dog.'

Alice made a little anguished face. 'I haven't decided yet. I thought it might be company, with the winter nights coming in and Greg away.'

'You've a few spare rooms, haven't you?'

'Yes, there's Betty's double room and a smaller, single one at the back.' She lifted a ham and tomato sandwich. 'I love dogs and it would be company at night.'

Emily leaned in towards her. 'Could I ask you a big favour?'

After what Sophie had asked her earlier on, Alice wasn't sure what to expect. 'It all depends... but go on.'

'You've heard me talking about the Guernsey children we have at the school? And the Guernsey teacher – Louis – who keeps a check on their home situations?'

Alice nodded, not quite sure where the conversation was leading.

'There are two nine-year-old children – twins – a boy and a girl, and they were with a lovely woman for the last four years. She's been very ill and has moved away, and Louis told me the children are desperate for a new home.'

'Where are they now?'

'They've been staying with the local vicar and his family, but his wife is due a baby any day, and they already have three other children.'

Alice's brow furrowed. 'Do you want me to put a notice in the shop window? Or maybe I could ask some of our customers if they could help out.'

They paused for a moment as one of the waitresses came into the room and rushed over to Sophie's table.

'I was wondering,' Emily said, 'if you might be able to help out.' Then, before Emily got a chance to say any more, Sophie called across to her.

'Emily! The waitress said you're wanted on the phone downstairs!'

'Me?' Emily said. She looked at Alice. 'Why would anybody phone me here? God, I hope there's nothing wrong at home.'

'It might not be anything serious,' Alice said. 'Go down and see.'

The waitress stopped beside her. 'It's a man on the phone.' She lowered her voice. 'A man with a funny accent.'

Emily wondered who she knew with a funny accent. Then, her stomach suddenly flipped as she remembered the handsome Italian she had met in the shop. She dismissed the ridiculous thought. She shrugged and said, 'I'd better go and find out...'

She followed the waitress down the stone stairs. They went along a small corridor behind the smoky bar – loud now with men's voices – to where the phone booth was. When she picked up the receiver, she smiled when she heard Louis's voice on the line. She was so used to him now, she no longer noticed his Guernsey accent.

'Ah, Emily, so sorry to disturb your ladies' night,' he said, his voice rushed, 'but we have an emergency with Philip and Gabriela. I am trying to contact any people I know while I can, use the vicar's phone. I remembered you saying you would be in the Bluebell Hotel.'

'What's happened?' she asked.

'The vicar's wife has had to go to hospital as her baby is suddenly arriving, and I am at the church house with all the children. I wondered if you had any luck finding a place?'

'Oh Louis, I'm sorry,' she said. Guilt struck her as she imagined him trying to manage five young children alone. He was very good with his pupils in school, but changing nappies was not an easy task for any men she knew. 'Most of the families I know have already taken in any children they can...' She could hear him taking a deep breath and could tell he was anxious. 'I hadn't time to ask around properly this evening, as I was getting ready to go out.' She hated to leave him with no hope. 'My friend, Alice, will put a notice in her shop window in the morning, and she'll ask any customers who she thinks might be able to help.'

'Maybe something good will happen tomorrow.'

'Do you need me to come and help tonight?'

'Some family relatives are coming from Poynton to stay with the children tonight, until their father is back home. I will stay until they arrive.'

'Are you OK with the younger children? With the nappies?'

He gave a little laugh. 'I am OK. I won't spoil your night of fun. I used to help with my young cousins back home, so I know what to do. The three small children are already in bed, and I am playing draughts with the twins. I'll go now and make some supper – it will help settle them.'

Emily was impressed and relieved that Louis was so resourceful. 'If I get any news tomorrow, I will ring the vicarage.' She went back upstairs, stopping at Sophie's table to reassure her nothing was wrong, and explained how Louis was helping to find accommodation for Guernsey children.

'He must really fancy you if he's ringing you here. You're obviously on his mind at night as well as during school time.'

'It's nothing like that,' Emily said, laughing. 'We just teach at the same school, and we get on well.'

'I've heard that before!'

'It's true, and anyway, he's engaged to a girl back in Guernsey.'

'What a pity.' Sophie pulled a disappointed face. 'You deserve to meet somebody special. It would be awful if you ended up a spinster schoolteacher.'

Emily caught her breath, taken aback that Sophie would say such a thing in front of the other girls. 'Thanks very much, Sophie,' she said, rolling her eyes, 'but I'm a bit young yet to be called a spinster.'

A girl called Josephine from the hat factory leaned forward. 'Ah, you're lovely! Any man would be glad to have you. It's an awful pity my brother is down in London working on the railways. He'd love to meet a girl like you. He's a surveyor, so he's like you, clever.' She gestured towards one of the other girls. 'You know our Alan, don't you, Daphne? Wouldn't they make a lovely couple?'

'Definitely,' Daphne agreed. 'Maybe when he's home on leave, you could set them up. You could write to him this week and mention Emily.'

Emily shook her head vigorously. 'Definitely not...'

'That's a great idea!' Sophie said, clapping her hands. 'When you go home tonight, Emily, find a nice photo. Remember the one we took when you and me and Alice went to Blackpool back at Easter? The one where you were wearing the yellow dress? You looked lovely in that.'

'I'm not sending any photos to a stranger,' Emily said, aghast.

'Our Alan is a lovely chap,' Josephine said, as though offended. 'Lots of girls like him, but he's just a bit shy.'

'I'm sure he is a lovely person, but I don't want a blind date.'

'We're only trying to help,' Daphne said.

Sophie held her hands up. 'When this bloody war is over, you'll meet some nice lad, Emily. Somebody perfect for you.'

'If we can all meet somebody,' Josephine said, 'there's no reason why you won't.'

Emily suddenly felt the object of everyone's pity, and her face reddened with embarrassment. Sophie held her arms out, gesturing towards all her friends. 'I just want everybody to have somebody special – somebody like my Tony.'

Emily watched as her friend lifted a schooner of sherry and took a long swig of it, then put it back on the table with a wavering hand, and she suddenly realised that Sophie was drunk! She went back to her own table, deciding to pay no heed to anything that Sophie said tonight.

Alice had kept a cup of tea and some of the sandwiches for her. 'I heard Sophie,' she said. 'Just ignore her, she's anxious about the wedding. In her own way, she's giving you a compliment, as she thinks any man would be lucky to have you.'

'It's a funny kind of compliment,' Emily replied, rolling her eyes. 'Sophie wasn't saying all that stuff before she met Tony, she always said she was happy being single.' She lifted her cup of tea and took a drink from it. 'Besides, not every couple is ecstatically happy, are they?'

'No, I'm sure they're not...' Alice said.

'The ones who get married really quickly are most likely to run into problems, because they didn't take the time to get to know each other.' Emily looked at Alice. 'At least you don't need to worry about that – you knew Greg a good while before you got married.'

'You can't guarantee anything,' Alice said. 'Nobody knows how things can turn out.' Something made her want to tell Emily how she really felt, but she stopped herself. This was a night for celebration. 'Was everything OK with your phone call?'

'God, I'd almost forgotten.' She quickly explained Louis's situation to her friend. 'He must be worried to have rung me here.'

'I was thinking about it while you were downstairs, trying to think of anyone who could help. I'd offer to help out temporarily, but I couldn't look after children properly while I was busy with customers.' She halted. 'I've been thinking that even getting a dog might be too much.'

'I wish we could take them,' Emily said quietly, 'but Mum's just not up to it. She doesn't even help much with our Mary's two girls, since . . .' She halted, biting her lip.

'Since Jack?' Alice said gently. Emily's older brother had been killed at Dunkirk, and her mother had never got over it.

Emily felt her throat tighten as it always did when she was reminded. 'She's still not herself. Some days she keeps busy cleaning and baking, but other days she goes off into a world of her own.' She shrugged. 'And she still won't go to mass – she keeps saying that there can't be a God if he causes all these terrible things to happen to families.'

'Oh, I'm sorry to hear that, I know she was very religious before . . .'

'Father Dempsey comes up to the house every few weeks, but nothing he says makes any difference. She just gets upset and angry, and I think he's more or less given up trying. Dad can't say anything right either.' She shrugged. 'So, you can see it's not the ideal place for two children.'

'Oh God, that's not easy for you, Emily. I was hoping she had improved.'

'We're all heartbroken about Jack, but we can't change it. Lots of families have people away from home. Greg is down south in training camps and Sophie will be no sooner married than she'll have to say goodbye to Tony. The worst has happened to us; Jack is dead and gone . . .'

Alice reached out and squeezed her hand. 'I hope things get better soon.'

'I'm sorry,' Emily said. 'I don't mean to cast a gloom over the evening...' She lifted her teacup and pinned a smile on her face.

'You've a lot on your plate, and you rarely complain.' There was a small pause. 'How's school going?'

Emily chatted about her recent school activities, and then she asked Alice about the shop.

'It's a completely different life now, but surprisingly, I actually enjoy it as much as school, and I have more freedom in a way.' She smiled. 'Little things, like I can have the radio on all day, and when it's not busy, I can stand and chat to people which I could never do at school.'

'And you can make cups of tea whenever you like,' Emily giggled, 'and read the newspapers and magazines without having to buy them. It sounds so good I think I might change jobs myself!'

'It sounds the perfect job, doesn't it?' Alice giggled, too. 'I must remember that when I'm getting up at half past six for the bread and milk deliveries, or if I'm dragging in wet boxes of potatoes and cabbages when the rain comes on.'

They suddenly stopped chatting when one of the girls at the other table stood up and tapped a teaspoon on a glass to get everyone's attention. 'I want us all to move the tables to the side of the room,' she said, in a high, excited voice, 'and drag your chairs into the middle. We're going to have a game of musical chairs!'

Everyone laughed, but before long the chairs were organised into a row in the centre of the room. A short while later the room was bursting with activity as the girls shrieked and laughed, chasing each other around the row of chairs in time to The Andrews Sisters singing, 'Don't Sit Under the Apple Tree'. The girls from the factory had also organised a few small prizes of perfumed soap, bath cubes and talcum powder for the winners of the games.

When the game concluded, there was another active half an hour, of dancing to The Ink Spots and Jimmy Dorsey, then the girls went back to their tables. At one point, an unsteady Sophie came over to flop in a chair beside Alice and Emily. 'What great fun it's been!' she said. 'I am so glad we organised tonight; it's done me the world of good.'

After a while, Alice left Emily and Sophie chatting, and lifted her bag and went downstairs to the ladies' toilets. When she passed the public phone, she remembered Emily's call earlier, and she wished that she could have done something to help with the children.

As she came back out into the hallway, she saw the hotel owner chatting to a slim, brunette, sophisticated-looking woman, a bit older than herself. She was wearing a floaty yellow dress cinched at the waist, and the way she held herself spoke of innate confidence. Alice was not surprised to see the middle-aged man was hanging onto every word the woman spoke, and it struck Alice that there was something familiar about her. She wondered perhaps if it was someone who occasionally came into the shop, although she looked more suited to somewhere like Bramhall than Edgeley.

The woman turned around, her eyebrows arched, and for a moment their eyes met in recognition and Alice's stomach suddenly lurched. The woman quickly turned back towards the hotel owner and carried on with her conversation.

Alice took a deep breath and moved past her as though they were strangers. Except the brunette was not a stranger. She was Marjorie Jones – the woman who had thrown a bomb into the middle of Alice's and Greg's marriage.

Back upstairs, Alice did her best to appear normal – to join in with the light-hearted chat and fun, and drink a complimentary sherry from the bar in two big gulps, which she hoped might make things fade further away. She moved around the room talking to the other girls, keeping focused on the conversation and away from the uncomfortable thoughts. She came back to sit with the bride again, and Sophie repeated the story about how her mother thought Tony was only marrying her for the factory, and how she was determined to prove her mother wrong.

As she moved back to chat to Emily again, she realised that both her friends had confided in her, and she wondered why she hadn't been brave enough to talk to Emily or Sophie about her own problems. She had considered it, but always pulled back. It was so big and so personal, that she felt her world would implode if she voiced what had happened. No one but Greg's mother knew about it, and she was gone now.

It was Betty who had comforted her and advised her through the situation, and who had suggested she say nothing to her friends. 'It'll only blacken Greg's name and it will tarnish your marriage in their eyes forever,' she warned. 'I've seen it happen before. They will never think the same of either of you again. Best to keep it private and quiet, and put it to the back of your mind. He's had a good fright now, and trust me, I know our Greg, and I know by his reaction to all this that it will never happen again.'

It had only been referred to one more time when Betty had taken Alice out for a meal to the Grosvenor Hotel. It was something so serious that they could not say the words out loud in case it led to a situation that could not be handled. It had lain silently between them in the mornings when Alice came downstairs to help Betty and Freddy bring in the milk crates, carry out the boxes of vegetables which lived outside the shop, and sort out the piles of daily newspapers for the delivery boys. But Betty knew how much it had affected Alice, and after Greg had gone down south to the training centre, she had made it her business to sort out the situation once and for all.

Whilst she adored her son as much as any mother, Betty had no illusions about Greg. When he was at school, there were several occasions when she had to put her hat and coat on and go and sort things out for him when his impulsive behaviour had got him into trouble. He had eventually knuckled down and got good results which allowed him to go to university, and he had successfully seen his course through to graduation.

Betty had been delighted when he met Alice, and couldn't believe Greg had been lucky enough to find a girl who was clever, kind and lovely-looking. As they got to know each other better – and as Alice had become more confident in their relationship – Betty began to look on her as the daughter she had always wanted. She knew Greg was unlikely to meet anyone half as good, and did everything she could to encourage the romance without interfering. After the sudden engagement, both women were on a firmer footing, and Alice was able to open up to the warm-hearted shopkeeper and soon began to view her as a second mother.

When Marjorie Jones first appeared at the shop looking for Greg, and threatening to tell Alice about their affair, Betty knew she had too much to lose if she allowed the situation to continue. It only took her a few weeks to find out what she was dealing with, and then she made her move.

After a few glasses of wine, she had told Alice that she had nothing more to worry about.

'I've been out to Didsbury to see that particular lady,' Betty told her. 'And I've left her under no uncertain terms about keeping well away from this area and our Greg when he comes home on leave. I told her not to write to him or contact him ever again, or I would see to it that her behaviour would become known, and it would hurt her in more ways than one.'

'What do you mean?' Alice had asked.

'Well, I told her I would let her family know what she'd been getting up to, but she didn't seem to be too concerned about that. Sounds like they were no better than her, but I had another trick up my sleeve that knocked her off her perch. I found out that she had a good job in one of the banks in Didsbury, and I told her that they wouldn't look too kindly on one of their staff making overtures to a married man. I warned her that I would write not just to the manager of the bank, but to the area manager as well.'

Alice had closed her eyes to hold back the tears that were threatening. 'It's awful,' she said, 'every time I think of Greg with her. I never suspected or imagined he would do that to me. I feel so stupid.'

'Well, don't,' Betty had told her. 'It's him that was the stupid one, and I'd say he knew it as soon as it happened. When I confronted him, he broke down and asked me to help him sort it all out so that he didn't lose you. He's learned his lesson.'

Although Alice had felt sorry for Betty having to deal with all this – for having to sort out her son's mess – she felt sick to her stomach reliving this nightmare again. During the day, she was so busy in school with the children, she hadn't time to keep thinking about Greg and this other woman.

Alice had gradually managed to put it to the back of her mind, and Greg had done everything to make up for his mistake, both in his letters and on his last two leaves home. But the incident left a wound that had still not healed, and seeing the woman again tonight had opened it up again. She had also been reminded that although undoubtedly glamorous, Marjorie Jones was older than Greg, and that somehow made Alice feel even worse.

Alice smiled now as Sophie told the girls about the lovely wedding presents she had received, and then giggled when asked about their honeymoon plans. They were all impressed when she said her Uncle James was paying for her and Tony to have two nights in the prestigious Midland Hotel in Manchester.

'He knows one of the managers,' Sophie said, 'so he got a good rate. I've been for afternoon tea there a few times, and it's gorgeous, so I'm really looking forward to it.'

'My older sister had her honeymoon in the Palace in Buxton,' Josephine said. 'It's posh there, too, but it's been closed down since the war started. It's been taken over by the government for some kind of offices.' She shrugged. 'I bet all the lovely furniture and carpets are ruined.'

'Well, the Midland is the top place in Manchester,' Emily said, 'so the carpets and furniture will be perfect – you'll be well spoiled there.'

'I doubt if they'll even notice!' Josephine said. 'The only thing that Sophie will be looking at will be the ceiling!'

The other girls screeched with laughter now, and one asked Sophie what kind of lingerie she planned to buy for her wedding night, and that brought more ribald remarks and laughter.

'That's for me to know and you to wonder!' Sophie told them.

'Well, just in case you hadn't thought of it,' Rosemary, a girl from the office in the hat factory, said, 'we clubbed together and bought you a little present.' She handed over a box wrapped in wedding paper with a big satin blue bow.

Sophie's eyes widened. 'I'm afraid to open this,' she said. She untied the ribbons then she carefully opened the gift paper to reveal a box with the name of Kendals department store in Manchester. She held her breath and then she lifted out two pairs of lace-edged, silk knickers, silk stockings and a white lace garter with blue flowers and a tiny horseshoe on it for good luck.

'It's too much!' Sophie protested. 'You've all given me lovely wedding gifts…'

'This present was for Tony!' Rosemary laughed. 'We thought he would enjoy unwrapping it all on your wedding night!'

Again, there were ribald comments and whoops of laughter.

Just as they settled back down again, the landlord of the hotel came in to announce that if they were interested, there was a three-piece band with a singer coming on downstairs in the lounge.

'Bring your drinks downstairs with you, girls,' he told them, 'and I'll make sure you all get seats and another drink on the house. We have a new singer, and from what I've heard, we won't be disappointed.' He lowered his voice. 'I'd be grateful for your opinion because we're trying to encourage the local lads to bring their women here on the weekend nights, and we want entertainment that appeals to the girls.'

As the group made their unsteady way downstairs, they could hear the band playing Glenn Miller's 'Moonlight Serenade'.

Alice, glad of the distraction, lifted her handbag and gin and orange and followed Emily to the bar floor.

'It's been a great night,' Emily said. 'It's done me the world of good to get out of the house and to have a bit of a laugh with everyone.'

'Me, too,' Alice said. 'I know I'll probably pay for the late night and having a drink in the morning, but it's been worth it.' She held her glass up and smiled. 'This is my last one, or I'll have to keep the "Closed" sign on the shop door all day.'

'I wish I could put "Closed" up on my classroom door!' Emily said, laughing. 'I'll probably regret it, but we don't get many nights out together like this, and who knows what tomorrow might bring?'

They were both surprised to see the crowds in the front hallway, spilling out from the lounge downstairs. The landlord appeared at the door of the lounge and beckoned the girls. 'You have seats in here beside your friends.'

The girls made their way through the groups and into the small, dimly lit, smoke-filled lounge. Sophie waved to them, indicating two seats over at the window. The band now moved on to play the opening bars of 'Lili Marlene', and as everyone cheered at the sound of the popular song, the male singer gestured towards the door, and said, 'We have our own Lili Marlene here tonight from Didsbury, and I'd like you all to give her a very warm welcome.'

Alice froze in her chair as she saw Marjorie Jones, watching her lift her head high before making her way through the crowded room. She was not conventionally beautiful, and Alice knew she herself was younger and prettier, but there was something about the woman that turned heads.

The band repeated the opening bars again and as she started into 'Lili Marlene' – her voice as clear and true as Vera Lynn – the crowd hushed into silence. Alice sat watching, both tormented and horribly mesmerised by this sophisticated and talented woman. And, as she listened to the lyrics – about a soldier pining for his lover – she pictured Greg and the singer together, and she was immediately taken back to that awful time again, when her heartbroken mother-in-law had had to sit her down and tell her that Greg had been unfaithful to her. And worse, that the woman now singing in this room had had the nerve to come into the shop looking for information about Greg and to tell Betty the sordid details of their brief relationship.

Alice had never known how and when they met, as Betty had told her that the less she knew, the less hurt she would be. She guessed now that he had come across Marjorie singing in one of the pubs or clubs in Stockport or Manchester that he went to with his friends. She could see how some men, especially after a few drinks, would be drawn to her, but it had never occurred to her that Greg would be like that. More fool her, she realised. She watched now as Marjorie Jones closed her eyes, swaying to the side, singing, '*Darling I'd caress you, and press you to my heart...*' A suffocating feeling came up her chest and into her throat, and she knew she had to get out of the place before she made a fool of herself.

She bent down for her handbag, and as she did so, she was suddenly distracted by movement further along the row. She looked and saw Sophie coming towards her, a stricken look on her face, trying to clamber past the other girls. Then Alice heard her saying, 'I need to get out, I'm going to be sick!'

Alice got to her feet quick and moved out of the seats. She then caught Sophie's arm as she came past, and steered her out of the dimly lit lounge and into the hallway. Sophie was weaving about, and at one point, fell against the wall.

'Oh my God... I feel terrible. I'm seeing everything double...'

'You've just had a bit too much to drink,' Alice told her. 'You'll be all right when it wears off.'

They just made it into the ladies' toilets in time for Sophie to throw up in the sink. She stopped for a few moments, then turned quickly to the toilet cubicle, retching loudly.

Alice was outside, opening a packet of paper hankies she had rescued from her handbag, ready to hand to her friend. She turned as the door from the hall was pushed open and Emily came in, her eyes wide with concern. 'Is she OK?'

Alice shrugged and made a little face. She took a few steps closer to the cubicle. 'How are you now?' she called. 'Do you feel any better?' Sophie didn't answer, then a few moments later, they could hear her being sick again.

When she was finished, she made a low, moaning noise, and a short while later the cubicle door opened. Alice and Emily rushed towards her in case she needed catching. 'I'm so sorry...' she said, slumping against the wall. 'I've drunk far too much...'

'Don't worry,' Alice said in a soothing voice. 'You'll feel better now you've got everything up.'

'I've never, ever... ever drunk that much before. Never...' Her voice suddenly rose. 'What will my mother say if she sees me like this? I can't go home. She'll go mad...'

'You can come back with me,' Alice said, 'and wait until you feel all right.' She handed her the paper hankies now, and Sophie dabbed her mouth.

She threw the hankies down the toilet and flushed it, and then made her wavering way back out towards the sink and mirror. She washed her hands, and then cupped them under the cold water and drank a little to freshen her mouth. Then she leaned both hands on the edge of the sink and stood with her head bowed.

Alice put her arm around her shoulder. 'Do you feel well enough to walk home now?'

Sophie took a deep breath and straightened up. 'I'll try,' she said, 'although I'm still seeing double of everything.'

'The walk out in the fresh air will do you good,' Emily said.

'What would Tony think if he saw the state of me?'

'He would understand that it was the excitement of the night, and he would probably just laugh. He'd want to look after you, and make sure you were OK.'

Sophie's face brightened a little. 'He would, wouldn't he? That's what he's like...' she said, her voice high and slurring.

'That's exactly what Tony's like. He's kind and he looks after me...' she smiled. 'That's why I'm marrying him, isn't it?'

'It is,' Alice said. 'He's a lovely chap.' She paused. 'Are you up to walking back?'

Sophie moved her shoulders in a helpless gesture.

Emily moved to one side and linked her arm. 'We'll get you home, won't we, Alice?'

Alice came to take her other arm. 'We certainly will. Isn't that what friends are for?'

'You are the most wonderful friends... and you always make me feel better. I don't know what I'd do without you.'

'The three musketeers,' Emily said, as they moved out into the hallway. As Sophie swayed, the other two caught her and steadied her up.

There was no one around in the corridor, and Alice felt her stomach clench as they came towards the lounge. She kept her gaze straight ahead as they passed the open door of the dim, smoke-filled room. She heard everyone laughing and talking, and then she heard the band striking up again. She realised, with great relief, that she was unlikely now to run into Marjorie Jones, if she was still on stage. As they made their way along the black and white tiled floor towards the main double-doors, she though how fortuitous it had been that poor Sophie had got sick. It meant that she could make her early escape without any explanations.

When they came to the inside doors, Alice held onto Sophie while Emily went ahead to push the heavy outer door open for them. Just as they moved forward, the band struck up the opening bars of Vera Lynn's popular song, and Marjorie Jones's voice could be heard clearly singing the immortal words, '*We'll meet again.*'

Alice felt a surge of anger. '*No, we won't meet again*!' she thought. '*No, we bloody well won't*!'

Chapter Six

Emily looked at Sophie, who was fast asleep in the armchair in front of the fire. 'What will we do with her?'

'Nothing for the time being,' Alice said. 'We'll let her have a sleep for an hour or two, and then we'll wake her up and give her some tea, and see how she is after that.'

'I've heard black coffee is good for people who've drunk too much,' Emily said, 'although I don't think I could drink it.'

'I have a tin of coffee out in the kitchen cupboard, Greg likes it now and again. We'll try to get her to drink some when she wakes up.'

'I hope she's OK – her mother will go mad if she sees the state she's in.'

'Hopefully she will come round.' Alice glanced at the clock. 'It's only half past nine. We have a few hours to sober her up.' She could just imagine how Dorothy Morley would be, especially with all the things Sophie had said about her mother earlier. Alice wondered if she had confided the same things to Emily, but thought it best to say nothing, in case Sophie woke up and heard them discussing her. She beckoned to Emily now. 'Will we go into the kitchen and have a cup of tea?' she said in a low voice. 'We don't want to disturb her here.'

Emily lifted her bag and followed Alice into the next room. She sat down at the table while Alice put the kettle on. When she was offered a tin containing digestive biscuits, she shook her head. 'I can't believe I'm actually turning down a biscuit, but I'm too full after the lovely food in the hotel.'

Alice put out cups and saucers, and then brought the pot of tea over to the table and sat down with her friend. 'I'm quite glad we got home early,' she said, filling the cups, 'because I've got a baker's delivery coming in the morning.'

'It seems much later,' Emily said, pouring milk in her tea. 'I feel we've been out for hours. I wonder how all the others are getting on back at the hotel, and if they minded Sophie leaving them in the lurch.'

'I don't think they would have minded; they could see she was more than a bit tipsy.'

'They probably stayed downstairs until the band was finished,' Emily said. 'And then they will have gone back upstairs to finish off any sandwiches or cakes that were left.'

'The girls from the factory are a lively bunch, aren't they?'

Emily rolled her eyes. 'To be honest,' she said, 'I found them all a bit much, too familiar, especially when they were going on about finding me a boyfriend. And I could have killed Sophie for telling them she's worried that I'm going to end up a lonely spinster schoolteacher.'

Alice touched her finger to her lips.

'I don't care if she wakes up now and hears me,' Emily said, 'because I'm going to tell her off for showing me up like that.'

Alice put her hands on Emily's arm and gave her a friendly squeeze. 'I'm sure she didn't mean to upset you, she was just so excited about the wedding and everything.'

'I felt mortified with them all going on about it. Did you hear them trying to arrange blind dates for me with people's brothers and any other waifs or strays they could think of?' She gave a huge sigh. 'Surely everybody doesn't see me as such a hopeless case?'

Alice wrinkled her forehead. 'Of course they don't. Sophie and I have always said you were the best-looking girl in the class.'

'Thanks, but it still doesn't make me feel any better.' Emily rolled her eyes. 'Those girls trying to give me advice and fix me up with anyone they could think of. Good God, I never imagined I would be an object of pity to girls like that. They all think that finding a man is the answer to everything.'

'They're not that bad,' Alice said. 'Everyone was just giddy and enjoying the night. I'm sure they would feel terrible if they thought they had upset you.'

'I'm not upset,' Emily said. 'I'm bloody *annoyed*! I'm actually happy on my own, I love my job and I'm happy going to the pictures or dancing at the weekend, or going into Manchester. I'm sure I have a far more interesting life than some of those factory girls.'

Alice started to laugh. 'You're taking it too seriously, Emily. The girls didn't mean any harm, they probably talk like that at work all the time. They won't realise you're more intellectual than them, and that you're not looking for the average type of fellow.'

Emily looked flummoxed. 'Me, intellectual?'

'Of course, you're interested in art and music and all that sort of thing.'

'You like cultured things, too,' she argued, 'but I never heard Sophie saying you might become a lonely old spinster.'

Alice started to laugh now. 'I guarantee you are not going to be a spinster! When you least expect it – when you're at an art exhibition or in a bookshop or somewhere like that – Mr Right will suddenly pop up, and you will know straight away.'

'Is that how it was with you and Greg? Did you find you had a lot in common?'

'I suppose we liked the usual things like the cinema and dancing. Greg loves music, jazz and the big bands, so we often went into Manchester where the popular bands play.'

'That small band was good tonight, especially the singer. She was very glamorous, too, wasn't she?'

Alice swallowed hard, trying to think of something to say. 'Yes, I suppose she was...'

'Have I said something wrong?' Emily rolled her eyes. 'Sorry if I went on a bit too much about the girls earlier...'

'No,' Alice said. 'It's not you. It was that woman who upset me – the singer.'

Emily's brow wrinkled. 'What did she do? Were you talking to her?'

'No, not tonight... but I know her.' She put her cup down on the saucer and closed her eyes. She suddenly knew that she could not keep this awful secret buried inside her any longer. She could not be a hypocrite, letting Emily believe that she and Greg were happily married, when part of her was dreading his return. She looked up. 'Greg had an affair with her.'

Emily looked at her in shock. 'Are you serious?'

'Deadly serious,' Alice told her. 'I got the shock of my life when I saw her earlier this evening, when I went down to the ladies'. I thought she was just in briefly talking to the manager, and then I nearly died when she appeared again and got up on the stage.'

'Oh, Alice...' Emily reached her hand out and covered her friend's. 'And you've kept this to yourself all this time?'

'Betty knew.'

'Greg's mother? Oh my God...'

'She sorted the whole thing out, so that I didn't have to deal with it.'

'How did you find out about it?'

'She turned up at the shop one afternoon, looking for Greg. It was a school day, so I wasn't around. Betty knew instantly that there was something going on.'

'Was Greg home at the time?'

'He had been home on leave and had just left that morning. Betty asked her what she wanted with a married man, and she could tell by her reaction that she didn't know he was married. It seems he had written and told her he would see her when he was home, and then he must have had cold feet. Betty didn't tell me the first time she came around, she just warned her off and hoped she wouldn't come back. It was when she came the second time, on a Saturday, that she caught me on my own.'

Emily's eyes widened. 'God ... what happened?'

'She just appeared in the shop and asked me if I was Greg's wife, then she told me her name and asked if Betty had mentioned her previous visit. When I said she hadn't, she said that she met Greg in a hotel in Manchester, and he had given the impression that he was a single man. They met up several times and then Greg was posted down to London. When she visited him down there, she said she saw a letter from his mother with the shop address in Edgeley. He had told Marjorie Jones that he lived in Davenport, so the letter aroused her suspicions. When she read on, she could tell from what Betty wrote that Greg was a married man.'

'What happened then?'

'She confronted him, and she said he broke down, telling her that our marriage had been a huge mistake, and that he was going to get a divorce when the war was over.'

Emily's hands came up to her mouth. 'Oh my God ... You don't believe it all, do you?'

'I was so shocked, I didn't know what to think,' Alice said in a flat voice. 'But she said he convinced her that it was only a matter of time until he was a free man. He said until he met her, he hadn't had the courage because his mother adored me, and he felt trapped.'

'If it's true,' Emily said, 'then Greg Fairclough is the best actor there's ever been. He always gave the impression he idolised you.'

'He wouldn't have been running about with another woman if he cared about me at all.'

Until Marjorie Jones walked into their lives, Alice realised that she had taken it for granted that Greg absolutely loved her. He had always had an easy, confident manner with women, which she had put down to working in the shop, but she had never once suspected that he was capable of being unfaithful to her. She had never questioned him going out with his army pals, and coming in at all hours because they had ended up in some place in Manchester with late-night jazz. Looking back, she felt ridiculous for trusting him so implicitly.

'She's a horrible woman,' Emily said indignantly. 'God knows what he saw in her. She's not as nice-looking or as classy as you, and she must be a good bit older than Greg.'

Alice shrugged. 'I thought all that, too, but she's still an attractive woman and a talented singer. Greg's always been fascinated by musicians and performers, so I can easily imagine that he would have got chatting to her when she came off the stage.'

'It looks like it was only a fling,' Emily said. 'Could you honestly imagine Greg being with a woman who was out every night singing? He would soon get fed up with that.'

'That was only her part-time job,' Alice said. 'Betty found out that she had a good job in a bank in Didsbury. After Marjorie Jones came to see me, Betty threated to tell her boss she had been running around with a married man.'

'Did it work?'

'She said she hadn't come to see me to cause trouble, and she had no intention of seeing Greg again. It was to tell me what had happened so I would know the kind of man I was married to.'

'So, what happened then?' Emily was intrigued now.

'The night after Betty visited Marjorie Jones, she sat me down and told me how disappointed and disgusted she was with Greg. She also said she would tell Greg she was one hundred per cent on my side whatever I chose to do. She then poured us both a brandy, and told me about couples she knew that had split up over affairs, and how difficult it could be for the woman. She then helped me to look at all my options, and said if I stayed, she would make sure I was well looked after, and that she would put half the shop in my name so if anything happened to her, Greg would only get half. She also said that if Greg misbehaved again, she wouldn't expect me to stay, and that she would still leave half the shop to me.'

'What a brilliant woman!' Emily said. 'She really must think the world of you to do that. So how did Greg react when he came back home?'

'Both Betty and Marjorie Jones had been in touch with him, so he had time to work things out. He said that Marjorie had known he was married and became obsessed by him. He also said that it hadn't been a full physical relationship, no matter what she says. It was just a terrible, stupid mistake that he had learned a very hard lesson from.' She looked up at Emily with sad eyes. 'I've never been sure whether he was telling the truth or not.'

'But you're OK now … aren't you?'

Alice sighed. 'I just don't know. I was still numb about it all when he came home, but I felt I had to at least give it a try – for our sake and for Betty. We got through that next visit home, and in fairness, Greg did everything he could to reassure me. He didn't move out of the house without me knowing where he was going, and was back in early every night. And then, of course, poor Betty died and when he came back everything was about his mother and the funeral. We didn't even talk about it.'

'It sounds awful,' Emily said, 'but as if the worst is over. A lot of couples have things like this happen and they get over it. Greg will be terrified of losing you; he'll know he would never meet anyone like you again. I read somewhere recently that the war makes a lot of men afraid, and they do stupid things – drinking too much, getting into fights, and carrying on with other women.' She paused. 'It even makes some women behave recklessly, too, not knowing what's going to happen the next day or the next week. Lots of them are just grabbing a bit of fun or happiness while they can.'

'I wish I could imagine feeling truly happy again.'

'You'll be fine,' Emily said.

'I hope so.' Alice managed a weak smile. 'If it makes you feel any better, I wish I was in your shoes at the moment. Being a spinster teacher with nobody to worry about but yourself seems like an enviable option.'

A noise in the other room suddenly startled them, then they both moved quickly as they heard the bride-to-be suddenly vomiting.

Emily and Sophie turned to wave goodbye to Alice, then set off with linked arms, down Aberdeen Street to Wellington Road to catch their late buses home.

'Thank goodness there's a bright moon,' Sophie said. 'I'm always afraid of tripping over something in the blackout, and it could easily happen the way I am tonight.'

'How are you feeling now?' After being sick on Alice's hearth rug, she had sunk back into a deep sleep for another hour, and when she reawoke, she was more compos mentis. After two strong coffees with a slice of toast and a Beechams Powder, she had rallied around to almost normal.

'Not as bad as before. At least I can see one thing at a time – that double vision was horrendous. I can't believe the state I got into. I've never drunk that much before in my life. What will all the girls think of me?'

'They won't care,' Emily reassured her. 'Some of them might end up worse as they probably had a few more after we left.'

'I can't remember the end of the night or walking back to Alice's. I hope I didn't do or say anything stupid...'

'Apart from calling me a lonely spinster and trying to pair me off with any man under the age of seventy, everything else was fine.'

'What?' Sophie attempted a smile. 'Tell me you're joking...'

'Half joking.'

'Did I really say stupid things like that? Oh God, I'm so sorry, Emily. You know I didn't mean anything – I would never upset you.' She shook her head. 'I don't know what else to say because I honestly haven't a clue what I said.'

'It's OK.' Emily's voice was more light-hearted now. 'I'll forgive you. Just don't go announcing that you're looking for a man for me at your wedding, or I'll be straight out of the door.' After listening to poor Alice's shocking revelation, she realised she had little to complain about. In fact, she was now beginning to think that she was actually lucky. Not that she fancied being single forever, but she realised she had more options in her life. There was no rush. Far better to take her time – making absolutely sure that she had found the right person – before she tied herself down. As Alice had done. As Sophie was about to do.

'I promise I won't ever say anything like that again,' Sophie said, her voice contrite. 'And thanks so much for looking after me tonight. You and Alice are great friends, and you are the last people in the world I would want to offend. You do know that, don't you?'

'Yes, I know you didn't really mean it.'

'I don't usually drink much either, and I'm going to be very careful from now on.'

'Forget about it,' Emily said. 'It was a special night, and everyone had a bit too much to drink.' She thought now of her own overreaction to Sophie and the girls. 'We should just remember the lovely parts of the night. It was such a laugh when we played musical chairs, I don't think I've giggled like that in ages.'

'We were lucky the Bluebell had a band on mid-week, even though we missed the end. The singer was good, wasn't she?' Sophie raised her eyebrows. 'And very glamorous – you can see she puts a lot of effort into her appearance.'

'Yes,' Emily said. 'You can.'

She was glad now that Alice was not with them, and hoped that things settled down when Greg came home.

Sophie got off the bus at the Alma Lodge and then walked for a few minutes back towards their house, still feeling the effects of all the drinks she had consumed throughout the evening.

When she saw the light on in the front room, she straightened herself up to try to appear sober when her mother opened the door.

'I have the kettle boiling, so we'll go into the kitchen,' her mother said as they walked down the hallway. 'I'm glad you're not too late. I thought we would have a cup of tea now before bed, as I'd like to have a little chat with you.'

Sophie took a deep breath and reminded herself to enunciate her words carefully. 'Is anything the matter?'

'Nothing at all to worry about,' Dorothy said. 'Just a little bit of news for you, darling. Good, I hope.' They headed into the kitchen, and she went to the cooker to pour the boiling water into the teapot. 'A change of wedding plan – but only if you agree. It's entirely up to you and Tony.'

Sophie felt slightly alarmed. 'What kind of change?'

'After I left you at Alice's tonight, I thought about your father. I thought what he would have wanted for you, and I know it would not have been a hurried wedding in a small, backstreet hotel.' Sophie opened her mouth, but before she could say anything, her mother rushed on. 'So, I drove straight up to the Grosvenor,' she said, 'and I went in and asked to see the function manager. To cut a long story short, they have a space on Saturday and – if you and Tony wish it – we can have your wedding breakfast there.'

Sophie stared at her. 'But the arrangements are all made . . .'

'Yes,' her mother said, 'and I explained that. I said that under normal circumstances we would have gone to the Grosvenor, but you were trying to be independent sorting things yourself. I told the manager I would speak to you and, if you agreed to change hotels, then I would speak to the Bluebell Hotel.'

'They might be angry,' Sophie said. 'They might have already started the arrangements.'

'I'm sure they won't mind, and I'll offer to compensate them for any money they have already laid out. I doubt if there will be any huge problems given that you booked it so recently. Besides, I know the owner's wife and I'm sure she will smooth anything over for me when I explain what happened. I'll also offer to book the factory summer dance there and a few of our ladies' functions, too, so they will get more business in the long run.' She hurried along before Sophie could interrupt her.

'I know it's absolutely what your father would want, darling, and I should have thought about it when you were making the arrangements.' She wrung her hands together. 'I was so flustered about everything happening so quickly that I didn't look at the bigger picture – what Daddy would have wanted for you.'

'I don't know what to think,' Sophie said.

'I'm sorry that I reacted the way I did, and I want to make it up to you by having the best possible wedding you can have under the circumstances.' She went over and put her arms around Sophie. 'You're my only child, and I don't want you looking back on your big day and feeling that it wasn't what we had all imagined. That it wasn't what you deserved.'

As her mother went to pour the tea out for them, Sophie tried to digest all her mother had said. Her brain was still foggy, but it seemed that she didn't need to do a thing. Her mother appeared to have it all under control. She imagined now how much more glamorous it would be in the grander surroundings, the space, the decorations, the bigger dance floor. Tony, she knew, would not care. He told Sophie to pick whatever place she liked and that they could afford, as she knew much more about these things than he did. If she was happy with everything about their wedding, then he would be happy, too.

Dorothy placed a mug of tea in front of her then lifted her own mug and sat down at the table next to her. 'Any thoughts?' she said quietly.

Sophie looked at her. 'Are you sure? It will be much more expensive.'

'It will be worth every penny,' her mother said. 'I had planned to pay for the wedding in any case. Your father was a traditional man and would not have heard otherwise.' She looked directly at Sophie now. 'This has got to be your choice. I will be equally as happy in the smaller hotel if that's what you truly want. There will be no more arguments. I want this wedding to be as close to the one you dreamed of before this wretched war. I want you to have it with my love and my blessing.'

Tears welled up in Sophie's eyes. 'Thank you,' she said. 'Giving us your blessing means more to me than anything.'

Dorothy moved now to put her arms around Sophie. 'Thank *you*,' she said. 'I will have all the arrangements made in the morning.' She paused. 'And I am looking forward to welcoming Tony into our family.'

Chapter Seven

Alice woke at three o'clock in the morning, her mouth dry and with a dull headache. She could only imagine how poor Sophie must feel, having drunk more. She went downstairs and got a drink of water and two aspirins, then headed back upstairs. She dozed until five o'clock and then she tossed and turned for a while.

At six o'clock she gave up trying to sleep and went downstairs to the kitchen in her dressing gown, grateful that her headache had gone, and that she felt almost like her normal self. She lit the gas stove and put the kettle on, and while it was boiling, she went to clear the ashes from the fireplace. Using a small black shovel and a wooden hand brush, she quickly emptied the end of the previous night's fire into a galvanised bucket, carefully laying aside the larger cinders to use in lighting the fresh fire.

She went out the back door to empty the bucket into the larger ash bin. All was quiet, nobody as yet moving outside from any of the other houses, not even a dog barking. As she turned to go back into the house, she stopped and stood looking beyond the rooftops of the red-bricked terraces at the grey, early morning sky. There were already patches of blue, echoing the forecast on the radio, which had said it would be a warm, sunny day, but Alice knew that the weather would make no difference to how she felt today. She had been through this before, thought that after Betty's death she had managed to put it all behind her. Seeing Marjorie Jones last night had brought back the dark memories as though it had just happened.

Once again, all the colour had been washed out of her life.

Back inside, Alice went through the mindless routine of rolling up old newspapers then placing pieces of Zip firelighter on top. She added the cinders and some small pieces of wood which she sold in bundles in the shop, then she placed half a dozen pieces of coal. She then lit a fire taper from the flame under the nearly boiled kettle and went back with it to set fire to the papers and firelighters.

She had just made a pot of tea and lit the grill to make a slice of toast when she heard the gate at the side of the shop banging open, and saw Freddy going past the kitchen window towards the back door. She glanced at the clock and wondered what on earth had brought him to the shop over half an hour early. She moved to let him in, and then stopped when she heard him speaking to someone.

Freddy gave a loud bang on the door, and when Alice opened it quickly, he looked surprised. 'I didn't know if you would be downstairs yet...'

'What's wrong?' she asked. 'Why are you up so early?'

'Me Dad,' he said.

Alice looked down at the brown and white bundle in his arms, which she recognised as his little dog, Bella. 'Come in,' she told him. 'We'll go into the kitchen.'

Freddy followed her down the hallway, talking as he went along. 'Last night me dad said if I didn't get rid of Bella, he was going to drown her. He got drunk in the afternoon and he's been in a bad mood ever since. Me mam was upset, and the two little ones were crying with all the shouting, so I took them down to my Auntie Elsie until he was asleep last night.'

'That's awful for you all,' Alice said, her voice gentle. 'Your father shouldn't be giving your poor mother such a hard time.'

'He can't help it,' Freddy said. There was a sad but slightly defensive note in his voice. 'Me mam says he wasn't like this before Dunkirk, and I remember him always being nice and funny.' He shrugged. 'He was in a boat that was bombed, and most of the others were killed. He was lucky he survived, but he got some kind of head injury, and Mam says it's changed him. He doesn't sleep very well, and it makes him cranky.'

'It sounds like he went through a terrible experience,' Alice said kindly.

Freddy looked over at her now. 'He would never have been cruel about the dogs before. Mam says it's when he's not well, the noise of them barking or whining grates on his nerves.'

'I suppose that would make him feel worse.'

'Me mam got Bella to keep her company when Dad was away, and she feels sorry for her now.'

Alice's gaze dropped to the little brown and white dog, which was shivering. She stifled a sigh. Her mood was already strained this morning, and this was the last thing she needed.

'Her pups are already gone,' he said. 'I don't know if he's given them away, and me mam said she came home and they were vanished.'

He looked up and Alice noticed the dark circles around his eyes, which made her think he hadn't slept much.

'I didn't want anything to happen to Bella,' he said. 'She's a good little dog, and she wouldn't harm a fly. I thought – if you don't mind – that I could tie her outside while I was working, and then ...' He stopped as the dog gave a little whimper.

Alice glanced down, and the dog was looking at her with sad, almost pleading eyes. She suddenly thought of Betty and wondered what her mother-in-law would have done. There was a pause and then she said, 'I'll make you some breakfast and we'll get a tin of Winalot for the dog, and then we'll see what we can do.' She saw the wave of relief wash over Freddy's face.

'Thanks,' he said. 'Bella's no trouble. She'll eat anything you give her.'

Alice could almost hear Betty's voice saying, 'Aye, just like yourself.'

They all went inside and when Freddy put the little dog down on the floor she moved to lie in front of the fire. Alice said, 'You go on into the shop and get her a tin of dog food, and I'll make the toast.' She looked at Freddy, thinking how skinny he looked. 'Would you like a few slices of cheese on top of the toast?'

'That would be great,' he said.

Alice found an old tin plate to put the dog's food on, and a chipped bowl for water. He lifted Bella over and she gulped down half of the plate quickly, then after a drink, she took a bit more, leaving a reasonable amount behind.

'She's not greedy,' Freddy said. 'Once she's had her fill she stops.' He stood up. 'I'll just take her to the grassy bit across the road to do her business.'

Alice watched him as he went outside, her heart heavy for the boy. She knew she wasn't as natural and easy with him as Betty had been, but in their own way they got on well. The more she got to know him, the more she liked him – and he was clever. He only had to be shown something once and after that he did it without any prompting. She remembered Betty showing him the list of deliveries for the paperboys and explaining how the names and street numbers had to be written on the corner of the newspapers, and then put into piles for the four delivery sacks that the boys took around the various streets.

Later, Betty had remarked that he did it in half the time she herself took. 'Sharp as a whistle,' Betty had said. 'As clever as our Greg at that age, and a more willing worker, even though he's hungry most of the day. He's great with book-reading, too, and history and geography. If he came from a half-decent family, that lad could be anything he wanted – a teacher or even an accountant, for he's good with figures. Pity he's going to have to leave school as soon as he's allowed, and get out to earn money.'

Alice already knew the father was a drinker and difficult from what Betty had said, but she hadn't realised how bad it was. She sighed, wishing there was something she could do to lift the burden on his young shoulders. She turned to the cooker to put the bread under the grill, to have the toast ready for him coming back, then she went to the cupboard to get another mug.

When Freddy returned, they sat at the kitchen table, covered with a floral oilcloth. 'How is your mother?' Alice asked.

Freddy shrugged. 'She wasn't up when I left this morning, but she'll probably be OK. After Dad's had a bit of a bender, he's usually quiet for a while. He won't remember half of it, and he tries to make it up to her. He doesn't hit her or anything really bad, but he shouts and says stupid and nasty things – like he said about drowning Bella and her pups.'

'Have the pups definitely gone?'

Freddy nodded. 'He might have taken them down the pub and given them away, or he has a mate who has a farm out in Cheadle, so maybe he gave them to him.' He lifted his toast and cheese in both hands.

There was a silence, and Alice thought it best not to probe any further. She moved the subject on to school and how he was doing, and his face brightened as he told her that he had got top marks for an essay he had written the day before, and then he told her about the books he'd recently read and how his favourite author was Charles Dickens. Alice told him that she liked Dickens, too, and said she had a good collection of his books if he wanted to borrow any.

'Thanks,' he said, 'but I've read most of them, as me dad has them at home.'

Alice was surprised. 'So, he's interested in reading, too?'

'Yes, he's very clever in a lot of ways... if he could just put his mind to it.' Freddy took a gulp of his tea. 'I was thinking,' he said, his face very serious now. 'You know you were considering taking one of the pups?'

Alice looked at him. 'I don't think it would have worked,' she said. 'I wouldn't have the time to train a pup, I'd have to take it out every half an hour or there would be a mess, and I couldn't leave the shop.' She shrugged. 'And then there's the chewing. My brother had a pup a few years back and it chewed up everything – even his glasses.'

Freddy took a deep breath. 'Could you take Bella?'

Alice looked over at the sleeping dog. 'I could manage her until you get home from school,' she offered. 'We can see how your dad is by then.'

64

'I didn't mean just today – I mean, could you keep her all the time? She'd be happier here.'

Alice's eyes widened at the unexpected request.

'She'd be much easier than a pup, I promise,' Freddy rushed on, before she could say anything. 'I can take her to the park for a walk before school, and I'll run straight back after school and take her out again before I start work. She's well trained and can last all day without doing anything,' he smiled. 'She'd be company here for you at night, especially when the winter comes in.'

Alice thought for a few moments. 'I'll keep her for today, and we'll see how things go.'

'A trial?' he checked.

'Your dad might change his mind and feel sorry about what happened, and your mother might miss Bella.'

He closed his eyes and shook his head. 'Me dad will do the same thing again next time he's drunk, and feeding Bella will be one less thing for my mum to worry about.'

Alice suddenly thought. 'What if she has more pups? I wouldn't have the space and time to deal with anything like that.'

'She only comes into season every six months and me mam always made sure to keep her inside. She only got caught last time 'cos me dad put her out all night.'

Alice looked over at the clock, then she finished the last few mouthfuls of her tea. 'I need to get washed and dressed or I'll be late opening the shop.' She gestured towards the sleeping dog. 'We'll see how she gets on today and decide what happens after that.'

'She won't let you down,' Freddie promised. 'Is it OK if I have another slice of toast before I take her out?'

'Take a couple of slices of bread from the loaf, and you can finish the bit of cheese there in the greaseproof paper.' She turned to check the cooker. 'I'll just put the grill back on and you can make it yourself.'

When she came back downstairs, Freddy had washed and

65

dried the plates and mugs and put them away, and then wiped the table and the work surfaces, leaving everything tidy. Bella was back beside the fire, asleep on top of a clean potato sack which he had found folded in the shop.

Alice said nothing, and instead they both got on with organising things so the shop was ready for the baker's delivery, and the first customers looking for newspapers, cigarettes and milk. Around nine o'clock, Freddy took Bella outside again, and afterwards – with a ham sandwich Alice had made in his pocket – he ran off to school.

It was only when she was in the shop for a few minutes on her own that Alice had time to think back to the events of the night before. Bella came over to sit by her feet. She patted her head and then ran a hand down her back. The dog looked up at her, and then put a paw on her knee. Alice patted her again, and, as she drew her hand back, Bella inched her paw closer, still looking straight into her eyes.

'What is it?' Alice asked. 'What do you want?' The little dog put her other paw on Alice's knee now, and instinctively she picked her up and put her in her lap, where she curled up.

Alice smiled and shook her head, then started stroking Bella. After a while, the dog looked up at her again, and as she gazed back, Alice unexpectedly felt tears rushing into her eyes. Everything from the night before suddenly hit her. The awful humiliation and shame she had felt seeing Greg's other woman on the stage in front of her. The woman who had given her a cool glance and turned away, as though she had been of no consequence. And the situation made even worse by her friends saying how sophisticated and lovely she looked, and the reaction of all the men towards her.

A nagging doubt had crept into Alice's mind about having blurted the whole story out to Emily. Her cheeks burned now at the memory, and she knew she would never have said anything, had she not drunk so much. There was nothing that could be done; she could not take the words back.

Tears trickling down her cheeks, she lifted Bella up, and

hugged her to her chest. After a while she felt Bella move and she halted, thinking the dog might be uncomfortable. She loosened her hold to let her jump down to the floor again. Instead, the dog went into a sitting position on her lap and edged her way forward to give a cautious lick to Alice's damp cheek.

When she realised that the little dog was trying to comfort her, she felt a wave of emotion. 'Thank you, Bella,' she whispered. 'You're just the loveliest little dog.'

In that moment she knew that she would keep her. Not just for Freddy's sake. She would keep the dog for her own sake.

Chapter Eight

Freddy arrived back at the shop, his face flushed from running all the way from school. Alice was serving old Mr Baxter from Fox Street, so he stopped to have a cheery word with the elderly man, and then he went through the back to get his brown coat. He came back into the shop, doing the buttons up, just as Alice was finishing packing the items into his shopping bag.

Mr Baxter looked at Freddy and grinned. 'You'll grow into that coat, one of these days,' he told him. 'You could nearly get two of you in it now.'

Freddy laughed at the well-worn joke. He liked Mr Baxter, he was a cheery man, and they always had a bit of banter. 'Is the bag heavy? Do you want me to carry it home for you?'

He looked down into the bag. 'Just a loaf, milk, a packet of dried egg and a tin of corned beef,' he said. 'Nothing too heavy, but thanks for offering anyroad, lad.'

After he left, Freddy turned to Alice, an anxious look on his face. 'How was she?'

'Bella?' Alice said. 'She was fine. No trouble at all.'

A relieved smile came to his face. 'I was worrying all day about her,' he said. 'Just in case the change made her have an accident or something. I'll take her out now, then I'll get a sack of potatoes to empty into the crates at the door. I noticed you were running low when I was coming in.' He turned towards the kitchen.

Alice touched his arm. 'Are you sure about me taking her full-time?'

Freddy's eyes widened. 'Yes,' he said. 'Oh, would you?'

She smiled and nodded. 'I think we got on very well, and she would be good company for me. It would be a lot easier than training a pup.' She halted. 'What if you miss her?'

'I'll see her here, won't I? And it means Mam won't have to worry about feeding her, or about Dad getting annoyed if she makes a noise.'

'Are you sure they will be OK about it?'

He nodded vigorously. 'I told my mother I was going to ask you, and she said it would be an answer to her prayers.'

'That's it settled then,' Alice said.

'I can come round here on a Sunday to take her out for a walk if you like,' he said, 'or any evening you need me as well.'

'I'm sure I'll manage,' she said. She saw the disappointed look on his face. 'Well, I might need you if I'm going out anywhere.'

'Especially when Mr Fairclough comes home. You'll probably be out a lot with him.'

'We'll see. We can make arrangements nearer the time, when I know what's happening.'

Freddy went off into the back of the shop to get the dog, an unusual bounce to his step. Alice smiled, heartened to see the difference in him since the morning. She turned to lift a cloth to wipe down the counter, when someone standing at the window caught her eye. She looked, thinking it might be Mr Baxter, stopping to catch his breath before stepping into the shop, but the man didn't look like any of her usual customers. He was around her own age, and had thick, dark hair, worn slightly longer than most of the local men, and he was wearing a casual, tan jacket, with a briefcase or some sort of bag slung over his shoulder. He was not conventionally handsome, but there was something striking about him, Alice thought.

She stepped further back, so he could not see he was being observed, as he studied the notices on the window, informing customers about rationing or when certain restricted items were likely to be arriving in the shop. It occurred to her that he might be a new commercial traveller, who was trying to gauge the sort of items that were in the shop, before coming in to sell her a new line in soap, toothpaste or cleaning fluid.

Alice gave a little sigh at the prospect of having to turn him away, because few of their customers had the money or ration allowance to try anything new. She turned her back to the window and busied herself wiping the counter and the shelves alongside, which held tins of prunes, fruit salad and rice pudding.

The shop bell rang as the door opened, and when she turned around, there he was, smiling at her.

'It's Alice, isn't it?' He gestured around the shop with his hands. 'I am at the right place?'

'Yes,' she said. 'I'm Alice, and this is Fairclough's shop.' She was pleasant, but she did not smile in case he was a travelling salesman, and it gave him false encouragement.

He slid the strap down from his shoulder to let the briefcase drop to the floor, then he stepped forward, hand outstretched. 'Louis Girard,' he said. 'I teach at the school with your friend, Emily.'

'Ah, yes,' Alice said, her mind working quickly. He was here about the evacuees. She shook his hand, feeling a tinge of guilt because she knew she was not able to help him. 'I've heard Emily talking about you. You're one of the Guernsey teachers.'

'I am indeed,' he said, his face friendly and warm. 'She said you offered to put a notice in the window about the two children who need a new home.' He handed over the notice which had been neatly written on a piece of white cardboard. 'The vicar's phone number is on it, for anyone who can help out. He will pass any messages on to me.'

She took a deep breath. 'I can't guarantee anything. It's a difficult time for people, and anyone who could help probably offered when they first arrived.'

'Of course, but people's circumstances might have changed.' He shrugged and smiled again. 'If we don't try, we will never know. Sometimes, when you least expect it, good things suddenly happen.'

70

Alice found herself smiling now, in spite of her reservations. 'That's a good way to look at things, and I hope it works out for the children.' She held the card up. 'I'll get some Sellotape and stick it on the door of the shop. More people will see it there than if I put it in the window.'

'That's kind of you. I've already given notices to some of the shops in Shaw Heath and in Stockport – newspaper shops and grocers. Hopefully, someone will offer space for them.' He paused. 'The right kind of people. Most Stockport people are very good and decent, but we have had occasional difficulties with children being neglected and made to do work for adults. Also, some of the accommodation was not acceptable – no heating or lighting and they were not fed regularly.'

'That's awful to hear.'

'Most situations are very good,' he stressed, 'but we have to be careful, as the children have no one to speak up for them.' His face lightened. 'The lady who had these children before was very kind – like a grandmother to them.'

Alice looked down at the card. 'Hopefully something will turn up.'

The door from the back of the shop opened and Freddy came through, carrying Bella. He glanced at the dark-haired man, and then suddenly stopped. 'Mr Girard!' he said, grinning. 'What are you doing here in Edgeley?'

The teacher smiled and looked from Freddy to Alice. 'I might ask you the same question, young man.'

Freddy straightened his back. 'I work here,' he said. 'Don't I, Mrs Fairclough?'

'He does,' Alice confirmed. 'He gives me a hand after school and on Saturdays.'

'And the mornings before school,' Freddy reminded her. 'I help sorting the papers and getting the boxes out the front.'

'You sound like a very industrious young man,' Louis said.

Alice suddenly remembered what he had said about the Guernsey children who were taken in by families and then made to work too hard. She hoped he wasn't wondering about Freddy's circumstances.

'I like working here,' Freddy said. 'They look after me well, and it gets me out of the house.' He smiled. 'And on top of all that, I get paid as well, and it helps me mam out.'

Alice felt a sense of relief that she hadn't had to defend herself. 'How do you two know each other?' she asked, interested now, as Freddy seemed so easy and confident chatting to this teacher, when he often gave the impression of not being keen on school.

Freddy grinned. 'Football. Mr Girard does the football training at Alexandra Park on a Sunday, and when I was at St Matthews, he used to bring his school team over to play us.'

'And we beat you a few times, too,' Louis said, winking over at Alice.

'And we beat you back a few times as well,' Freddy said, laughing. He held Bella up. 'I better get her out now to do her duty, and then I'll get the potato boxes sorted.' As he went out the door he said, 'See you Sunday, Mr Girard.'

'You will, Freddy,' he replied. 'Be good until then.'

'I'll try my best, but I can't promise nowt!'

When the door closed behind him, Alice shook her head and said, 'He's a little character, but we're very fond of him.'

'And he seems fond of you,' Louis said.

Alice looked at him, and as their eyes met she felt herself blush, but he just smiled back without saying anything. She went back behind the counter now, not quite sure what to say to him as she was rarely on her own with a man like this. She was used to male customers coming in for newspapers and cigarettes, but they were in and out quickly. Some would ask after Greg, and would chat about the war, but usually they were elderly men, out for a morning walk and in no great hurry to go home. Unsure what to say next, she lifted her cloth as though ready to start work again.

'Freddy seemed very at home in the shop.'

'Freddy's a good footballer, and a cheery fellow. I should

imagine he's easy in the classroom, too, as he's a respectful sort.' He paused. 'Emily told me you're actually a teacher.'

'I am,' Alice told him, 'but until the war ends, I'm a shop-keeper.'

'Many of us are in places we never imagined before this war,' he said. 'And I wonder where we will be when it all ends?'

There was a silence and then Alice said, 'Do you miss Guern-sey?'

'Yes,' he said. 'I especially miss my family and some good friends back there. But I like Stockport and when we leave, I am going to miss it very much, too. It's strange how people and places grow on you...'

Alice laid her cloth down on the counter. 'It must have been very hard for you all, coming over here so quickly, leaving every-thing behind...'

'It was.' He raised his brows and sighed. 'Especially the first few years, when letters weren't allowed, and we didn't hear anything from the island for a long time. That was very, very hard. And when we did hear news, so many terrible things had happened under German rule. People died, people were sent to prisoner of war camps in other countries, and other people just got on with their lives, not knowing what had happened to us.' He paused. 'Of course, we're not special. People have suffered all over the world, so many have lost their husbands and sons, and of course the women who are nurses or in the services abroad, too.' He shrugged. 'How do you count all that loss in all those countries?'

'Yes,' Alice said, 'so many people are affected by it, even in Stockport alone. You probably know Emily lost her brother in Dunkirk?'

His face darkened. 'Yes, she told me, and I was very sad for her, and two of the older teachers lost their sons as well. That's why I think that, in many ways, the ones who came here from Guernsey have been very lucky. Most of the children and adults are alive and well, and that is something to be very, very grateful for, when we consider all those poor Jewish people who, I believe, have been treated worse than anyone.'

She could tell his concern was heartfelt by the way he spoke and the seriousness of his face, and it made her warm to him. Emily had said how good and kind he was with the Guernsey children, and with the other children in the school. She now remembered Emily saying something about him being married or engaged to someone back in Guernsey, when Sophie had teased her about a new male teacher joining the school. Having met him now, Alice was suddenly curious to know more about him and wished she had paid more attention to what Emily had said.

Louis looked at his watch. 'I must go,' he said. 'I have books to mark at home before I go to help out at my friend's house. They have a new baby, and he is going to hospital to visit his wife later.' He lifted his bag and hoisted it up on his shoulder again.

Alice held up the notice he had given her. 'I'll put it on the door now, and I'll let you know if I hear anything.'

'Thank you,' he said, offering a handshake. 'It has been lovely talking to you.'

Alice felt his grip warm and firm, and when she looked up, he was smiling straight at her. 'It's been lovely talking to you as well,' she said.

As he left the shop, Alice thought that even without Emily's praise of him, she could tell he was a good and decent man. With a little start, she realised he was also the most attractive and interesting man she had met in a long time.

Chapter Nine

When Sophie arrived home, Mrs Wilson came down the hallway to greet her, wielding a mop in one hand and a bucket in the other. She came to a halt in front of Sophie, a big smile on her face. 'Not long now until the big day, love! I'd say you're all excited?'

'I've never been so excited in my life,' Sophie told her, her eyes shining. 'I can't believe it's actually happening. I've just been into town to the registry office to sort our special licence.'

'It's complicated enough at the best of times,' Mrs Wilson said, 'and even worse when you're trying to do everything in a rush.'

'Hopefully it's all sorted now. All we have to do is get Tony home from London and then we all turn up on the day.'

'Your mother has been busy phoning about the wedding car and the flowers, and she seemed happy enough with the way things are going. She went upstairs a few minutes ago, and I think I heard her talking on the phone again.'

Sophie held her shopping bag up. 'I'll just go and get rid of these and put my feet up with my new magazine for five minutes.'

'Will I bring you a cup of tea?'

'I'm thirsty, so I'll just have a glass of lemonade.' She smiled at the elderly woman. 'Don't stop what you're doing, I'll get it myself.'

She went down to the sitting room and dropped her bags on the coffee table, throwing her coat on the back of an occasional chair. She picked her magazine out of the bag and leaned on the chair as she flicked through it for a short while. She stopped at the problem page, which she loved, and glanced over the questions sent to the agony aunt.

One problem drew her attention, about a woman who had recently got married and wanted to know if it was the proper thing to wait for her husband to make the first move in bed. He was a shy man, she explained, and she was afraid that he might be shocked if she approached him. She had been told that women didn't enjoy sex, and it was just a part of marriage that had to be endured. After the honeymoon, the woman had been most surprised to discover that it was something she found immensely pleasurable. The agony aunt had replied saying that her husband was a lucky man, and that many men would be thrilled if their wives were to, on occasion, make the first move.

Sophie closed the magazine, her cheeks tinged with red. Alice had reassured her that sharing a marriage bed was natural and this confirmed it. She glanced over at her shopping bag, thinking of the silk underwear she had bought on her way back from the registry office, and Tony's face when he saw her wearing them. Sophie was filled with a mixture of excitement and anxiety, and couldn't wait to get her wedding night over to see what all the mystery was about.

She gave a little sigh and then she slipped off her stilettos, padding out into the hallway in her stockinged feet and down towards the kitchen. She poured herself a glass of lemonade and then wandered over to the door to look out into the garden. It was more perfect than she had ever seen it. The sight of the straight-topped hedges, the tidy rose beds and the regimented rows of cabbages and lettuces, brought a little ache to her heart. It would never have been that perfect if her father was still in charge. He had always planned and talked about getting it tidy and everything under control – as it was today – but it had somehow eluded him.

He had hugely enjoyed gardening, yet he always seemed to leave things half done or abandoned. When Mrs Wilson called to say dinner was ready, he would leave the vegetable patch where he was digging up carrots, and then return to start a different job. At certain times of the year, he had Mr Simpson, a local man, to help with cutting the higher hedges and the trees, as he knew climbing ladders with his bad leg was more than foolhardy. Her mother suggested employing him on a regular basis, but her father said he preferred to work on his own.

After her father died, Mr Simpson worked in a similar, lacka-daisical way to her father. Earlier in the week, Sophie's mother decided she was going to get a gardening firm in to do a proper job on the front and back. The three men the firm sent had been quick and thorough, leaving everything perfect.

Sophie looked now at the meticulous lawn and borders – the paths clear of barrows and shears and spades – and she was reminded that her father would not be there to give her away on her wedding day. It was something she could never have pictured – this special day without him. His loss still caught her heart more often than she could bear. She took a deep breath, and she knew he would not want her to be sad. He would want her to be pleased that her mother had thought the wedding important enough to have the garden perfect. To have the place her father spent all those hours in, beautiful for the guests who would return to the house from the hotel.

Sophie forced her thoughts away from sadness to practical issues – how Tony's family might mix with her father's cousins from Disley and her mother's friends. They had few close family members as her father's only brother had left Stockport years ago, and was now in America. Dorothy's mother was too old to travel from Leeds, and the sister who cared for her could not leave her to come. Dorothy's older brother was in Scotland and was involved in the Home Guard and therefore he, too, could not travel at such short notice.

Tony had two brothers and three sisters, and they were all coming to the wedding. Sophie had met his parents and his sisters and got on well with them, although she felt that they might be a bit intimidated by her mother and the house. The

Shaws lived in an ordinary terraced house in Levenshulme – one of hundreds of similar houses – which Sophie knew was different in every way to the house she had grown up in. She also knew that the lives they lived in those houses were very different, too, and she hoped her mother would talk in a more relaxed, down-to-earth way to them, as she did with Mrs Wilson and Mr Jackson and some of the older workers in the factory whom she had known for a long time.

She took a drink of her lemonade, and then turned away from the window and went back out of the kitchen and down towards the sitting room. She put her glass on the small side-table and chair where her coat was, then lifted her handbag. She took out the various envelopes with the formal documents she had needed for the registry office, placing them on the table.

Her eyes fell on the envelope with Tony's birth certificate inside and she took it out to have a proper look at it. She read through all the details, smiling as she thought of him as a new baby, and imagining how he might have looked. It occurred to her that she must ask Mrs Shaw if she had any old photographs of him. She put the document back in the envelope and then lifted the one with her own birth certificate in it. Her mother had given it to her sealed, telling her to make sure that the person in the registry office gave it back sealed, too.

'The last thing we need is documents going missing during a war,' Dorothy had warned her, 'as it would be impossible to replace them. As soon as they copy the details down, ask them to reseal the envelope so they don't slide out of your handbag on the bus or anything like that.' She had paused, and then put her hand on Sophie's arm. 'And, darling, don't go reading things and getting upset when you see your father's name and handwriting. I'm just thinking of the way you reacted when you found that lovely poetry book that he bought you. Getting through the wedding without him will be hard enough.'

She started going through her shopping bag, lifting out the elegantly wrapped bottle of perfume and the bath oil that she had bought to use the morning of her wedding, so she smelled lovely for Tony. She had a bottle of men's cologne for him, too, some handkerchiefs with a 'T' embroidered on them and some new fine wool socks. She had noticed that he wore rough ones even with his smart polished shoes, and knew it was the sort of little thing that her mother would pick up on.

Tony had laughed in a bemused way when she commented on them, and said that socks were socks unless you were in military uniform and you had to wear the ones issued to everyone. There had been a few other differences that marked him out as being more working class than the other young men she had gone out with, and men like Alice's husband, Greg, who always wore the finest of clothes. The sort of clothes that made an impression and told you something about their backgrounds and their family. But none of it really mattered to her. Tony was the only man who had made an impression on her heart, and that, she knew, was the main thing.

Sophie smiled to herself, thinking of all the little details that would gradually change him into a more sophisticated man. A man who dressed like her father with subtle but stylish silk ties and matching handkerchiefs. The little items she was lifting out of her bag now would be the start of that change. She did not really care about those things, but she knew it would make life easier for Tony with the new world he would be mixing in both socially and when he became involved in the factory business.

Whilst she had defended him to her mother, and had made an issue about him being a telephone engineer, she most certainly wanted her husband by her side in the factory when the war was over. Within a few years she hoped to start a family, and she imagined she would be quite happy to be at home looking after her lovely children while Tony took over the factory business.

Even though making hats would be a new area to him, Sophie knew he was clever and capable, and just needed time to acclimatise himself to it all. She would ask the factory foreman to take him under his wing and teach him everything that was needed about the world of hat-making. He would pick it up easily, she knew, and would have little trouble adapting to the paperwork and accounts, as he was used to that kind of work with the telephone exchanges.

She paused for a moment, thinking how well her father and Tony would have got on. Whilst they looked very different, they had similarities in that they were both quiet but warm and kind, and had a sensitive, understanding side to them, which Sophie thought was not always the case with men. She heard her friends and the girls in the factory complaining about their boyfriends and husbands and how they hadn't a clue when it came to feelings. When she was a little girl, her father had always noticed if she was upset or wasn't her usual, bubbly self, and he would want to know what he could do to help. In the short time she had known Tony, she saw that same quality in him, and it had been a big deciding factor in agreeing to marry him. Of course, his looks and his lovely eyes had been the first things that attracted her, but they would have counted for nothing if he had not been a kind and caring man.

She lifted Tony's documents and put them safely in her handbag; she would keep them in her bedroom until he returned. Her eyes then moved to the envelope with her own certificate, and she thought again about her father. Impulsively, and without allowing herself to consider it, she peeled the Sellotape from the back of the envelope and slid out the certificate.

She unfolded it, closing her eyes for a few moments, and then she opened them and started to scan down the printed columns on the yellowed, parchment paper. Her gaze stopped when she came to the space which had her father's signature. She paused, waiting for her usual reaction, and then to her surprise, she found herself smiling. Instead of feeling upset at seeing his neat, slightly slanted writing, she felt a warm glow run through her, as though her father was actually there beside her. As though he was sending some sort of comforting message to her about Tony and the wedding.

Her gaze moved to the column where her father's occupation was listed, and her face became more serious as she read that he was officially documented as being a factory manager at the time. Only a few years later, she knew, when the hat business went up for sale, he had actually become the owner of the factory. He had done so well in life, given his difficult childhood with polio and then having to live the rest of his life with the disability it created.

She gave a little sigh and then moved to look at her mother's signature. She was surprised to notice that it was quite different to the one that Sophie was used to seeing every day in the factory office. The signature on the certificate was that of a young girl, written in a careful but uncertain cursive script with some letters written separately. Dorothy Morley's distinctive flowing signature now indicated a confident, very different woman. Her father's signature, she mused, had remained almost identical throughout his life. She then moved on, in an almost idle way, to look at the writing in the date of marriage column, written in the perfect script of the registrar.

Her brow creased as she took in the date, and then her gaze moved upwards as she considered it. She looked again, and this time she felt her heart suddenly lurch. Surely the dates were wrong, she thought. The year they had put in could not possibly be right. She stared at it intently, and then sank down into the armchair as she calculated it again.

Her mother's voice suddenly came from the doorway behind her. 'Mrs Wilson said you were back. I was upstairs sorting out some things.'

Sophie whirled round, startled. She had been so engrossed that she hadn't heard her mother come downstairs and into the room. She went to speak, and then discovered she did not know what to say, how to begin to voice her thoughts.

Dorothy moved into the room to look squarely at her daughter. Her gaze fell on the open document on the table. 'What are you doing, Sophie?'

Sophie looked at her mother and noticed that her face had suddenly drained of all colour. She picked the certificate up. 'This is the first time I have ever seen my birth certificate.'

'It's not something we need very often,' her mother said evenly.

'That's why I keep all those old documents safely upstairs.' She reached out for it.

Sophie turned away, so that it was out of her mother's reach. 'I don't understand... what does this mean? These dates, they don't make sense...'

Dorothy's face tightened, then she turned her gaze towards the window. 'This is not something that we need to discuss now. We have a wedding in a few days' time and a lot to do beforehand. I wanted to talk to you about the drinks in the hotel before the meal, whether we should offer both whisky and sherry or just sherry?'

'Have you read this properly?' Sophie held her birth certificate up. 'Is it wrong? Have they made a mistake with the year?'

Dorothy swallowed hard as though her throat had gone dry. 'I haven't looked at it recently...'

Sophie saw a red tinge rising on her mother's neck and then move up to her face, a familiar tinge that occurred when her mother was upset or agitated about something. 'Mummy...' Sophie said, her voice choking. 'I need to know if this is correct.'

Her mother remained silent.

'According to the dates on my birth certificate, it states that you and my father got married *ten days* before I was born. Is that a mistake?'

Her mother still did not speak.

'Did they print the wrong date on it?' Sophie's voice faltered. 'Should it have been the year before?'

Dorothy took a deep breath. 'There were reasons for it,' she said. 'And I will explain it to you someday... at a better time.'

Sophie digested her words. Her mother, she realised, was not shocked or even mildly surprised. She was, in fact, confirming that there was no mistake in the dates.

'I want to hear it now,' Sophie said quietly. She walked over to one of the armchairs at the side of the fire and sat down. She pointed to the other one. 'We have time to talk now. Mrs Wilson won't have dinner ready for another hour.'

'I can't,' her mother said. 'I'm not ready... I wasn't prepared for this...'

'You don't need to be prepared or ready. You just need to tell me the truth.'

There was a painfully long pause, during which Sophie dug her nails into the palms of her hands to keep both still and silent. To not say anything that would give her mother a reason to throw her hands up and walk out of the room as she sometimes did when she was angry and frustrated. She did not want to give her mother a way out of this situation. For a change, she was not the person having to explain herself.

Eventually, her mother started. 'I am not prepared for this, Sophie...' Dorothy Morley's voice was higher now, filled with the usual, steely determination, which at times Sophie admired, but at other times she feared. 'With the wedding and everything, it's just not the right time.'

Sophie knew that if she let things go, it would be too difficult – probably impossible – to find the right occasion to bring this up again. She looked down at the certificate in her hand – amazed that a mere piece of paper could hold such power.

'It's quite obvious that you were expecting me when you got married, and it is the biggest shock I have had in my life. The most unexpected news...' She halted. 'I'm not naïve or stupid, I know these things happen – and can happen to anyone.'

'Well,' Dorothy said, her head tilted defensively, 'if you understand that, then we don't need to talk about it any further. Especially not now.'

'It has to be now,' Sophie said. 'You owe me an explanation. You can't just leave it like this.' A sudden feeling of courage came over her. A feeling of being in the right, so much so that she was afraid of letting this one chance go to stand up against her mother. 'I won't let you...'

A tap came on the sitting room door and they both whirled around. Mrs Wilson opened the door and tentatively stuck her head in. 'Mrs Morley,' she said in a careful, placating tone, obviously aware it was a bad time, 'it's the lady from Clarke's florist shop. She said she wants to check about the buttonholes.'

Dorothy's forehead creased 'Buttonholes?' Then she took a deep breath. 'Ah, the roses for the men's jackets.'

'She's at the door… She said she was out on a delivery and was passing by the house and thought she would call in and check.'

Dorothy moved towards the door now. 'I'll have to go to her,' she said. 'She squeezed in the wedding flowers at the last minute because your father and hers were old friends. She's the sort who would take it as a snub.'

Sophie understood her mother's reasons for going, but she also knew that it was a perfect excuse to avoid the uncomfortable situation she was now in. 'I'll be waiting here for you,' Sophie said, straightening her back in the chair.

As soon as the door closed, Sophie's shoulders slumped in relief. She took a long, deep breath and assessed the situation. Some moments later she got to her feet and went over to the cabinet that held the drink and glasses. She felt light-headed and almost unsteady on her feet as she took down a bottle of sherry and two of the larger sherry glasses. She poured one glass half full, and then lifted it to her lips and drank it down in several gulps. Hopefully, she thought, it would help steady both her mind and her legs. Then, she refilled both glasses almost to the brim, and brought them over to the coffee table in front of the fire.

She sat down now, making herself take deep breaths and relaxing as much as she could. She would wait here in this room and in this chair until her mother came back. She would not move until she knew the true circumstances of her birth, regardless of how long it took Dorothy to tell her.

This was something that Sophie could never have imagined. That her mother had had a hastily arranged wedding, within days of giving birth. Why had her father left it so late to marry the woman he had adored and worshipped? What circumstances could have led them into such a situation? They had always been the most rule-abiding people she could imagine. Her father served on local council committees and was involved with several charities; her mother was on the social committee in the local church and in the Women's Institute. She had been very involved with the Guernsey evacuees, and had even taken in a mother with three children for six months until the council had found them somewhere to live. Sophie shook her head. None of it made any sense.

Chapter Ten

Sophie was just about to lift the sherry glass when she heard her mother's heels tapping along the hallway. She sat up straight in her chair and waited.

Dorothy came in, and then closed the door behind her. She took a deep breath. 'I am imploring you to leave all this business until after the wedding... until Tony has gone back.'

Her mother's tone and strained face made Sophie realise, for the first time in her life, she had the upper hand. She might have gone against her mother's wishes by insisting on marrying Tony, but she knew full well that particular battle was only starting. She knew her mother would constantly be on the lookout to prove that she had made a mistake. If she was sad and missing Tony, that would be her own fault because she knew he had to travel all over the country for his work. If she decided not to stay at home brooding, and went out with Emily and her other friends, that would be interpreted as regret at having married and being tied down.

If she allowed her mother to gloss over this massive issue of her birth, it was as good as saying that she would not stand up for herself over anything. That her mother would always win. 'I'm sorry, Mummy,' she said quietly, 'but I'm not prepared to wait. I want to know the truth. It's my life and I deserve to know all the facts about it.'

Dorothy put her hands behind her back and leaned against the door as though for support. 'This is not the time to be raking up the past...'

There was a stony silence. Eventually, her mother gave a deep sigh and came across the room to sit in the chair opposite.

Sophie lifted both glasses and handed one to her mother. 'This is terribly upsetting for both of us,' she said, 'but I am a grown woman, and entitled to know the truth.'

Dorothy took a drink of the sherry. 'I did plan to tell you, and would have explained it all properly at the right time. With your father dying last year . . .' She shook her head. 'I couldn't face it, and of course I didn't think you would need your birth certificate. I would have explained it in good time, but, of course, you needed the certificate . . . and this has been sprung on me.'

Sophie took a sip of her drink and waited silently. Part of her felt bad for putting her mother in such an awful situation, but she knew it might be extremely difficult to revisit this conversation again.

Dorothy lifted her head and looked directly at Sophie. 'I am so sorry you had to find out this way . . . that I was pregnant when your father and I married.' She paused. 'I can see it must have been a great shock for you, and I really am sorry for that.'

Sophie could see how wounded her mother was, but something propelled her on. 'It was a shock, especially with the way you have always viewed things. How you've disapproved of other women in that position, talking about "shotgun weddings".'

'You have to understand that it's a mother's duty to protect and guide her children, Sophie,' she said, 'and that includes preventing them from making the same mistakes we may have made.' She halted. 'And, yes, sadly these things happen in life. As I said to you recently, in my younger days I didn't always do the right thing, but hopefully, I made up for any mistakes.'

As she listened to her mother, Sophie realised that she did not feel overly shocked or upset about the circumstances of her birth. If anything, it was more a feeling of surprise and bemusement. She knew that many girls her age would be horrified to discover they were so close to being illegitimate, but she didn't feel like that. In a way, it just made her mother seem more ordinary and human. She took a sip of sherry and then looked over at her mother. 'I feel there are still things you haven't explained to me.'

'Well, I have confirmed what was on the birth certificate,' Dorothy said now, 'and I've said I'm sorry about the way you found out. Yes, I was expecting you when we got married, but you were a very wanted child.' Tears came into her eyes. 'You know you've been well loved by both your father and me; there can't be a single doubt in your mind about that.' She shrugged. 'There's really nothing more to say about it ... is there?'

'I would like to know a bit more ...'

'We haven't the time now. I've done what you asked, and we really need to get on with things.' Dorothy finished her sherry and then stood up.

'Why did you leave it so late to get married? Didn't you want to marry Daddy?'

'Of course, I did. It was just how things worked out ...'

'But he adored you. Why would he have left it so late? Why would you both have left it so late?'

'I told you ... it was how things worked out.'

Sophie got to her feet now. 'That does not answer anything!' she said, her voice high and emotional. 'You didn't rush to do the decent thing. You left it so late, I was almost illegitimate.'

'Do not use that word, and please keep your voice down.' Dorothy had one hand on her hip and the other shielding her eyes. 'We don't need Mrs Wilson hearing all our business.'

'You have to tell me!' Sophie said in a heated whisper. 'Why did you wait to get married until ten days before I was born? It seems to me you didn't want to marry Daddy and then changed your mind at the last minute because you didn't want to have a bastard child!'

'My God ...'

'It's the truth – if I had suddenly been born premature, I would have been classed as illegitimate. In other words – a bastard.'

'How can you say such things, Sophie?'

'You must have been very unsure about getting married to Daddy.'

'It was the opposite – the absolute opposite. Marrying your father was the best thing I ever did.' Dorothy went to move and then suddenly swayed and had to catch onto the chair to steady herself.

Sophie rushed over and caught her arm. 'Are you OK?' She guided her mother back into the chair, then stood close beside her. 'Are you OK?' she checked again.

'Yes, yes ... I just felt a little dizzy for a few moments.'

Sophie put her hand on her mother's shoulder and after a few moments, she felt her Dorothy's hand covering hers. 'I didn't mean to upset you,' she said, 'and I'm not naïve or totally old-fashioned. I know these things can happen to anyone, but I feel I will have no peace until I know why you and Daddy didn't get married sooner. It's a reasonable thing to ask.'

'It was personal. It was just the circumstances we were in ... with work ... with a number of things.'

'Your answers don't make sense, Mummy. If you don't tell me, this will hang like a long shadow over us both. It will hang over my wedding day.'

There was an agonising silence, then a little choking sound and she realised that her mother was crying.

'What is it? What happened?' Sophie asked. A thought suddenly struck her. 'Was Daddy married before? Were you having an affair? Was he waiting for a divorce?'

'No, no ...' her mother said, appalled at the suggestions. 'Not at all ... Your father was the most decent, respectable man. He couldn't have been kinder.'

Sophie threw her hands up. 'I have a right to know why – if Daddy was free to marry you – why he took so long to do the decent thing.'

Her mother reached out and took Sophie's hands in hers and squeezed them tightly. Then she kissed the back of one hand and then the other. Sophie's heart almost stopped at the unexpected, loving gesture.

Dorothy looked up, slow tears trickling down her cheeks. 'I hope you can forgive me, for giving the wrong impression of your father. He actually knew nothing about my pregnancy until a month before you were born. We hadn't seen each other for over six months. As soon as he found out, he offered to marry me almost immediately.'

'So why didn't you tell him before? Why did you wait until I was ready to be born?'

'Because I didn't know him that well, and it wasn't the sort of thing that women went shouting about in those days. I used to see him through work, every week or so. We happened to meet in a café in Stockport, and of course, he immediately saw my condition...'

'But why hadn't you told him? Given him a chance to marry you earlier?'

'Because, Sophie,' Dorothy said in a quiet, sad tone, 'it would not have been fair.' Her hands came up to her face. 'The truth is, the kindest, most generous man – George Morley – was not your real father.'

Sophie felt the world suddenly stop. This was not something she had considered. All the feelings about having the moral upper ground faded away. Moments passed and during that time she became aware of an awful sense of loss. A sense of loss as bad as when her father died – even worse.

She wished now that she had never opened that envelope and never seen her birth certificate. More than that, she wished she had never opposed her mother. She could have carried on with their relationship, with the ups and downs, because underneath it all, they loved each other. They understood each other. At least, she thought they had. She now realised she had understood nothing.

Dorothy reached out and touched her hand. 'Darling...'

Sophie flinched and moved away. She stood in the middle of the floor, her eyes wide and staring ahead.

'Are you all right?' Dorothy asked in a fearful voice. 'I can see this has come as a terrible shock.' She swallowed hard. 'That's why I couldn't tell you before. I was always afraid of this... afraid of hurting you.'

Sophie moved across the room. She lifted her coat and her handbag and then she went out of the room and straight down the hallway.

Dorothy followed her. 'Where are you going? You can't go out now... Mrs Wilson will have dinner ready soon.' She watched as Sophie headed towards the front door. 'We have things to sort out for the wedding. Please come back in so we can sort things out—'

She froze as the door banged shut, drowning the rest of her words.

Sometime later, Sophie found herself sitting on a bench near the Bear Pit in Mersey Square. As though awakening from a dream, she lifted her head and looked around her, realising where she was. It was quiet with few people around and the shops were closed.

She tried to calculate the time it would have taken her to walk down from Davenport, and then she wracked her brain to remember when she had arrived in the centre of Stockport and how long she had been sitting there. Half an hour? An hour? She had no idea. She also wondered if she had come direct down Wellington Road or whether she had detoured off the main road and walked through some of the backstreets, perhaps down Hillgate? She had no idea.

She sat for longer, replaying the scene over in her mind, where she discovered that her whole life had been a tissue of lies. Everything that she believed to be true, now no longer was, and the only person she could have asked more questions of, was gone. Her father was gone. Whether he was her real, *real* father or not, he was the person she would have wanted to comfort her through this. He would have explained why he had not told her. He would have said everything in the right words, that would have made sense, because she knew he loved her.

She sat there for a while longer, and it was only when someone came to stand in front of her that she was jolted back to reality.

'Are you all right, love?' a woman asked, moving her umbrella back to see better.

Sophie looked up to see a rough-looking woman, a little older than herself, with peroxide-blonde hair staring down at her. 'Yes... yes,' she said. 'I was just taking a rest.'

'It's just that it's pouring rain, love... and you're gettin' soaked through.' She gestured towards the nearby bus shelter. 'Some folk at the bus stop noticed you, and were a bit worried that you might be poorly or upset, like.'

Sophie glanced around her and could see a group of four or five people staring over at her and the blonde woman with great curiosity. Embarrassed, she quickly got to her feet, then she smiled at the woman. 'Thanks for being so kind, but I'm fine. As I said, I suddenly felt tired and decided to sit down.'

The woman's eyes narrowed. 'As long as you're OK, love.'

Sophie thanked her again and then turned in the opposite direction to the bus stop. As she went along, she felt drops of water running down the back of her neck and was suddenly aware that her hair was soaking wet. It had obviously been raining for a while – how could she not have noticed?

Chapter Eleven

Dorothy whirled around as a tentative knock came on the door. She could tell by the cautious way Mrs Wilson entered that she had heard the row between herself and Sophie. She squared her shoulders. 'Yes?' she said, gathering the documents from the table as though she had been busy with them and was now tidying up.

'Just checking about dinner,' the housekeeper said. 'I thought I heard the door going and wondered if there was any change in the time?'

'Ah,' Dorothy said, thinking quickly, 'I was just going to come and tell you that Sophie has had to go out. The wedding arrangements and everything.' She halted. 'She's getting a bit anxious about things... a bit more highly strung than usual. I suppose we both are...'

'It's only natural,' the housekeeper said, smiling in understanding. 'These things always seem bigger than they are at the time. It's harder for the younger ones, especially with the war going on and nothing the way it was.'

Dorothy's shoulders eased a little. 'Yes, and with everything being arranged so quickly.' She smiled back at the housekeeper, grateful that she had not alluded to the raised voices and the banging doors.

Edna Wilson was not a woman to step out of her place and make comments about the family she had cared for all these years. Mrs Wilson had been working as a cleaner in the hat factory with George, but left to help care for her invalid mother.

He liked the hard-working, middle-aged woman, and suggested to Dorothy that she come and help her in the house – tactfully saying it was more as a favour to Mrs Wilson. At first Dorothy wasn't sure, as neither she nor George had grown up in families with domestic help.

After a period of sleepless nights with a new baby, an exhausted Dorothy agreed, and Edna Wilson arrived to help. She checked out where things were in the kitchen, and how to operate the gas cooker, then she encouraged the new mother to go back to bed for a few hours after lunch.

By the time Dorothy awoke, the housekeeper had systematically worked her way through all the rooms, cleaning and tidying, and generally getting the house into the order that Dorothy had never managed.

And somehow, whilst every part of the house was being cleaned, Edna managed to find time to put in place a laundry system. This meant that there was always a pile of freshly bleached nappies every morning, and clothes seemed to magically appear ironed and folded in the baby's chest of drawers. Over the first few weeks, without any guidance, but without stepping on her employer's toes or being too familiar, Edna had organised every aspect of the house apart from Dorothy and George's room. By the time Sophie was sleeping all night, Mrs Wilson had become a fixture in the home.

'I'm glad to come here to get a break from them all,' she told Dorothy. 'I enjoy looking after little Sophie and doing the housework – it clears my head – because I'm always running from pillar to post at home, listening to a litany of complaints. Being here gives me a bit of peace and quiet.' She also admitted the hours and the money suited her perfectly. 'I can fit all my other jobs in around this, which I couldn't have done with the factory hours, and the money lets me keep my bit of independence.'

There were times over the years where Dorothy felt overwhelmed and could have easily cried on Edna Wilson's shoulder, but, knowing that the older woman had enough on her plate,

94

she never did. Her own mother was too far away, and would never have understood the situation that Dorothy had got herself into, becoming pregnant by one man and marrying a completely different one. When Dorothy had turned up on 'a surprise visit' with both a husband and a child, a few months after the wedding, it had been received with shock and suspicion by her mother. Dorothy had expected this reaction and had prepared George for it, and they endured the visit, fending off as many questions as possible. Later, occasional visits followed and the issue of the wedding and the question marks around Sophie's birth faded into the background.

Through those early years, Dorothy often wished she had a more understanding mother-figure close by to confide in, and to ask advice of. She made a few friends – young mothers her own age – who she could go to the cinema with on the occasional night when George was at home to look after Sophie, but there was no real depth to the conversations, mainly talk about when their children had taken their first steps or grown their first tooth.

When Sophie reached school age and she had more time on her hands, Dorothy decided to join the local Women's Institute. There, she quickly made two friends – Frances and Gwen – who were a little older than herself. Within a short while, Frances confessed to her that before getting married to Len, she had foolishly been involved with a married man. Dorothy revealed her own situation about being duped by someone who was already engaged, and was eminently comforted by the fact that Frances was neither shocked nor in any way judgemental about what had happened.

Later, when an unexpected and most unsettling letter arrived for her and George, she found herself confiding in Frances about the circumstances of Sophie's birth. Again, Frances was supportive and gave her good advice, gleaned from her own difficult experiences and those of her three sisters.

That friendship had endured all through Sophie's early years, when George had worked as manager in the factory and when he was dealt a devastating blow when the owner, Mr Altman, called him into his office and told him that he was retiring and moving down to Devon. He then said that he was selling the factory, and that he already had an offer for it from a bigger hat manufacturer based in London. He was even more shocked when the owner said he was going to give George first option on buying the factory himself, and at a lower price than his competitor. George, Mr Altman stated, knew everything there was to know about running the place, and would be a fair boss to all the staff who had been working there for years.

George was very uncertain. He was content with his position as manager, and had never envisaged himself as the actual owner of a business. He told Mr Altman he would need time to discuss the situation with Dorothy, and depending on her reaction, he would then have to find out if the bank were willing to loan him some of the money to fund it. When he told Dorothy the news, she was fearful about repayments on a big business loan, along with a mortgage and the school fees for Sophie's school.

Dorothy had turned to Frances, who listened as she poured out her worries about George losing his job as factory manager. The London owners had already intimated to Mr Altman that they were planning on moving their own staff up from the city and therefore most of the staff would be made redundant – including George.

After a nerve-wracking week, George was called back to the bank to be told that they could only loan him three-quarters of the money that was needed. Devasted, George went to his boss to explain that he couldn't come up with the full amount, and Mr Altman immediately agreed to sell the factory to him for the amount of the loan. When things were up and running, George could then repay the remainder in instalments.

Mr Altman said he advised him strongly to buy the factory, as there could be problems with his employment status if the factory was bought out by the London company. There could also be an issue with George's disability and insurance if he started work in a new place.

Dorothy was almost speechless when George related the conversation. 'But your health record has been a hundred per cent since I've known you,' she told him.

'It's the future Mr Altman was thinking of,' he explained, 'and how it would affect me if my condition deteriorates.'

'In that case,' Dorothy told him, 'we must look to the future, too. Whatever it takes, you are going to buy that factory. I had already been thinking about it, and if you become the factory owner, I could help manage the office for you.' Before he had a chance to argue, she continued, 'Sophie is well settled in school now, and I have been thinking that it's time for me to go back to work. Besides, the extra income will at least pay for the school fees. Rather than paying a manager's wages to one of the workers, the money can go into our bank account instead.'

As George digested this suggestion, Dorothy then went on to tell him how she could be of help finding new markets for the hats they manufactured, as she had contacts from her previous job. She then said that if they felt things were going well in the future, they might even expand to adding their own trimming department to Morley's factory.

He had been amazed by his wife's vision of how the factory could be under his ownership, and even more amazed by Dorothy's faith in him. Consequently, he had taken the biggest step in his life, of buying the hat factory he had imagined he would always remain an employee of.

Over the following years, they both realised that Mr Altman's and Dorothy's faith in George had been well placed. The factory ownership passed seamlessly from Altman to Morley and production carried on as before, then had to be stepped up as fresh markets were found by the new manager. Before three years had passed, a modern building was erected, and staff taken on to start work in the new hat-trimming department. Month after month the money he owed to Mr Altman was delivered to his account until the debt was paid off.

At times George could not believe how well life had turned out for him, both at work and at home with his family. He knew a lot of this was down to Dorothy as she worked tirelessly as factory manager to make sure that standards were kept high and delivery deadlines met. All of it was done quietly and discreetly, giving George full credit for the success of the business as though the positive and lucrative changes had been something that he had planned all along.

As their fortunes improved, George initiated the next change in their life when he arrived home with a brochure from Thornley's Estate Agents, with details of a large, five-bedroomed house that had come on the market. The price was low for the prestigious house as it needed renovations and updating, but George suggested they could employ the men who had built the trimming department extension, as they had been thorough in work and fair in price.

After the move, life settled down for the Morleys in their new house with the addition of a young lady named Ivy, who shared the domestic work with Edna Wilson, and was there to take care of Sophie after school.

Throughout all the moves and changes, Dorothy had kept up her friendship with Frances and Gwen, and when the war started, all three had been involved with the Women's Institute project to welcome the Guernsey evacuees who had arrived in Stockport. Dorothy had taken in a mother – Sally Brock – along with her three little girls, whilst her friends did likewise. The Guernsey children were younger and very different to Sophie, but they had rubbed along together until Sally had been given a two-up two-down terraced house in Edgeley, which was nearer to a group of her Guernsey friends.

Dorothy's friendship with Frances and their weekly lunches had remained constant, until Frances's mother died, and she was left a large house in Knutsford that was perfect for their growing family. Meeting up was more difficult, due to the petrol rationing and the long country journey during the blackout, but they kept up their regular chats on the phone.

Frances and Gwen were two of the few friends invited to Sophie's wedding. Dorothy had confided to Frances her disappointment at both the choice of groom and the hastily organised event.

'Of course I can understand your feelings about it,' Frances had said, 'but I am sure it will all work out. The wedding itself will be lovely, and the Grosvenor will pull out all the stops regardless of it being smaller and during this awful war.'

'And the choice of groom?' Dorothy had said in a low voice. 'Will that work out just as well? I am terrified he's a gold-digger and only proposed when he heard about Sophie owning half of the factory. Do you think if anything happens to him after the wedding that his family could have any claim on the business?'

'I very much doubt it,' Frances said. 'I'm sure it would remain in Sophie's hands, but I don't think it would be a good idea to mention your worries to her. Since she is determined about marrying him, it could cause a rift between you that might never heal. Just support her decision and then cross each bridge as it comes.'

Dorothy thought of her friend and wondered what she would advise now. She looked at the empty sherry glass in front of her, then got up and went over to the drinks cabinet. The situation warranted something stronger, so she lifted the brandy bottle and poured a large measure, then opened a bottle of ginger ale and filled the glass two-thirds of the way up. She took a good gulp and then went over to the armchair beside the phone table and dialled Frances's number.

When her friend's voice sounded on the line, Dorothy said, 'The very worst has happened, and I really need your advice now.'

'The wedding?'

'No, Sophie has seen her birth certificate and knows that George is not her real father.' Then, her voice anxious and her

99

heart beating in an almost frightening manner, she outlined the situation.

'OK,' Frances said, 'Sophie now knows that you were pregnant with her when you met up with George again, and that he asked you to marry him?'

'Yes,' Dorothy confirmed, 'and she was terribly upset and has walked out of the house. I don't know where she is or if she's coming back. It's days until the wedding and her fiancé is due back in England tomorrow.'

'Can I ask – is that all she knows?'

There was a pause. 'Yes,' Dorothy replied.

'What about her real father? Did she want to know about him?'

'I explained that he disappeared to London, and I never heard anything more after that.'

'And do you plan to tell her who he actually is?'

'God, no! I couldn't ... especially not at the moment.'

'How do you think she will react to that?'

There was a pause as Dorothy closed her eyes and then her hand came up to her chest as though to still her heart. 'I can't bear to even think about it ... It was something that George and I always planned to tell Sophie together, when we heard of his return. I think I told you before, the first few times he came back for his mother and then his father's funeral, she was too little to understand. And then, when he came back to the area about five years ago, we planned to tell Sophie – and, if she understood, maybe even introduce her to him – but of course, he and George had that awful row. We never heard from him again.'

'Until George's funeral ...'

'Yes, well, you saw him there yourself, and you didn't have to ask me who he was.' She halted. 'I did introduce them,' Dorothy said, 'but I couldn't tell her who he really was.'

'Of course not, that would have been absolutely the wrong time ...'

'It was always there at the back of my mind, like a big, black shadow, knowing that I should tell her the whole truth, but I had always imagined George by my side. He would have been able to explain it much better than me – in a way that made it more acceptable to Sophie. But now, I don't have that choice. George is gone, and I have to deal with it on my own. Sophie has reacted so badly to the news that George isn't her real father that I just can't take the risk of saying any more. To tell her now who that person is – on top of the arguments about her wedding – could do irreparable damage.' Dorothy paused. 'I'm so sorry for ringing you about this . . . but I just needed to talk to someone about it, and you are the only person I can fully trust. I just need to know, when she comes back, whether I should take that risk, and tell her the whole truth?'

'No, no . . .' Frances said, her voice high with concern. 'I don't think you should – not now. Not in the days leading up to her wedding.'

'You don't think it's best to get everything out in the open?'

'Absolutely not, you don't know how she will react. You don't want any further upset before the wedding – for either of you.'

'Thank you,' Dorothy said, tears coming to her eyes. 'I feel that's the right thing, but I've lost all confidence in my own judgement, and needed to hear it from someone else. I've made so many mistakes, and I don't want to make a bigger one now.'

'Don't be so hard on yourself,' Frances told her. 'You've done everything with Sophie's best interests at heart, and don't forget that George wanted it this way, too. She's a sensible girl, and she must know these sorts of situations happen to people, and that even her parents make mistakes.'

'Oh, she certainly knows that now,' Dorothy said in a shaky voice. Tears were now falling onto her cheeks.

'Try to relax,' Frances advised. 'Wait until after the wedding, until Tony has gone back to work. Do everything to make sure the wedding goes off as perfectly as it can for her.'

'I owe her that at least . . .' Dorothy nodded and wiped her damp cheeks with the back of her hand. 'Thank you, Frances. I can't tell you how much I appreciate your advice. I was so used to talking things out with George, and I now realise I find it very hard to make decisions on my own.'

'I wish I was closer to you, but ring me any time – and I'll be there by your side at the wedding, too.'

'I can't tell you how much that means...'

'My dear,' Frances said, 'that's exactly what friends are for.'

Chapter Twelve

Alice opened the door to see a white-faced, wet Sophie standing on the step.

'Can I come in?' she asked, pushing a damp strand of hair away from her eyes. 'I need to talk to someone, and you are one of the only people I can trust.'

Alice's chest tightened, knowing something serious had happened. 'Of course you can.' She stepped back, then held the door wide open to let her in. Once inside, she put her hand on Sophie's shoulder. 'What on earth is wrong?'

'My mother. She's just shattered my whole world. You won't believe what she's just told me.'

'She won't mean it,' Alice said. 'She's just highly strung before the wedding. She'll be fine by the time it comes around to the actual day. Come in and sit down. Take your wet things off first, and I'll go and get you a towel to dry your hair.'

'You don't understand,' Sophie said. 'It's nothing to do with the wedding. She's just told me that Daddy wasn't my real father.'

Alice looked at her, wondering if Sophie had become slightly hysterical with all the pressure of the wedding. 'Are you sure that's what she said?'

Sophie's eyes were clouded with tears. 'Absolutely sure. I looked at my birth certificate and discovered that my mother and father got married only ten days before I was born. *Ten days* – can you imagine? If I'm honest, it didn't bother me as much as I would have thought. In a way I was glad to see my mother was human like everyone else and had made a big mistake, but then, when I asked her why they hadn't got married sooner, I knew things didn't add up.'

'Oh, Sophie, what a shock for you,' Alice said quietly. 'Although she's not the first woman to find herself in that position...'

'I know all that,' Sophie said wearily, 'and I'm not being hard on her about that – it's the way she's gone about things. She refused point-blank to have any conversation in the beginning, but I wouldn't let it go, and it took ages before she would even talk about the birth certificate.' She closed her eyes and shook her head. 'I just can't believe it. Imagine finding all this out days before my wedding. Knowing that the man I loved and adored as Daddy, is no relation to me at all. And that some other man out there – a total stranger – is actually my father.'

Alice hesitated, then she asked, 'Did she say who your real father is?'

'No, we didn't get that far ... I wasn't ready. I'm still not ready. It was something I had never envisaged.' Her hands were moving in agitation. 'I have no idea who he is. None! He could be the local coalman, or he could be the king of England for all I know. In some ways, I don't even care. It's all a complete nightmare, and the more I think about it, the worse it gets.'

'Come into the kitchen and sit down, and let's get you dried off, and then let me make you a cup of tea,' Alice said kindly. 'It might help – even a little.'

'Thank you,' Sophie said, 'but *nothing* can help. All I can say is that it's lucky I'm getting married in a few days because at least I will know who I am. I'll know I am Tony's wife – because Sophie Morley does not exist anymore. She never did.'

A few minutes later Alice came over to the kitchen table with two cups of tea and a plate with two slices of fruit cake, then she and Sophie sat opposite each other at the kitchen table.

'I know it's a shock,' Alice said, 'especially with the wedding and Tony coming back, but you are one of the strongest girls I know, and you will get over this.'

'Do you think so? At this moment, I don't feel I will. I feel I can't forgive my mother for all this deception, and because I know she would have continued except for me catching her out with the birth certificate.'

'I am trying to be careful, because I don't want to make you any more upset, but if you look at it in one way, nothing has really changed.' When she saw that Sophie was listening, she felt encouraged and continued, 'All that has really happened is that you now know your parents got married later than you thought, and your mother has confirmed that the man who brought you up since you were a baby absolutely loved and adored you.'

'It's the lies,' Sophie said. 'And the fact that my mother has been such a hypocrite.'

'Yes,' Alice said, 'but she absolutely loves you as well.' She raised her eyebrows and smiled. 'I know she drives you mad with her ways, but she always has your best interests at heart. Lots of women have done things like that – concealed the truth – because they thought it was for the best. I'm sure I've told you before that my grandparents brought up my mother's nephew, Gerald, and pretended he was their own?'

'Yes,' Sophie said. 'I do remember, because I thought how brave you were talking about it. Most people keep family things like that secret.' She forced a little wry smile. 'Just as my parents did.'

Alice nodded. 'Gerald was Mum's older sister's child, and I remember overhearing Mum telling a friend that an older man took advantage of her. I don't recall the details, but I know she had to go into service to work in a big house up in Newcastle.' She shrugged. 'Maybe it was to get away from the man, who knows? In any case, my grandparents decided it was best to bring him up as though he was their own child. In those days older women often had babies without announcing it beforehand to the neighbours, and they wore big dresses and aprons so no one would really notice if a girl was pregnant,' she smiled. 'Apparently, he was the little pet of the family, they all spoiled him rotten. My mother was more open about it – she said he gave her parents a new lease of life having him.'

'And how did he react when he found out that they were really his grandparents?'

'He never did find out.' Alice took a deep breath. 'I thought I might have mentioned it, but obviously not. He was killed in the Somme in the last war.'

Sophie's hand came to her mouth. 'Oh God, I'm sorry . . .' She could not remember now whether Alice had told her that sad story. Her mind was so full of her own situation that she couldn't think of anything else.

'Gerald being killed was awful for everyone,' Alice continued, 'but in all honesty, his actual background made no difference to anyone. My mother said Gerald was just Gerald to everybody, and it was no great issue. They all loved him.' She halted. 'I think in time you might be able to look at your own situation in that way. It really doesn't change a thing. You are still the same Sophie regardless.'

Sophie caught her lip between her teeth. 'I don't feel I am the same person,' she said in a flat voice. 'I was OK when I thought my mother had been pregnant when they got married, that didn't really bother me at all. In fact, it made me warm more to my mother, realising that underneath all her pomp and glory she made mistakes like any other woman.'

'Knowing your mother,' Alice said, smiling now, 'I can understand that. But you must know that she only wants the best for you?'

Sophie lifted her cup and took a sip of her tea.

'Cake?' Alice pushed the plate towards her.

'No, I couldn't, thanks. My stomach is still in a knot.' She gave a weak smile, as they both usually laughed over her sweet tooth when it came to cake.

Alice reached out and squeezed her friend's hand. 'Try to let it all go,' she said. She remembered her mother-in-law's advice when she had felt she could not carry on. 'Don't torture yourself over this one thing. You have so many other good things in your life, and so much to look forward to.'

Sophie looked at her with tear-filled eyes and nodded.

'Just remind yourself that you are seeing Tony soon, and think of your lovely wedding day. It was one of the happiest days of my life, and I know yours will be the same.'

'I really want it to be, and I am so looking forward to seeing Tony.' She wiped away a tear. 'I need to talk to my mother again, and after that I hope I'll feel more normal.'

'You will,' Alice said. 'It was just the shock of it all happening now. There's probably never a right time for difficult things like this, so try not to judge her too badly.'

'The right time was when my father was alive,' Sophie said. 'They should have both sat down with me and explained it all.'

Alice thought for a few moments. 'It might have been your father who didn't want you to know. He worshipped you so much that maybe he found it too difficult and was worried you might not look at him in the same way.'

'That would never have happened,' Sophie said, a catch in her voice now. 'I would have loved him even more ... I would have loved him for knowing that he happily took me on as his own child even before I was born.'

'I know you might not feel it,' Alice said, 'but I think you're already coming to terms with it.' She squeezed her hand again. 'I promise you it will get easier.'

'Thank you,' Sophie said. 'I can't tell you how glad I am that I found my way to you. You always seem to know the right thing to say.' She rolled her eyes. 'I'm useless, I put my foot in things all the time. I upset poor Emily the other night. I didn't mean any harm, it was just silliness.'

'I'm sure she's forgotten all about it by now, and I know she's really looking forward to the wedding.'

'Thankfully that's one thing that my mother has done her best to get completely right – after she realised that poor Tony wasn't after me because of the factory. She has lists pinned up on the kitchen noticeboard about absolutely everything.'

They chatted for a while about the wedding arrangements as they finished their tea, then they suddenly stopped as a snuffling noise sounded in the corner.

'You got the dog after all!' Sophie exclaimed. She watched as Bella stretched then stepped carefully out of her basket. 'I thought it was a pup you were getting.'

'Yes,' Alice said. 'It's a long story, but I ended up getting the mother instead.'

'She a lovely little thing.' Sophie finished the last mouthful of her tea. 'I need to go home now. I have a hundred things I need to do, but first I need to sort things with my mother. Exactly how I'm going to do it, I have no idea, but I have a few more questions I need to ask her, so that will be enough to be going on with.'

Chapter Thirteen

When she arrived home from school, Emily's mother was waiting for her in the kitchen. 'I have a pan of homemade soup ready for you,' she said. 'I got a ham bone from the butcher this morning that had a good bit of meat on it.'

Emily was pleased that her mother seemed brighter than normal. 'It smells lovely.' She left her gas mask and leather school briefcase on top of the marble-topped chest of drawers, which held the cutlery, dishtowels and tablecloths.

'Your father got me some potatoes and leeks and carrots from the allotment this morning, so it should be nice and thick.'

'Thanks, Mam,' Emily said, sitting down at the pine kitchen table. 'I'm really tired after my late night.' She rested her chin in her cupped hands. 'I could have dozed off in the afternoon when the class were taking turns at reading out from *Heidi*.'

Her mother smiled. 'You used to love that book when you were a little girl.'

'I still do, but today I was so tired it was sending me off to sleep,' she laughed. 'Especially when we were reading about the little bed with the straw-filled mattress – I was picturing myself lying down in it.'

'Late nights never suited you.'

'When we finished, I took the class outside for a five-minute run around the playing field. Thankfully, the fresh air woke me up, so I managed to get through the last hour without falling asleep.' She indicated towards her briefcase. 'I decided not to stay behind marking books, and brought them home with me to do tonight.'

'Have a lie-down after you've eaten and you'll feel brighter later on.' Hannah Browne went back to the cooker. 'We don't have to wait for your father.' She looked up at the clock. 'He's later than usual, whatever has kept him back.' She took her ladle from the old earthenware jug that held her utensils, and then lifted one of the deep bowls from the worktop. She filled it with several spoonfuls of the steaming soup and brought it over to the table. She had just half-filled another bowl when they heard the front door open, and then Emily's father came in.

'I got held up,' he explained, hanging his cap and working jacket up. 'There was a bit of a to-do outside the shops.' He came into the kitchen, smoothing his hair down as he always did when he removed his cap. He then went over to the sink to wash his hands. 'I'm not sure exactly what was going on, but it seems there was some kind of fight.'

Emily's mother looked at him. 'A fight?' she said, putting her ladle down in the bowl. 'In the middle of the afternoon? What kind of fight?'

'Serious enough, as the police and the priest were there, and so were two of those bloody Italian prisoners from the camp.'

Emily felt a start at the mention of the Italians. She remembered the friendly young man she had met – Marco – who had given her the rosary beads. She hoped he wasn't involved.

'Good Lord!' her mother said. 'Were they stealing from the shops and got caught?'

'It seems they gave a young lad a bit of a hiding,' her father said. 'I came upon it when it was all over. I stopped for a few minutes and was talking to Tommy Breslin, and he said the priest was out for his afternoon walk and saw a group of young lads gathered and could tell there was a commotion going on. By the time he crossed the road over to them, one of the Italians was on the ground fighting with the oldest lad in the group and a couple of men had gone over to separate them.' He shrugged.

'Tommy said it was something to do with a bike, but he wasn't sure. One of the shopkeepers must have called the police and the men held onto the Italians until they arrived a short while later.'

'What happened then?' Emily asked.

'I've no idea, as I didn't want to stand around gawping. They were all still there when I left. No doubt we'll hear more about it later.'

'It's a disgrace having that Italian prisoner camp here, near ordinary people,' her mother stated. 'I said it at the time that we would all be in danger, and now look what's happened.'

'I've never heard of any problems with them before,' Emily said. 'Have either of you?'

'That's not the point,' her mother said. 'It doesn't mean things aren't going on, or might go on as long as they are here. If enough local people complain, the authorities should move them. They should be put somewhere far off like the Highlands in Scotland or out in the mountains in Wales. We shouldn't have to tolerate enemies of our country living beside us.'

Emily's father nodded. 'That young lad who helps the priest out with the garden was there ... the young Neville lad – Harold. That's probably why the priest got involved.' He raised his eyebrows and gave a little sigh. 'The poor lad that's not right ...'

'In some ways he's cleverer than most, and his mother wouldn't let them put him into an institution. I believe he can even read and write. He would never get into trouble, he's a lovely young lad.'

'What kind of people are those damned Italians?' her father asked. 'Who in God's name would get into a fight with an innocent young lad like Harold and his friends? I wonder, were they trying to steal a bike belonging to one of the local lads?'

'The Italians are nothing but cowards,' her mother said. 'They followed the Germans into the war and then when things got tough for them, they turned tail and gave themselves up.'

'That bloody Mussolini was hoping to become another Hitler,' her father said, 'and he had the Italians all dancing around him like puppets, and then when the tide turned for his party, he scuttled off looking for Hitler to rescue him and left them all to their own misfortunes.' He thumbed behind him. 'And we're stuck picking up the pieces for Italy, having that lot in the prisoner of war camp just up the road from us. And from what I've heard, they're letting some of them roam about like free men, up and down to the shops and all sorts. The fact two of them were about today proves they can do whatever the hell they want.'

Emily felt a wave of despondency wash over her. She felt she should speak up for the decent Italian she had met, but she knew it would only cause an awkwardness between them. It would particularly agitate her mother, and make her go over all the war stuff about Jack again. She decided to say nothing.

'It's a disgrace having those Italians nearby,' Hannah Browne said again. 'That's all I can say.' She looked at her husband. 'I'll get your soup now. Poor Emily is dead on her feet after her late night. I've told her to go up to bed for an hour when she's finished eating.'

'Are you all right, love?' her father asked. 'You seem a bit washed out.'

'I'm just tired.'

When they had finished eating, Emily went upstairs to her bedroom. She undressed down to her satin petticoat and then climbed in between the cool cotton sheets. Within minutes she had slipped into a deep sleep.

She awoke half an hour later, her heart pounding, as though something was terribly wrong – and then she realised she had been dreaming. She tried to remember, but could only recall snippets of it. There were children in scenes, she thought, from school, but she could not be sure. She closed her eyes again and drifted back into sleep for another hour, and when she awoke the second time, she remembered dreaming that Father Dempsey had been speaking to her very seriously about the rosary beads that the Italian prisoner had given her. She could now clearly picture herself passing them around in the class, so that each pupil could examine them and see how they had been carved from wood.

The dream had then switched to her in the playground during the morning break and seeing Louis, talking at the school gate to a group of policemen, who suddenly became angry. She had watched, frozen to the spot in shock, as they pushed him around and then put handcuffs on him, dragging him towards the police car. As Emily turned away, she heard her name being called, and when she looked back, Louis had transformed into the Italian prisoner. In the dream, she had run towards the police car but then everything changed, and she found herself in the Bluebell Hotel playing musical chairs with the children in her class.

She sat up in the bed now, trying to make sense of it all, and concluded it was a weird amalgamation of the conversations from earlier. Although her head felt fuzzy and she was still tired, she decided to get up, as she did not want to risk having more unsettling dreams. She would be fine after a cup of tea, and then she would tackle marking her schoolbooks.

She put her skirt and blouse back on, then she went to the wardrobe to get her comfortable sandals, brushed her hair and went out of the room. As she came down the stairs, she heard a familiar voice and stopped to listen, surprised that it was the priest. She wondered now if she had heard his voice earlier, when she was half asleep, and that it had prompted her dream.

As she went towards the kitchen, she wondered if the priest had come to encourage her mother to go back to mass again. He was good in that he kept trying, and didn't take offence when she refused. Emily thought he was also good with her father, given that he wasn't even Catholic, and only attended church for special occasions.

When she went into the kitchen, both her parents and the priest were seated comfortably at the table, drinking tea. She was relieved to see her mother smiling. Smiling as much as she did these days.

'Hello, Father,' she said. 'How are you?'

'I can't complain, Emily,' he said, 'and anyway, who would want to listen to me?'

'We were just talking about you,' her father said. 'We were saying how much you love your job in the school, and how you sit here marking books most nights or sorting out bits for your nature table and art classes.'

Emily felt herself cringe, as she always did when her father started bragging about her teaching in the school. 'I'm just doing my job,' she said, going over to stand by the sink.

'There's tea in the pot,' her mother said. 'It should still be warm enough.'

'Father Dempsey called in to let us know about that trouble outside the shop,' her father said.

'Ah, it gave me an excuse to look in on you,' the priest said, 'and I saw Tom amongst the crowd that had gathered at the shops, but he was gone by the time we had sorted things out. I just thought I would call in and bring you up to date on what happened.'

Emily's father looked over at her. 'It seems,' he said, 'that young Harold was in the shop, and he left his bike outside and when he came out it was gone. Father Dempsey was just saying that this has happened to him before and it was the same lads.'

'Was it the Italian men?' she asked. 'Did they try to steal his bike?'

The priest's eyebrows shot up. 'No, no, they did not. I was explaining to your father that it was the other fellows, the local ones. Harold told me about this recently. A gang of them have been bullying him, and any time they see him they take the bike off him just to taunt him.'

Emily felt relieved it was local boys.

'You couldn't be up to the young pups,' her father said.

'Harold was in the shop, and he saw them at the bike,' Father Dempsey explained, 'and when he ran out, the brats surrounded him, and were making a fool out of the poor lad. Jeering and imitating the way he speaks.' The priest held his hands out.

'You know how cruel some people can be with those who are different in any way.'

Her mother looked upset. 'The poor lad...'

'They were acting like they were giving the bike back to him, and then when he went for the handlebars they would whip it away from him again. Of course, Harold lost his rag with them, as they knew he would, and he was shouting and kicking out at them. This played into their hands as they love teasing him, and they started pushing and shoving him around, which only made him worse.'

'I wouldn't blame him for losing his rag,' Emily said. She felt almost sick picturing the scene.

'Anyway, it was lucky that the two Italian men happened to be passing by, and they stopped to help. When one of them went to take the bike to give it back to Harold, one of the bigger lads made a swipe for him, calling them all the ignorant names you can imagine. Then the other lads piled in on top of the poor Italian, and had him down on the ground kicking him, so naturally the other Italian had to help his friend.'

Emily could see her father looking across at her mother and shrugging.

'That was when I came upon them,' the priest said, 'and it didn't take long to see quite clearly who was to blame. The Italian lads were innocently walking down the road on their way home from Mrs Fox's house. You might know her, she's an elderly lady who attends our church.'

'I think I do,' Hannah said. 'She's a small, neat lady.'

'And what in God's name were prisoners doing up at her house?' her father asked. 'Why would they be allowed outside the prison?'

Emily noticed the patient smile that came on the priest's face, as though used to dealing with this kind of question all the time.

'They were cutting her grass and weeding and digging vegetables up for her.' He left a little silence as though to allow his words to digest. 'Two of the Italian men have been going to Mrs Fox and any elderly people on their own who need help with gardening and odd jobs. They have been doing voluntary work for months.'

'I suppose when the church organise it,' her mother said, 'people are more likely to trust them.'

'That's true, but it's not just the Catholic church parishioners, they help elderly people from all denominations. I think they are just glad to get out of the camp and mix with ordinary people.'

Her father gave a weary sigh. 'I'm amazed that people would allow them anywhere near their houses,' he said. 'And with all due respect to you, Father, they are still our enemies. They fought on the side of the Germans until the Allies defeated them, and that Mussolini was as bad as Hitler if he'd got the chance.'

The priest nodded his head. 'I know that there were some who followed Mussolini,' he said, 'but there were as many who were against him and had no choice in the matter. They were treated very badly and would have been killed if they hadn't done as they were told. I heard the women and elderly people who were left at home were abused and starved if they didn't fall in with the fascists.' He paused. 'A lot of the men in the camp have lost family members while they were away, as a lot of the cities have been bombed as badly as London. Some of them have no homes to go back to.'

'It's the same here in England, Father, and our country only got involved to help others,' Tom said. 'You can't compare the Italians to us. They were with the instigators of the war, and were to blame for some of our lads being killed.'

'I agree with what you're saying,' the priest replied, 'but I visit the camp regularly and I've spoken to all the men there, and there are only a couple who would be on the side of the fascists. The vast majority were relieved when they were taken prisoner because they didn't want to be associated with the fascists or the Nazis.' He paused. 'It would have been the same thing if Britain had been overrun with Mosley and the British Union of Fascists and they joined up with Hitler, and we all had to do what we were told.'

There was a silence now during which Emily felt a coward for not speaking up and agreeing with Father Dempsey, but she had her mother to consider and the family's feelings about losing Jack.

Her mother looked over at the priest. 'And was Harold OK?' she asked quietly.

'Shook up as you can imagine,' Father Dempsey said. 'But he wasn't hurt as such. It would have been easy to let the bullies go with a telling-off, but they have been getting away with it for far too long. I thought he hadn't been himself for a while, but I never imagined there was anything so serious going on.'

'And how was he at home?'

'I don't think Harold mentioned every time there was an incident,' the priest explained, 'but his mother noticed he had become awkward about going down to the shops on his own and she didn't know why.'

'The poor lad, and his mother's such a nice person.'

'When the police arrived, I could see a change in the bully boys,' the priest said. 'I knew that they had been given a fright, but I couldn't be sure if it was enough. For all I knew they might make things worse for Harold when he was on his own, and I didn't want to take that chance, so I decided to let the police deal with it. They carry more weight with young lads than a priest would, especially if their families are not from our religion.'

'How did the police react when they saw the Italians were involved?' her father enquired.

Father Dempsey shrugged. 'All the witnesses confirmed that the Italian fellow had come to Harold's rescue, and that the lads attacked him first. The second Italian lad was only trying to stop it, and never even struck a blow. When me and the other men tried to pull them apart, the tallest of the thugs was still kicking out.'

Emily wondered if Marco had been one of the Italians, and the thought of him being attacked sent a little shudder through her. Having listened to the priest, her conscience also told her that she needed to speak up. 'It's awful those boys were bullying poor Harold, and worse that they turned on two innocent men who tried to help. And it doesn't matter which nationality they were, they didn't deserve that.'

'I'm glad to hear you saying that, Emily,' the priest said.

'Were they hurt badly?'

'A few cuts and bruises,' the priest said, 'but it could have been a lot worse if we hadn't intervened. Those boys were big enough and a kick to the head can cause serious damage.'

Her father shook his head. 'They might have to stop the Italians mixing so freely in the area. Those lads likely wouldn't have reacted so badly if it had been local men who intervened. People who would have known their fathers and mothers.'

'Maybe so, but the police told me that they have never had any trouble with the men in the camp, and they had their own reservations when they first heard about it. They said it's well run, and they go up and down to it regularly, so they would know. They said that in the majority, they're all decent enough people.'

'And how has Mrs Fox found them?' Hannah Browne asked, in a disapproving tone.

'Thorough gentlemen,' Father Dempsey said. 'That's exactly how she described them. One of them brought her a lovely handmade bird box for her garden. It was so well done, I told her to tell the chap he should sell them in the local shops.'

Emily thought about the rosary beads and guessed that most of the men in the camp probably had hobbies like carving things from pieces of wood.

There was a silence then her mother said, 'Your tea, Emily. You haven't poured your tea yet.'

After Father Dempsey left, there was an uneasy silence in the house as Emily sat drinking her lukewarm tea and her mother washed up the dishes. Her father lifted his newspaper again and started to read.

When she finished, Emily took her cup and saucer to the sink and then helped her mother dry the crockery. Afterwards, her mother went upstairs, and her father went out into the garden. Emily sat at the table, pondering the conversation, and wondering why it had left her feeling uneasy.

She shrugged to herself, and then got her schoolbooks out and began to mark them.

Chapter Fourteen

Sophie got off the bus and walked towards the house. As she went up the driveway, she could see the sitting room light on, and knew her mother would be there waiting for her.

By the time she reached the door, her mother had already opened it for her, white-faced and anxious. 'I was so worried . . . are you all right?'

Sophie walked in past her without speaking, and down the hallway to the sitting room. Without taking her coat off, she went over and sat in the armchair. 'You might as well tell me everything,' she said. 'Because Tony will be home tomorrow and he needs to know who he is marrying.'

Dorothy took a deep breath. 'Surely, there's no need to tell him anything – well, not at this time. Your birth certificate states your legal name as Morley . . .'

'I don't want to start our married life under false pretences.' Sophie's voice was dull and flat. Talking to Alice – crying with her – had drained away her energy. 'I want him to know the truth about me – and the truth about you. He didn't get to know Daddy, but I'm sure they would have got on. Unlike you, Daddy wouldn't have judged him for coming from an ordinary background.'

'I was afraid of you making a mistake . . .' She halted. 'Of making the same mistake I did with your real father.'

'Well, thank you for that,' Sophie said bitterly.

'I want you to know, I have no regrets about having you, Sophie. Not for one moment. The regrets were about how it all happened, before George stepped in to make everything all right.' Dorothy lifted her head. 'We would have managed. I'm a strong person and I would have found a way to make things work, but we would never have had the lovely life George gave us.'

Sophie looked directly at her mother. 'What happened? Why did you end up pregnant with me and unmarried?'

Dorothy came to sit in the chair opposite now. 'Because I foolishly fell in love with the wrong man. I had moved from Durham to Manchester when the textile firm I worked for opened a new branch, and I was living in a flat on the outskirts of the city. I didn't know many people, and I was lonely and homesick when I met him. He was handsome and funny, and extremely confident, and he became like a lifeline to me.'

'Where did you meet him?' Sophie asked, suddenly curious.

Dorothy tightened her lips together, remembering. 'On a train. I used to catch the train from my flat in Heaton Moor into Manchester every morning, and one day it broke down and we were stuck in a railway siding for hours. He was in the seat beside me, and he started chatting and when we finally moved onto another train he asked if I would like to go to the cinema with him after work.' She shrugged. 'And that was that. For weeks we met practically every night, going dancing, going to cafes and cocktail bars and to the pictures.'

'And what went wrong?'

'He eventually told me he was engaged to marry a girl down in London, but he told me he loved me in a way he had never imagined. He said he was going to do the decent thing and break the engagement off.

'I believed every word he said.' Dorothy's face was dismal now. 'I was so innocent and stupid, I thought that if I agreed to sleep with him, that it would somehow bond us together. That he would feel responsible towards me because it was something that I had told him I would only do with my husband. After he promised to marry me, we went away for a weekend.' She sighed. 'I thought it would be OK, because I truly believed we would be together forever.'

'What happened?'

'He disappeared. He said he was going down to London to tell his fiancée about us, but...' She closed her eyes. 'But he never came back.'

Sophie paused, trying to take it all in. 'Did you see him again?'

'No. He literally disappeared.' There was a pause. 'Of course, I tried to find him. After some weeks I rang his parents. I had only met his family briefly, and I didn't want to tell them what had happened.' She looked at Sophie. 'About you, I mean. They confirmed he had gone to London, but they had no address for him. They took my work phone number and said they would ring if they heard from him.'

'And did they?'

'They rang about a month later to say that he had written to them to say he had left London and had gone to America.'

'With his fiancée?'

'I couldn't ask,' Dorothy said. 'His mother seemed a lovely lady, and I knew she was telling the truth.'

'What did you do then?' Sophie asked, her voice more weary than angry now.

'I went back to work and carried on as usual, without telling a soul about my situation. I went to the local vicar and asked for advice. He was young and I knew he was more open-minded than the other ones.' Dorothy's eyes moved slowly to the ceiling, as though she was trying to picture the scene again. A scene she had pushed to the darkest corner of her mind. 'He immediately suggested adoption,' she said in a low voice, 'and he offered to arrange it for me, but I knew by the end of our conversation that I was going to keep you. I told him I had to go back to Durham to get help from my parents, and he said that parents often wanted their daughters to have the babies adopted, too. He said he could refer me to a mother and baby place in Manchester, where I could go before I was due to have you.'

Sophie felt the person she was listening to was not like her mother at all. The words and the unexpected humility in her tone showed a vulnerability that she had not thought her mother possessed. Then she remembered the accusations her mother had hurled at her when she first said she wanted to marry Tony. Knowing what she did now, Sophie suddenly felt aggrieved and angry again. How unfair and hypocritical of her mother to have been so hard on her.

She lifted her head, her eyes narrowed. 'So where did Dad come into all this? What made him suddenly rush to your rescue?' She gave a hollow laugh. 'Well, I suppose rush is hardly the right description when you only made it to the altar days before I was born. Had he been waiting in the wings, ready to step in when you decided that you had no other option?'

'Sophie!' her mother snapped. 'Don't talk about your father like that... I'm surprised at you. Under the circumstances I can understand how you feel about me, but not your father.' She lifted her head. 'I always cared for him – always. And after we married, I grew to love him very much.' Dorothy cleared her throat. 'I knew George from when I worked in the office at Cooke's Trimming Factory. I dealt with the orders from Morleys, so I spoke to him on the phone regularly and he often dropped in to check out new stock.'

'Did he ask to court you?'

Dorothy lowered her head. 'Not as such, because he knew I was already seeing someone else, but if you are asking if he had feelings for me, then yes, I knew he did. He was a quiet, reserved young man back then, and it took him a while to come out of his shell.' Tears suddenly came into her eyes. 'I often wondered if he had been brave enough to ask me out earlier, how differently things might have turned out. But then, I wouldn't have had you – and I wouldn't change that for anything.'

Sophie sat in silence.

Dorothy clasped her hands tightly together now. 'I had left the factory before it became obvious that I was pregnant, and when my savings were beginning to run out, I went to the big house for mothers outside Manchester. I hadn't seen George for months, and one day – just a month or so before you were born – I went for a check-up at Stepping Hill Hospital, and we ran into each other.' She shrugged. 'There was no hiding my condition by then, and no point in lying about the situation. I told him the truth and he was very kind to me. He drove me to a hotel for lunch and by the time it was over he had proposed to me.'

'That's extraordinary,' Sophie said. 'Didn't he mind you were carrying another man's baby?'

'It was extraordinary,' Dorothy said, 'and I thank God every day for it.' Her eyes widened. 'But I didn't rush into it. I didn't accept him immediately, although I really wanted to. I told him it was much too quick to propose within hours of knowing my situation, and that I wanted him to go home and think about it very carefully. To take another week or so to work out all the ramifications.' She held her hands up. 'It wasn't as though he was short of options. Apart from the fact that he was a lovely, kind man, your father was very good-looking and women found him attractive, but he wasn't confident.'

'His leg,' Sophie said, nodding her head.

'Yes, he was always self-conscious about his leg, and he avoided dance halls and sporting events because of it. I was worried he might regret his decision later, and I wanted him to be really sure of what he was committing himself to. He came back within days, and he convinced me that he knew exactly what he was doing, and that he wanted us to marry as soon as possible.' She looked straight at Sophie now. 'So now you know why everything was such a last-minute rush. It was me who delayed things, not your father.'

'Did he wonder about the other man, or think that you pre-ferred him? Did he not worry that if the other man came back, you might leave him?'

Dorothy shook her head vigorously. 'George was a far su-perior man in every way, and, having made such an error the first time around, I was hardly likely to be misled again. I knew I had been given a wonderful chance for both of us, and nothing on earth would have made me risk it. And that was how things were from the day we married until the day your father died.'

'What about me?'

'What do you mean?'

'Surely he must have had some reservations about taking on another man's child? He would have had to be a saint not to have some feelings.'

'Absolutely none. Don't you think you would have known, felt something, if he harboured any resentments?'

Sophie looked at her. 'I don't know.'

'You must know that your father and I adored you. Absolutely adored you. From the day you were born he always thought of you as his own.'

Since everything else now seemed to be out in the open, Sophie asked a question she had always wondered. One she had asked as an innocent child, but never as a grown adult, feeling that it was too sensitive. 'Why didn't you have any more children?'

'It just never happened. I had two or three little episodes – so small I wasn't sure whether I had ever been pregnant or not. The doctors couldn't find any reason for it, with either me or George.' Dorothy gave a little sigh. 'It might have been nice for you to have had brothers or sisters, but it wasn't meant to be.' She shrugged. 'I don't know what more to say ... I have told you everything.'

Sophie put her head in her hands. 'I don't know what to think ...'

'I'm so sorry if it has spoiled your wedding. I would never have wanted to do that.'

'Finding this out has been a bombshell, but, if I am entirely honest, your attitude towards me marrying Tony before was almost as hurtful.'

'I am so sorry for that, and I hope in time, you will forgive me.'

Sophie viewed her mother now, and Alice's words came back to her. 'Let it go. *Don't torture yourself over this one thing. You have so many other good things in your life ...*' She moved towards the door. 'I'm going upstairs to sort a few things out, and when I come back down later, I want us to pretend this nightmare has never happened. I want to get on with the wedding plans and to make this as happy a day as possible.' She looked her mother straight in the eye. 'What happens afterwards I do not know.'

Chapter Fifteen

Alice woke with a start, surprised to see Greg standing by the side of the bed holding a cup and saucer. He had been home a few days now, but she still hadn't become used to it. She looked at the bedside clock and was even more startled to see that it was almost seven o'clock. 'God, I've slept in...' she said, moving into a sitting position. 'I didn't hear the alarm going off.'

'I woke earlier,' he said, 'and I thought I'd go downstairs and get things started so there's no need for you to rush.' He waited until she had sorted the pillows behind her back, then handed her the tea. 'You're up early every morning, so I'm glad I could let you have a lie-in.'

'But I need to sort the newspapers,' she said, 'and bring the milk crates inside.'

'All done,' he said. 'And I can hold the fort until Maeve and young Freddy arrive, so you can take it easy for a change.' He looked towards the door. 'I have toast under the grill for you, and I'll bring it up in two minutes.' He smiled. 'Butter then marmalade?'

Alice suddenly felt flustered. Part of her felt strange and almost vulnerable, still in bed while he stood there beside her fully dressed. 'Yes,' she said, 'that would be lovely, thanks...'

'And I have the boiler on for you, so the water should be hot enough for a bath in the next half an hour. I heard you saying to Sophie last night on the phone that you wanted to have your bath before going to the hairdressers.'

'That's great,' she said. 'Thank you...'

He turned away and went back downstairs, leaving her to ponder over this new thoughtfulness. Alice could not remember him ever making breakfast for her before. In the few days he had been home, Alice also noticed that he had seemed kinder and more considerate. Usually, when he came back after weeks or months away in one of the army camps, he couldn't wait to get out to meet up with any of his old friends who were around. He would meet them for a drink in Stockport and on a couple of occasions, he had even caught the train to Manchester or Liverpool and be gone for most of the day and home on the late-night train.

It had crossed her mind that he may have been seeing Marjorie Jones at that time, and that the army friends were a cover for their affair, but she pushed the unsettling thoughts away. Dwelling on that situation would only colour the short time they had together, and Alice knew she needed to make the most of it. She needed to work out how things were between them, and whether her old feelings for him had come back. Meanwhile, she would enjoy this considerate side of him.

This new thoughtfulness was a side that his mother would have approved of, because she had often quietly criticised him to Alice.

'He's like a bloody cat on a hot tin roof,' Betty had said, 'full of energy and wanting to be doing things. He was always the same, even when he was young, that's why life in the army suits him so well, because there's always something going on. There's many a poor lad would give their right arm to be out of it all, and back home in a quiet routine, but our Greg seems to thrive on army life. I'm not saying that he would like it so much if he was back on active duty, but the job he has in the training camps suits him down to the ground.'

Alice wondered if he had matured since losing his mother, had realised that the important things in life could just fly by, while he was busy looking towards the next exciting adventure. Perhaps, she thought, he may have been reflecting over what had happened to him at Dunkirk, and those who had not survived.

Perhaps he had eventually realised that life did not have to be lived at a fast, exciting pace all the time.

He had been more considerate in other ways, and on their first night together in bed since his return, he had been slower and more attentive to her than usual. Alice had not been sure how she would react to him because they had little physical contact when he was home for his mother's funeral, other than the night before he left. This time, he had lain with her in his arms first, asking her about her days in the shop and then telling her random things about the training camp, and what he thought might happen next in the war in Europe.

When he had turned towards her, her body had felt rigid, and she found that she did not quite know how to respond – what to do with her hands and her arms, and when he kissed her, she felt as though she was kissing a stranger. She wondered if it was something to do with him having been away so long, that she had forgotten all the little things she had learned early on in their marriage. But when her mind went back to their first physical encounters, she remembered the intense feelings and longings, which she now realised she had lost when his affair came to light. She closed her eyes to block out the painful memories, and tried to remember Betty's advice, and how one mistake need not spell the end of a good marriage.

Alice had willed herself back to the time when things were good and natural between them, and eventually, her body began to relax and after a while they were making love as they used to – or almost used to. Afterwards, when she turned away from him, she realised that there was a part of her that was still separate from him, a part which was going to take some time to fall back into place. If it ever fell into place again. Alice wondered now if their marriage had ever been a 'good marriage' at all. A strange sadness came over her, and she buried her face in the pillow to hold the tears back.

After finishing breakfast, Alice dressed in slacks and a jumper for working, then went downstairs. She would have her bath later, before going to the hairdressers up in the main street in Edgeley. As she came down into the living area, she could hear the cheery sound of the radio playing 'Boogie Woogie Bugle Boy'. Greg loved all kinds of music – jazz and even classical, and the radio was on night and day when he was home.

She could hear voices in the shop and when she entered, Greg was there, leaning against the counter and chatting with young Freddy and Maeve, who was there to cover for Alice when they went to the wedding later in the morning.

Freddy looked at her with big eyes. 'Mr Fairclough was telling us about some of the aircraft down at the training centres. We were asking him about where he's going to be posted, but he can't tell us. He said he's learned Italian – so I'm guessing it's somewhere in Italy.'

'That sounds like a fair enough guess,' she said, smiling at him. 'We'll have to wait until he comes back when the war is over to find out.' She suddenly remembered. 'I had a lie-in this morning, Freddy, so Bella might be ready for a little walk.'

'Already done,' Greg said. 'I've taken her out twice since I got up, and fed her, and she's having a little nap now.' He pointed towards the door. 'You might like to check the boxes outside, I've done them the way—' He hesitated. 'The way we used to do them, but you might want to change them around.'

Without saying anything, Alice knew he meant the way his mother did things. 'That's great,' she said. 'I'm sure they're fine.'

She went over to the rack where the newspapers were, and rifled through them, making sure the right names were on any ordered papers. She then moved to check the bread delivery on the shelves. 'I'm putting two loaves underneath the counter for Mrs Knowles,' she told Maeve and Freddy. 'The bread was all gone when she arrived yesterday, so I said I would make sure she got some today.' She raised her brows. 'I know we have a rule of first come first served, but she is trying to feed a houseful with children and elderly parents.'

Freddy's face suddenly flushed. 'Is it OK if I put one by for my mam?' he asked in a low, embarrassed tone. 'You can take it out of my pay…'

'Take one now and leave it in the kitchen,' Alice told him. 'We'll sort it out later.'

'The wedding sounds as if it will be lovely, being in the Grosvenor and everything,' Maeve said. 'I've only been there once myself, and it was lovely. Very posh indeed.'

'I'm looking forward to it,' Alice said. She glanced around the shop. 'Well, if you're all sure you can manage, I'll go and start getting myself organised.'

As she went out of the shop and into the hallway, she heard Greg behind her.

'What time did you say we're leaving for the church?' he asked.

'I have to be dressed and up at Sophie's house for eleven o'clock,' Alice told him. 'It's not far from St George's, so if you drop me up first, that would be great. I can't be late this morning with being a bridesmaid, and I know Sophie will be anxious everything goes well.'

'That's no problem,' he said. 'I'm just checking if there's anything you want me to do beforehand.'

'I think everything is OK…' she said, trying not to sound surprised by his concern for her. It was always she or his mother who had made any arrangements for functions or outings, and usually had to remind him nearer the time. 'Maeve and Freddy should be fine, they are here every Saturday and know the routine, and Freddy will sort Bella.'

'She's a nice little thing,' he said. 'I'm glad you have company. It must have been lonely here for you when my mother died. I often thought that when I went back… I felt guilty for leaving you on your own.' He paused. 'But we all have to do our bit with this bloody war.'

'I'm fine,' Alice said. 'If I'd known how much I would enjoy having her, I would have thought of getting a dog before.'

He paused, then he put his hand on her shoulder. 'We live and learn, don't we?'

Alice looked at him. There were a few moments of silence and then she said, 'I hope we can learn.'

'I definitely have learned.' He moved now and put both his arms around her neck and drew her into him. 'I promise you, with all my heart, that I'll never make that same mistake again.'

Alice leaned against him and closed her eyes.

Chapter Sixteen

When Alice came back from the hairdressers, there was a queue of women outside the shop, holding ration books in their hands, and waiting hopefully for the fresh bread that they knew had been delivered. She nodded and spoke to them as she passed, and quite a few complimented her new hairstyle. She explained about going to the wedding, and they all wished her friend and new husband well.

'They might as well make it legal, love,' one woman joked. 'With rationing and blackouts, there's nowt much else to enjoy these days!'

Another joined in saying, 'At least you'll get well fed today!'

'Hopefully!' Alice joked back, then went quickly inside before anyone asked her where the reception was being held. The Grosvenor was the most expensive place in Stockport, and she was sensitive to the fact that it would be well out of the price range of most of her customers. When she saw that Maeve and Freddy were busy serving customers, she just gave them a quick wave and went on into the house to get dressed for the wedding.

Greg was in the bathroom, so she went into the bedroom to where her blue bridesmaid's dress and matching stole were hanging up. She took off her slacks and sweater, and then went to her underwear drawer for her suspender belt and stockings. Stockings were precious and only for very special occasions these days, and she could not think of a more special day for them. Before putting them on, she went to the bedroom door and checked that it was tightly shut, as she did not want Greg to walk in on her. Before, when they were newly married, she would not have minded, knowing that she looked attractive in the flimsy things, but those uninhibited ways had all gone, and she felt self-conscious with him now. Whilst they had resumed marital relations, it was mainly in darkness and with the bed-covers over them. Alice wasn't comfortable to be viewed in lacy underclothes and stockings because she could not bear thinking that she now might be compared to another woman.

She sat on the edge of the bed, and deftly hooked the white lace suspender belt and then she very carefully pulled on her silk stockings. She slipped on her white slingback sandals and then she went over to the wardrobe to lift the blue satin dress down.

She had just stepped into the dress and slid the wide straps up on her shoulders when the bedroom door opened, and Greg came in. He looked tall and handsome in his dark suit, and his blue tie and handkerchief emphasised the blue in his eyes.

He saw her hands move to the back of the dress to do the zip up. 'Let me do that for you,' he said, smiling.

She turned her back to him and stood with her eyes closed as he pulled the zip up for her. When she turned around, he was staring at her, his face serious.

'You look beautiful,' he said. 'Absolutely beautiful...'

Alice felt herself blush. 'I don't know about beautiful,' she said, 'but I'm glad I look OK, for Sophie's sake.'

'You do,' Greg said, stepping back to look at her properly. 'Everything about you – your hair, the dress and your face. You smell lovely, too.'

'Thank you,' she said, a warm glow coming over her.

'Everything about you looks perfect,' he said, coming to put his arms around her. 'You are perfect, Alice. No wonder my mother thought the world of you.'

Alice leaned her head on his shoulder. 'It's awful, isn't it?' She suddenly felt emotional. 'I know it must be much worse for you, but I still can't believe she's gone.'

'She was always proud of the fact I married you, and loved you from the first day I brought you home.'

'That's nice of you to say...'

'It's true,' he said. 'She would have been proud of the way you've taken over the management of the shop. I can see how smoothly everything is run, exactly as she would have done, but in a more modern way. I felt bad leaving you in the lurch so quickly after the funeral, especially since you had to give up teaching to work in a corner shop. I know it was a comedown for you, after all your studying, and then to have to give it all up at a moment's notice.' He moved back now, to look directly at her. 'I just wanted to say, it won't always be this way. You will be able to go back to teaching at some point in the future. I'll make sure of that.'

'When the war is over,' she said. 'When things are back to normal, we can look at the shop again.'

'As long as you know I don't expect you to bury yourself in here,' he said, gesturing around him. 'Not for the rest of your life. We need to be clear on that.'

They were downstairs and ready for the taxi fifteen minutes before it was due. Alice sat in the dining room flicking through a magazine, while Greg had gone into the shop to chat to a customer he knew. After a while, she heard Greg's footsteps coming back in again, and, guessing it was the taxi, went over to the table to lift her blue stole and her handbag.

Greg came to the door. 'There's someone asking to see you,' he said. 'There's no sign of the taxi yet, so I said you had a few minutes.' He looked at his watch. 'I'm just going to get a different pocket handkerchief from the bedroom – I'm sure I have a patterned silk one that matches the tie better. I'll catch you back here in a few minutes.'

'Who is it?' she asked.

He gave a vague shrug. 'A chap with a child, I think.'

Alice stifled a sigh. She didn't have time to chat, but she had no option, since Greg had obviously said she was there. She went cautiously along the hall towards the shop.

When she walked in, negotiating her way around a box of potatoes, she heard a familiar voice. She looked up and saw Louis Girard standing just in the doorway, out of the way of the other customers, who were being served by Maeve and Freddy.

He smiled awkwardly. 'We were passing, and I thought I would introduce this pair to you. We've just been to Stockport Library, and are going to Alexandra Park.' He moved backwards and it was then Alice noticed the two children: a boy with a serious, shy face, and his sister, pretty and smiling confidently, with two long dark plaits.

Alice smiled at them. 'I think I can guess who you are ...'

Louis stretched his hand out. 'Philip,' he said, then moved to the girl, 'and Gabriela.'

'The twins from Guernsey. I have heard all about you.'

'Louis said you are a teacher,' Gabriela said, her eyes bright and interested.

'That's right,' Alice said, 'but I work in this shop now.' She looked at Philip. 'Did you pick some nice books in the library?'

'Yes,' he said. 'I got *Treasure Island* and *Robinson Crusoe*.'

'They are very exciting books,' she told him. 'I'm sure you will love them.'

'Louis said reading them at night before bed will help me to sleep.'

'I always read before I go to sleep, too.'

Louis patted Philip's head. 'I can see we've come at a bad time, and you are on your way out to somewhere special.'

Alice indicated her dress. 'A wedding. Emily and I are brides-maids.'

'Ah!' He tapped his forehead. 'I should have realised ... the same wedding that Emily has been talking about in school. It never occurred to me this morning.' He rolled his eyes. 'I didn't pay attention really, the talk was more for the female staff – about the dresses and the fashion.'

'Well, I can quite understand that,' Alice said, rolling her eyes and laughing.

'Forgive me if it's inappropriate to say, but you look very nice . . . lovely.'

Alice felt herself blush at the compliment and was glad that the radio and the noisy meat slicer drowned out the conversation. 'Thank you,' she said, smiling self-consciously. 'It's a change to get dressed up for something these days.' It was a long time since she had been complimented by someone like Louis Girard who, she knew, would be attractive to a lot of girls.

'I am sure that Emily will look lovely, too,' he said.

'She always does,' Alice agreed, nodding. She looked over at the counter and saw Freddy was free. She beckoned him over and quietly asked him to get two lollipops from under the counter, and when he came back, she gave one each to the children.

The children were delighted and thanked her.

'You wait outside,' Louis told them. 'I want to check something with Alice.'

The children moved towards the door, and then Philip turned back and looked up at her. 'Thank you,' he said, his big eyes looking into hers. 'You are a very kind lady, and I am sure you were a very nice teacher, too.'

Alice was surprised and touched by his comment. 'That's very nice of you to say.' She thought few children, especially at his age, would have the confidence to say something like that. As she smiled back at him, she felt something shift inside her, as she saw the vulnerability in his expression. Something she often recognised with children in school, who were struggling with life.

When the twins went outside, Louis turned to her. 'I'm sorry about catching you at the wrong time . . .'

'It's fine,' she said. 'It was nice of you to call in. Have you had any luck with finding a new place?'

He shook his head. 'The vicar and his family have been very good, but they have enough with a new baby who is not sleeping well. Also, I still think it would be best if we found a quieter place for them. Philip is not so good with noise and crowds.' He shrugged. 'That's why I try to get them out of the house if I can.'

Alice felt guilty she had been so absorbed with Greg and the wedding that she hadn't made a bigger effort to help. 'I'll keep trying,' she told him. 'When I'm at the wedding this afternoon, I'll talk to my friend's mother, who is in the Women's Institute, and ask if she knows of anywhere suitable.'

'That would be great,' he said. He looked towards the door. 'I hope you didn't mind me dropping in, but I feel I know you with Emily being a friend to both of us.'

'I don't mind at all,' she said, feeling an unexpected blush coming to her face.

'I don't want Mrs Ponsonby's good work with them to be undone,' Louis said, 'and I wish I had my own place so they could live with me, but I'm just renting a room in a house with two other teachers. It's even pushing things when I bring the twins to my place at the weekend.'

'You really couldn't do any more for them,' Alice said. 'They are lucky to have you.'

There was a pause. 'I must go.' He smiled at her. 'I hope you and your husband enjoy the wedding.'

'Thank you,' she said. 'And I'll tell Emily that I spoke to you.' As he turned now to leave the shop, she suddenly heard herself say, 'Why don't you bring them for tea some evening after school? We close for a half-day on a Wednesday, so I'm off in the afternoon.' Greg would be gone, she thought, and things would be back to normal.

'Really?' he said. 'Wouldn't that be a lot of trouble for you?'

'It would be no trouble. I would like to have them.'

'Next Wednesday,' he said, nodding. 'They will be very happy to come here again.'

He went out and as Alice turned away, she saw the taxi pull up across the road. She went back down the hallway and called to Greg that it was time to go. She paused to look in the hall mirror and check that she looked her best for the wedding – looked her best for Sophie. As she checked her reflection, Alice was pleasantly surprised. She looked better than she had imagined. She thought back to the compliment Louis Girard had given her and a light flush came to her face.

Chapter Seventeen

As the taxi turned onto Wellington Street, Alice looked over at Greg. 'I hope Sophie isn't too nervous.'

'As long as it's not one of those hasty war marriages, trying to bring a bit of glamour and excitement into their lives. You hear of so many of them happening now.'

'I don't think so,' Alice said. 'Sophie is sensible. She's had a few boyfriends and never given the impression she would have rushed into anything serious before. She seems sure that Tony is different to anyone she has ever met.'

'All we can do is wish them well,' Greg said. 'And help them to enjoy their big day.'

The taxi slowed up and then turned into Morley's driveway. Greg got out his side of the vehicle and then went around to help Alice out.

'I'll see you at the church,' she said, stepping down carefully, so as not to tread on her dress. 'You should be OK on your own now, you'll know a few people there.'

'Don't worry about me,' he said, smiling at her.

Alice walked towards Morley's front door, and then she turned back and smiled at him. 'See you later.' He was only home for a few more days, she thought, and he was trying his best to make up for his mistakes. Alice decided she needed to buck herself up and try to meet him halfway.

Sophie's mother came to the door, looking sophisticated in a lovely lilac dress and matching jacket and a beautiful floral hat. 'Come in, Alice, dear, you look lovely,' Dorothy said, a warm smile on her face. Alice stepped inside and was ushered into the hallway. 'Emily arrived a few minutes ago, and Sophie is almost ready, just touching up her make-up. They are both upstairs if you would like to join them. Sophie looks wonderful... like something from a wedding magazine.'

As she climbed the staircase, Alice thought Mrs Morley's happy demeanour had to be a good sign, and she was relieved for Sophie's sake. She walked along the thickly carpeted hallway towards Sophie's room. Alice paused for a few moments at the door of the lovely bedroom. Sophie's beautiful home had always been a world away from the ordinary houses both Alice and Emily had grown up in. The two girls were chattering away and didn't notice her at first.

Emily was sitting on the end of the bed, adjusting the strap on the back of one of her slingback shoes. The bride – resplendent in her lace dress decorated with pearls and tiny flowers, and looking more glamorous than ever – was sitting in front of the white, French-style dressing-table which matched the double-sized wardrobe. A small chandelier hung in the middle of the room, and a tall standard lamp with a fringed, Victorian shade stood by the window. Above the bed was a gilt-edged mirror, decorated with entwined cherubs, and two gilt lamps flanked either side of the bed.

As Sophie's mother had described, the scene looked like a feature in a bridal magazine. Alice tapped loudly on the bedroom door, and the two girls whirled around and made little squealing sounds when they saw her and then came rushing towards her to give her a hug.

Alice looked at Sophie. 'You look spectacular! The most beautiful bride I've ever seen.'

'Really?' Sophie said, her eyes wide with delight. 'I hope Tony thinks so...'

'He won't be able to believe his eyes.' She looked over at Emily. 'And you are gorgeous, too – the perfect bridesmaid.'

Emily came over and hugged her. 'Oh, thanks, Alice,' she said. 'You look lovely as well.' She gestured towards Sophie. 'I can't believe she has organised these gorgeous dresses and everything else in such a short time.'

Sophie pulled an anguished face. 'We still have the wedding service to get through, and then the photographs and the reception and everything. What if something goes wrong?'

'I'm sure everything will be perfect,' Alice said. 'Your mother seems relaxed, as if everything is under control.'

'She's got over the wedding happening so quickly, and her and Tony have had a few good chats, and they're getting on very well.' Sophie raised her eyebrows. 'Tony said his own family had reservations about the wedding being so quick, too, but I didn't tell my mother that.'

'There's always tensions with families about weddings,' Emily said. 'I can just imagine what my family would be like, coming from a mixed religious background – Catholic and Church of England. In Dad's case, nothing really, because he doesn't really believe in anything and never goes to church. That religious mix causes problems with both sides of the family.'

'I think you told us years ago that some of your relatives criticised your mother for letting you go to Hilltop School because it wasn't Catholic?'

Emily rolled her eyes. 'They thought my mother should have made me go to a Catholic school even though it was miles away, and I would have had to travel on two buses by myself every day. Thankfully, they've quietened down since they know I teach in a Catholic school.'

A tap came on the door and Dorothy came in carrying a silver tray and five champagne glasses. 'I'm delighted to hear all the laughter,' Dorothy said. 'I was afraid you might be nervous.'

Frances came behind, smiling and carrying the bottle of champagne and a box of biscuits.

'This is my friend, Frances,' she told Alice and Emily, and then introduced the two girls. 'Frances suggested that we all had a little toast to Sophie, to wish her well on her way to her wedding and help to calm any little nerves.'

'Mummy, that's a lovely idea,' Sophie said.

'We managed to pop the cork in the kitchen,' Frances said, smiling, 'and thankfully we didn't break any windows.'

The champagne was poured and then Dorothy held her glass up. 'To my darling Sophie – our beautiful bride – wishing you and Tony every luck in your future married life.'

As they held their glasses up, Alice noticed that although Sophie was smiling, there was no real warmth towards her mother, and realised that the situation between them was not yet resolved. As she lifted the champagne glass to her lips, Emily caught her eye and smiled at her, checking she was all right, reminding her that she hadn't forgotten the difficult situation her friend was in. Alice smiled and gave a little nod to reassure her she was fine.

Hopefully, Alice thought, they would all be fine. Sophie and Tony, starting their new life together. Herself and Greg, trying to put the past behind them. And Emily – and whoever the lucky man was, who eventually found her.

Chapter Eighteen

Dorothy discreetly turned to see Sophie coming up the aisle on the arm of her slightly awkward-looking Uncle James – Dorothy's younger brother. A beautiful vision in a long white dress and veil, held in place by a pearl-studded crown. Her blonde head – perfectly coiffured – was held high as she turned every now and again to acknowledge the guests and smile at them. As she came nearer, Dorothy stole another glance to reassure herself. She saw that Sophie's eyes were smiling and sparkling with happiness, and she felt a wave of relief so intense it left her almost weak.

This day *had* to be the happiest of Sophie's life. Regardless of anything – that it had been hastily arranged, Tony having to go away within the week, the wartime shortages – today had to go perfectly because it would determine how they would move forward as mother and daughter. They had spent little time together since Tony had returned, and neither had referred to the day when Sophie saw her birth certificate.

Each time they had spoken since, Dorothy had hoped to see even a glimmer of their old relationship, but that had not happened until last night. She was not deluded and knew they did not have the light-hearted comradeship that some mothers and daughters had. She knew she irritated Sophie because she preferred things done in the proper way, which young people did not always appreciate, and that she was a little more formal than some of Sophie's friends' mothers. But they had never had any major disagreements that were not sorted out, and in their own way, they had what she thought was a close and loving relationship. She hoped with all her heart that Sophie could put the secrets she had uncovered from the past behind her, and not let it jeopardise their future.

She watched now as a smiling Tony stepped forward to meet his bride and then James – self-conscious of the eyes that were on him – answered the vicar's question about giving Sophie away. The bride was then manoeuvred to stand beside her groom, and James turned away from the altar and came towards Dorothy's pew.

'You did it perfectly,' she whispered to him, as he came to stand in the space beside her.

'As long as it's over and done with,' he said, brushing a shaky hand through his hair.

The small congregation sat down as the vicar began the wedding ceremony, and Dorothy was grateful to have James beside her – filling the space where George should have been. Things, she thought, would have been so very different if he were still alive. In his own quiet way, he had been the foundation stone of the family as he was in the factory.

George would have been there comforting and reassuring her that things would work out, and that he would help sort them for her. Instead, she felt that the dark cloud of deception, which had hovered above her, had slowly descended and was like a shadow hovering around the edges of her life. Nothing she could do could change the circumstances of Sophie's conception, and concealing them all these years had been easier when life was busy, full of work and routine and much less complicated. Now, there was nothing she could do to escape the consequences of it all. She knew one day the whole truth would be revealed, perhaps just as suddenly and simply as Sophie had found out from the birth certificate. At least they had got this far without the entire fallout happening.

They had reached Sophie's wedding day without the truth being revealed to her by someone who was a total stranger to her. Someone who could have walked into their lives again and demanded to be known to his daughter. George had done everything to ensure that did not happen, but he was gone now.

Whatever came next, Dorothy knew she would have to face alone.

Chapter Nineteen

When the speeches were finished and the dishes from the wedding breakfast all cleared away, the family group at the top table were now relaxed enough to speak to each other in a more natural way. James had taken the first opportunity to vacate his prominent seat, and had gone to join his equally quiet wife at her table with their two sons.

Dorothy watched as Tony's mother got to her feet and went to the table where her daughters and her sisters were sitting. She then looked along the table and saw that Sophie was engaged in an animated chat with Tony and Emily. Alice's husband had come up from where he was sitting and had his hand on the back of her chair talking to her.

Just as she began to feel conscious of being on her own, Frances appeared at the table with a glass of white wine in her hand, and sat down in James's seat.

'You must be delighted at how well everything has gone,' Frances said. 'The meal was excellent – as good as any wedding breakfast I had before the war began.'

'I was relieved about that,' Dorothy said. 'I would have felt very responsible if it hadn't been good, having changed the wedding venue.'

'The Grosvenor is always top-notch, although no hotel can be sure at the moment that they will get all the things they need – but they pulled out all the stops today. The trifle was perfect, one of the best I've ever had.' She smiled and tapped her slightly rounded hip. 'Not that I need to add more inches here.'

'Nonsense,' Dorothy said. 'Your figure is every bit as perfect as the trifle.' They both laughed and then her face became serious again. 'And the speeches?'

'Tony did very well, he's a competent public speaker. What he said was lovely, too, he put a lot of thought into it.'

'He certainly did, and I was pleased for Sophie.' Her brow furrowed. 'What did you think about James?'

Frances looked down at the white damask tablecloth. 'He did well, too, considering he was obviously very nervous, but lots of men are when it comes to wedding speeches.' She lifted her glass and took a mouthful of the wine.

'I meant the part about George … Did you see how Sophie reacted?'

'Yes,' Frances said. 'It obviously had an impact on her when James said those lovely things about how proud George would have been to have given her away, and how much he adored her. I was glad to see how she turned so naturally to Tony, and that he comforted her.' She paused. 'I know you didn't want him to know before the wedding, but I think it was the right thing that she told him. It might have been more difficult if she had bottled it up, and then became overwhelmed and it all came out during or after the wedding. You could see that Tony was looking after her, and that shows the strength of their relationship and her trust in him.'

Dorothy took a deep breath. 'Yes, you're right,' she said. 'It does bode very well for their marriage that Tony is the sort of man who will care for her. It's what I always wanted for her, and it's what George would have wanted.' She took a sip of her wine. 'I just feel hurt that she didn't even glance at me when her father's name was mentioned. Before all this happened – even during our little spats – she would have checked how I was.'

'Give her time,' Frances said. 'She will come round, and Tony will be the one to help her see things in a different light. He could turn out to be your best ally, you know. A good son-in-law is a wonderful asset.'

'I hadn't looked at it that way,' Dorothy said, sounding

surprised. She reached over and squeezed her friend's hand. 'Thank you so much for coming to the house last night, and again this morning. You have been like a shield for me through all this. I will never forget it.'

'That's what friends are for, and you have been there for me when I needed you.'

'You must go back to Arthur now and rescue him from those two women from the factory,' Dorothy said, smiling. 'God knows what they are saying to the poor man. And I must go and mix with Tony's family or there will be another black mark chalked up against me.'

Later, when she had talked to everyone she should talk to, and checked everyone had plenty of drinks, Dorothy went back to the top table where Sophie was still sitting with a group of her friends. She came behind Sophie and put her arm on her shoulder. 'Everything OK, darling?' she asked. 'I have been around the room making sure everyone is enjoying themselves, and I've told them the band will be playing soon. Is there anything you would like me to check on?'

Sophie turned to look at her, a smile on her face. 'I think everything seems fine, Mummy,' she said. 'The hotel staff are checking everyone has drinks, and they will be bringing more tea and coffee later with the wedding cake.'

'The wedding service was lovely,' Dorothy said, 'and I am sure the photographs will be wonderful. The woman took great care sorting your veil for each photograph, and checked that your dress and the bridesmaids' dresses were hanging properly before her husband took the photos. The most professional photography business I have ever seen at a wedding.'

'Yes, I must thank Frances for recommending them,' Sophie said. 'She has been such a great help.'

'She has,' Dorothy said, feeling a wave of relief wash over her. 'If there is anything else you want me to do, just let me know.' She moved towards Tony now. 'How are you, young man, now all the formalities are over?'

'Fine, Mrs Morley,' he said. 'Delighted with how smoothly

everything has gone off.' He put his arm around Sophie's chair. 'And I couldn't ask for a more beautiful bride – she is absolutely stunning, isn't she?'

'Absolutely,' Dorothy agreed. She halted then said in a low voice, 'I wish you both all the happiness in the world. I know I was a bit taken aback with it all happening so quickly, but I just know that everything will work out fine for you both.'

'Thanks, Mrs Morley,' Tony said, turning in his chair to look at her. 'And thanks for treating us to this lovely day. I was talking to my mother and the family, and they were all saying what a grand time it's been, and how good you are paying for it all. It's much appreciated.'

'You're welcome, Tony,' she replied.

He smiled warmly at her. 'As I've said to Sophie, my own mother got a shock when I rang to tell her about the wedding being so quick. It's only understandable that you should have been worried, when you hardly knew me.' He touched her hand. 'When this war is all over, I promise I will do everything to look after Sophie. You won't need to worry about a thing.'

Frances was right, Dorothy thought. Tony sounded much more level-headed and mature than she had given him credit for. He might indeed turn out to be a good ally.

Sophie looked at her now. 'Thanks, Mummy,' she said, looking directly at her for the first time that day. 'Apart from wishing Daddy had been here, we couldn't have asked for a better day.'

Dorothy could see that Sophie was sincere when she thanked her for the wedding, and she had referred to her father as she always would have. She could relax now and enjoy the rest of the reception.

Some time later, Dorothy was chatting with Alice and Emily, and then Alice got up to go to the ladies'. 'I think I will accompany you,' Dorothy said. 'I'm sure I could do with touching up my make-up.'

When they arrived in the marble bathroom, the two women stood chatting for a few minutes about how well the church service had gone and how lovely all the ladies looked, then they went into their separate toilet cubicles.

Dorothy was adjusting the catch on one of her suspenders when she heard the main bathroom door open, and some women came in laughing and chattering. She smiled to herself as she recognised Tony's mother's voice, and could tell by her giggly, high-pitched tone that the small, rotund woman had taken a few more sherries since she last spoke to her. She was a nice enough woman, albeit a touch overfamiliar, and Dorothy reckoned they would all get on fine when mixing at future family occasions.

To save getting into another big conversation with the Shaws, she decided that she would stay put in the cubicle, to give the women time to go into their own cubicles. She would then quickly wash her hands and powder her nose, and be gone by the time they had finished.

'What a lovely wedding,' Dorothy heard Mrs Shaw saying. 'I can't wait to get home to tell that nosey Mrs Platt from down the road how lovely the reception in the Grosvenor was. Imagine her catching the bus up to Stockport to come and stand outside the church, so she didn't miss a thing.'

One of Tony's sisters went into a fit of giggles. 'I nearly wet myself laughing,' she said, 'when I saw her peeking through the church railings, thinking we couldn't see her, and trying to get a good look at everything.'

'I gave her a big wave,' Mrs Shaw said, 'then before she had a chance to scarper, I went over and thanked her for coming to see us all.'

'It gives her something to talk about with all the neighbours when she gets back home.'

'She can go straight back and tell everyone what a lovely wedding our Tony had, and how posh a lot of the guests were, and how everyone was dressed up to the nines.'

Dorothy suddenly felt awful, realising that she was now eavesdropping on what the Shaws thought was a private family conversation. She wondered if she had made the right decision about hiding away after all, and hoped they would stop talking now, and go into their respective cubicles so that she could get out. Then she suddenly realised that there had been no sound from Alice, and that she must be waiting in her cubicle, too, until the ladies were out of the way.

'There certainly wasn't a thing Mrs Platt could pick holes in,' Tony's mother said, 'and we all know that if there was a hole to be found, she would find it.'

They all started giggling again, and then his sister said, 'I hope she got a good look at Sophie's fabulous dress and saw her mam in her lovely suit and fancy hat. Mrs Morley is beautiful and so young-looking, isn't she? You can see where Sophie takes her good looks from.'

'She is that,' Mrs Shaw said. 'She's like something out of a magazine, and she's a nice woman, too, given that they're so well off. Fair dues to her, she came around the tables and checked we were all right and made sure we had plenty to drink. A lot of their kind wouldn't even talk to you, but she's a very nice lady.'

Dorothy suddenly felt a bout of nervous laughter coming on. She was relieved the family had enjoyed the wedding so much, and it was nice of them to give her such lovely compliments, but she found it all a bit absurd. The comments about their neighbour, Mrs Platt, watching the proceedings through the church railings, would have been very funny in a different situation. She put her hand over her mouth now, wondering whether they were ever going to use the toilets, and if Alice would stay hidden.

'Let me just comb the back of your hair, Mam,' Tony's sister said. 'There's a little bit sticking out that's annoying me.'

There was a silence then Mrs Shaw said, 'God, girls, can you believe how our Tony has fallen on his feet? Him going to be a factory owner. Who would have thought it?'

Dorothy's heart suddenly plummeted.

'We can all get jobs there when the war's over,' his sister said. 'He'll be the owner by then, won't he?'

'Well, it's Sophie officially,' Mrs Shaw said, 'but in my opinion, it's not the sort of place for a woman to be running. It's OK to work in it, but it's a man's place to be the boss. Anyroads, I'm sure our Tony will have Sophie in the family way soon enough, and she'll be happy to stay at home like the rest of us.'

The other sister spoke now. 'Do you think our Tony would have married her so quickly if she didn't own the factory?'

'Ah, Sophie's a lovely girl,' Mrs Shaw said. 'But you never know, he's always been ambitious, and he's probably fed up travelling about in his own job. Working in the factory might suit him a lot better. Whatever way you look at it, he's going to benefit from marrying into that family, will our Tony.'

'What about her mam, doesn't she work at the factory, too?'

'She's been the owner since the dad died, so I'm sure she'll be glad to retire and let our Tony run things for her. She looks well for her age, but when all is said and done, she's no spring chicken.'

'Do you think they'll change the name of the factory to Shaw? Could you imagine a factory with our name on it?'

'You never know,' Mrs Shaw said. 'But remember, not a word outside the family. It's early days, and if our Tony gets to hear we've been talking about it, all hell will be let loose.'

The outer door opened, and a cleaner came in and lifted the bin, bringing the conversation to an abrupt halt. The three women scattered into the cubicles, and almost simultaneously, Dorothy and a shocked Alice came out of theirs.

Dorothy put her finger to her lips and pointed back to the cubicles, and they both washed their hands and tiptoed out as quickly and quietly as they could.

When they were back in the foyer, Dorothy took Alice's arm and said, 'Let's go into the small lounge at the front of the hotel.'

Alice nodded and asked, 'Are you all right, Mrs Morley?'

'I've had worse happen, dear,' said Dorothy, 'but I'm not ready to go straight back into the main function room... I couldn't face everyone just yet.'

'I understand,' Alice said. 'Nobody will miss us for ten minutes.'

They walked down the carpeted hallway, their steps quickening when they heard women's voices laughing loudly, in case it was the Shaw women exiting the ladies'.

There was a young waiter in the empty lounge, polishing glasses.

'Two large gin and oranges, please,' Dorothy said. 'As quickly as you can, as we only have a few minutes.'

They sat down in the corner over by the window, and as Sophie's mother went to take her compact out of her handbag, Alice noticed that her hand was shaking. She wondered what to say, but was afraid of sounding too familiar or dramatic, so she remained silent.

When the waiter came with the drinks, Dorothy gave him a two-shilling tip and told him to put the drinks on the wedding bill. Then, she lifted her glass and downed half of it in one go. She put the glass back down on the table and looked at Alice. 'I am so glad you were a witness to what happened because I almost felt I was listening to a radio play.' She shook her head. 'If only it had been a radio play.'

'I think they've had a lot to drink . . .'

'Alice, dear,' Dorothy said in a strained voice, 'I'm sure that Sophie told you I had reservations about Tony? That I was concerned about him proposing so quickly, after she told him she owned half the factory?'

Alice bit her lip. 'Sophie is such a good friend, and I don't want to be disloyal.'

Dorothy reached over and clasped Alice's hand for a few moments, her own hand still trembling. 'I understand that and applaud you for it. I would be the same with my own close friends.' She lifted her glass and took another drink. 'You've been friends with Sophie for a long time, and I hope you have always known that I only have her best interests at heart? I hope that's been clear?'

'Of course,' Alice said.

'It's not easy for mothers . . . for the different generations to understand each other. You must know that from your own family.'

'Yes, I do,' Alice said, 'and our family are not as close as you and Sophie. It's bigger and we're more spread apart in age and in the places we live.'

'There's only the two of us now,' Dorothy said, 'and Sophie means the world to me. I just can't bear the thought of anyone taking advantage of her. It's my biggest fear ...'

'Of course,' Alice said again, as she could not think of anything better to say.

'Can I ask you honestly, what you thought about the conversation we overheard in the ladies' toilets?'

'I think they had too much to drink and said things they should not have said even in private.' She halted. 'Although they did pay you and Sophie some very nice compliments.'

'Yes, they did ... apart from me no longer being a spring chicken. Thankfully, Mrs Shaw's opinion does not concern me in the least, and neither do I take any notice of her compliments.'

Alice bit her lip, trying not to see anything funny in the exchange. 'I don't think Tony or Sophie would have been happy with what they said about the factory.'

Dorothy moved her gaze to the window. 'Especially when his sister suggested that Tony had set his sights on Sophie because of the factory.'

'I'm sure it's not true.'

'How do we know whether it's true or not? His mother said how ambitious Tony was, and the factory would suit him much better than his usual job.' She paused. 'What was it she said? Fallen on his feet?' Alice nodded. 'That is exactly what I was afraid of, and of course now, it's far too late.' Tears came into her eyes. 'They are married now, and there's not a single thing that can be done about it.'

'All we can do,' Alice said, 'is wait and see. It may well be absolute rubbish made up by Tony's family – just speculating about things, the way some families do.'

'But they knew all the details about the factory,' Dorothy sighed. 'They could only have known that if Tony told them that Sophie owned half of it. All the times I warned her to keep quiet about it, so that she would know if a man showed interest in her, it was for herself and not for anything she had.' Dorothy lifted her bag and took out an initialled, lace-edged hanky and dabbed her eyes. 'How am I going to get through the rest of the afternoon?'

Alice squeezed her hand. 'You will get through it. You are one of the strongest women I know, and I've always admired you for it. Just pin a smile on your face when you meet anyone and try to put it out of your mind. Enjoy the rest of the wedding – the band will be on soon and everyone will be up dancing.'

Dorothy nodded, picturing Mrs Shaw and the girls whirling around on the dance floor. 'I will,' she said. 'I've had to get through worse recently...'

The lounge door opened, and Frances came through. She put her hand to her head in a gesture of relief when she saw them sitting by the window. 'We thought you'd run off,' she said, laughing. 'The bride was wondering where her mother and bridesmaid had both got to. The band are getting set up and they will be starting the dancing soon and you will be needed for the bridal waltz.' She came to stand at the table, then looked from one serious face to the other. 'Is anything wrong?'

'Oh, Frances,' Dorothy said, giving a great sigh. 'I had hoped today would go off perfectly, but...' She held her hands up in a helpless gesture.

Alice got to her feet. 'You stay and chat to your friend,' she said. 'I'll go back and check on Sophie now, and I'll say we were just having a little chat. She won't start the dance without you.'

'We will be back in a few minutes,' Frances said, sitting down beside her friend. 'Whatever is wrong, nothing is going to spoil today. We won't let it.'

156

Chapter Twenty

'You invited Louis and the twins to tea? Why?'

Alice felt her heart sink at Emily's reaction. 'I have no idea why I said it.' She shrugged. 'The invitation was out of my mouth before I had time to think about it...' She now felt that the niggling doubts at the back of her mind about asking Louis Girard and the Guernsey twins to tea were well founded.

'And what did Greg think?'

'I didn't tell Greg. He met them in the shop this morning, so I explained who they were and about helping find the children accommodation, but he didn't seem overly interested.' She shrugged. 'The only reason I can think that I invited them, is guilt. Guilt that I wasn't able to help your friend, Louis, with finding somewhere for the twins. Guilt that I have two empty bedrooms upstairs when those poor children are looking for a home.'

'We know you're not in a position to help them,' Emily said. 'It was just to ask around.'

'I've put a notice in the shop window and in the Post Office in Edgeley, but we've had no luck so far.'

'I'm sure Louis doesn't expect you to do any more. I felt the same when he asked me, but my mother is just not up to having children.' She shrugged. 'We can only try our best and hope that something will turn up.'

Alice bit her lip. 'I was thinking that it might be easier if you could come for tea on Wednesday as well. You know him much better and will be able to chat easily to him.'

'Me?' Emily said, then an incredulous smile came to her face. 'Please don't say this is all a plot to match-make me with Louis now? One of Sophie's schemes?'

'No, of course not,' Alice said quickly. 'I wouldn't do that, and besides, I haven't even talked to Sophie about it.' She raised her eyes to heaven. 'I don't know why I invited them, I really don't. I just felt so sorry for both Louis and the children.'

'You could back out of it.'

'I know the children will be really disappointed if I cancel.' She shrugged. 'I just don't know what I'm going to talk to him about whereas you can easily talk to him about school and sports and things like that.'

Emily shook her head. 'Even if I wanted to – which I don't – I've got a netball match out in Marple and I won't be home until after eight o'clock.' She halted. 'Don't you think it might look a bit odd to Louis if I am suddenly invited? He might think I fancy him or something, and got my friend to set it up.'

'He is a nice chap,' Alice said.

'Yes, and I like him as a colleague, but I don't fancy him, and I don't want him to get the wrong impression.'

'He told you he's engaged to a girl back in Guernsey, didn't he? So he won't think anything like that.'

'He told us about being engaged when he started at the school last year, but he's not said much since.' Emily shrugged. 'He's talkative about school things, but when it comes to himself, he's very private, especially about the people who are back in Guernsey. I think it probably upsets him. You can only imagine what it must be like for them, not seeing their families for years.'

Alice's gaze moved to the ceiling. 'Oh God, what have I done?' she said. 'What are we going to talk about if you're not there? Do you think it would look bad when he arrives, if I said that I only meant the children to come for tea?'

'Don't disinvite him,' Emily said. 'It's only an hour or so, to give the children a little treat and give the vicar's family a break. He's really easy to talk to, honestly.'

Alice's brow furrowed in thought. 'Maybe I could invite young

Freddy to come as well. He knows Louis through the football, so they can sit together and talk about that, while I look after the twins. We might even walk down to the park with Bella.'

'That's a great idea,' Emily said. She looked over at Greg, who was in deep conversation with another man at the end of the table. 'How are things going at home?'

'Better,' she said in a low voice. 'I wasn't sure what to expect when he came home, but he's been much more thoughtful, and he's referred to his mistakes several times and apologised.'

'That's great news,' Emily said, covering Alice's hand. 'And you know I won't breathe a word about what you told me.'

'I know I can trust you.' She thought now about telling Emily what she had overheard in the ladies' earlier but decided against it. It would only spoil the remainder of the wedding for her and taint her view of Tony and Sophie's marriage before it had even got off the ground.

Alice herself managed to put any thoughts about her evening with the Guernsey children out of her mind and was determined to enjoy the rest of the wedding. The incident in the ladies' room with Sophie's mother had left her unsettled, but she decided that it was best to say nothing for the time being. Let Sophie find things out for herself.

Greg had been very sociable, mixing with the other guests and chatting to Tony about his work, and when the dancing started, he sat back smiling, happy to see Alice up dancing with the best man. Later, when they waltzed around the floor together, he told her how lovely she looked and whispered in her ear how proud he was that she was his wife.

Alice felt warmer towards him, but it was a long way off the feelings she had before Marjorie Jones barged into their marriage. Better than the anger and deep resentment she had wrestled with all those months. It gave her hope that her old feelings might return, especially if these few days together resulted in her becoming pregnant.

It would make all the difference to their future together.

Chapter Twenty-One

Sophie emerged from the lift, Tony's hand guiding her across the deep carpet towards the reception desk of the Midland Hotel. She wore black wide-legged slacks with a deep blue silk blouse that had a loose bow at the neck, and a triple row of pearls. Her make-up was perfect, and her blonde hair had a light bounce to it as she walked along, a fan-shaped straw bag under her arm.

'You find us a seat in the lounge area,' Tony said, smiling but with a slightly anxious look in his eye, 'and I'll go and check everything is OK with the room bill, as we put a few extras on it.'

Sophie was aware that her new husband felt intimidated in palatial surroundings like this hotel, but she knew he would become used to them. He would probably have felt more comfortable in a homely, family-run hotel out in the Derbyshire countryside somewhere, but Sophie felt it was best to have him jump in at the deep end – get him used to the places they would go to regularly when the war was over. The sort of places she had been used to going on special occasions since she was a young girl.

She glanced around at the surprisingly busy lounge, and then spotted a table over in the corner. She strode confidently across the floor, aware that eyes were on her unusual outfit. Wearing trousers gave her a small feeling of defiance, as they were still regarded by many as being a rather provocative fashion. They were mainly worn by the independent sort of young woman like Sophie – or eccentric upper-class older ladies – although they were undoubtedly becoming more popular in the last year. She had deliberately worn them today, in celebration of going back home as a newly married woman – and an unspoken message to her mother that she would do as she pleased.

Although her mother wore trousers occasionally for practical purposes, Sophie knew she was still unsure of the fashion for more formal occasions, and would probably disapprove of her having worn them in the elegant surroundings of the Midland.

When Tony came back and told her that he had paid for the extras on the bill – like the bottle of champagne for their first night together – she smiled at him.

'It's been worth every penny,' she said. She lowered her voice. 'Especially the champagne, even though half of it ended up spilling all over the bed.'

'I have no complaints,' he said, raising his eyebrows, 'in any department.'

'I'm glad to hear it, Mr Shaw,' she said lightly.

As he looked into her eyes, Sophie remembered the amazing two nights they had shared in the lavish hotel room together. After leaving the Grosvenor wearing her pink suit and white shoes and bag, they had climbed in a taxi and reached the edge of Manchester just as darkness fell, and the driver had had to slow down to negotiate his way through the blackened-out city.

Their luggage had been brought up to the room, and Tony had tipped the porter, but when the door was closed and they were on their own, she had suddenly been overcome by shyness. When she glanced at the large, richly dressed bed, she had felt her breath quicken.

'Let's go back downstairs for a night-cap before the bar closes,' she had suggested. She thought she saw a look of relief flicker in his eyes, which made her feel even more nervous, and made her think that Tony was feeling unsure as well.

She had a gin and orange, and Tony had a whisky, and they fell into chatting as they watched the other guests – young couples like themselves and groups of people of all ages. Then, Tony had gone off to gents' room, and when he came back, he said it was time for them to go up to the bedroom as he had ordered a surprise to be delivered.

Intrigued and feeling more relaxed after the drink, they both headed up to the room to find the bottle of champagne in a bucket of ice, alongside two glasses. Sophie was thrilled and they sat opposite each other in armchairs, going over the wedding again and laughing at the slightly suggestive jokes Tony's best man had made, and both saying how sorry they felt for her shy uncle, stumbling his way through the speeches.

After two glasses of the bubbly drink, Sophie kicked off her shoes and went to sit on Tony's knee where they kissed and whispered to each other, until he suddenly stood up and carried her across the room and laid her down on the bed.

Within minutes Tony had helped to peel off her wedding suit and then stopped to slowly take in the vision his bride presented in delicate lace-edged underwear and silk stockings. His own clothes were quickly discarded, and Sophie felt a little pang of alarm as she saw him naked and fully aroused for the first time. As he came to lay on top of her and kiss her slowly then fiercely, she found herself carried away beyond the place where they always stopped.

Afterwards, as they both lay breathless after that first sexual encounter, she understood all that Alice had tried to explain to her, and was glad she had been warned about the initial discomfort. She had found Tony's first attempts to enter her almost painful, but he had been kind and offered to stop. Sophie had shaken her head and reached for her half-filled glass of champagne, downing it in two mouthfuls. She had then taken deep breaths and forced herself to relax, and when they moved close again the barrier between them just seemed to suddenly melt away. When Tony was reassured that she was OK, he relaxed more and they fell into a natural rhythm that aroused more intense feelings in Sophie than she had imagined were there, and which she knew were leading her to a bigger unknown.

The second night Sophie left Tony in the bar with an after-dinner drink while she went to their room and bathed and perfumed herself and was waiting for him, in her wine satin slip. There was no hesitation between them this time, and they had lain this morning wrapped around each other, after she had unexpectedly reached an almost unbearable pleasure she hadn't known existed.

The lingering memories of those physical encounters now made her reluctant to leave this magical place, and to walk outside the hotel into the real world of Manchester city centre, filled with people and noisy with cars and trams.

'Why don't you sit down, and we'll have another drink before we catch the train back home?' Sophie suggested. 'It's the last few hours on our own; after we get home my mother and Mrs Wilson will be around. We'll be lucky to get much time on our own together after this, especially in these lovely surroundings.'

'That's a very good idea.' He looked over towards the bar area. 'What would you like?'

'A waiter will come to us,' she said, patting the chair next to her. She knew he was acting as he would in a local pub, ready to walk over and order his drink from the person behind the bar.

'The time has suddenly flown,' he said, sitting down. 'We only have a few more days and I'm gone.'

Sophie didn't want to think about him going away again. 'We have to go out to your parents' house tonight. Some neighbours have dropped off wedding presents and she wants us to see them before you go back to work.'

'The last thing I want to do is have to sit and talk to neighbours.'

'It's for your mother,' Sophie said. 'And she's been so good about everything.'

'She just wants to show us off,' he said, shaking his head and laughing. 'Well, *you* off really, and have you telling every little detail about the wedding in the Grosvenor, in case they don't believe her version of it.'

Sophie started laughing. 'Oh, Tony, you are so funny about them. But really, your family have been great, accepting me so quickly.' She paused. 'I wonder what they would think if they knew the truth about me? That I was almost born illegitimately, and how Daddy isn't my real father at all.'

Tony reached out and squeezed her hand. 'It's nobody else's business, and certainly not my family's. Anyway, I'm sure there are plenty of skeletons in our family.'

Sophie's face crumpled. 'Oh, Tony ... you have been just wonderful about all this. It almost spoiled the wedding for me, worrying that you might change your mind about me when you knew.'

He looked at her as though she were mad. 'But nothing has changed – you're still the same Sophie, aren't you?'

'I suppose so ...' She saw a waiter coming across the floor towards them now, and cleared her throat to alert her husband.

'What's the point in looking back to the past?' Tony said, lowering his voice. 'We have a whole exciting new future to look forward to.'

As he turned to give the waiter their order, Sophie felt a wave of gratitude wash over her. She was lucky to have met someone like Tony. Someone who was so handsome and attractive, but most of all, someone who was kind and caring. Someone who she knew had married her because he loved her, and not – as her mother thought – because of the factory.

Sophie and Tony travelled back to Stockport on the train, and then, enjoying the sunshine, walked at a leisurely pace from Davenport Station all the way home. They had looked at the houses as they walked, from the small two-up two-down to the larger semi-detached and then onto the substantial detached houses that the Morleys lived in. They discussed prices and what kind of house they might buy in the future when Tony returned home.

'You're OK staying at your mother's until we're all sorted, aren't you?' Tony checked. 'Until the war's over?'

'Yes,' she said, 'I think so ...'

'She's been very good to us,' Tony said, 'with the wedding

and everything, and it makes sense for you to stay there until I get back.'

'I suppose it does,' Sophie said, 'but it won't be easy. I still don't know if I can forgive her.'

'You have to try,' Tony said gently. 'I think it must be difficult for your mother dealing with this all on her own. I don't think you would have been as hard on your father if he had told you, would you?'

'It's my mother who made all the mistakes,' Sophie said. 'She's the one who got pregnant by another man and then married Daddy, and kept it secret all these years.'

'But your father chose to keep it a secret, too,' Tony pointed out.

They stopped talking as they crossed over the busy Buxton Road, and when they reached the other side, Sophie squeezed his arm. 'I don't want this to cause a problem between us, and I need you on my side.'

'I'm always on your side, and I'm sure both your mother and your father were always on your side, too. Maybe they should have told you earlier, but I think they were afraid that the truth would hurt you.'

She pondered his words for a few moments as they walked towards the house. 'What would I do without you? You've made me feel much better about it all.'

He raised his eyebrows. 'So, are you going to make it up with your mother?'

'I'm still very hurt, but I'm going to take your advice, and not make things any worse.'

'Good girl,' he said, winking at her. 'I'm going to make a list of all the things I can give you advice about and have it with me next time I'm back on leave.'

'Oh, Tony!' she said, laughing and shaking her head. 'What would I do without you?'

Chapter Twenty-Two

Emily went around the desks, handing out black and white printed pictures of Jesus with a group of children to each of the pupils. Under the picture was printed the words: *Suffer little children to come unto me.*

When she finished, she came back to stand at the front of the class. 'I want you to colour in the picture with your crayons, as perfectly as you can. When they are finished, we are going to hang them up on the walls for Father Dempsey to see, when he comes this afternoon to ask you your catechism questions.'

She then went to sit at her own desk in the corner, to correct a pile of arithmetic exercise books, while the class worked on their pictures. After a while, boys and girls came to her desk with the completed pictures, some coloured in very well, others with the crayon marks going outside the lines. She offered words of praise and advice, and discreetly helped some of the lesser-abled children with their pieces.

By the time Father Dempsey appeared in the staffroom during the lunch break, the classroom walls were filled with the colourful pictures. The secretary went off to get the priest a cup of tea, while he chatted to the headmaster and some of the other teachers, before coming to sit at the table beside Emily.

'How's your mother?' he asked quietly. 'Any improvement?'

Emily gave a small sigh. 'She was out working in the garden, so that's a move forward, and she's eating better, too.'

'Oh, I'm pleased to hear that. Getting out in the fresh air makes a difference.' He paused. 'If we could get her back into the church, I'm sure she would feel the better for it. Not just for the religious aspect, but to get her mixing with other people.'

'She used to go every day, when Jack was missing in action,' Emily said. 'But when the bad news came, she just felt it had all been a waste of time.'

'She's told me that many times,' the priest said, 'and I can understand how she feels. But there are families I know who thought they could never return to church, and when they did, they found help from it – in a different way.'

'I'll keep trying, but it's not easy to bring it up without her getting upset all over again. Thanks for being so good with her; some of the other priests wouldn't have come back after the first time.'

'Some priests are easily put off doing their duties,' he said. 'We won't name any names, but some of them would sooner be sitting in front of the fire with a glass of whisky in their hand than be out visiting their parishioners.'

Emily gave a little nod, then she asked, 'Did everything settle down with young Harold?'

'He's fine now,' the priest said. 'Nobody is giving him any trouble. He's back helping me in the church garden, and he seems like his old self again. The good thing is, he's able to talk about it, and I'm confident he'll let us all know if anything else happens.'

'That's good news,' Emily said.

'That's why I took more drastic action than I normally would have done,' Father Dempsey said. 'Between you and me, I tracked down some of the lads involved and Sergeant Timmons and I paid their families a quiet visit. We told them about their sons bullying Harold, which got a few of them a clatter around the head from their parents, and then we told them about the attack on the Italian chap.' He shook his head. 'That was a disgrace. Do you know, I found out that that poor fellow was actually a doctor? Imagine, those young pups kicking and punching a clever chap like that. Someone who helps others.'

'Awful,' Emily said. 'How did the parents react to that?'

'Mixed,' he said. 'Some of them were shocked, but some reacted with pure ignorance, just because they were Italians.' He shook his head. 'I pointed out to the parents that if they encourage that violent trait to be used against people who have done them no harm, then they are taking the same attitude that the Nazis showed towards the Jews. I said that most of those Italian chaps – like the doctor – were dragged into the war, and would have been killed if they had refused. Some of them have even told me that they were glad when they were captured.'

'People don't realise the full story, do they?' Emily said. 'I didn't really know anything about their circumstances myself until you told me. When you hear the word "prisoner"...' She shrugged. 'You just think of people who have done bad things.'

'We're all guilty of making assumptions,' he said. 'When I went up to the camp for the first time, I didn't know what to expect, and I got a surprise to find that most of them are lovely lads.' He shrugged. 'There's the odd Mussolini supporter, but the others give them a wide berth. They have enough on their minds as so many of them have lost their families in the war – they have no homes or people to go back to.'

'I suppose we never think of that...'

'We're all human beings,' Father Dempsey said, 'one way or the other.'

'Are the men still working locally?'

'Yes, and being of great help to the elderly.' He lowered his voice. 'Sergeant Timmons told me that they're allowing the men a bit more freedom now. They're allowing them to go out to work on farms or in local businesses where the men are away.'

Emily looked surprised. 'Are there many families who would bring them into their homes?'

'Mr Barlow down in the newsagents' shop has a lovely chap there who helps them out in the garden at home – he's called Marco.'

Emily caught her breath.

'He often goes to them for Sunday dinner,' the priest continued, 'and they took him off with them to visit their daughter out in Cheshire. She has a big farm there, and some of the men from another camp are working out on the land.'

Emily thought of the rosary beads, still pushed to the back of her bedside cabinet drawer, and then she thought of the friendly, attractive man she had pushed to the back of her mind, and felt it would be dishonest to say nothing. 'I met him in Barlow's shop a few weeks ago.' She explained about knocking over the box he was carrying. 'Very clumsy of me, but he was polite and nice, and Mr and Mrs Barlow seemed very relaxed and familiar around him.'

'That'll be Marco,' the priest said.

'He's not the one who was attacked, is he?'

'No, no. It was another two fellows, equally as nice. The chap you met is definitely Marco, very clever chap, and well educated—' He stopped then as the bell rang, and the teachers all started to move to go back to the classrooms. 'I'll be down with you in a few minutes.'

Emily greeted him at the door of the classroom, and when he came in, the children were sitting upright with their arms folded. He took his hat off, and then walked up and down in front of the rows of desks. 'I'm going to ask you all a question now, so be ready with your answers.'

The children turned to look at each other with wide, anxious eyes, hoping they could remember the catechism questions they had been learning.

He went to stand at the front of the room, his face suddenly very serious. 'I want everyone who is a Manchester United fan to put up your hands.'

There was an incredulous silence and then a ripple of giggles, as over half the class put their hands up.

'Hands down,' he said. 'Now, I want everyone who is a Manchester City supporter to put their hands up.'

Emily smiled bemusedly at the questions and watched as the remainder of the class then put their hands up.

'Now I want all the United supporters to go to a City supporter,' the priest said, 'and shake hands with them.'

There was a moment's stunned silence, then Emily smiled and clapped her hands, understanding the priest's intention. 'You heard Father Dempsey,' she said. 'Up you get, and go to the nearest person who supports the other team, and shake hands with them.'

The first brave pupil to move was a girl, who went to offer her hand to the boy at the desk opposite. The giggling started again, then another girl moved and then a boy, and then more joined in until the whole class was shaking hands with each other.

'Well done!' Father Dempsey said. 'You can all sit down now.' He looked around the rows of smiling faces. 'And what did you learn from that?'

One girl put her hand up. 'That some of us like Manchester City and some of us like Manchester United.'

'Correct. And did anyone learn anything else?' There was a silence. 'How did you feel,' he asked, 'when you shook hands with one another? Did you like it?'

'Yes,' a boy said. 'It was good fun.'

'Hands up all the people who liked shaking hands,' he asked. He watched and then smiled as everyone put their hands up. 'And when you were laughing and smiling, did you think that it mattered whether that person supported the same team as you?'

There was a lot of shrugging and shaking heads.

'OK,' he said. 'Hands up who likes jelly?' Almost the whole class put their hands up. 'And who likes ice cream?' Everyone's hand went up. 'Shake hands with the nearest person who likes the same as you.' The same fun and laughter went on and then they all went back to their places. 'And what if I didn't like jelly or ice cream?' he continued. 'Or if I didn't like football, but I was a great swimmer? Would I be left out?'

He made a sad face. 'Would nobody shake my hand?'

A girl at the front stood up. 'I would shake your hand.'

'Thank you.' He glanced all around him. 'Stand up everyone who would shake my hand.'

A scattering of the class stood up immediately, and then

gradually, the whole class stood up. 'So you would all shake my hand?' he said. 'Well, that's great news because I think that's exactly what Jesus would have done, don't you?'

He walked over to the wall now, and pointed at the pictures the children had coloured in. 'Look at all the great pictures you made, aren't they lovely? And look at the words below them: *Suffer little children to come unto me.* Do you think Jesus said only the children who like Manchester United were allowed to come to him? Do you think he said only those of you who like jelly were allowed to come to him?'

The children, beginning to understand now, shook their heads.

'Of course not.' The priest went to one of the pictures, then pointed to each child kneeling in a circle around Jesus. 'He wanted *all* the children to come unto him, and he loved them all. It didn't matter whether they were big or small, thin or heavy, curly-haired or straight-haired, white-skinned or dark-skinned.' He paused to let the words sink in. 'And we must learn to do the same. We have to make friends with *everyone*, not just the ones who we think are the same as us.'

He looked at Emily. 'What do you think, Miss Browne?'

'Oh, I agree,' she said, nodding her head vigorously. 'And I know everyone in the class has been listening to every word you've said, and I'm sure they're going to remember that Jesus wants us to be friends with everyone.'

'Now it might not always work out,' he said. 'Not everyone can be great friends with everyone else, but we should at least give people a chance.' He paused. 'I had to remember that myself when I moved over here from Ireland. I was very nervous because I didn't know a soul in Stockport, and I wondered if the people in the parish would like me – if they would give me a chance.'

Emily could tell by the looks on the children's faces that they were listening to every word now.

Father Dempsey continued to talk about the changes when he moved from the country to a big town, and getting used to different accents, then described all the nice people he had met, and how he discovered that many of his parishioners had come from Ireland, too.

'I felt better when I heard that,' he told the children, 'but as time went on, I got to know more English people, and after a while I hardly thought about whether they were Irish or English or from another country. That's what happens when you get to know people, you don't see the differences, you begin to only notice the things you like about them.'

Emily had never heard any member of the clergy talking in the way Father Dempsey was speaking just now, not in a church, and not in a school. As she looked around the class, she could see that all the children were taking in every word that the priest was saying. Talking about himself had gripped their attention more than anything he could have said about Jesus or from passages read from the Bible.

'And while you might be surprised to hear about a grown-up like me finding it hard to come from a different country,' he said, 'you can imagine how the children who came over to Stockport from Guernsey might have felt. They had to leave their homes and families behind, and come to live amongst strangers and go to new schools. Wouldn't that have been hard to do if people didn't welcome you and be friends with you? I know you have some of the Guernsey children here in the school, and that you've come across more of them when playing football and netball with the other schools.' He looked back at Emily. 'And of course, one of your teachers in the school here, Mr Girard, is from Guernsey, too.'

'Everyone knows Mr Girard,' Emily said, smiling at the class. 'He trains our football team. And do you know, the school have done much better in the inter-school championships than we've ever done before. Isn't that right?'

There was another babble of chatter then the priest signalled with his hands and they quietened down. 'Well, that just shows us another lesson that Jesus teaches us in the Bible – about how God gives us talents and how we can use them to help ourselves and to help others. Mr Girard is using his talent at football to teach the boys in this school.' He looked at his watch. 'I'll have to be going soon as I have sick calls to make in the parish. We'll talk about talents the next time I'm here, in a few weeks' time. In the meantime, you can be thinking about all the things you're good at, or could become good at if you practised hard enough.' He indicated the pictures on the wall. 'I can already see by your lovely work that some of you are talented at art. And every time you look at the pictures, don't forget what we said about Jesus welcoming everyone.'

Emily moved towards the door now, then she saw a boy put his hand up.

'What is it, Alfred?' she asked.

'I wanted to ask, what about the catechism answers we had to learn off by heart?'

Emily looked at the priest with raised eyebrows.

'Did you learn them?' the priest asked.

'Yes,' Alfred said.

The priest turned to the class now. 'How many of you learned all the catechism answers?'

The whole class put their hands up.

'Well done,' he said. 'And we'll see if you remember them the next time I'm here.'

As Emily saw him to the door, he said, 'I hope I haven't spoiled your catechism lesson?'

'I think they learned a lot more listening to your stories than they would have done from that,' she said. 'And I think they also enjoyed it a lot more, too.'

'Well, keep them at it anyway,' he said, going out the door. 'You never know when Canon Whitelaw or even the bishop might call in, and they like to keep the kids on their toes with the more abstract things about religion that none of them will understand.' He gave a sidelong grin. 'They only have to memorise the answers and that will be enough to tick all the boxes – they won't be expected to understand anything.'

Chapter Twenty-Three

Alice looked at the dining table, and then she suddenly went over and lifted the five linen napkins. *Paper*, she thought, going back to the dresser drawer, *paper will be more suitable for the children and less fussy.* She put the linen ones back into their drawer and took out five white paper napkins, placing them on the table instead.

As she looked over the bowls of freshly washed lettuce and tomatoes, pieces of pickled beetroot, and the platter with slices of cold ham and beef and boiled eggs cut in half, she wondered what had possessed her to invite a strange man and two children for evening tea. The feeling was only consolidated when Emily wondered why she had invited them, too.

She hadn't mentioned it to Greg at all, as it just hadn't cropped up during his few days home. She had seen him off at the train station in Stockport, as he headed back to the training camp down south. He would only be there a short while longer, he thought, then he would be moved to one of the schools for military intelligence for further training. After that, he expected to be sent somewhere like Italy, but he could not confirm for sure, as things could easily be changed at the last minute. All he could say for definite was that he would try to phone her and let her know when he was being moved out of England. Alice had felt better knowing that when he did go abroad, he would not be in active service, and would be safely behind a desk, in an area away from any conflict.

After he left on Tuesday afternoon, she had walked back up to the shop to find a queue of customers out in the street, as they had heard about a recent delivery of tinned vegetables and fruit, and crates of fresh oranges. As she hurried towards the shop, Alice hoped that Maeve had remembered to put out the sign, stating only one orange per customer. Oranges were one of the popular items that often created awkwardness between the local shopkeepers and customers.

She gave a quick, cheery greeting to those in the queue, and then rushed inside to get her working overall on to give Maeve a hand. The shop was busy for most of the afternoon and then when Freddy appeared after school, Maeve attended to the counter, while the two of them unpacked boxes of cleaning materials which had been delivered while she was out.

She had little time to herself, and it was only when the shop closed and Freddy took Bella out to do her business, that the house felt strangely quiet without Greg. She switched on the gas oven to warm for cooking her lamb chop, and then went back into the shop to get a couple of potatoes and some of the smaller carrots to peel and boil for her evening meal. She had just put the vegetable pan on the cooker, when Freddy appeared back with the dog.

She gave him a loaf she had put aside, and two oranges. 'Don't tell a soul I gave you two,' she said, 'but I know one orange won't go very far in your house, and they are good for the children.' She had paused then asked, 'How is your father?'

'Still doing OK, touch wood,' he said, tapping his fingers on the countertop. This was a little mannerism he had picked up from the hours he had spent in the shop with Betty. 'The thing is, my da is like a different man when he's not drinking. My mam says she doesn't know whether it's his nerves that causes him to drink, or whether it's the drink that sets his nerves off. Chicken and egg, she says.'

'Is he sleeping better?' Alice asked.

'Yes, and he's not having the bad dreams as much.' He gave a little sigh. 'That's one of the things that sets his nerves off, that and a lot of loud noise – like when the council workmen were drilling outside our house that time there was a burst pipe. He was bad then, and was sticking lumps of cotton wool in his ears and putting a pillow over his head to try to block the noise out.'

'That must be very hard for him,' Alice said, shaking her head, 'and as hard for your mother trying to help him and look after you all.'

'He is definitely getting better, and he told me he was sorry about Bella, and that the farmer he knows is training the pups to work on the farm. He even said if I wanted to bring Bella home again there would be no trouble.'

Alice had looked at him, sensing a small defensive note in Freddy's tone. 'Do you want to take Bella back?' she asked softly.

His eyes widened. 'No, no – definitely not. She's much better off here, and she's better fed and everything. She even looks better since she came, younger like.'

'Are you sure?'

'Definitely, and I get to see her every day, don't I? She's much more settled 'cos I think she likes the peace and quiet and everything.'

Alice felt a tinge of relief, as she had become very fond of Bella. 'That's fine then,' she had said, 'because I like having her here, too.'

'I think you keep each other company, don't you? With you not having a husband or children around.'

'The shop keeps me busy enough,' Alice said, her voice deliberately light, as Freddy had unwittingly touched on a raw nerve.

When she saw Freddy gathering up his school bag and gas mask, and the bag with the bread and oranges, she reminded him about coming to tea the following night.

'I like Mr Girard, although it will be funny having tea with a real teacher.'

'But you often have something to eat with me,' Alice said, smiling, 'and I'm a teacher, too.'

'That's different...' Freddy's brow wrinkled. 'Mr Girard is

good fun, but he can be tough on the pitch, and strict with anyone messing around. I've never seen you in a school, being strict like a proper teacher.'

'I suppose you haven't seen me being a teacher at all,' Alice said, amused at his description. 'But I try not to be too strict at school, and when the children are mainly good, you don't have to be. It's nicer for everyone when you all get on well.'

'I think it's different for men teachers,' Freddy said. 'They have to be hard on you, 'cos it wouldn't look well for them if they got the mickey taken out of them. They have to show who's boss.'

'Mr Girard doesn't strike me as the type of teacher to be hard on anyone.'

'He's one of the nicest and fairest I've come across on the pitch, but he's still a man.'

Freddy had gone off in a cheery mood, saying he was looking forward to tea tomorrow. As she stood watching him from the shop doorstep, Alice realised how fond she had grown of him, and she hoped that things had settled down at home for him. The evening had passed quickly as she gave the kitchen a good clean and hoovered and polished the dining room, which was only used on special occasions.

She also had two phone calls, one from an excited Sophie telling her how wonderful the honeymoon nights were in the Midland Hotel in Manchester. 'Everything was perfect,' Sophie said in a low voice. 'Absolutely *everything* ... much better than I could ever have imagined. I don't know why I was worried – but I suppose every girl feels the same when it's the first time.'

'I am sure they do,' Alice had agreed, happy for her friend.

'I will bring you up to date on it all when Tony goes back – he's here for another two nights.'

Alice wondered how things were going between Tony and Mrs Morley, after all the things she and Dorothy had overheard Tony's family saying. 'Where is Tony going next?'

'He's going up to Newcastle,' Sophie told her, 'and then he's back to London after that, as the telephone engineers are needed down there with all the bombed-out buildings. God knows when I will see him again, but if things settle, I might go down to London for an overnight.' She had giggled. 'Now I know what there is to look forward to, I want to see him as much as I can.'

Alice had hardly put the phone down when it rang again and this time it was Emily, calling from the local phone box.

'I was thinking about you in school today,' she said, 'and hoping you're not worrying too much about having Louis and the children tomorrow night?' She had paused. 'After the wedding I felt bad about letting you down, and I hope you weren't upset about it? If I hadn't had the netball tournament on, I really would have come.'

'It's fine,' Alice said, glad her friend cared enough to check on her. 'I decided it would have been rude to cancel Louis, and it will be fine with Freddy here, as they already know each other from football training.'

'I also think it's really kind of you, inviting them to tea,' Emily said. 'The twins have been through a lot and need something nice.'

Emily's words had taken the edge off her anxiety. She felt happier afterwards, as she buttered and cut bread into triangles, and then covered it with a damp, linen dishtowel so it would not dry out.

She went into the shop and came back with a bottle of lemonade and a bottle of dandelion and burdock, which she knew Freddy liked. She would make tea for herself and Louis, and she also had a tin of coffee – just in case – as she heard some Guernsey people were more French in their ways.

By half past five, everything was ready on the dining room table apart from the portions of fresh chips that she planned to send Freddy to the chip shop for. He appeared early as planned and went running off to get them. She went over to the record player, to check the pile of LPs and 78s, wondering what music might suit the occasion. She had a few favourites amongst them, but most were ones that Greg and his mother had collected over the years.

Her eyes lit up when she came across one of Betty's, called *Old Music Hall Favourites*. She scanned down the list of song titles, and then smiled, thinking they were perfect. 'Me and My Gal', 'The Laughing Policeman', 'You are my Sunshine', 'Any Old Iron' and similar tunes. Lively, silly and funny, and suitable for all ages – she even liked a few of them herself. *Good old Betty*, she thought, and then had to catch herself as tears unexpectedly filled her eyes.

She had just plugged in the record player when Freddy came rushing in the back gate and tapped on the kitchen door. Alice let him in and took the three parcels of chips off him, and then she unwrapped the newspaper and greaseproof paper, and placed the chips into a dish, putting them into the oven to keep warm. A few chips had clung to each of the greaseproof paper sheets, so she offered them to Freddy with a smile, saying, 'When you've finished, wrap the paper up tight and put it in the kindling bin at the door, for lighting the fire.'

After devouring the chips, Freddy went to the bin, glancing into the dining room as he passed. 'Everything looks lovely, Mrs Fairclough,' he told her when he came back. 'I've never been asked to a proper sit-down tea in anybody's house before.'

'I didn't get asked to tea when I was your age either.' It struck Alice as strange him calling her Mrs Fairclough – which he had called Betty – and then she realised that Freddy rarely addressed her at all. 'You can call me Alice if you like,' she said.

He looked at her, surprised. 'OK,' he said. 'I'll try to remember.'

The shop bell went, startling Alice, and, as she rushed to answer it, she realised that she was still anxious about her Guernsey guests. She had hardly opened the door, when Gabriela almost tumbled into the shop.

'There's a big dog out there, following us!' the young girl exclaimed, as Alice stepped back to let her in. 'Louis said it's an Alsatian.'

Philip followed behind. 'It wasn't following us, Gabriela,' Philip said scornfully. 'It was just out for a walk with its owner.'

Louis was laughing and shaking his head. 'It did come a bit too close to Gabriela for comfort,' he told Alice, 'but it did no harm.' He lowered his voice. 'She's a little nervous around dogs.'

Alice smiled at him and nodded knowingly.

Philip went into the middle of the floor, turning around in a full circle. 'It's funny to be in a shop when it's closed,' he said. 'You wonder where all the people are.'

Alice was used to this reaction with her nephews and nieces. 'Yes,' she said, 'it's a bit like going into an empty school without all the noisy children.' She smiled at them. 'It's lovely to see you all again.'

'And it was very kind of you to invite us,' Louis said. He held out a large brown paper bag. 'Some little gifts from us.'

'You shouldn't have,' she said, caught by surprise. Her hand moved up to her throat as she saw the colourful blooms peeping out of the top of the bag. 'It's just a simple tea...'

Louis raised his eyebrows and smiled. 'I hope you like them.'

She thanked him and when she took the bag from him, she was surprised that it was quite heavy. She indicated towards the door that adjoined the house. 'Freddy is joining us, as I thought the children would like to meet him.' She turned to Gabriela. 'And our little dog, Bella, is here, too.' She saw the alarm in the little girl's eyes, and said quickly, 'She is a bit nervous of people, so I know you will be very gentle with her.'

'We will all be very careful,' Louis said.

Alice led them through the door to the narrow hallway, and down past the kitchen. 'We'll go straight into the dining room, as everything is ready,' she told them. Freddy was already in the dining room, looking through the pile of records that Alice had left out on top of a side table.

Alice introduced them, and said, 'If you would all like to sit around the table, I'll bring the plates through, and you can choose whatever you like.'

'This looks beautiful,' Louis said, looking at the table. 'Can I help? I'm sure Freddy will entertain the children here.'

'OK,' Alice said. 'You could bring the plates through if you like.'

They worked easily together in the kitchen, as Alice put the chips out on each plate and Louis carried them through. When the three children had been served, he then helped Philip and Gabriela pick out slices of cold ham and tomatoes and eggs, and gave them bread. He looked at Freddy. 'You can sort yourself, can't you? A big lad like you.'

"Course I can,' Freddy said. 'And will I pour out the lemonade, too?'

'Good idea,' Louis said. He came back into the kitchen as Alice was taking the second tray of chips out. 'Have you looked at your presents yet?' he asked her.

'No,' she said, putting the tray back in the oven.

'Maybe you should look at them now,' he said, 'as you might want to put them on the table.'

Alice went to the paper bag and found a colourful bunch of garden blooms – roses, sweet William, sweet pea and pansies, mixed with trailing pieces of ivy and wrapped up in white tissue paper. 'What beautiful flowers,' she said, 'and so nicely wrapped.' She held them to her nose. 'And they smell gorgeous, too.'

'I think most women like flowers,' Louis said. 'My mother grew flowers at home, and we were used to having colourful vases all over the house.' He paused. 'These came from the vicar's garden, and Gabriela and Philip enjoyed picking them for you.'

'That is so kind,' Alice said, touched that the children had made such an effort for her. 'I have a favourite vase that will be perfect for them, one that was my grandmother's.'

'There's another gift in the bag from me,' Louis told her.

'This is too much... the tea is just a little treat for the children.'

'Well, it's also a treat for me,' he said, 'and we've been really looking forward to it.'

Alice looked up at him, and he smiled at her, and she suddenly felt herself flush. She hadn't noticed he had such deep blue eyes before. She turned back to the bag, to discover a bottle of rosé wine. 'Goodness!' she said. 'That's really kind of you...'

'I wasn't sure if you drink wine?' he said. 'Or what kind you might like, so I picked a rosé, as it's in between white and red.' He shrugged. 'I know wine is not so popular with some English people, and they might prefer beer or sherry. If you don't like it, please keep it for Christmas or whenever you have visitors who will enjoy it.'

Alice thought it best to be honest. 'I've never tried rosé,' she said, 'but I would love to.' She felt her heart beating quickly now, as though she was about to do something exciting or dangerous, and almost smiled to herself, since it was only a glass of wine. She pointed to a rack on the wall behind her. 'There's a corkscrew there,' she said, 'hanging beside the butter curler.' While Louis opened the wine, Alice went to take the chips from the oven and put them on the warmed plates. She suddenly remembered, saying, 'Wine glasses!' a little flustered now. She had left plain tumblers out for soft drinks at their places.

There was a variety of glasses in the dining room, some of which had been Betty's and some that she and Greg had received as wedding presents. 'They're in the cabinet in the dining room...' She turned quickly with the plates in her hand and almost bumped into him.

Louis stepped aside and made a small sweeping bow with his hand. 'You go on in,' he said, 'and I'll follow.'

Alice moved on ahead, carrying the plates and trying not to drop any chips. She felt self-conscious now, and wondered if he thought her unsophisticated compared to the women back in Guernsey. She wondered if they drank wine regularly, the way the French did, as she had heard that the islanders were more similar to the French than English people. She knew little about the place, apart from what she had read in the newspapers, when the families were first evacuated to England. She knew they had undoubtedly suffered when they were invaded by the Nazis, and for a long time were cut off from their loved ones and the rest of the outside world. She was sure Louis Girard probably talked about Guernsey to the staff in school, and she wished she had asked Emily a bit more about him and his life on the island.

'Is this where you keep the glasses?' Louis asked, indicating the mahogany cabinet.

'Yes,' Alice said. 'Have a look and see what you think best.'

He set the wine on the table then went to open the doors on the cupboard. A few moments later he held up two crystal stemmed glasses. 'These are perfect!'

The crystal glass suddenly reminded her of the flowers. She went quickly back into the kitchen and found the vase on a shelf, and half-filled it with water. She then deftly arranged the colourful blooms in a simple display and brought them back to sit in the middle of the table.

Gabriela's face lit up. 'They look absolutely beautiful!' she said. 'You would think they came from a flower shop.'

'I think garden flowers are much nicer than ones from a shop,' Alice told her.

'I agree,' Louis said, winking over at her. He came back and then filled the two glasses three-quarters of the way with the rosé wine. He handed Alice hers and then he held his glass out and said, 'Cheers, and thank you so much for asking us to your home.' He tipped his glass against hers and then did the same to Freddy's glass of dandelion and burdock then Gabriela's and Philip's glasses. All three children looked at each other, grinning and rolling their eyes at what they obviously thought was a funny little ritual.

Alice passed the plates of food over to Louis, and he had something from each one, then she checked that Freddy and the children were all happy with what they had. 'There's more bread and butter,' she said. 'And there's some extra chips in the oven.'

All except Freddy said they had enough. He held his half-full plate up and said, 'I'll have more chips if they're going, thanks... Alice.' He suddenly grinned. 'I don't know if that sounds funnier than calling you Mrs Fairclough.'

'You'll get used to it,' Alice said, smiling. 'We both will, and you can go into the kitchen and help yourself to more chips.' She took a drink of the wine and found it different to the white and red she had drunk on a few occasions. It was lighter than red, but she could not decide if it was lighter or sweeter than white. After a second sip, she thought it an interesting combination of both.

When Freddy was out of earshot, Louis leaned over to Alice and said, 'He's a nice boy, and you're very good with him.'

'He's actually a great help in the shop,' Alice said. 'He comes before school in the morning and lifts and carries all the boxes outside and that kind of thing, then he helps me sort out the newspapers for the paperboys. He's also very good serving the customers, although he gets me or the other lady, Maeve, to work the till. I'm going to get him to come into the shop when we're closed some Wednesday afternoon to show him how to work the till properly. He's clever enough to do it, and it would be a great help and speed things up when there's a crowd waiting to be served.'

'That's excellent,' Louis said. He took a drink of his wine. 'You obviously bring out the best in him.'

'I don't know how I would manage without him,' Alice said, 'and he's cheery and brightens up the place.'

'I would love to work in the shop when I'm older,' Gabriela said. 'It would be great fun putting all the tins and packets on the shelves.'

Alice smiled at her. 'Maybe you could come and help some time when you're bigger.' She noticed that the little girl had picked up a Stockport accent, and supposed it was inevitable since she had been in England since she was five or six years old. Alice wondered, with a feeling of trepidation, how the children would adapt again when they eventually went home. Would their parents even recognise them? The thought sent a shiver through her.

Philip then asked Freddy what school he was in, and in between eating mouthfuls of chips, Freddy told him all about it.

'What's your favourite thing?' Philip asked.

'Football,' Freddy said without missing a beat. 'After that, it's woodwork.'

'Do you like reading?'

'Sometimes, it depends on the books.'

'I love reading, especially Sherlock Holmes and Tom Sawyer,' Philip said.

Freddy's eyebrows shot up. 'You must be brainy if you can read Sherlock Holmes,' he said. 'I tried it and found some of the words really hard.' He speared a piece of tomato with his fork and put it in his mouth. 'Mind you, that was last year. I might try it again, if somebody younger than me can read it.'

'Philip is particularly good at reading,' Louis said. 'He could read when he arrived in Stockport, Mrs Ponsonby said.'

'And she read with us every night,' Gabriela added. 'She really helped us.'

'Our house is too noisy for reading,' Freddy said. He took a big glug of his dandelion and burdock. 'My da listens to books on the radio, and when the younger ones have gone to bed, sometimes me and him listen to them while Mam is doing the ironing or cleaning up. We like Charles Dickens, things like *Oliver Twist* and *A Christmas Carol*.'

'They are brilliant classics,' Alice said. 'And it's nice for you and your dad to listen to them together.'

'He only likes quiet things on the radio, not loud jazz or anything with drums – that kind of music sets his headaches off, or kids screaming and dogs barking loud.'

'That happens to a lot of people,' Louis said, 'but I think it gets less and less as time goes on.'

'That's good to hear,' Freddy said.

Alice looked across the table at Louis and he caught her eye and just nodded.

Philip swallowed his bite of bread. 'At the moment I'm reading a great book called *The Hobbit*. The librarian in Stockport Library recommended it.' His brow creased. 'It's very good but you have to really concentrate on it, as it's not about the real world. Everything in it is made up, the writer has a brilliant imagination.'

'Absolutely,' Louis said. 'It's one of my favourite books, too. I think you would like it, Freddy.'

Freddy raised his eyebrows. 'I might,' he said. He looked at Gabriela. 'What ones do you like?'

'*Black Beauty*,' she said, putting her finger to her chin, 'and *Rebecca of Sunnybrook Farm*, and my absolute favourite is *The Railway Children*.'

Freddy's face lit up. 'I liked that one, too. It's all about them moving from a big posh house to an old one, isn't it?'

'Yes,' Gabriela said, 'the old house is called *The Three Chimneys* and their father is away.'

'He's in prison, isn't he?' Freddy said.

Philip leaned forward. 'He was falsely accused...'

Louis leaned towards Alice now, as the three children recalled their favourite bits of the book. 'Tell me about the school you were teaching in,' he said. 'Was it far from here?'

Alice told him that it was near Davenport, and about a twenty-minute walk from the shop, but Louis hadn't heard of it.

He smiled and shook his head. 'If it's not in our football league, I don't know it.'

'Emily is the same with the netball leagues,' Alice said, laughing. 'I wasn't very involved with sports, so I probably know less schools than you do.' She took a sip of the wine, which she now found to be very pleasant.

'Are you enjoying the wine? You said it was one you hadn't tried before.'

'Yes, it's lovely,' she said. 'And thank you for bringing it.'

'I'm really enjoying this, too.' He indicated towards the children, who were now laughing and chatting easily together, as if they had known each other much longer. 'You've no idea how nice this feels, the mixture of adults and children all eating together and different conversations going on.'

'It is nice,' Alice said, looking across the table, 'and the children all seem to be enjoying it by the sounds of things.' She glanced at their plates, and saw they were all nearly finished. 'More chips and bread or eggs or salad for anyone?' she asked.

'Chips!' Freddy and Gabriela said together then laughed, Freddy adding, 'I'll have bread, too, and make it into a chip butty.'

Alice finished her wine and then went into the kitchen and came back with the remainder of the chips and more bread. Louis had a few more chips and tomatoes and another slice of bread. She smiled when he held up his hand and said in an overexaggerated manner, 'I don't know about everyone else, but I'm done! I can't eat another bite.'

'If you keep eating like that, you'll get fat, Louis,' Philip told him, wagging his finger like a teacher.

Freddy and Gabriela went into peals of laughter.

Bella suddenly got out of her basket and went to the door.

Louis reached for the wine bottle and then moved it over in the direction of Alice's glass. 'A little more?'

'Lovely,' she said, as she watched him filling her glass. 'The rosé wine is really nice and a lovely treat, especially in the middle of the week. Normally it would just be me here, with Bella. I've only had her a short time. I would be catching up on household things or going over the books for the shop. This is a very different Wednesday evening for me.' She took a drink from the glass and smiled.

'And me,' he said. 'I can't think of a nicer evening since I came to Stockport – or nicer company.'

'That's kind of you to say, but drinking wine here in an ordinary house in Stockport must be very different to what you're used to back in Guernsey. You have the sea there, and beautiful scenery, don't you?' She shrugged. 'I don't really know anything about it, but I've always thought the Channel Islands sounded lovely.'

'Guernsey is a lovely place,' he said, glancing to check the children were not listening, 'but for now, it is very difficult to think about it. Everything has changed.'

Alice suddenly realised she had been insensitive, talking about Guernsey as a place of beauty, as though things were normal. 'Of course, and the people have been through a terrible time. I'm so sorry...'

'We are all in strange times and have to deal with difficult things.' He shrugged. 'At times it feels unreal – like a far distant memory—' He halted as Philip suddenly dropped his fork.

'Louis... my stomach is sore again...' Philip clutched his side.

Louis's brow deepened in concern. 'Stand up and have a little walk around,' he suggested. 'You said that helped you when you had it in school this afternoon. Or maybe you need to go to the toilet?'

'No...' Philip shook his head, and then got to his feet. 'I'll have a little walk around again.'

'I think Bella needs to go out,' Freddy said. 'It's a while since she's been.' He looked over at Alice. 'Maybe Philip has trapped wind, and a little walk might sort it out.'

'It's not trapped wind!' Philip said indignantly. He bent over, rubbing his side.

'You don't know,' Gabriela said, looking at Freddy and starting to giggle.

'That's enough of the laughing,' Alice said. 'It's not funny when poor Philip doesn't feel well.'

Philip straightened up now. 'I think it's easing off...' He shot his sister a look, and when she started laughing again, he joined in, too, and so did Freddy.

'Right, out for a walk,' Louis said. 'That should help.'

Freddy moved out of his chair. 'I'll get Bella's lead,' he said. He called the little dog and went out into the hallway to the hook by the back door where the lead was hanging.

As the twins went after him, Louis looked at Alice. 'Is it far? Do you think I should go with them?'

'It's only across the road and down to the area with grass,' she said. 'You can practically see it from the shop door, it's not even five minutes.' She thought how caring he was towards the children, and she could imagine he would make an excellent father, when he returned home and married his fiancée.

Freddy gave a lop-sided grin. 'You don't need to worry, I'll look after the twins,' he said importantly. 'I'm well used to it with our younger ones.'

Gabriela's brows shot up. 'We're not babies, you know,' she said. 'We walk to school on our own every day.'

All three went out the back door and as they passed by the window in the hall, their laughter could be heard.

'That sound is good for your heart,' Louis said, leaning his arms on the table. 'Especially for the twins, hearing them sounding happy and carefree, and teasing each other. It's how children should be.'

There was a small, not uncomfortable silence, and then Alice said, 'You were talking about Guernsey.'

He took a sip of wine and then he sat back in his chair. 'I was just saying that as time has passed, Guernsey seems further away. The same with all the people and the places I've known since I was a child. Sometimes the memories are clear enough, but other times they are very foggy, and everything seems strange, and I can hardly picture it at all.'

'That must be hard for you.'

'The war has changed things for lots of people, but recently, I've realised that life is for living in the present.' He lifted his glass and took a large swallow. 'When we arrived here, all we thought about was Guernsey and how things were when we left. We hung onto that – thinking that there was no point in planning a life in Stockport – thinking we would be back home soon, and just pick up where we left off. Even when weeks and months turn into years, you still keep hoping that things will somehow stay the same.'

'That's only natural,' Alice said, 'when you have been forced to leave everything behind.'

'But there comes a time when you have to realise that the future you had planned doesn't fit anymore.' He took a deep breath. 'That the circumstances and the people and places you left behind can suddenly – or even gradually – change. If it's a sudden change – like hearing people you knew and loved are killed – you are in shock, and it makes you immediately realise that things will never be the same when you eventually return. When the changes are gradual, you hardly notice it until one day you realise what you thought was always there – had taken for granted – has just disappeared.'

'It sounds very hard... and very sad,' she said, wondering what he was referring to, as what he had said left it unclear. 'Something that only people who have gone through can really understand.'

'You're probably right.' He took another drink of wine, then looked at her and smiled. 'But this evening has not been hard or sad in any way – it has been easy and natural.'

'It has,' Alice said. 'It sounds silly, but I actually felt a bit nervous after I had asked you all, wondering if I had done the right thing.'

'But why?'

'Well, I suppose it's because I don't really know you or the children,' she said. 'I didn't know what we would have to talk about, and whether the children would feel OK coming to a strange house.'

'And how do you feel about it now?'

She gave a slightly embarrassed smile. 'I've enjoyed every minute; they are lovely children.'

'That's good, because I can tell they really like you. Philip can be a little awkward or self-conscious with people, but I haven't noticed that this evening.'

'Freddy being here has helped,' she said. 'I thought he would be younger company for the children, and I can tell he has enjoyed it.'

Louis's face lightened. 'He certainly enjoyed his chips,' he said, laughing.

'He certainly did!' Alice said, rolling her eyes. 'But it wouldn't have occurred to me to ask Freddy to tea before. I thought a boy like that would have been bored with just me, so it's great that all three have got on so well.'

A strand of hair escaped from behind her ear now, and as she brushed it back in place, she thought that she had never talked like this before with a man. And she had never felt this comfortable with anyone so quickly. She could not remember a man being so open about their feelings, and she wondered if the wine had made them both open up more. And yet, something told her that they would have got on easily with or without the wine.

Louis leaned forward. 'I can't imagine anyone being bored with you.'

It seemed a long time since Alice had felt so interesting to a man, and she experienced a real glow at the compliment, but made light of it, saying in a jocular manner, 'Well, thank you, kind sir...'

His eyes looked directly at her now and, as she met his gaze, she felt a quick sensation deep inside. Flustered, she lifted her wine glass and took a gulp of it. She hadn't done or said anything wrong, but she felt she had.

There was a silence and then he stretched his hand towards her and covered hers. For a few moments she froze, and when she glanced up at him again, he was still looking at her, as though studying her carefully. Her heart racing now, she turned her hand around and his fingers entwined with hers.

'I know you're married,' he said quietly, 'and I respect that. But I feel there is something, a connection, between us. Something that tells me in a different time and place, that we would have been more than friends.'

Alice knew she should move away from him, but something stopped her. She sat there silent, looking down at their clasped hands, her heart beating so fast she almost wondered if he could hear it.

'Have I upset you?' he asked quietly. 'Perhaps I should have kept those thoughts and feelings to myself?'

'No,' she said, 'you haven't upset me...'

He looked anxious. 'I want you to know I am not the sort of man who often goes after women, and I have not been with any women since I arrived in Stockport. Also, I don't talk about personal things to many people.' He shrugged. 'I don't know why, but it feels easy to talk with you, as if I've known you before.'

'I've never talked like this with another man since I got married. It's not something I could ever have imagined.'

'I am not asking anything of you.' He held her hand between both of his, then lifted it to his lips and kissed it.

That small, intimate touch felt like an electric jolt through her. 'Louis...' She bit her lip. 'I don't know what to say...'

'I know you are not free,' he said, 'and this is enough. I don't expect any more physical closeness from you. Just to be here and to talk to you – and to feel like this. It's enough.'

They sat, hands clasped together, until the distant sound of children's laughter made them sit back in their chairs. A few moments later Alice heard the familiar rattle of the latch being lifted on the back gate and she heard Freddy's voice.

Louis looked over at her, smiled and shook his head. 'I'd almost forgotten about them. How is that possible?'

'I don't know,' Alice said, a breathless note in her voice, 'because I had forgotten everything else, too.'

All three came in loudly, talking over each other, each trying to tell the story about a young woman who they met down the hill, who had asked them to help catch her new puppy that had run off.

'Me and Gabriela caught it just before it ran into the road,' Freddy said. 'It was dead lucky because there was a big coal lorry coming down the road one way, and an ambulance on the other side.'

'Well done for catching it,' Alice said, 'but I hope you wouldn't have run into the road to rescue it and got hurt yourselves.'

Freddy looked at Alice as if she was mad. 'No chance,' he said. 'And I wouldn't have let Gabriela go into the road either.'

Gabriela put her hands on her hips and looked at him mischievously. 'Do I look stupid?'

Freddy mirrored her pose. 'Do you really want me to answer that?'

'Sit back down at the table,' Alice told them. 'I'm going to bring out the pudding now.' She halted, remembering her earlier plans. The plans she had made when she thought she would have to fill awkward silences between her and Louis Girard.

'I have some music I thought you might like to listen to.' She went over to the record player, followed by an interested Freddy. The record she had purposely left on top of the pile was now mixed somewhere in between the others, when her young shop assistant was rifling through them.

Louis looked over at Philip. 'Are you OK?' he asked. 'Did the walk help your stomach?'

'I think it's a bit better. I held Bella by the lead while they went to get the pup.'

'Good boy,' Louis said. 'Tell me if it continues – we might have to take you to the doctor.'

Philip shook his head. 'I don't like doctors, I'll be fine.'

Alice glanced over at Louis, and he just nodded and mouthed, 'It's OK.'

How, she thought, had they come to be on this same wavelength so quickly? Emily's teaching colleague was a virtual stranger, and yet, at this moment, she felt closer to him than anyone she had met in her life. There was no sense to what was happening between them, and she had no experience to help her navigate her way through these sudden, overwhelming feelings. This, Alice recognised, was the sort of situation she knew led to love affairs. The sort of dangerous situation she would have been critical of other women for becoming involved in.

As she plugged the gramophone in, she suddenly wondered what Emily would make of this. What would any of her friends or family think, if they had seen her sitting at the table, holding hands with another man – allowing him to kiss her hand? An image of Greg flew into her mind, and she didn't have to wonder what he would think. She knew the answer only too well.

As she slid the music hall record out of its cover, and placed it on the turntable, she told herself that they had done nothing wrong. They had hardly touched each other; some people would laugh at the innocence of it all. As Louis had said, he expected nothing from her, that he would not interfere in her marriage. That maybe – at a different time – they could have found a lot more between them.

In many ways it was such a small thing that had happened, and, in all probability, would never happen again. But it meant something, and Alice knew that the memory of those moments would stay with her forever.

As the record began to spin on the turntable, the childish gaiety in the room was heightened by the sound of the familiar, favourite songs. Alice left them and went into the kitchen to sort into bowls the large dish of strawberry jelly she had made – which had a whole tin of tropical fruit embedded in it – and a carton of ice cream. She came out with three dishes and gave them to the children, then she looked at Louis. 'Would you like the same or some apple tart?'

'Jelly and ice cream, please,' he said, looking up at her the way he did earlier. 'It's party food and it feels like a little party here tonight.'

As she came back in with two more portions for them, 'I Do Like to be Beside the Seaside' suddenly blared out.

'Oh, I do really like the seaside!' Gabriela said. Her face suddenly became solemn. 'I miss the sea back in Guernsey. I wish we could go back there again and make sandcastles and have ice cream sitting on the benches.'

Freddy stopped with his spoonful of ice cream in mid-air. 'What about Blackpool?' he said. 'That's the best seaside place ever. Have you been there?'

'Yes,' Philip said, nodding his head vigorously. 'Mrs Ponsonby took us to see the lights a few times, and we went in a bus with one of the Guernsey groups last year.'

'I wonder if she'll come back to take us again,' Gabriela said.

'I'll take you to Blackpool during the summer holidays,' Louis said. 'We'll have a lovely day out; we can go on the train.'

'Can I come too?' Freddy asked. 'I could help you carry things and look after this pair. Stop Gabriela running into the road after dogs, like.' As he anticipated, there was an over-loud protest from the twins, followed by more teasing and laughter.

When they finished eating and the music was turned down to play in the background, Alice presented her final piece of entertainment – a jigsaw puzzle of a corner shop window. The puzzle was an unopened present she had been given as a joke when she started work in the shop – a thousand pieces – which she guessed was just at the right level for everyone. The window was filled with items such as tins of peas and beans, jars of jam, Marmite, boxes of Oxo cubes and packets of washing powder and scouring powder. All the familiar, essential things that could be found in a typical corner shop.

She looked up at the clock then over at Louis. 'Have we time to play?' It was after eight o'clock and she was conscious the children were up for school in the morning.

He nodded. 'I don't think anyone will mind,' he said. 'They are not over-strict at the vicarage, and I'm in no big hurry.'

She smiled and handed the box to him. 'If you unwrap it and lay out the pieces on the table, I'll go and get everyone a fresh drink.'

'This is good,' he said, studying the picture on the box and nodding. 'It would be great for school, for the children to learn the labels on the tins and jars.'

'You can have it when we're finished,' she told him.

'If you're sure?' he asked. 'The class would love it.'

Alice didn't mention that the puzzle had been a joke, as she was pleased he had seen something worthwhile and useful in it. She came back with the drinks and then produced a bowl of Liquorice Allsorts from the drinks cupboard. 'Your very last treat,' she told them, smiling, 'otherwise I'm afraid you might come back again.'

Philip looked at her, not sure if she was serious, then he looked at Louis. 'Can we come back again?' he asked.

'I think we might, if Alice has time.'

'Yes,' she said. 'I've enjoyed having you all very much, so we'll organise another visit.'

Freddy lounged back in his chair with his legs out straight and hands hanging down at the sides. 'I'm here nearly every day, so I don't need to worry.'

'You'll be worrying in a minute if you don't sit yourself up straight at the table,' Alice told him, her finger wagging as in mock-censure. 'You're supposed to be the older one, setting a good example.'

He straightened up, then gave a half-salute, signalling surrender.

The pieces of the puzzle were spread out on the table, and then divided into three piles. 'The Laughing Policeman' started in the background, but nobody noticed the ridiculous song, as a serious atmosphere suddenly descended on the room. The children studiously began to sort through their pieces, three heads bent intently in concentration, while Alice hovered behind them checking if any of them needed any guidance.

Alice glanced towards Louis, and she saw he was engrossed in watching them work. His quiet willingness to join in with the activity and his easy connection with the children impressed her. He looked up at her and as their gaze met, she saw the warmth in his blue eyes, and wondered again at how being with him felt so natural. She moved and sat beside Philip, and as she examined a couple of pieces of the puzzle, she was aware of a sense of contentment within her, which made her wish that this scenario around the table was part of her life. The children took a drink or reached out to the dish of liquorice sweets every so often, relaxed and easy.

After a while, Louis lifted the bottle of wine and filled their glasses with the remainder of it. He did not ask this time if she wanted more. It was just a natural movement between two people, now at ease with each other, and it did not occur to

Alice to even question it. The record finished playing and no one noticed except Louis. He quietly got up and went over to the gramophone and changed the record to the Ink Spots.

As the familiar opening notes of 'Whispering Grass' came on, Alice took a sip from her glass and then she looked at the colourful, tumbling flowers in her grandmother's vase. She reached out and slid the flowers closer to her, to smell the damask roses again. She inhaled the beautiful scent, then she closed her eyes for a few seconds, thinking that she had never had a Wednesday evening like this. The relaxed, simple meal, the easy – sometimes silly – conversation, and sitting now completing the jigsaw puzzle with Freddy and the Guernsey children. It had filled the house with real life. She could not remember any evening when she had wine and flowers, jazz music playing and the company of an entertaining and intelligent man. A man Alice found to be frighteningly attractive.

When half past eight came around, Louis looked over at Alice. 'We should think about moving soon. It will be after nine by the time we get up to the vicar's house.'

Gabriela looked at him pleadingly. 'We haven't much to go with the jigsaw,' she said. 'Can we have a bit longer to try to finish it?'

He gave a good-humoured sigh. 'A few more minutes,' he said. He glanced over at Philip, and noticed he was suddenly pale. 'Are you OK?'

'That pain is back,' he said, giving a little whimper. 'It started a while ago and it's getting worse.'

'Let's get you to the bathroom again,' Louis said, standing up. 'It might be all you've eaten.'

Philip pushed his chair back and then as he went to move around the table, he suddenly doubled in two. 'Argh!' he said. 'It's really bad...' He took a deep breath and then he stood up and took a few steps, before falling into the table, clutching his stomach.

Alice rushed towards him. 'Sit down again and see if it eases.'

Philip closed his eyes and then he stepped away from the table, made a choking noise and vomited on the floor.

Alice suddenly felt alarmed. 'Don't worry,' she said, 'you might feel better after being sick.' She grabbed some of the paper napkins on the table and brought them over to him.

Louis caught him by the shoulders and gently guided him back into the chair. 'Take some deep breaths and see if it helps.'

Freddy and Gabriela were standing now, looking frightened and unsure.

Philip closed his eyes. 'The pain is terrible... it's got much worse.' He started to cry, and a short while later he was sick again. 'I'm sorry, Alice,' he said, 'for all the mess...'

'Forget about that,' she told him. 'That will be easily cleaned.' She gave him the bundle of napkins to wipe his mouth and then she looked at Louis. 'You said this started this afternoon?'

Louis confirmed with a nod.

She mouthed 'appendicitis' at him, and his eyes widened and then he shrugged, unsure.

'Can you drive?' she asked, and he confirmed with a nod. 'The shop van is outside, and we could be down at the casualty department in the Infirmary in five minutes.'

'OK,' Louis said. 'Let's get everyone ready.' He moved to gather up their things.

Alice turned to Freddy. 'I don't know when I'll be back, so it's best if you go home now.'

'Will I take Bella out first?'

'No, she was out not too long ago, so she'll last.' She looked now at Philip and saw little beads of perspiration on his forehead and above his lip, and felt a knot of anxiety starting in her chest. 'We need to go quickly to get Philip checked out.'

Within minutes the group was out in the street, Louis and Freddy supporting Philip, while Alice locked up the shop door. She then guided them to the side entry where Greg had parked the van, and she gave Louis the keys. They helped Philip into the passenger seat, then she and Gabriela climbed into the back of the van. As she looked out of the back window, she thought

Freddy cut a forlorn figure, waving them off from the pavement outside the shop.

As they walked Philip from the car to the door of the Infirmary casualty department, they had to stop to let him be sick again, and then clean him up with a box of tissues which Alice had brought just in case. She felt a pang of guilt thinking of the jelly and ice cream and the Liquorice Allsorts she had given him, and hoped the sweet treats had not contributed to making him sick.

The casualty department was quiet, and a nurse brought them into a small side-room and after listening to the description of Philip's symptoms, he was put in a wheelchair and taken down to an examination room. Louis asked if he could accompany him, and the nurse asked him to stay in the waiting room until she checked with the doctor.

'Some doctors are OK about parents being there and some don't like it.'

'Please let me know when the doctor decides,' Louis told her. When he went back to Alice and Gabriela in the waiting room, he said quietly, 'They think I am Philip's father, and I didn't contradict it, as the doctor might not let me in.'

Alice was sitting with her arm around a very quiet Gabriela. 'You did the right thing,' she said.

Louis ran a hand through his thick dark hair. 'I feel sorry for poor Philip being in such pain and hope he is sorted soon.' He looked over at Alice. 'And I am very glad you are here.'

Gabriela suddenly sat up. 'And I am, too. I am glad we were at Alice's when this happened. If we were at the vicar's house, it would have been very difficult if Philip was ill, with the other children and the baby.' She bit her lip. 'What would have happened to us?' Tears suddenly came into her eyes. 'Children are supposed to have their mothers to look after them when they are in hospital, and ours is far away in Guernsey. We have no mother to look after us here in England.' The tears now trickled down her face and Alice put her arm around her shoulder and pulled her in close.

'You have lots of people who care about you here,' she said. 'Louis is a great friend to you and Philip.'

'He is,' Gabriela sobbed, 'but he's not our mummy, and what if Philip is very, very sick? What if he dies and I'm left all alone here in England? What will happen to me?'

Alice's stomach clenched as she saw the panic on the little girl's face. She wanted to say something to make her feel better, but she knew she was not in a position to say or do anything.

Louis leaned over now and put his hand on Gabriela's head. 'Philip won't die,' he said in a reassuring voice, 'and the doctors will take great care of him.' He ruffled her curly hair. 'And I promise I will look after you both, whatever happens.' He looked the child straight in the eye. 'Haven't I looked after you both, since Mrs Ponsonby moved away? Haven't I called up to the vicarage almost every day to check you are OK?'

Gabriela nodded. 'Yes...'

'Well,' he said, 'I am hoping to get a house of my own very soon, and when that happens, you can both come and live with me until it is time to go back to Guernsey.'

Alice looked over at him, a questioning look in her eyes, and he nodded his head.

'Don't worry about anything,' he told Gabriela. 'Things will work out.'

The nurse came down the corridor towards them now, and Louis went over to her. She spoke quietly to him for a short while, and then he nodded. He looked back at Alice. 'I'm going to see the doctor now and then we'll know what's happening.'

Fifteen minutes later he appeared, his face dark and serious. 'It is his appendix,' he said, 'and the doctors are taking him straight to the theatre now.'

'How is he?' Alice asked. Her heart dropped when he gave a little shake of his head. He smiled at Gabriela. 'The doctors will look after him now, and we'll know how he is in a few hours. So, I'm going to take you back to the vicarage to get a good night's sleep, and then I'll drop Alice and the van back home before it gets dark.'

'No!' Gabriela said, cuddling into Alice. 'I don't want to go back there on my own... I want to stay with Alice.'

Louis sat down beside her. 'I know how you feel,' he said kindly, 'but we have to be sensible. You and I both have school in the morning, and Alice has to get up early to open the shop. All your school things are at the vicarage, so we need to go back there to get them. If the doctors allow us, we'll go in to visit Philip after school tomorrow.'

'I don't want to go to school,' Gabriela sobbed, burying her face into Alice's side. 'I don't want to go without Philip...'

'But you've never missed a day of school,' he said. 'You get a prize every year for perfect attendance.'

'I don't care about prizes... please don't make me go on my own.' Gabriela's shoulders heaved up and down now. 'I want my mummy and daddy. I want them to look after me and Philip.'

Alice looked at Louis. 'Why doesn't Gabriela come back with me tonight? There's a spare room and it won't take long to sort out. I can phone the school in the morning and explain about Philip. I'm sure they will understand.'

'Oh, please!' Gabriela said, wiping tears away with the back of her hand. 'Please let me stay with Alice, Louis.'

Louis shook his head. 'Surely this is too much? It's putting you in a difficult position.'

'It's OK,' Alice said.

Louis paused, thinking it through. Having weighed up all the other options, he said, 'Are you sure?'

'Yes,' Alice replied without hesitation. 'It's absolutely fine. I'm sure I will find this young lady something that she can wear in bed tonight, and we can sort out her own things tomorrow.'

'Thanks, Alice,' the little girl said. 'I liked being in your house, it's nice and quiet.'

'I'm glad you like it, and I'm sure Bella will like your company.'

Louis had another quick word with the nurse, and then he

came back to Alice. 'I'll have to stay at the vicarage tonight,' he said. 'They want me to be near a phone, and I don't have access to one where I'm living. I'm sure they won't mind; I can sleep in Philip's bed.' He paused. 'If we stop at my digs in Shaw Heath, I'll collect a clean shirt and a few other things, then I can take you and Gabriela back to the house, and leave the van and then I'll walk to the vicar's.'

Alice turned to Gabriela. 'Do you see the door at the end of the corridor?' she said, pointing. 'You go down there and wait on the bench for a few minutes, while Louis and I talk to the nurse.' She smiled. 'If you're very good, I'll make you hot cocoa before you go to bed.'

Gabriela's face lit up, and she went off down the corridor.

Alice turned to Louis. 'What did they say?'

'Worse than we thought,' he told her. 'The doctor is concerned that Philip's appendix might be ruptured, so they had to get him to surgery immediately. I asked if I could wait until he comes out of theatre, but they said there was no point as they won't know anything until they operate and see how things are. Whatever happens, they won't know how he is until after he comes around in the morning.' He paused. 'They have asked for a phone number, in case anything goes wrong.'

'Oh God,' Alice said. 'Poor Philip...'

'The doctor said it would have happened at some point, and it could have been in the middle of the night.'

'And that would have been much worse for poor Phillip.'

'I can't tell you how grateful I am to you for offering to have Gabriela tomorrow.'

'It's no trouble,' she said, 'none at all.'

He looked at his watch. 'There's a phone box outside the main door, so if you don't mind waiting, I'll go and make a quick call to the vicar to let him know what's happening.'

'Before you do,' she said, 'I have a suggestion – a purely practical one. Why don't you just stay at my place? It's much closer to the infirmary and we have the phone in the shop.' Her gaze moved to the floor. 'And if something unexpected happened, you can jump in the van and be here in a few minutes. You can also use the shop phone to let school know if you have to go in late or anything like that.'

His brow deepened as he thought it over. 'Oh, Alice, that would make things much easier... but are you sure?'

'It just makes sense, and Gabriela will be happier knowing you're there. We don't have a bed in the spare room, but you can sleep downstairs on the couch.' There was no point, Alice felt, in going into long explanations about how she got rid of Betty's old bed after she died and hadn't got around to replacing it yet.

'You've been so good with the children, I don't know what to say. If I was given to that sort of thinking, I would say fate led me in your direction today, so that I would have someone...' He shrugged. 'Someone beside me to get through this.'

'I'm sure you would have managed fine without me,' she said, 'but I'm glad that it's worked out this way.'

They walked towards the door now, where Gabriela was standing reading a poster about how people could prevent common accidents that happen during the blackout.

'Thank you,' Louis said once again. 'I hope this doesn't put you in a difficult situation... I don't know how your husband would feel about you having a strange man in the house overnight.'

Alice slowed up now, so Gabriela was not in earshot. 'What my husband thinks is not a concern,' she said quietly. 'At one time it might have been, but for a number of reasons, it's not now.' She looked him straight in the eye. 'What we're doing is right and perfectly decent, looking after two vulnerable children, one who might be seriously ill. It's no one else's business.'

He nodded. 'As long as you feel OK.'

'Lots of people are doing what they like now, and we're not interfering with them or judging them. I have spent my whole life doing the right thing...' Alice suddenly felt as if she could cry. 'At this point, I don't feel I need to answer to anyone. With

Philip seriously ill and Gabriela needing you, staying the night at my house is the right thing, and that's all there is to it.'

'You have suddenly made a difficult thing seem easy,' he said.

She smiled at him. 'Well, that's a lot better than making an easy thing seem difficult.'

Chapter Twenty-Four

When they arrived back at the house, Alice put the kettle on and then Louis took Bella for her last walk, while some nightclothes were found for Gabriela. The best Alice could come up with was a cream satin petticoat which came down to Gabriela's ankles, and a white cardigan with floral embroidery on the top half, which looked decent enough.

Alice then went to the airing cupboard and got fresh sheets and pillowslips and an eiderdown for the small guestroom. She glanced in Betty's bedroom at one point and reminded herself to order a new mattress for the old cast-iron bed.

When Louis came back, she made tea for him and herself and cocoa for Gabriela, and the little girl helped her make toast for everyone. Afterwards, they sat at the kitchen table with the wireless on in the background, and eventually Alice noticed Gabriela's eyelids starting to flutter and she gently guided her off upstairs to bed.

'In the morning when you wake up,' Alice told her, 'if there's no one here, you don't need to worry, I'll only be in the shop. If you can remember, it's the door past the kitchen and at the end of the hall.' Alice put an arm around her. 'And don't worry about Philip, the hospital will take very good care of him, and we'll take you to visit him as soon as it's allowed.'

'Thank you for letting me stay with you, Alice,' Gabriela said. 'You're a very kind lady. I can't remember her very well, but I think you're a little bit like my mummy.'

Alice's throat tightened. 'Goodnight,' she said, trying to keep her voice steady and normal, 'sleep tight.'

When she came back downstairs, Louis was still sitting in the kitchen. She told him what Gabriela had said, and he just nodded slowly. 'Being away from their families for this long is even worse than I thought. When I think of poor Philip having to go through an operation on his own tonight with no family to come home to...' she said.

'They're not the only ones,' he said. 'And they are lucky compared to some. There are children who have been living with unsuitable families for four years now, and we still don't know when they will be able to go home.'

'I almost cried when Gabriela said she couldn't remember her mother very well...' She put her hand over her mouth now and shook her head. 'I didn't know what to say.'

'You've been very kind to her, and that has made her feel better tonight,' he said quietly.

'It must be terrible for her, not remembering her mother or her home.'

'That's one of the worst things – how everything has changed since we've all been away.' Louis's voice sounded flat. 'Time has moved on and we have changed by being here, and of course those we left behind have changed during that time, too. It's hard to imagine how things will be when we go back. You don't think of these things until something happens to yourself or you hear about someone else from Guernsey who has lost someone back there. Time moves on and things just keep on changing. The only thing we can do is adapt and wait and see what happens in the end – when the war is over. We will find out then what is really left.'

There was a silence and Alice looked up at the clock. It was half past eleven. She was normally in bed and fast asleep at this time, and although her body felt tired, her mind was still going over everything that had happened that night. 'Would you like some more tea?' she asked.

'No, thank you.'

She suddenly thought. 'Do you want me to bring the bedding down now?'

'Whatever suits you,' he said, spreading his hands out. 'Can I help you to carry them down?'

'I won't be a minute,' she said, heading back out into the hallway. She tiptoed upstairs so as not to waken Gabriela and went quietly into the airing cupboard, finding a sheet and eiderdown. She realised she had no spare pillow, and for a few moments considered giving him the one from her own bed – the one Greg used. It didn't feel right somehow, for reasons she didn't want to think about.

When she came back along the hallway, she saw Louis was waiting halfway up the stairs to help her. Silently, she threw the eiderdown and he caught it, and then she followed him down carrying the sheet. He took them into the sitting room and put them on the couch.

'You can use the cushions on the couch, if that's OK?' she told him.

'It's perfect, thanks.' Then he said, 'If you are ready to go to bed now, please don't let me hold you back.'

Alice hesitated, unsure what to do.

'I'm not actually tired at the moment.' He indicated his bag on the table. 'I picked up a book when we stopped off at the house in Shaw Heath, so if you want to go to bed, I'm happy to read for a while.'

She stood at the door, knowing she should go.

'Up until Philip got sick, I was enjoying every minute with you. But I know that situation is not fair on you... and things seem different this time of night, compared to earlier on.' He ran his hand through his hair. 'I just don't want you to feel you have to spend more time with me than you want – or feel is right.'

'I don't feel that tired either. Would you like a drink?' She thought quickly. 'I don't have any wine, but I think there are bottles of whisky and brandy, and maybe port.'

'I don't want you to stay up just to be polite... you've done so much already.'

'I'm not being polite,' she said. 'I'm asking you because I think it would be nice for us to have a drink and a chat. To take a little bit of time to get to know each other better.'

A short while later they came to sit opposite each other in the armchairs by the empty fireplace. Louis had a large whisky and Alice had a brandy with lemonade. On the side table was the remains of the fruit cake she had cut earlier.

They talked for a while about school and how the shop was dealing with rationing, then Louis told her about his involvement in the evenings with the Home Guard. He explained how they had recently let him juggle the rota while he was helping find accommodation for the twins.

'I wouldn't normally be free on a Wednesday,' he told her, 'and I'll be back to duties most evenings as soon as things are settled. That's why this has been a very different evening in more ways than one.'

Alice looked at him. 'It's been a very different one for me, too.'

There was a pause as though neither was sure where to take the conversation, as though both were skirting around anything that might be too personal, or might allude to the intimate way they had been earlier in the evening.

'Tell me more about Guernsey,' Alice said. 'I'm ashamed to admit I know very little about it.'

He smiled and said, 'Why would you? I had never even heard of Stockport until the train pulled up at the station, and we found ourselves in this strange mill town somewhere near Manchester. I knew London because my older brother moved there about ten years ago, and I visited him a couple of times, but that's the only place I knew in England.' His face darkened. 'Although my best friend from childhood, Paul, was born in England and lived in Liverpool, until he was around six or seven. He used to talk about the trains and the trams, and we had never heard about things like that.'

'That's something you never think about,' Alice said, 'the difference between places and how people have to adapt – like the twins.'

'Until the war came, I suppose everyone's world was much smaller. Now we are listening carefully for news from France and Italy, and countries like Poland and Russia that we knew nothing about.'

'What was it like to grow up there?' Alice asked.

'I had a happy, contented childhood,' he told her, and went on to describe his mother, who was a nurse, and his father, who had a small farm, and his older brother who always seemed like an adult to him. His mother, he explained, had lost several babies in between them, two at birth and then tragically another who had been born with a heart defect and only lived to be a year old. 'I came two years after he died, and I think that helped lessen the grief she has always carried about losing the others.' He gave a small sigh. 'It was something I was always aware of, and I felt as though those lost children were as much a part of our family as if they had lived. My mother remembered each of their birthdays and we always took flowers up to the graveyard.'

Alice could almost feel his sadness. 'I'm so sorry, that must have been hard for you all. Can I ask, are your parents still in Guernsey?' When he slowly nodded, she said, 'Have you heard from them?'

'Nothing for the first two years,' he said, 'and then after that the Red Cross were allowed to organise a postal service – a very slow postal service – and we received and sent occasional short notes of only twenty words.'

'And they were OK the last time you heard from them?'

'I think so . . .' He moved in his chair as though suddenly uncomfortable, and then he took a gulp of his whisky. 'The last few times I heard from my mother it was to send me news that she thought I should hear.'

Alice wondered what he was referring to, but she stayed silent, and waited to see if he wanted to tell her.

'The English friend I mentioned, called Paul,' he cleared his throat. 'He was called up for military service before the island was invaded and I never saw him again. My mother kept in touch with his parents, and they told her when he went missing in action some time back.'

'Have they heard about him since?' Alice asked.

'No, they heard nothing further about Paul, and then I got another shock when my mother wrote last year, and said his parents were taken away by the Nazis.'

'Why? What reason would they have to take them?'

'Because they were not born on Guernsey,' Louis explained. 'They recorded all the people on the island and rounded up Jewish people and those not born on the island. Paul's parents must have managed to remain undetected, but his father took ill and when he was in the hospital his documents were examined again, and they discovered his English origins. So, his mother and father and younger sister were arrested, and sent off to an internment camp out in Germany somewhere.'

'It's just awful – totally inhumane,' Alice said, clearly shocked. 'I know it's been difficult for the children and people like yourself who had to leave, but harder not to hear what has happened to people left behind for so long.'

'At least we have some contact now,' he said. 'Before that you just feared the worst, not knowing what had happened to people. The short notes at least confirmed those who were still alive and got some news out to you. The rest of the news about the island comes from the radio or in newspaper reports, but you are never actually sure what is going on. The people from the Guernsey Islanders, who meet in the Stockport area, often have news that they say has been smuggled out, but there is no way of checking how true it is. We just have to rely on those short Red Cross letters, which are censored by the Germans, and try to read the truth between the words.'

'What about the twins' parents and family? Have they managed to make contact?'

'As far as I know they are still alive and surviving, and the children have had several letters from them. Some reports say the Germans are treating those on the island reasonably well, but it's difficult to know the truth. There is a difference between living a normal life and surviving under another nation's rule. A nation that has killed hundreds of thousands of people – maybe millions – in different parts of the world.'

'It's hard to imagine it. Some terrible things have happened to our troops abroad and in the bombings here – but we are very lucky we haven't been invaded.'

'The Germans have ruled the Channel Islands from June 1940,' Louis said, his voice dull and emotionless now. 'As soon as they arrived, everything began to change. They imposed a curfew, made everyone carry identity cards, then they banned radios so the island was completely cut off from any news about the outside world. I also heard that they have brought in these poor prisoners from places like Poland and Russia, and they have used them as slaves to build fortifications and hospitals on the island.' He held his hands up. 'Our people knew nothing like this before – we were just a quiet island where almost everyone knew everyone else. The only changes in the year came in the summer, when visitors came from England and France and helped boost our small economy. Now, after all that the people have been through, I don't know if it will ever be the same again. I don't know if I will even recognise my homeland when I am allowed to return to it.'

'You must miss it very much,' Alice said, 'and after all this time I'm sure you can't wait to get back.' There was a question that had been lingering at the back of her mind – almost since she had met him. A question she had been afraid to ask in case it unsettled or even upset him. In case it changed the relationship between them.

'As soon as this war is over,' he said, 'I need to get back to check how everyone is, to see my parents – and others I left behind – to do what I can to help them rebuild their lives again. To maybe even help rebuild the island again. But after that...' He shrugged. 'Who knows? Who can see into the future? I have given up trying to do that.'

'It's the same here,' Alice said. 'Nobody could have imagined we would still be at war and lost all those men fighting abroad and all the people killed in the Blitz in London and places like Liverpool. We weren't so affected here, but in Manchester hundreds were killed in air raids early in the war. You almost forget these things.'

'I suppose we have all suffered,' Louis said, 'and we have to look at both sides. Britain has undoubtedly suffered in huge ways, but it was very hard when they pulled the British military defence out of the Channel Islands, and the people were left to the mercy of the Nazis.'

'I can't imagine how frightening that must have been.' Alice took another mouthful of the brandy and lemonade. It was not a drink she had very often, but on this strange and unpredictable night it felt soothing and comforting.

'In many ways, those of us who were evacuated were lucky, and everyone has been safe here in Stockport. The people could not have given us a bigger welcome. Stockport is a town to be proud of.'

'I'm glad you feel that,' Alice said, 'because I've always found it to be a good place.'

'The people are down to earth and decent,' he said. 'I don't know what the future holds, but I know it's a place that will always mean something to me.' He lifted his glass and drained the last of the whisky.

There was a silence now, and perhaps due to courage fortified by the brandy, Alice suddenly found herself asking the question at the back of her mind. 'Emily mentioned some time ago that you are engaged to a girl back in Guernsey. I imagine that must be very difficult for you, and I do understand if you don't want to talk about it.'

He looked up at her now, and then he gave a small, bitter laugh. 'Now, that is a subject I am going to need another whisky for.' He got to his feet and moved towards the side table where Alice had left the bottles.

Alice felt a sense of alarm. 'You don't have to tell me anything. Some things can just be too difficult...' Something told her that it was time to go, that forcing him to open up about private matters was not the right thing to do. They didn't know each other well enough for that, and as Emily had told her, he didn't talk much about his personal life. She moved to her feet. 'You enjoy your drink, but I really think I should go on to bed now. You know where everything is in the kitchen for the morning if you want to make tea and toast. There's a jar of instant coffee in the cupboard above the sink if you'd prefer that.'

'Don't go,' he said. 'Stay a little while longer. Have another drink or a cup of tea or something. Please stay...'

The look on his face made her turn back. 'OK,' she said, 'for a few minutes longer.' He gestured towards the drinks, and she nodded. 'I'll have a tiny brandy with lemonade.'

He poured the drinks and they both sat down again opposite each other. 'I suppose I'll have to talk about this at some point, and you seem to be the right person.' He took a mouthful of whisky. 'The engagement with Rose didn't work out.'

'I'm sorry to hear that,' Alice said.

'Looking back, it was done in the heat of the moment – when we realised how serious things were with the war, how things could change so quickly. It was as if we needed something to hang onto, to have something familiar when we came out the other end.'

'Did you change your mind when you came over here, and then decide to break it off?'

'It wasn't as simple as that,' he said. 'Don't forget we had no communication for two years. As time went on, I realised we'd rushed things, but I decided to wait until I got back home to be sure, to give us a fair chance, see how things worked out when we saw each other again. Of course, we had no idea how long I would be over here. At the beginning I only looked a month ahead at most, thinking the war would surely end soon.'

'What made you change your mind?'

'It was kind of made up for me.' He took another sip of his drink. 'I got a message that changed everything. One of those carefully worded messages that can say a lot in a little space.'

'From Rose?'

'No, the message was from my mother. I know it off by heart. She wrote: *As explained last message Rose not around anymore. She had baby boy yesterday, blond hair, blue eyes like doctor father.*'

Alice was silent as she digested this. 'She met someone else and had a baby since you left?'

'Yes, and if I'm reading the situation correctly, the father is a German doctor who works with my mother in the hospital. She hinted at it, in the letter before, saying that Rose was working in the office in the hospital, and that she seemed to have impressed some of the new government officials.' He shrugged. 'Well, he was obviously more than just impressed with her, if she became pregnant.'

'Oh my God...' Alice did not know how to react. 'Are you OK?' she asked. 'Were you very upset?'

'At first, I didn't know what to feel. Rose is a kind, decent girl who always tried to do the right thing. But knowing that she's involved romantically – had a baby – with a Nazi, is hard to take in. Human nature is human nature, however, and I suppose there will be good men amongst the Germans, too. I imagine he must be one of them, if Rose has fallen in love with him.' He gave a long, low sigh. 'It will be very difficult with her family and the local people who have suffered at their hands. By all accounts it's happened to a number of women, and they even have a name for them – an awful name – Jerrybags. Some poor women may have been forced into it, but I think Rose fell in love.'

'I don't know what to say...'

'I haven't told anyone this before now,' Louis said. He looked straight at Alice. 'Although I need to make one thing clear – I am not upset for any loss over the relationship. I just wish Rose had told me herself, rather than hearing it from my mother.'

'Had she been in touch with you?'

'Two letters or notes, saying very little. Saying she missed me and how the war had completely changed her life. That she hadn't imagined I would be gone so long.' He gave a wry smile.

'Something like that squeezed into twenty words. I was relieved she was OK, but it was like hearing from an old friend rather than a fiancée.' He shrugged. 'So now you know everything.'

'Are you OK?' Alice asked. 'That has been a difficult thing to listen to, so I can't begin to imagine how you must feel.'

'You have to get over things,' he said, 'and a lot worse has happened to people. I had to put it behind me and concentrate on my job and duties with the Home Guard. In a way, it made me stop living in the past – it's made me settle down more in Stockport and make the best of life.'

'I'm relieved to hear you say that,' Alice said. 'It's the right attitude.'

'I enjoy my job,' he said, 'and all the inter-school sports and that kind of thing, and I've made some good friends. People from all different backgrounds, the vicar and an Irish lad called Tommy who has one of the rooms in the house I share in Shaw Heath. He has a great wit and yet he's clever and well-read. Before this difficulty with trying to find accommodation for the twins, any spare time I had I went to art galleries and museums. I bought a gramophone and I listen to music, all kinds. At the weekends, if I've time off from Home Guard duties, I've gone into Manchester with Tommy to the dance halls or to concerts.'

'You seem to have a much more full and interesting life than I have. Apart from the wedding and the bit of excitement before it last week, I've hardly been further than the Plaza.'

'But you're married,' Louis said, lifting his glass from the table. 'From listening to the female teachers in school, most married women settle down at home. They don't seem to go dancing or to music halls very often. I'm not saying it as a judgement or anything, or saying they shouldn't be out enjoying themselves. It's just an observation.'

'That's true for most women,' she said, 'and of course I'm busy with the shop and everything.'

Louis raised his eyebrows and looked directly at her. 'It's your turn now, Alice . . .'

'What do you mean?'

'I've told you what you wanted to know about me. Are you happy and living the life you hoped for?'

Alice looked down at her brandy glass, then she shifted her gaze over to the window. 'No,' she said, 'I'm not happy. I used to think I was, but my marriage is not the way it was at the beginning.'

'But there's a war on,' he said, 'and your husband is away a lot of the time, so it must be hard to get that back, especially at this time.'

'It's not that,' she said quietly. 'The truth is, Greg is not the husband I thought he would be. He was unfaithful and since I found out, I just don't see him in the same way. The trust is all gone.'

'Oh, I'm sorry, Alice . . .'

'It's OK,' she said, her voice surprisingly matter-of-fact. 'It was a while ago and I've had time to get used to it. I was upset for months, but now I just feel nothing – or very little – towards him.' She sighed. 'It would be easier if I could just put it out of my mind, but I can't. I can't get around the fact that he wanted another woman when everything was fine between us, when I thought that we were happy and planning to have a baby together. How could I ever trust him again?'

'And how is he? You saw him a few days ago.'

'He's trying – in fact, he's better than he's ever been. His mother died recently, and I think it's had an effect on him, made him re-evaluate everything.'

'Maybe he has changed,' Louis said. 'Maybe he realises what he almost lost.'

'Maybe,' she said, and shrugged. 'We'll have to see.'

As they sat finishing their drinks, Alice told him the rest of the story and about Marjorie Jones.

When there was nothing left to tell, Louis asked her, 'Where do you see things going from here?'

'I honestly don't know. There have been so many changes in my life recently – school, losing my lovely mother-in-law – that I feel I need to just take things as they come for a while.' She turned her glass around in her hand. 'And with Greg being away, there's nothing that can really be done.'

'We've both been through times we never imagined...' He paused. 'Earlier on this evening I asked you if things had been different, if we met at a different time, do you think something might have happened between us. How do you feel now?'

Alice knew there was no point in lying or being evasive. After all the things they had just told each other, how could she? 'I still feel the same,' she said. 'Apart from what's happened to poor Philip, I've enjoyed every minute with you.'

'Me, too,' he said. 'I want to spend more time with you – to keep that connection and see where it goes – if you feel the same. I know that won't be easy and I don't have any expectations, given your situation, but it would be nice to do things together. Get to know each other properly.' He paused. 'I'm not sure what you think...'

'I'm not sure what I think either,' she said. 'I'm afraid of letting this thing between us go, but then I'm also afraid of what we might get ourselves into. What if things were to develop and then you had to suddenly go back to Guernsey?'

'But what if we never see each other again? What if we never felt this way about anyone else again? I never felt like this about Rose. I never felt the same connection when we talked, and I never felt the same attraction for her that I feel for you. From the very first time I saw you through the shop window, I knew there was something special about you.'

She felt a heat rising to her face now. 'Well, I felt like that, too... but I quickly put it out of my mind.'

'There's something I should be honest about,' he said. 'I have met other women since I've been here in Stockport.'

Alice's eyes widened at that news. She shouldn't be surprised, she thought, as it had registered at the back of her mind that four years was a long time for anyone to be deprived of the opposite sex's company.

'After the letter about Rose and the baby, I decided I wasn't going to waste any more time than I already have. For a while

I became close to one of the teachers in school, but after a few dates at the cinema and dances, I guessed it was going to end up like me and Rose.'

'Emily didn't mention anything about that.'

He looked at her in surprise then laughed. 'I'm glad to hear it,' he said. 'We kept it private because we didn't want anyone on the staff to know our business. I didn't realise Emily was keeping a close eye on me.'

Alice gave an embarrassed laugh now. 'She wasn't, it was because Sophie – the girl who got married – was teasing her about you. When she heard there was a decent-looking man working in Emily's school, she thought you and Emily might have matched up. Emily said you were just friends and colleagues, and she thought neither of you were the type to go out with someone from work.'

'I've no interest in anyone at school – Emily included – although she's a nice person and a good teacher.'

'You've had other romances, you said.' Alice was curious, although thinking about him with someone else felt like rubbing salt in a wound.

'Nothing worth talking about,' he said. 'Just girls I met at dances and had a few dates with, same story as the teacher from school. No one like you.'

His words filled her with such a mixture of feelings that she found she could not speak. She had heard of love at first sight, and she knew she hadn't felt that bolt of lightning when they first met. She had definitely registered him as an attractive man, but that was about it. That was all she would ever have allowed herself to feel about another man, since making her wedding vows. But she knew that from the first time they had spoken, deep inside her, a little spark had ignited. Something that was strong enough to turn her mind away from Greg and Marjorie Jones. Something that made her feel more like herself again. She thought she had buried that little spark, until the next time he appeared. And then it had ignited into a flame, which had resulted in her inviting him to tea.

'Where do we go from here?' he asked. 'Or is there anywhere we *can* go from here?' He shook his head. 'I have to leave that decision with you because you are the one who it will affect most, and I understand that.'

Alice stared at him, not sure what to say.

'In the morning,' he said, 'I will be up and gone as soon as it's light – I can go before that if that's what you want. I will go straight to the hospital and if all is well with Philip, afterwards I'll come straight back and pick Gabriela up, and take her to the vicarage to get her organised for school.' He looked straight at her. 'After that, I promise you I won't come here again. I'll forever be grateful for all the help you gave us tonight, but I won't come back again because I don't want to make things any harder for you.'

His words struck right through her. The picture he painted of him disappearing out of her life suddenly made her realise how colourless and empty her world was before she met him. How colourless and empty she would feel if she never saw him again – and, she realised, Gabriela and Philip.

With all that had happened, a bond had been formed with them. She had come to understand how being evacuated had affected them – how losing their parents had affected them. For them to go through the same thing again when Mrs Ponsonby took ill had undoubtedly shaken them. Louis had explained to her that they couldn't stay in the vicarage forever, and since there was no other family available to take them, he would have to find a place where he could keep them.

'I doubt if a bank would lend me money to buy somewhere,' he said, 'so I would have to find a house to rent that's big enough for us.' It would not be easy, he had explained, and there would be the issue of finding someone to help when he was out with the Home Guard. He hoped that some of the Guernsey families would step in on those nights.

Alice pictured the three of them now, trying to make yet another new start. A cold hand clutched at her heart. She took a deep breath. 'Philip and Gabriela can move in here with me.'

Louis looked at her for a few moments. 'Really?' he said.

'It's the only thing that makes sense.' Alice pressed the palms of her hands together. 'I wouldn't have thought it was possible before, but after meeting the children – getting to know them and understanding what they've gone through – I just think it's the right thing to do.' Her voice was calm but firm. 'You can keep your own routine in your own place, but you can come down here whenever you like to see the children.'

'Are you sure you've thought this all through? And what about your husband? He might not agree.'

'I know what it means, and I'll tell Greg when the time is right.' She tilted her head. 'He's not going to be here, so it won't affect him. He won't be home full-time until the war is over, and the children will go home to Guernsey when that happens.'

'This is so good of you...'

'I've become very fond of them, and I would feel awful now if I didn't help.'

'And us?' he said.

Alice spread her hands out. 'We'll probably be spending time together with the children, and that will give them two adults they can depend on.' She looked directly at him. 'It will also give us time to get to know each other properly.'

'So... we could be sitting together like this at the end of the day, when you've finished work, and I've finished whatever I'm doing? I can help the twins with schoolwork, and then when they've gone to bed, we could spend some time like this on our own?'

'Yes,' she said. 'Just like tonight, only more relaxed.' A huge smile spread on Alice's face. 'As far as anyone else is concerned, you're visiting the twins, which is the absolute truth. Anything else is our business.'

Alice stood up now, and he moved out of his chair and went towards her. He put his arms around her and drew her close to him – so close she could feel his heart beating alongside hers. As his cheek touched hers, she closed her eyes. As they stood there, she felt a sudden surge of happiness that she had never felt before. Being with Louis Girard, she realised, now seemed the most natural thing in the world to her.

'This,' Louis said, 'is more than I could have imagined. This is the answer to everything.' He then moved to hold her at arm's length, as though studying every little detail of her face. As he looked at her, his eyes held a question.

She moved her head and he bent towards her and kissed her.

Chapter Twenty-Five

Ten days later, Alice and Louis helped a pale-faced Philip out of the shop van and then down the back entry and into the house. The steps up into the shop, Alice thought, might just be too much for him, as the doctor had said stairs were out for a few weeks. To everyone's great relief, his appendix operation had been fairly straightforward, and it was just a matter of taking time to recover.

Maeve was closing the shop for lunch, and as they passed by, she told Alice the kettle was boiled and she had left corned beef and ham sandwiches and an apple tart on the kitchen table for them, along with a bottle of lemonade for the children.

'He's doing well,' Alice told her, 'but it will be a few weeks before he's back to himself. He's got to take it easy and not move around too much. Lucky he's a good reader, isn't it? We have a pile of books and comics to keep him occupied.'

Maeve gave Philip a sympathetic smile. 'I don't know if it's good or bad,' she said, 'but the schools are on summer holiday from next week, so he won't get much time off school.'

'I don't mind school,' Philip said, his voice a little weak, 'but I much prefer to read my own books and comics. And when I'm allowed to sit up, I can play games and do jigsaw puzzles, and Louis says he's going to teach me how to play chess.'

'As long as he's well for going back to school in September,' Louis said, 'he can take it easy at home for the next few weeks, and gradually get back to doing his usual things when he feels up to it.'

'No doubt Alice will spoil him,' Maeve said, 'and rightly so.'

Gabriela looked up at her. 'We will all look after him. If he needs things brought downstairs or anything carried, I can do it for him.'

'They're a lovely pair, God bless them,' Maeve said. 'And the place will be livelier now with two of them.'

Louis had been given the afternoon off school to go with Alice and Gabriela to the hospital to collect Philip and help settle him back in his new home. The boy had been almost overwhelmed when Louis told him the news a few days after his operation. 'I hope you will be as pleased as Gabriela was, that Alice has said you can live with her in the house.'

'It's like a miracle,' Philip said, his eyes glistening with tears. 'I like Alice's place because it's so quiet in the house but it's interesting in the shop, too. And I'm glad because I'll see Freddy as well.'

Alice had told Philip that he could sleep on the couch for the first few weeks and use the outside toilet in the backyard, which would save him climbing stairs to the bedroom and bathroom.

'I collected all your things from the vicarage,' Louis said, 'so your clothes and your books and games are in bags in the dining room.'

'You can decide what you want to keep downstairs with you,' Alice told him, 'things like your books and games, and the rest can go up to the bedroom that will be yours when you are ready.'

Alice had already ordered a new mattress from a furniture shop in Castle Street, for Betty's old room, and that's where Philip would sleep. Over the next week she planned to finish emptying the wardrobe and tallboy of the remainder of her mother-in-law's possessions. She had kept anything useful, and given Betty's good coats and suits, dresses and shoes and scarves to Maeve or anyone else she knew well enough to offer them to. She had kept a few handbags and scarves for herself, and put aside Betty's jewellery for Greg to decide what to do with, when he came home.

Freddy came rushing into the shop after school. He threw his satchel down and took off his jacket and then checked with Maeve if it was OK to go through to the house to say hello to Philip. He had knocked on the adjoining door and when Alice brought him in, she noticed that he suddenly seemed a bit awkward and even shy.

He looked at Philip, who was lying on the couch with a pillow and eiderdown, and then went over to stand beside him. 'How are you feeling?' he asked, his voice almost formal.

'Not too bad when I'm lying down,' Philip said, 'but it hurts when I move or walk. I won't be able to take Bella a walk for a while.'

'Have you still got your stitches in?'

'Yes, I don't get them out until next week.'

Freddy had looked over at Alice and Louis, his face grave. 'Don't let anyone tell him jokes or say anything funny...'

'What?' Alice said.

'Somebody I know at school had their appendix out,' Freddy explained, 'a lad called Colin, and he wasn't feeling very well after it, so his father started telling him jokes to cheer him up, like. Anyway, he told him a really funny joke and Colin started laughing so hard he couldn't stop and he burst all his stitches.' He looked over at Philip. 'He had to go back to hospital and have the operation done all over again.'

Philip's eyes widened now, and he looked at Louis then to Alice. 'Could that happen to me?'

'No, of course not,' Louis said, his voice comforting.

'Freddy!' Alice looked at him and shook her head. 'What a thing to tell somebody who's just come out of hospital.'

'It's true,' Freddy said. 'Honest to God, it happened to Colin... although it might have just been two stitches that burst, not all of them.'

Alice put her hand on her hip. 'Do you know what they call people who say things like that? A Job's comforter.'

Freddy's brow wrinkled. 'What does that mean?'

'It means a friend who is supposed to be cheering someone up, and instead they end up making them feel even worse.'

'Philip knows what I meant, don't you, Philip? I was only warning him what could happen if he laughs too much.'

Alice glanced over at Louis, who was trying not to smile, and she ended up grinning back at him. 'Well, there's no fear of him laughing while you're around giving him dire warnings.'

There was a silence then Freddy said, 'Will I take Bella out to do her business?'

'Yes,' Alice said, 'I think that would be a good idea.'

She smiled when Gabriela said, 'Wait for me,' and ran to put her shoes on to join Freddy and the dog.

How much has changed, Alice thought. Only a few weeks ago, taking Bella in had seemed like a huge decision. Since then, her life had become unrecognisable. Gabriela was now in the single bedroom upstairs and had settled into the house and the surrounding area of Edgeley as though she had been there for ages. She had recently made friends with two girls her own age in nearby Fox Street – who came into the shop and had got chatting to her – and had been out the last few evenings playing hopscotch and skipping ropes with them.

She also got on well with Freddy, and, given the fact that there was a difference in age of a few years between them, she was well able to hold her own with him. He had also saved the day when Alice was trying to work out how to get Gabriela safely to school in Davenport each morning, as she had to walk down to Wellington Road to catch the bus. It was at the busy time of the morning when bread and meat was being delivered and people were coming in for cigarettes, pipe tobacco and newspapers on their way to work. Freddy had come to the rescue saying he could escort her down and put her on the bus safely, and then run back to Edgeley in time for school himself.

Over the following weeks, things settled into a routine at the house. Alice kept an eye on Philip during the day, going into the house every time the shop was quiet and making breakfast for him and Gabriela, and then later, lunch for Philip and herself when the shop was closed. Louis called in most evenings when he was not on duty and had the evening meal with Alice and the children.

Alice waited a few weeks, and then took the chance to tell Greg about their Guernsey guests when he rang from a call box near the army training unit.

'How did you get involved with that?' he asked, clearly taken aback by the news.

'Emily asked me,' she said, quite truthfully. 'She explained about these twins who had lost their home and needed new accommodation. At first, I told her I couldn't help, but as time went on, I just felt I had to do something. We have two spare bedrooms and these poor children had nowhere to live.'

'It just seems to have come out of the blue,' Greg said. 'One week we have a dog, and the next we have two strange children living in our house.'

'You actually met them the morning of Sophie's wedding when they called into the shop with their teacher.' Alice felt a flush steal over her neck. She knew she had referred to Louis in a deliberately vague way, and felt a pang of guilt, even though they had spent little time on their own. 'And I'm sure I mentioned to you that I had put a notice in the window asking for any family who could take them in. Don't you remember?'

'Ah yes,' he said. 'I think that might ring a bell.'

'The situation has actually been going on for months,' she explained, 'and there was literally no one else to take them in. The local vicar stepped in, but they have four children of their own and it was just too much for everyone.' Alice suddenly felt she was babbling, and she made herself slow down. 'It just hit me how desperate the situation was when the young boy was taken into hospital to have his appendix out. They were both very upset and crying, saying they wanted to go back to their families in Guernsey. Of course, no one really knows what the situation is back there.'

'Oh God...' Greg said. 'I know what's happening in the Channel Islands is pretty bad.'

'It's not forever,' Alice said. 'They will be gone as soon as the war is over. They will probably be gone when you get back home. I hope you don't mind?'

'No,' he said, 'how could I?' The line was muffled and hard to hear. Eventually, his voice came through again. 'How are you? I hope things are not too much for you with the shop?'

'I'm OK,' she said. 'It's fine. Maeve is a great help and Freddy is improving and learning new things.'

They talked a little while longer about his training, but as usual he could not tell her much about any future plans, just that he would be moving again soon. Alice asked about his back, and he said it was still improving and that he had new painkillers which helped when it was bad.

'I'll ring again when I know what's happening,' he said. 'I just wanted you to know that I was thinking of you . . .'

'Yes,' Alice said. 'And I'm thinking of you. Do everything you can to keep safe and well, until you come home.'

Chapter Twenty-Six

August 1944

Everyone Emily met on Saturday afternoon in the market in Stockport was talking about the liberation of Paris, which had taken place the previous day. The effect the good news had on both stallholders and customers was apparent, and the general mood was one of relief and cheery optimism.

The whole country had listened to the radio on Friday 25th August, hearing the accounts of how, after many days of fighting, Germany had surrendered Paris to the Allied forces, ending four years of occupation.

Like everyone else, Emily was hugely relieved to hear that the war was at last coming to an end, and hopefully the British troops would soon be returning home. Her parents' reaction the night before had been bittersweet: relieved and pleased to hear the news, but once again reminded that their only son would not be amongst the returning servicemen. Emily dearly missed her brother and had grieved for him sorely for almost a year, but she had then picked herself up to get on with her work and the other areas of her life. What still broke her heart was witnessing the effect it had on her parents, especially her mother. Jack's loss would always remain; for the rest of their lives, they would have to live without him, and nothing Emily could do would change that.

She wandered around the 'Glass Umbrella' covered market hall looking for pink buttons for a cardigan her mother had knitted for her little niece, and for some hairgrips for herself. When she found the haberdashery stall, she sifted through the little drawers of buttons to find just the right ones, and then she spied a card with eight mother-of-pearl buttons which were perfect for a blouse she had lost two buttons on. She also found a plain, white satin waist underskirt she had been looking for, as she had scorched the one she wore to school most days by carelessly not checking how hot the iron was.

She stopped at the baker's stall and was lucky to find a display of Eccles cakes that had just been delivered. She bought six, as both her mother and father loved them, so it would be a treat for them with their usual cup of tea after the evening meal.

She thought about bringing some buns or biscuits up to Alice, but decided that it was like the old saying 'taking coals to Newcastle', bringing things to a shopkeeper. Alice was the one person who could get these things easier than most, although she was still fairly strict about breaking any ration rules.

Emily had rung her friend from a phone box on Princess Street to say she would walk up to Edgeley after she had been to the market, and would try to make it for around one o'clock for Alice's lunch break. Alice told her that would be great, and that she was actually taking the rest of the afternoon off and leaving Maeve in charge.

'Philip and Gabriela go back to school soon,' she told Emily, then she laughed. 'Not that you will want reminding that your summer holidays are over! I haven't had much time with them at the weekends, so I thought I would take them up to Bramhall Park this afternoon. We're not leaving until after lunch, so it's perfect for you calling up. Louis said he might drop out this afternoon, so he might come with us, and you're welcome to join us if you're free.'

'I would have loved to go to Bramhall Park,' Emily said, 'but I'm going to a concert in the town hall tonight. One of the older teachers in school had tickets and asked me to go with her as her husband is sick.'

'What kind of concert?'

'I'm not sure,' Emily said, 'probably big band or something like that.'

Emily spent another half an hour idly walking around the market, browsing at the various stalls. She glanced at a children's second-hand one as she went by, and then halted as she spied some games, thinking they would be a cheap and welcome gift for the twins up at the house. She picked up a snakes and ladders game and, after thinking about it for a few moments, put it back down again. They were bound to have the popular game. She looked at some of the others – Ludo and draughts – and came to the same conclusion. In fact, she thought, she was sure that Louis had mentioned in school that he was teaching Philip chess, so would probably find the other games a bit too easy. She browsed a bit more and then she lifted a jigsaw puzzle entitled *Children of The World*, the cover of which depicted a map of the world in the background, with children from various countries in their national dress. She decided it would suit Philip, and it was in very good condition and only sixpence. The stallholder, a heavy woman with a shawl around her head and shoulders, asked her if she could help, and Emily asked if she had another puzzle that might suit a girl. The woman disappeared under the covered stall and rooted around for a few minutes, then came back up – breathless from bending – holding one that pictured young girls at the beach, which Emily thought was perfect.

On her way out of the market she stopped at a grocery stall and bought a jar of local honey, which was something that she had not seen in Alice's shop, and knew that she liked.

She walked down into Underbank and bought a new lipstick in the chemist shop. She carried on to Mersey Square, and then she walked up to Edgeley and within minutes she was in Aberdeen Street. As she approached the shop, the door was open, and she could see Alice busily wiping down the countertops. Emily tiptoed in to surprise her friend. 'I'm glad to see you're still working and keeping the country going.'

Alice whirled around and then laughed when she saw who it was. 'I was watching for you and thought I would give the shop a tidy around while Maeve is on her dinner break.' She went over to the sink and ran her cloth under the hot tap then squeezed it out and left it back in its place. 'We'll go through into the kitchen, I've already boiled the kettle,' she said, 'and I've made us some sandwiches.'

'You look great,' Emily said as she followed her friend along the hallway.

'You told me that last time,' Alice laughed. 'I think you're hoping I'll leave you something in my will.'

'I *am* hoping you'll leave me something in your will,' Emily joked back, 'but I do think you look the best I've seen you in ages. Your hair is lovely and wavy, and your eyes and whole face are glowing.' She narrowed her eyes. 'You have to tell me your secret. Are you wearing new make-up? Is that what it is?'

Alice rolled her eyes. 'I might have got a new mascara since I last saw you, but I can't think of anything else.'

They went into the kitchen and Alice headed over to the cooker and lit the gas under the kettle to let it come to the boil again.

Emily studied her friend again. 'Well, you definitely look and even seem different – much lighter in yourself.' She put her bag down on the kitchen table, then took off her jacket. 'I know you enjoyed teaching, but I wonder if you're happier working in the shop.'

'I'm so busy these days,' Alice said, 'I hardly have time to think about things like that.' She shrugged. 'I like working in the shop, so maybe you're right.'

'Where are the twins?' Emily asked, looking around.

'They went to change their library books,' Alice said. 'They should be back any minute.'

'How are things going? I haven't seen Louis much since the school holidays.'

'Fine, there's been no major problems, just the odd squabble between them now and again.' She smiled and rolled her eyes. 'Gabriela's much noisier and livelier and at times she drives poor Philip mad when he's trying to read or if he's doing a crossword.'

'That's brothers and sisters for you.' Emily suddenly remembered and lifted her bag. She gave Alice the honey, which she was delighted with. 'And I've got something for the twins,' she said, lifting out the jigsaws.

Alice looked at them. 'Oh, they will love those,' she said. 'It was really kind of you to think of them.'

'You're the kind one, taking them in the way you did.' Emily shook her head. 'The difference in Louis after you said they could stay with you was unbelievable. It was as if a weight had been lifted off his shoulders. You were definitely the answer to all his prayers.'

'I don't know about that,' Alice said, 'but it just seemed the right thing to do after Philip had such a scare with his appendix. He needed somewhere quiet to come home to and give the operation time to heal, and then build himself back up again. The vicar and his wife were very kind, but they have enough on their plate with their own children and a new baby.'

'It's still a lot for you,' Emily said, 'with the shop to run.'

'They're lovely children,' Alice said, 'and it wasn't just Philip being ill. Poor Gabriela had got herself into a state and she was crying about her mother and wanting to go back home to Guernsey.'

Emily's face was suddenly serious. 'You see them running around and laughing with their friends and you think they're happy, but of course it must be there at the back of their minds all the time.'

The kettle began to whistle, and Alice went over to lift it off the cooker. 'Well, it just hit me that night, and I couldn't find the heart to send her back to the vicarage on her own, when she was so worried about Philip.'

'And I think they've become attached to Louis,' Emily said, 'and he can't have them staying where he lives as he only has one room. He's over the moon that you offered to have them, it just solved everything.'

Alice poured the water into the teapot and put the lid back on. 'I think it's the sort of thing that Betty would have done if she'd been here that day,' she said, 'and for all we know, it might just be for a few months. The way things are going with the war, it could all be over by Christmas and the children could be going back to Guernsey.'

'Let's hope so,' Emily said. 'It's hard to imagine things going back to normal, isn't it? Have you heard from Sophie this week?'

'Yes, and she asked me to check with you what nights you are free next week, so the three of us can go to the pictures.' Alice lifted the plate of sandwiches over to the table, and then put a side plate in front of Emily with a linen napkin, adding one opposite for herself.

'That would be great, so we can all have a good catch-up,' Emily said, thinking now. 'Any night suits me really, I don't have anything planned apart from the concert tonight. I'm glad to have places to go to get me out of the house. Things are much quieter during the school holidays with no Brownies or netball games.'

'I'll check what night's best for me,' Alice said, 'and if you ring me tomorrow, I'll know.'

'Who will you get to look after the twins?' Emily asked.

'Maeve will come down or if Louis is not on Home Guard duties, he might do it.'

Emily raised her eyebrows. 'Does Louis come to see them often?'

'Now and again,' Alice said vaguely. 'He's coming this afternoon. It's a pity you weren't free to come out with us to Bramhall later, I'm sure he would have been glad to see you.' She smiled. 'You could both have a good chat about getting ready to go back to school next week.' She poured the tea into the cups and brought them to the table in matching saucers.

'Don't remind me,' Emily said. 'I'm not looking forward to having to get up in the mornings again, although I love school when I get back into the routine.' She paused. 'You seem to get on well with him.'

Alice placed the sugar bowl and milk jug on the table. 'Who?'

'Louis, of course.'

'He's very nice and so good with the twins,' Alice said. 'He often comes when I'm working and takes them out, or if it's a bad day, he'll read or draw with them or play chess with Philip.'

'I suppose it helps fill his day, too,' Emily said, pouring milk into her cup. 'He must be thinking about getting back to Guernsey. We'll all miss him in the school, he's so good with the kids. I wonder how he'll find settling back after nearly five years in Stockport.' She shook her head. 'And I wonder how things will be with him and his fiancée after all this time. He never really mentions her.' She looked at Alice. 'Don't you think it would be strange to go back to someone after all that time? I think it would feel like starting again, almost like two strangers.'

'I suppose so,' Alice said briefly. She lifted the plate of sandwiches, cut neatly into triangles, and held them out to her friend.

Emily suddenly thought Alice looked serious and wondered if she might have put her foot in it, mentioning couples being apart for long periods. She took a ham triangle and an egg one. 'Any news from Greg?'

'Still in Naples,' Alice said, 'and seems to be doing OK. He's staying with the lawyer's family in the big house, and he says the local people are mainly nice and friendly even though they are living in terrible circumstances.' She shrugged. 'It's very sad, I think the whole of Naples was bombed.'

'I often think it must be hard for all the soldiers, getting used to being in such different countries, and not speaking the language.'

'Greg's been in much worse places earlier in the war,' Alice said. 'At least Italy is a civilised country and a place we hear a lot about. It's not as foreign or different as some other places. From what he's said, he's got used to the Italian food, and enjoys the wine as well. Although he did say that meat and fish are very limited in the restaurants, and you don't always know what you're eating.'

'The thought of it ...' Emily said, pulling a face. 'Well, at least he'll be home soon and be able to recognise everything he's eating.' She paused. 'It's good you and Greg sorted things out. When he comes back home, you'll feel you have a new start all over again.'

'It will be the same for everyone,' Alice said. 'Look at poor Sophie, she's hardly had any time with Tony since they got married. He's been stuck in London most of the time because there's been so much damage done to the phone lines.'

'I felt sorry for her last time we were all together, when she said she had been hoping there might have been a honeymoon baby.'

Alice thought of her own situation but decided to say nothing. 'She has plenty of time when Tony comes home.' She took a drink of tea. 'You didn't have second thoughts about the lad you went to the pictures with last week?'

'The doctor from Stepping Hill?' Emily gave a little shudder then laughed. 'Definitely not. He was the most boring fellow I've ever been out with and the worst kisser I've come across.' She held her hands up. 'Not that I've kissed that many, but I know enough to know when it's not right.'

'I had high hopes for you,' Alice said, 'especially when you said he was a doctor. I was imagining you getting married to him and living in a big house in Bramhall with a surgery attached to the side of it. I could just see you answering the door to all the patients, dressed up in a nice suit and looking all prim and elegant.'

Emily laughed aloud. 'You have a very vivid imagination! I know everybody thinks I must be getting desperate, but I am not going to get landed with someone who is dead boring and a terrible kisser, just because he's a doctor.'

Chapter Twenty-Seven

Emily got off the bus and walked back towards the town hall. She could see people queuing to get into the door at the side, which led into the main hall, where she presumed the concert would be held.

She had made an effort for going out, so was wearing her good blue suit with the flared skirt and matching jacket with the nipped in waist and three-quarter length sleeves. The jacket had a lovely, shaped collar and there were lots of little pearl buttons down the front. She thought it would be too much with her usual pearls and chose a gold filigree brooch to wear on the collar instead. She pinned a blue beret on her long dark hair, and then powdered her face and put on a touch of brown eyeshadow to complement her dark eyes, and mascara. She then applied the new lipstick she had bought and was pleased that it was a light berry shade rather than bright red, which she found too conspicuous.

Her teaching colleague, Celia, spied Emily coming off the bus and came down from the hall, waving her hand in the air, to meet her. Celia was almost Emily's mother's age, and the tiny, slim, auburn-haired Celia was interested in music, art and designing and making her own clothes. Tonight, she was dressed in a red floral frock with a matching swing coat, and a red, feathered half-hat.

'The queue has just started moving in,' Celia said, 'so we should get a good seat up near the front.'

When they reached the door, Alice saw a stand outside,

showing they were attending an evening of classical music, but hid her disappointment that it wasn't a big band concert.

Inside, settled in their seats in the fourth row, Celia turned to Emily. 'I'm so grateful to you for coming, as I bought the tickets ages ago and at the last minute Edward discovered he had something else on.'

'That's a pity,' Emily said.

'It's not a pity,' Celia said, 'it's an excuse. It clashed with a golf meeting tonight and he's gone off to that instead.'

Emily looked at her colleague in surprise. 'I thought you both liked going to concerts and plays, and the ballet in Manchester.'

'I don't mind him ducking out occasionally, but at times it annoys me. Anyway, tonight I am delighted to have some young, female company for a change.'

'I don't know much about classical music, but I am looking forward to it.'

'You will love it, and I have a little treat for us for later.' Celia opened her large patent bag to reveal a quarter-pound box of Milk Tray chocolates.

The hall gradually filled up and then the lights in the main hall dimmed and the orchestra moved to take their places. The male musicians appeared on stage in black suits, the jackets with long tails, and the women in long dresses. Emily had never been to a full concert of classical music before and she was delighted when she recognised the first piece, 'Morning', which was on a record she used in class for music and movement. She smiled to herself as she pictured her little pupils attempting to make their arms move like feathery branches of a tree in the wind.

The pieces of music that followed Emily found to be pleasant and relaxing, and she was listening intently when she felt a gentle nudge at her elbow, as Celia held out the Milk Tray. As each piece went on, she concentrated on the introduction by the conductor and tried to memorise the names of them. She loved the light and airy 'Pachelbel Canon' and the more sombre but beautiful Symphony no 5 Adagietto by Mahler.

When the lights came up for the break, Emily turned to Celia and said, 'I'm so glad you asked me; I had no idea I would enjoy this sort of music so much. I'm used to livelier dance music, but I was surprised I actually recognised some of the tunes.'

'It's simply beautiful, isn't it?' Celia said. 'It takes you off into a different world.' She raised her eyebrows and gave a little conspiratorial laugh. 'How Edward can prefer golf to this is totally beyond me. Now, we are going to go into the bar, and we'll have another little treat.'

Emily held her hand up. '*My* treat this time,' she said. 'You got the tickets and brought chocolates, so it's the least I can do.'

'In that case,' Celia said, 'I won't argue then. I'll have a brandy and ginger.'

They went over towards the bar area and Celia went through the crowds looking for a table, or at least somewhere to perch their drinks while they stood. The bar was busy, so Emily walked around to the side, where she hoped she might be seen more easily. Two elderly men were standing there talking, and when they realised she was there, they stopped and moved to let her in closer. After a couple of minutes, during which she felt none of the people serving seemed to notice her, the taller of the men caught the eye of one of the barmen and beckoned him over to serve her.

Emily thanked the men and then ordered Celia's drink and a sweet sherry for herself.

Somehow, Celia had managed to find two seats at the end of a table for them, and they sat chatting about the new term which was speedily approaching, and then moved on to more general talk about the war and the wonderful progress the Allies were making abroad.

The bell sounded and the groups began to disperse and move back to the main body of the hall. The second part of the evening started off with a lengthy introduction to Vivaldi's 'Four Seasons', which Emily knew nothing about, so she listened with great interest as the conductor explained how the composer had attempted to capture scenes of life from the different parts of the year and translate them into music. She was taken aback when he said that all four pieces would take just over forty minutes to be played. As before, when she concentrated on the music and tried to imagine the scenes for each of the seasons, she became engrossed in it and was almost surprised when the audience started clapping enthusiastically and she realised it had come to an end.

The conductor bowed to the audience and then gestured to the orchestra, who all stood up and bowed to more applause. They went back to their places and then the conductor came back to the microphone to explain that the orchestra had the privilege of having two guests with them who would close the evening. The first, he said, was a young soprano from Scotland who was going to perform 'O Mio Babbino Caro'.

Celia nudged Emily. 'This is beautiful,' she said, 'one of my all-time favourites.'

When the piece was finished, Emily stood and clapped loudly with everyone else and then she leaned close to her friend and said, 'I think this will be one of my favourites from now on, too.'

The conductor then came to the microphone again and said the second performance would be given by a pianist who had also been part of the orchestra in the first part of the evening, as he had stepped in at the last minute to cover for one of the violinists who had been delayed.

'To play one instrument proficiently is a great achievement,' the conductor said, 'but to play a second one to an equally high standard is rare.' He then motioned to the side of the stage, and everyone watched as the musician in question came to the forefront.

The audience watched as the conductor and pianist spoke for a few moments, and then as the young man turned to fully face the audience, Emily was surprised that he seemed familiar to her. She stared intently at him, trying to work out how she might know someone in an orchestra. It didn't seem possible to her, as she did not attend many concerts where orchestras were playing, and if she had, she was sure she would have remembered meeting someone of such eminence. She listened now, waiting for the conductor to say his name.

Just as the conductor went to introduce the pianist, Celia leaned in close to her.

'What a handsome young man,' she said. 'If he can play as well as he looks, we're in for a treat.'

'Yes,' Emily said, nodding to cover up her frustration that she had missed his name.

The musician bowed low and then walked across the stage to the grand piano. She watched as he went to sit at the piano stool, sweeping the tails of his jacket behind him. Where, she wondered, would she have come across someone like this? Her eyes narrowed to try to see him better, while her mind worked out how she could possibly know someone who was a classical pianist.

He sat up straight and started to play.

'"Für Elise"...' Celia whispered.

Emily remembered her programme, which gave the list of performers, and bent to retrieve it from her handbag. She squinted her eyes to read the small print in the dimness of the hall, scanning down until she came to the bottom of the list. She looked at the name Marco Benetti, which baffled her further. And then, at the back of her mind, something fell into place. She looked up at the stage and realised, with some shock, that this was the young man who had given her the rosary beads. The Italian man from the prisoner of war camp. She looked at the dark hair and his handsome side profile as he stared ahead in deep concentration at his piano score. She thought about how he looked that day in ordinary work clothes, and compared him now to the man wearing the formal tuxedo. There was no doubt in her mind that the friendly young man she had met that day in the shop was indeed this gifted pianist. She would never have imagined that someone from the prisoners' camp could look so imposing, and be the sort of person who could command total attention in a room filled with hundreds of people.

Her hand came up to her mouth. 'I don't believe it...' she murmured amazedly to herself.

Celia turned to look at her. 'What's wrong?' she asked.

'I know him... the musician,' she whispered. 'I met him in a shop in Heaton Chapel and I knocked a box over that he was carrying. He was really nice...'

Celia's eyes widened. 'Lucky you,' she said. 'If I were twenty years younger, I wouldn't mind knocking him over myself!'

'It was his box I knocked over,' Emily said, shaking her head in bemusement.

They started to laugh and somebody behind made a shushing noise. Both women looked at each other with mock guilty faces, and then moved their gaze to the stage again, and stayed completely silent as Marco Benetti continued with his piece.

As she watched him play, Emily was aware of a sense of discomfort – something akin to guilt. A feeling that told her when she had met him first, she had immediately judged him on his status as a prisoner of war and given no thought to his life before that. Her mind went back to the afternoon they met, how kind he had been when she almost broke the things he had spent hours carving. She remembered how awkward she had been when she realised he was from the prison camp. She could picture him now, embarrassed as he explained his circumstances, and struggling to find the words to explain that he, too, was a professional – a teacher and well educated. A real person with his own personality and talents, and not just one of hundreds of prisoners.

Although her own instinct had told her that he was as decent as he appeared, she had dismissed it and had shown her discomfort when he suggested they might meet up again and form some sort of friendship.

She wondered now if she had first met Marco Benetti tonight – as this person of prestige who was up on the stage – whether she would have viewed him differently. When he finished, there was loud applause, which he automatically stood up to acknowledge with a bow. Emily watched him smiling at the audience, registering the slight awkwardness – the same awkwardness she had seen that day in the shop, when he was aware of his poor English. Given the enthusiastic reaction to his performance, she could tell it was also innate modesty. He sat back down and composed himself again, before starting his second piece, which the conductor said was an adaption where Marco Benetti would play the piano in an accompaniment with the cello.

'"Swan",' Celia whispered, 'from "Carnival of the Animals". It's just beautiful...'

This was a piece that Emily didn't recognise. She listened intently, then sat back in her chair and closed her eyes, and let herself be carried off by the delicate, slow melody. It was so beautiful, she thought, it was almost painful.

As she listened to the final strains of 'Swan', tears came to her eyes, and she knew that she would always remember listening to it for the first time, on this particular night, in Stockport Town Hall.

When it finished, she watched Marco and the celloist bow to loud applause before leaving the stage. The orchestra went on to play a selection of livelier tunes, after which the concert drew to a close. As they filed out of their seats, Emily's eyes kept flitting back towards the stage, and she realised she was hoping that Marco might suddenly appear from behind the curtains. What she might say to him if he did appear, she didn't know.

As they walked up the aisle, she suggested to Celia that they might have a last drink.

'That would be lovely,' Celia immediately agreed.

A waiter met them at the door and took their order of two sherries, and then the two women went inside and found a table in the corner. The waiter was back in minutes, and Emily insisted on paying for the drinks again to balance the cost of the tickets.

When they were settled with their drinks, Celia tapped her hands on the table. 'Now, tell me all about that wonderful pianist. Who is he, and where did he come from?'

Emily started to quietly explain about Marco being an Italian prisoner of war and meeting him in Barlow's shop, when a figure in black came striding towards their table. They both looked up to see Father Dempsey beaming at them.

The priest looked at Emily. 'Did you recognise the amazing pianist at the end? It's Marco, the chap you met in the shop.'

Emily told him she did, and Celia said how wonderful he was.

'Lovely young chap, I'm so delighted that the orchestra leader decided to give him a chance.' He shrugged. 'When the orchestra heard through the grapevine that one of the Italians from the camp was a talented musician, and it was suggested he join them, a few objected. When he came to rehearsals and they heard him play the piano and the violin, all doubts vanished.'

'I'm not surprised,' Celia said. 'He is amazingly talented to be able to play both instruments so proficiently.'

Father Dempsey brought a spare stool over and set it down between the two teachers. He then went on to tell them that Marco was trained in conducting as well. 'It was only a month ago he was introduced to the orchestra, and they changed their programme around to include his performance.'

'Talent overcomes everything, Father,' Celia said. 'And I only hope that if any of our boys are out in those dreadful camps abroad, that they are treated well and allowed the pleasure of making or listening to music. It can only improve the direst of circumstances.'

The priest nodded. 'The Italian lads have had a choir going in the camp since shortly after they arrived, and they sing at the masses we hold there.'

'I didn't realise you were so involved with them,' Celia said.

He shrugged. 'When they first arrived, feelings were still so high about Mussolini that we had to keep any church involvement quiet. We weren't quite sure ourselves how it would work out, but on the whole, things have been very positive, apart from the odd run-ins with some of the local men since they've been allowed to mix more freely in the town. The more people get to know the prisoners, the less they realise they have to fear.' He gave a small sigh. 'One of our elderly parishioners had two

Italians helping in his garden and invited them for a Sunday meal. Apparently, the poor men broke down in tears, saying it reminded them of having meals with their parents back in Italy, who they haven't seen for years.'

Celia looked at Emily. 'We must do more in school about them,' Celia said. 'Educate the children about how ordinary people get caught up in wars, and how each is an individual.'

'I agree,' Emily said, her face serious now, 'but it's hard to change people. My own parents are very down on the idea of them being here at all, and when they hear of them being allowed to mix, it makes them upset and angry.'

'I know it's hard because of their own loss in the war,' the priest said, 'but if they could meet them properly, they might feel different.' He paused. 'In fact, I am planning to ask the camp boys to come and sing in the church at eleven o'clock mass one Sunday instead of our usual choir. They've learned the words of all our well-known hymns, and they've sung a few in Italian as well. They're all very good singers.'

Emily hesitated for a few moments, then said, 'I'll make sure I'm at that particular mass when they are singing.'

Father Dempsey stood up. 'Try to get your mother to come along with you,' he urged. 'I have a feeling it would help her.' Then, just as he turned around, he saw someone coming towards him, and a smile broke out on his face. 'Marco!' he said. 'The very man! I was hoping to catch you. I've just been talking about you.'

'I saw you from the stage,' Marco said, gesturing with his hands, 'and afterwards ... I come down after the concert, looking for you ...'

'I was with these lovely ladies,' he said, indicating towards the table, 'teachers from the school. Celia and Emily.'

Marco held his hand out to Celia, who told him how wonderful his performance was.

He thanked her and when he turned towards Emily, a look of amazement came over his face. 'Emily ...' For a moment he seemed almost struck dumb, then he took a deep breath. 'How are you? After the shop... I didn't see you again.'

Emily felt herself flushing, aware that both Celia and Father Dempsey were watching them. 'No,' she said. 'Your performance was wonderful. I didn't recognise you at first...'

He touched the lapels of his tuxedo jacket. 'Very different from my work clothes.'

'I didn't realise you were a musician, so it was a surprise seeing you on stage.'

He then smiled at her, in the same warm and friendly way he had before, and Emily felt a small pang inside – embarrassment mixed with guilt – that she had deliberately avoided him.

'When we met, my English was very, very bad,' Marco said, then he joined his hands together as though praying. 'But I have been studying, so I am a little better, I think.'

'I can tell a difference,' Emily said, 'you have really improved.' He smiled again, and she felt that same awe at how handsome he was. His features were perfectly balanced, his eyes a darker brown than her own, and with a depth that showed intelligence and sincerity. His skin was tanned and smooth and, as she looked at him, she thought the most perfect thing about Marco Benetti were his lips. She had noticed that the first time she saw him.

Father Dempsey put his hand on Marco's shoulder. 'Your English has certainly improved, although I am not too sure about your football playing. Your lot didn't do so well against the team from the railway club in the last game.'

A grin broke out on Marco's face now. 'You joke me now, Father!' he said. 'We are much better. The referee was blind. My God – he could not see at all!'

Everyone laughed now, then Celia asked Marco where he had studied and how he had come to play the different instruments. He explained that his father was also a musician, and that his grandfather had actually made violins and had a shop in Rome, where their family were originally from. Celia was fascinated as she and Edward had visited Rome before the war, she told him, and had stayed near the Vatican.

He then talked about the family house in Rome, which his oldest cousin now owned, as Marco's family had moved to his mother's area in Florence. His face suddenly became very serious. 'My cousin was living in the house before the war began, but now...' He shook his head. 'We have not heard anything... the house and the family may all be gone.'

'That must be very hard for you,' Celia said, 'the same as it is for families in Britain. But the war may all be over soon, and hopefully things will get back to normal.' She paused. 'When you do get home to Italy, I hope all your family are well.'

'Our own home near Lucca was destroyed, but thank God my mother is safe and living with my oldest sister in another town. I hope to see them when this war is done.'

'I have Italian friends who lived in Manchester,' Celia said, 'and who were deported several years ago to the Isle of Man. I hope they can come home to England after the war.'

'It is hard for everyone,' Marco said, 'but thank you for your kind words. I am very grateful.'

'We all need to understand each other better,' Father Dempsey said. 'In God's eyes, we are all the same – including the Germans.' A little glint came to his eyes. 'Although I'm sure even God will have to make an exception with Hitler.' There was some muted laughter at his comment, then he put his hand up and said, 'Apologies, sometimes I forget I'm not in the pulpit.'

'We do need reminding about things at times,' Celia said, 'and you can speak about subjects – in God's name – the rest of us can't.'

Marco stood up now. 'Sorry, I must go,' he said. 'I have to make arrangements for another concert in Manchester for next week. There is also a taxi coming soon to take me back to the camp.' He shrugged and looked slightly awkward. 'The concert people kindly arrange the taxi for me.'

'I'll be up at your place later in the week,' Father Dempsey said, 'and we'll discuss arrangements for your choir to come to the church very soon.'

As Marco said goodnight to everyone, his eyes lingered for a few moments on Emily, and she thought he was going to say something. Instead, he just smiled and turned away. As she watched him go, she felt a small pang, as though she had lost something.

Father Dempsey suddenly got to his feet. 'And I must leave you, too,' he said, lifting his hat. 'I'm going to be bold and ask Marco if I can travel in the taxi with him since it's going down past the church. I couldn't take the church car out for a social event with the petrol shortage, and I was planning to walk back.' He looked at Emily. 'What about you? You're going in that direction as well.'

She paused for a moment, thinking that it would be nice to talk to Marco again, but she knew it might only make the situation more awkward than it already was. 'I was going to wait a while longer,' she said. 'I'll catch the bus back home.'

'If you're sure,' he said, moving off. 'I should go, otherwise I might miss him.'

Celia looked over at Emily. 'I only have a short walk home from here,' she said. 'You might have been wise to take the chance of the taxi home.'

'I wasn't sure . . .'

'Apart from saving you waiting on a bus, it would give you a chance to chat a little with our Italian musician.' Celia arched her eyebrows. 'Aren't you curious to know more about him? He's very handsome, too.'

Emily looked at her. 'He's a prisoner of war,' she said quietly. 'And I don't think it would be a good idea to become more familiar with him.' She shrugged. 'What would people think? I know what my own mother and father feel about the Italians in the camp.'

'Surely there's a difference, when you can see the sort of person he *really* is. You only have to see Marco on stage and hear him play to realise his background and his education.'

'That would all be fine if he was English...'

'He likes you,' Celia said. 'I can tell by the way he looks at you. More than likes you.' She paused. 'And how do you feel towards him?'

Emily's face flushed. 'I hardly know him,' she said. 'And this is only the second time we've met.' She shrugged. 'He's a prisoner of war and... he's very nice... but my parents...' She fumbled for the words, but they did not come and instead her eyes filled with tears.

'Oh, Emily,' Celia said. 'I'm so sorry, I didn't mean to upset you.'

'No, no, it's not you.' She reached down for her handbag and scrabbled around inside for a hanky. 'It's me, I'm being stupid.'

'What is it?'

'I suppose things are hard at home. My mother is just not the same, and the atmosphere is very depressing, and at times it gets to me.' She rubbed her hanky to her nose. 'About the musician – Marco – when I met him for the first time, we got on really well. I was shocked when he told me he was from the camp, but there was still something I liked about him. He makes things carved from wood, and he gave me a beautiful set of rosary beads he had made.'

'He really is a talented and very industrious young man.'

'When we were saying goodbye, he told me the days he came to the shop and he said that he hoped to see me again.'

Celia raised her eyebrows. 'And did you?'

'No, I was afraid it might encourage him when I knew that nothing could come of it. I've heard both my mother and father talking about the prison camp, saying that the Italians were almost as bad as the Germans.' She bit her lip. 'If I told them I was friendly with one of the prisoners, I think they would probably disown me, and God knows what would happen if I wasn't there...'

'I'm so sorry to hear that, Emily, and I feel sympathy for your mother and father.'

'So, you can see there's no point in me getting to know him better.'

'I hope your poor mother gets some help,' Celia said. 'She is so lucky to have such a very caring and supportive daughter, but you have to live your own life at some point. Marco is an exceptional young man and I think he likes you very much.' There was a silence. 'And I think you like him, too.'

'I do,' Emily said. 'I liked him the first time I saw him, and after seeing him tonight I like him even more – more than anybody I've ever met – but I know even thinking about it is pointless.' She smiled. 'I've never spoken to anyone else about him – not even my two best friends. I was afraid people would be shocked and think I was so desperate to find a boyfriend that I would even consider one of those Italians.'

Celia's eyes widened. 'No one would think that, Emily, and I'm sure you are not the only young woman who would consider such a good-looking, talented musician.' Her eyes narrowed. 'Did you notice the attractive young lady in the orchestra – one of the violinists – who was standing next to the piano?'

Emily thought back then shrugged. 'I can't really remember.'

'Well, she never took her eyes off him as he played, and she wasn't the only one. As we were leaving, I saw two other girls rushing out of their seats to go up to the stage to speak to him.'

'I'm not surprised,' Emily said. 'He is talented . . .'

'And very handsome,' Celia finished for her. 'Of course, I'm quite sure there are a lot of handsome young men who would be delighted to have you on their arm. And, if it wasn't such a horrendous time, with all our young men out abroad, there would be even more.'

'Surprisingly, I have had quite a few dates with the ones in reserved occupations.' She rolled her eyes. 'I was at the cinema with a doctor from the hospital last week – he was nice enough and very keen, but I knew immediately it wouldn't work. I just never meet anyone who seems right for me.'

'What if someone like our musician friend is right for you? What if you let that chance go and you never meet anyone like him again? What if every man you meet afterwards is the wrong person for you?'

Emily looked at her. 'But I hardly know him...'

'Maybe it would be worth getting to know him properly.' She paused. 'At least give yourself a chance. Edward's parents weren't keen on me when we started going out. Apart from me being a Catholic, his mother had set her heart on him marrying the daughter of a family friend.'

'What happened to change things?'

Celia arched her eyebrows and smiled. 'Nature intercepted, and I became pregnant.'

Emily caught her breath, taken aback. 'Oh...'

Celia continued, 'Our situation suddenly gave Edward the impetus to stand up to his family. We went off and quietly got married and there was absolutely nothing they could do about it.'

'How did they react?'

'With great reluctance in the beginning. They hardly ever visited us, and his mother showed no interest in the children when they were little. Thankfully, my own parents were more understanding and they helped us out enormously.'

Emily thought for a few moments. 'Didn't Edward's mother come to live with you?'

'Yes, after his father died. She took ill shortly afterwards and ironically, during those two years before she died, we got on better than we ever did. She loved being with the children; she realised then how much she had missed out on, and she apologised for the way she was in the beginning. I actually felt sad for her because nothing could bring back all those lost years.'

'Weren't you resentful?'

'After we got married, it didn't really matter to me anymore.' She smiled. 'Even though we drive each other mad at times, I love him dearly. I'm glad we didn't give in to his mother at the beginning, and I'm glad nature sorted it out for us.'

'I would never have guessed you'd gone through all that.'

Celia put her hand over Emily's now. 'As you get older, you

will realise that *everyone* goes through difficult times. The old saying *"To be human is to err"* is correct, and it's easy to judge if you have not been in that position. I was guilty of condemning others for getting pregnant before marriage until I met Edward and discovered how strong physical attraction can be.' She leaned in closer to Emily. 'A little word of advice, something many women don't talk about. If you feel that special spark, it can make a world of difference to a marriage.' She gave a wry smile. 'It helps you put up with all the other things, such as when your husband doesn't want to come to a concert with you.'

Emily laughed, then her face grew serious again. 'I'm grateful for the advice. I've never had anyone speak so honestly to me before, and ... well ... you've given me a lot to think about.'

Celia craned her neck to look over Emily's shoulder. 'Well, don't take too long, dear,' she whispered, 'because it looks like you might have to make a decision fairly soon.'

Emily looked at her quizzically, just as a shadow came over the table. She turned to see Marco Benetti looking at her.

'Excuse me, Emily,' he said, with a hesitant look on his face, 'but Father Dempsey said you might want to come in taxi ...'

She looked back at him then over at her friend. Celia's head was bent so she could not see her face, and Emily knew that she didn't want to influence her in any way. Father Dempsey, she thought, was oblivious to anything between her and Marco; he would have suggested giving a lift to anyone going in that direction. His suggestion about the taxi was purely practical. The decision had to be hers and hers alone.

She looked back at Marco and registered the impassive look on his face. It struck her that he might have regretted seeming too friendly the first time they had met, and he was now being more careful. Or perhaps, since being involved with the orchestra – and getting out into the local community more – he had discovered there were other girls who were more appreciative than she had been.

'If you don't mind,' she said, 'the taxi would be quicker than the bus.'

His eyes lit up. 'I will go check if it is out in street.' He smiled. 'I will come back to tell you.'

When he left, Celia held her sherry glass up to Emily. 'Now, that's a good start!'

Emily lifted her glass and took a gulp. 'I'll just see how things go …'

Five minutes later, Marco came back into the bar. 'Father Dempsey is waiting in the taxi,' he explained. 'He does not like travelling in dark.'

They quickly finished their drinks and then the three of them went out into the main hall towards the door. As they walked along, Emily thought that Marco was a little taller than she remembered and wondered if his formal outfit made his height more obvious.

Marco checked whether Celia would also like a lift home, but she thanked him and said she only lived a short walk away. She shared a few words of farewell with Father Dempsey, and then she said goodnight to Emily and Marco.

Emily climbed into the taxi and sat alongside the priest.

'I'm glad you changed your mind, Emily,' Father Dempsey said. 'You can't be too careful with this blackout still going on and all the road accidents. I've even heard about someone being robbed at a bus stop.'

Marco got into the taxi, smoothing down the tails of the jacket before sitting down. Emily glanced at him and noticed once again how good-looking he was. He caught her eye and smiled warmly at her, and she smiled back.

As the taxi driver swung the cab around, the priest asked her about the classes for the coming year in school, and which particular teachers would be taking each class. As she spoke, Marco listened intently as though it was of great interest to him.

When there was a lull in the conversation, Emily asked Marco if he would be playing with the same orchestra again, and he said he was playing in Manchester the following week. She asked who his own favourite musicians were and he talked about Mozart and Chopin, whom she knew, and other names like Debussy and Massenet that she had never heard of.

He explained that he taught music in a college and played in the orchestras on certain weekends. 'I am only new teacher, just one year then the war came, and I had to leave.' He shrugged. 'I hope I will go back to college again as I love music and also teaching.' He smiled. 'But I like other things like woodwork and playing sports.' He grinned at Father Dempsey. 'Football especially.'

'I'd say you need plenty of time to practise that,' the priest said, winking at Emily.

The light and easy conversation continued until they reached the junction to turn down Emily's road.

'I asked the driver to drop you off first,' Father Dempsey told her, 'so we can see you in safely.'

Emily directed the driver as to which house, and then she turned to lift her handbag. When they stopped, Marco acted quickly to get out first, and held the door open for her to climb out more easily. As she stepped down, he moved forward to take her arm and Emily felt her heart quicken as his hand touched her skin. She looked up at him to thank him, and again their eyes met.

'Thank you for the lift,' she said, her voice breathless and different from normal. 'And I really enjoyed your music. You are very, very good.'

'No, thank *you*, Emily.' His voice was low and serious. 'It was an honour you came in taxi. Also, to see you at the concert. It made me very happy.' He paused. 'If you would like to come to another concert, maybe Manchester, I can get a ticket for you – like Father Dempsey – and perhaps for your friend.'

She thought quickly. She did not want to snub him as she had done before. 'Yes,' she said, 'that would be lovely. I would really like to come and hear you play again.' She didn't need to tell her parents about Marco or where she got the ticket from. She just had to mention that Celia and the priest were going.

'The concert is next Saturday,' he said. 'I can meet you at shop next Thursday to give you tickets.'

Anyone, she thought, might see them together in the street or inside the shop. 'I'm not sure, I might be doing sports after school...'

'I could give them to Mr Barlow?'

Emily thought of the ramifications of the shopkeeper knowing. He might mention it to her father when he called in for his papers or tobacco, and explain about Marco dropping them in. Mr Barlow was very open about being friendly with Marco, and he might casually mention her to someone who knew her parents. She did not want her friendship with him becoming gossip. 'Maybe if you give them to Father Dempsey,' she suggested. 'I can call down to the church.'

He quickly put his head inside the taxi and explained to the priest, then came back smiling. 'Yes,' he said, 'that would be very good.'

'I'll look forward to it,' Emily said. She glanced towards the house, thinking she heard a noise. Her throat tightened at the thought of her father suddenly appearing and seeing her with Marco. 'I have to go now,' she said. As she moved towards the gate, the side door opened, and clouds of thick black smoke came billowing out. Her father stepped out to lean on the side of the house, coughing and spluttering.

Emily's heart dropped. 'Dad!' she shouted, then she opened the gate, and rushed up the path towards the door. 'What's wrong? What's happened?'

When she reached him, he was still trying to catch his breath. 'The chip pan...' he choked out. 'I fell asleep... it caught fire. I've thrown it in the sink... it's still burning... there's smoke everywhere!' He went into a paroxysm of coughing again.

'Where's Mum?' Her voice was verging on hysterical now.

'Upstairs in bed,' he wheezed. 'Get her out the front door...' He started coughing again, and he had to turn and lean on the wall at the side of the house, his head on his trembling hands.

As Emily turned to go around to the front of the house,

fumbling for her keys, she met Marco and Father Dempsey running towards her. 'There's a fire!' she told them, terrified tears streaming down her face. 'In the kitchen at the back of the house... I don't know how bad, but my mother is upstairs in bed. I'll go in the front door for her, it's safer.'

'You go quickly to your mother!' Marco said, taking his tailed jacket off as he ran. 'We will check the father and fire.'

'Holy Mother of God!' Father Dempsey said, rushing towards her father. 'How are you, Tom?'

Emily's hands were shaking so badly, she struggled to get the Yale key in the lock. Eventually it clicked and she threw the door open, to find the downstairs hallway engulfed in a thick grey smoke. She put her hand over her mouth and rushed upstairs, screaming as she went, 'Mum! Mum! Get up! Quickly!' By the time she reached the room, her mother was sitting up in bed with a dazed look on her face.

'What's wrong?' she asked vaguely. 'What's all the shouting about?'

'There's been an accident downstairs, and something caught fire... we need to get out of the house in case it spreads.'

'Where?' her mother asked. 'What's happening?'

Emily realised her mother had taken her tablets to help her sleep, so she must have been in a deep slumber and wasn't wholly awake. 'Put on your slippers!' Emily urged, turning to grab her mother's dressing gown from the back of the door. There was a strong, cloying smell from whatever was burning in the kitchen, but she was grateful that so far only thin trails of smoke had reached upstairs into the room.

Somehow, she got her mother down the stairs, grateful to note that the smoke was no worse than when she had gone to rescue her mother. They went straight out the front door and then around the side where she could see her father still leaning on the wall.

'Tom,' her mother said, in a thin, trembling voice. 'In the name of God, what's happened? Are you OK?'

He looked at her and shook his head. 'Stupid... stupid!' he

said. 'I thought I was doing a good turn. When I came in from the pub, I thought I would make a few chips to have ready when Emily came in because I know she likes them.' He gave a hacking cough to clear his throat. 'I put a pan on with a good bit of lard, and I was listening to the radio, and I must have dozed off...' He coughed again and shook his head. 'The next thing I knew the place was full of smoke and when I went into the kitchen the pan was in flames.' He closed his eyes, looking tortured. 'I threw it into the sink and put a towel over it. The fire had just caught on the curtains, too, but I managed to pull them down into the sink as well...'

'Is the fire out?' Emily asked. 'The smoke doesn't seem as bad.'

'I don't know... the priest and the other fellow went straight in.' He shrugged, a helpless look on his face. 'They told me to stay out here.' He started coughing again, though not quite so bad.

'You look after Mum,' Emily said, 'and I'll check what's happening.' She went quickly towards the side door and as she did so she could hear both men coughing inside. Tentatively she stepped over the threshold, and was relieved to see that the smoke was clearing, although the burning smell was still strong. 'Are you all right?' she called.

'It's out now,' the priest said, coming towards her with a hanky at his mouth. 'It's all OK.' His face was red and shiny with sweat and there were streaks of black on it. 'Marco damped a towel and managed to calm it down, and then we got the window open. If you give it a while to let the smoke all clear, it should be fine. There might be a bit of damage to the walls but nothing terrible. Nothing compared to what could have happened...'

'I don't know how to thank you,' Emily said. She pointed back outside. 'I was able to get my mother downstairs and she's fine, the smoke wasn't bad upstairs.'

'I'll go and have a word with them and let the taxi driver know what's happened. You might want to give Marco a hand to clean himself up, he was more in the thick of it than me.'

Emily went with him to the door and called to her parents,

'It's OK now, I'm just making sure it's safe to go back in.' Her father lifted his arm in acknowledgement. 'Give it a few more minutes,' she said. She went into the kitchen, relieved it was much clearer, and saw Marco over at the sink. 'Are you OK?' she asked.

'Yes,' he said. 'Just checking all OK.'

When he turned to look at her, her hands flew to her mouth. 'Oh my God! You've been burnt!' His face was blackened, and her eyes were drawn to several small but angry, raw marks which would undoubtedly blister.

'I'm OK,' he said, smiling at her. 'It's not bad, it will soon get better.'

Her gaze moved to his white shirt and black bow tie – which had been pristine earlier – all streaked now with a fine black soot and splashes of grease. There was also a layer of dust on his thick, dark hair. 'Oh, Marco, your lovely clothes! I am so sorry...' She suddenly felt weak and shaky. 'Let me get some cloths and towels to help clean you up.'

'No, no,' he said, shaking his head. 'You look after mother and father. My clothes OK – I clean up at camp.' He shrugged. 'When we work on farm or fields, we get very dirty.' He gave her a reassuring smile. 'It is no problem.'

Emily rushed over to the cupboard that held the clean dish-cloths and towels and lifted several out. She handed Marco the largest towel and then she went to the tap to run water on a smaller one to wipe his face. The pan that her father had used was in the sink now, filled with brown greasy water. She looked dismally at the window above and the area surrounding – all splattered with splashes of blackish, burned lard. The tattered and burned curtains, which her father had torn down, now trailed in a sad, bedraggled mess from the worktop to the floor.

When she turned back, Marco was putting on his jacket. She went over to give him the damp cloth to wipe his face. He took it from her and started to rub at his forehead, but he suddenly winced and closed his eyes when he touched one of the raw

257

spots where the lard had hit him. Emily indicated to the kitchen table. 'Sit down,' she said, 'and I'll clean it for you.'

Obediently he sat down at the table, and as she started to carefully wipe away the worst of the soot marks, he gave a shuddering sigh of relief. 'All OK now,' he said, nodding and looking around the kitchen. 'After cleaning, maybe some paint.'

'Don't worry about that,' she gasped, amazed he could even think of it after what he had done. 'My mother will make sure my father sorts it all out.' She forced a smile. 'She said last week that it would need painting soon, so he will have to do it quicker than he planned.' She touched the cloth around his hairline, and as she did so, he looked up at her – his face cleaner now but revealing more of the small burns than she had realised. The only flaws on his perfectly smooth, tanned skin. 'Oh, Marco,' she said, tears now filling her eyes. 'You have some marks on your face... I'm so sorry...'

'It is small,' he said, waving her fears away with a movement of his hands. 'Don't worry – soon will be OK.'

Tears trickled down her face. 'You looked so handsome tonight on the stage, and now look at your lovely suit and shirt... and your face.'

'Thank you,' he said. 'I feel very happy you say that.'

She turned the cloth around to a clean part, and then carefully dabbed it to the streaks on his nose and chin.

Then, very gently, he caught her hand. 'Emily,' he said, 'I am really OK. My face, I have hurt...' He couldn't find the words. He shrugged. 'Before... in war. Many things happened other people – terrible things I try forget. This is not so big.'

Visions of him now as a soldier fighting with his countrymen flashed into her mind. It was something she had never considered – she had always envisaged him in the camp. Never had she thought back to what might have happened to him before, what he might have endured or witnessed. Any thoughts of war were always linked to Jack – what had happened to him – and her mind automatically pushed them away.

She nodded and touched the cloth to a mark on his forehead.

Then, as she bent closer to him, some instinct made her move forward and she pressed her lips to the mark. For a few moments, neither of them moved, then she stepped back. Marco suddenly jumped to his feet and put his arms around her waist, and when she didn't move away, he put his hands on either side of her face and kissed her tenderly on the lips.

They drew back and then Emily tilted her head towards him, so he drew her into him and kissed her again, harder this time. Emily felt every part of her body react to him, and she was reminded of Celia's words about physical attraction.

Footsteps coming towards the door suddenly alerted them, and they moved apart just as her father and the priest came in the door, followed by Emily's mother.

'It's all out,' she told them, waving the cloth in the air. 'And the smoke has almost gone.'

'Thank God,' her father said. He went over to Marco and shook his hand. 'I don't know how to thank you, sir,' he said. 'You and Father Dempsey. If you hadn't turned up when you did, I don't know how we would have managed...'

Marco held his hands up. 'I am very glad to help.'

Father Dempsey went into the centre of the kitchen to survey the damage. 'It was Marco,' he said, 'who tackled the worst of it. He managed to climb up to get the window open to get rid of the smoke.'

Her father gave a long, tortured sigh. 'I can see that by the state of his face and his fine clothes.' He looked straight at Marco. 'I'll pay for replacing or cleaning your suit and shirt.'

Marco shook his head. 'I have another,' he said, smiling reassuringly. 'People from orchestra very kind... find second-hand suit for me.'

'I don't care about that. I'll make amends to you somehow for what has happened tonight.' He shook his head. 'I'll never understand what came over me – I rarely fall asleep in the chair.'

'It wasn't the falling asleep,' Emily's mother said. 'It was putting on a pan with lard and leaving it on a gas flame – and then falling asleep.'

'I know,' Tom said. 'I don't need reminding.'

Emily, embarrassed at her parents arguing, looked over at Marco and rolled her eyes.

Her mother went to Marco and stood in front of him. 'Thank you, Marco, from the bottom of my heart. If that fire had got out of control – if the smoke had reached upstairs – we would have stood very little chance.' She closed her eyes and shook her head. 'It doesn't bear thinking about.'

'Well, it didn't happen,' Tom said, 'so we'll just thank our lucky stars, and make the best of things.'

'I think God was looking after you tonight,' Father Dempsey said. 'It could have gone either way when those curtains caught fire because the next thing would have been the cupboards beside them.'

'That's what I was thinking,' Emily's mother said. She tutted and shook her head. 'Who in God's name would have thought to make chips at that hour of the night?'

'Ah, Hannah, there's no point in going down that road again. I've told you it's the last time I'll put a hand anywhere near the cooker.'

Emily could see a circular conversation coming around again. 'We have to put it behind us now,' she said, her voice firm. 'It was an accident, and that's all there is to it. We'll have it cleaned up properly in the morning, and then see what needs doing.'

A tap came on the door, and they looked around to see the taxi driver.

'Are you staying, or do you want me to wait?' he asked.

'Yes, we're coming now,' the priest said. 'We have to get Marco back, he's later than we anticipated.' He looked at Emily's father. 'I think you'll manage fine here now with Emily to give a hand. I'll say goodnight, and I'll call in on you tomorrow.'

Marco moved as well. 'Goodnight,' he said, looking at Emily's parents, 'I hope you sleep OK.'

'Goodnight, Marco,' her father said, 'and we'll be in touch.'

Emily looked at her father. 'I'll see them out,' she said.

Father Dempsey strode on ahead to speak to the driver, and Emily and Marco walked slowly down the path together.

'When can we meet again?' Marco asked.

Emily knew the sensible thing to say, but she could not. 'Monday,' she said. 'I'll be at the shop for four o'clock.'

'We have many things to talk about.'

'Yes,' she said. 'I'll look forward to it.'

He touched her arm. 'I would like to kiss you again...'

The thought of him taking her in his arms again sent a little shiver of excitement through her, but she knew she had to be sensible. 'I would like it, too, and I hope we can another time.' She placed her hand over his. 'But now, you have to go.'

Chapter Twenty-Eight

Alice looked up from the cheese slicer as the postman came in. She smiled at him. 'I won't be a second,' she said. 'Let me just clean my hands.'

She had spent the last fifteen minutes, while it was quiet after the morning rush, cutting the large lumps of cheese into smaller pieces. She then weighed them on the white enamel scales and wrapped them in greaseproof paper ready for her customers. She went quickly to the sink and washed her hands, then lifted a towel and came towards the counter still drying them.

The postman gave her four brown envelopes and a long white one. 'Looks like you have something from Italy,' he said, smiling at her. 'If you're throwing away the envelope, will you keep the stamp for me?'

'I'll do my best,' she said, 'but you have a competitor now for the stamps. Philip, the young Guernsey boy who is staying with me, has begun collecting stamps, so I might have to start giving him one and you the next.'

The postman laughed. 'No problem at all,' he said. 'I'm glad to hear some of the younger ones are taking an interest in stamp collection – or philately, if you want to be technical.'

'He's at school now, so when he comes in later, I'll check whether he has one similar, and if so, I'll keep it for you.'

'That's fine,' he said, hitching his sack up on his shoulder. 'And don't worry if he wants to hang onto any foreign stamps from now on. I have a few people on my round who keep their stamps for me. Some of the elderly ones get them off their families as well, and they're always waiting by the window to catch me when I'm on their street. It's very good of them.' He shrugged. 'I suppose it gives them something to do.'

As soon as he left, Alice put the brown envelopes on the counter and then studied the long white one, addressed to her in Greg's long script and stamped with a Naples postmark. She took a deep breath and then opened it.

Dear Alice, she read,

I hope this letter finds you well and that everything is going fine in the shop. I think of you often and miss you very much.

Thank you for sending me the information about Uncle Charles, and I will contact his solicitor some time this week. It is sad to think that my mother's only brother has died, too, so soon after her. I know you only met him a few times, but he was a quiet, likeable man, not unlike my own father in nature. It is also a bit unsettling to hear he died just as suddenly as my mother, but I suppose he was close to seventy and had almost reached his three score years and ten. At least he left no wife or family behind – his whole life was that bicycle shop where he spent more time than at home. I am not expecting any significant inheritance from him as my mother's sister, Agnes, and her family have helped in the shop and looked after him for years. If I do receive anything, it will come in useful to replace the shop van with something newer and bigger when I come home.

I am recovered from the stomach sickness that I mentioned in a recent letter, and was back to work after a few days, catching up on the mountains of letters and documents we receive daily. I am lucky it was not typhus or smallpox, which are circulating in some areas of Naples.

Alice put the letter down on the counter, and then gave a deep sigh. She had a myriad of feelings about the missive, but the overriding one was of relief that Greg was safe and well. She was thankful for that. She was also thankful that he had recovered and that it had not been one of the other frightening diseases he had mentioned. The thought of anything serious happening to him – especially while he was in a foreign country – filled her with dread. Whatever her personal feelings towards him, she wanted him back home in England, safe and well.

She read on:

Things remain the same here, all the staff working in Field Security are kept busy trying to bridge the gap between the military and the civilian population in the city. Generally, I have no complaints. Compared to the servicemen still in active duty, we are very lucky. But there are times it is not easy, being amongst people whose homes are in ruins and whose families have been killed in battles with our German predecessors. Many are starving, including several Italian men who work in our office. Thankfully, we can share our rations with some of them, but it is very hard to see young and old who have been without decent food for months. In England you could never imagine a trained lawyer dropping to the ground because he had not eaten in almost two days. The poor man has lost everything in the war – family, home, books acquired over a long number of years – and possesses only a few items such as photos and silver dining pieces from his bombed home, which he carries around with him.

To see mothers and children begging in the streets for scraps of food is heart-breaking and many of them walk miles out into the countryside to find orchards that might have the odd apples left or to forage for herbs and anything that can be described as edible. Petty crime in the area continues on a daily basis along with constant black-market activity. We are kept busy with local people reporting on each other (often neighbours or people with grudges against another) to our office via anonymous letters, which keeps us busy and at times amused, as the English is often confused.

On the whole the Italians are decent people, and amongst the kindest-hearted I have ever met. If you donate a few slices of bread or even the smallest piece of cheese, you are given in return a miracle prayer to keep you safe, scribbled on a scrap of paper or a shred of material, which they insist has come from some miracle-working saint. Most people in Naples are religious in the extreme and every few weeks there is a celebration of some saint or other which brings a bit of jollity to their days.

The family we are billeted with continue to be very hospitable. Although their home is beautiful, some parts are so damaged as to render them uninhabitable. Some of the FS men have helped repair areas of the house, but it will take a lot of time and work to restore it. The mother and the older children often entertain us on their piano in the evenings, and the staff remaining in the house are happy to cook for us whenever we can get ingredients.

Since my last letter writing about this, I have become more accustomed to Italian food and enjoy the odd glass of local wine. In the midst of all the devastation around us, I find great pleasure in the home-cooked dishes, especially when eaten outside on a warm evening. Something I could never imagine us doing in dear old Stockport! Whenever we have the rare opportunity to eat out in the cafes, I particularly enjoy the local pasta dishes cooked in tomato and herbs.

Alice, I have a favour to ask. One of the older children in the family has a birthday next month. I wondered if it would be possible for you to send me chocolates as a gift to them? The biggest box of Milk Tray would be great, to share around. Also, if you could find something like ribbons for the girls and anything that is easily posted for the two little boys. The smallest gift will mean a lot to them as the family live day to day, and any money goes on food.

At the moment I have no idea how much longer I will be here. The weather at this time of year is still hot, and we are lucky to have the courtyard garden which is sheltered from the extreme sun during the day, and cool to sit in at night. When things are calm in the city, it is very pleasant to sit outside, listening to music coming from the house.

Another interesting feature of Naples life is that some families spend their days living outdoors in the street. First thing in the morning, they are to be seen carrying tables, chairs, a vase of flowers, which they prop against the wall of the building. I even saw one family who had a clock and framed family photographs on the table!

I hope the shop is going well and that the work is not taking too much out of you? I am glad Maeve is there to help you out when needed and young Freddy.

Alice, I often think, with no small feeling of guilt, that this is not what you had planned to do with your life. To have spent all that time studying to be a teacher, and enjoyed your work in school so much, and to now be stuck in a small cornershop day in, day out must be hard. I am sorry about that, but neither of us could foresee what happened to my mother. It all took place so quickly, at times I feel as though it was all a dream, and that she will be there when I come back home. To *think of the shop is to always think of her there, where she was happy, doing what she wanted.*

But I am very aware that her life was not yours. I promise you that when this war is finally ended, and I come back to Stockport, we will sort this out and have you back in school, where you belong. One thing I have learned during my time involved in war, is that life is too short and precious to spend it doing something that is the opposite of what we truly want. I hope that makes some sort of sense?

I must go now, and I look forward to hearing from you very soon.

Sending my dearest love to you, and wishing you much happiness,

Greg

Alice read down the pages quickly, then went back to the start again, taking in all the details about Greg's life in Naples over the last few months. It was to his credit, she thought, that he managed to find things that were uplifting in a situation which sounded truly awful. It was a quality she did not know he possessed, as he had no reluctance in complaining about things he didn't like at home, whether it be food, music on the radio and local or national political situations he did not agree with. Living with, and witnessing, much more serious problems in Naples had obviously softened his approach to certain aspects of life.

From what he had written in this letter and previous ones, the city had appalling poverty, with broken buildings and worst of all, starving people. And yet, he somehow had managed to find positives in the midst of it all – the food, the wine, the music and the hospitality of the Italian people. He had also said in several letters how lucky his Field Security office was to be billeted in such grand surroundings, and with a family who worked so well with their temporary British governors. She was glad to hear that his conditions were so tolerable, and to have real hope that with the advance the Allies had made in Europe, that the end of the war was in sight.

As a customer appeared outside the shop window, Alice slid the pages back into the envelope. Whilst the letter had reassured her about her husband's safety, it had also unsettled her, as did each one that arrived. Each letter marked another two or three weeks nearer the time when Greg's work would be finished in Italy and he returned home.

There was another issue about his letters that caused her to feel unsettled, an issue she felt that she herself had caused. In his earlier letters from the training camps, and when he first went out to Italy, he had written telling her how much he loved her and how much he missed her. Whilst she had replied with concern and affection, she had been more muted than he, as she felt the spectre of Marjorie Jones still hovered over them.

Alice noticed that Greg's last few letters were written in a more low-key manner, and she wondered if he had deliberately toned down the romantic nature of his letters in response to hers. It may be that he was busier than normal and didn't have so much time to spend on letter writing. With the real possibility that the war would end soon, perhaps the need to express his feelings so strongly was no longer necessary.

Initially, she hoped when he came home that her feelings would return to the way they had been. She wanted to give him the loving welcome a serviceman deserved, and then move forward together as a united couple. To be once again the wife he had married, and the person who placed him at the centre of her life.

Since meeting Louis Girard and discovering a different kind of relationship, she wondered whether any of that was still possible. Alice knew she would have to decide soon. So far, Louis had stuck to his promise when they first admitted their feelings towards each other. He had put no pressure on her to be anything other than a close, platonic friend, and had understood her loyalty to her marriage and respected it. The undercurrents were all there between them, and there were times when Alice felt her natural passion for him running so high, she had to pull away from him and go and sit upstairs for a while. There were also occasions when Louis's hands wandered further, and before things got out of control, he suddenly moved to his feet and got his coat to set off for home. Their commitment to the children also served as another barrier against those feelings, preventing their friendship from turning into anything more serious.

When Louis visited on the nights he was free, he came just after the shop closed, in time to have tea with the three of them. He would sit for a couple of hours with them, checking over the twins' homework and hearing them read aloud, then discussing the books they were reading. He also talked to them about any news that had come through on the radio or in the newspapers about Guernsey, tentatively speculating what might happen when the war was over and how they might return home. He also encouraged the children to talk about any memories they had of their family life on the island, before they were evacuated, to keep the connection alive.

Both Philip and Gabriela were settled in a routine now, and Alice was heartened to hear that the vicar and his wife had seen a notable difference in both of them since coming to live with her. They seemed happy with their new situation, and were back to feeling safe and secure again, as they had been with Mrs Ponsonby.

The summer holidays had given Philip time to quietly recover from his appendix operation. He had slept downstairs for the first week and when he was recovered enough to walk upstairs comfortably, he'd moved into Betty's old room across the hall from his sister. Louis had brought him books from the library, and a beginner's set for stamp-collecting, which had a magnifying glass and a magazine that explained all the basics. The new hobby had absorbed him for hours on end, whilst Gabriela was happy out in the fresh air skipping and playing ball games with her new local friends.

Alice did not rush the children off to bed on the long summer evenings, and it was often past ten o'clock when they went upstairs. Afterwards, she and Louis would sit together with tea – or occasionally at weekends, with a glass of wine – talking or companionably listening to the radio.

When they talked, they told each other about both the trivial and the more important things in their lives. Little details about when they were growing up in Stockport and Guernsey, telling family stories and of the joys and difficulties with parents and siblings. They often told each other things they had never mentioned to anyone else. Never once was Alice bored in Louis's company and never once did she feel that he was not being open and honest with her.

There were a few things that they did not discuss. One was what was going to happen when Greg came home. The other was what would happen when the time came for Louis to go back to Guernsey.

In recent weeks, a new topic that Alice could not discuss emerged, one that she could hardly admit to herself or begin to broach with her friends. At time moved on, she realised – whether she was ready or not – the subject would have to be addressed and discussed. It would have to be addressed with Louis before it made itself shown. Afterwards, she would have to be prepared to make the biggest decision in her life.

Alice had discovered that she was pregnant, by the husband she no longer loved.

When she knew without a doubt that the baby she had longed for was confirmed, she had several nights where she lay awake trying to imagine how her life would now change. Because she knew, without a doubt, that change it must. Whilst a part of her was thrilled to think of herself as a mother, there was another part of her which felt betrayed that fate could intervene so cruelly at such a time.

Chapter Twenty-Nine

After her mother had left to go to the cinema with her old friend, Gwen, Sophie went upstairs to freshen up before her friends arrived. She changed into her wide-legged black trousers and a burnt-orange silk blouse, with flowing sleeves and tiny pearl buttons down the front. It was a blouse her mother had passed down to her, and more glamorous than anything in the shops at the moment. She had been to the hairdresser's the previous day, and her curly blonde hair was still tamed into the looser waves that she preferred.

After touching up her make-up, she dabbed on some Shalimar perfume, then went downstairs to check everything was ready. In the sitting room she looked over the dainty sandwiches and carrot cake buns that Mrs Wilson had left covered with damp dishtowels. The housekeeper had found yet another recipe which didn't require much of their butter or sugar rations, and only half of the small bag of raisins she had bought in the shop that morning.

Sophie then put out three crystal tumblers for the port and lemon she was going to serve when Alice and Emily arrived. She was looking forward to entertaining her two friends this evening, as it had been difficult to sort a night when the three of them were free. Alice was kept busy with the shop and the Guernsey children, and since Emily had gone back to school, she was occupied with schoolwork in the evenings and her usual netball practice and matches and Brownie meetings.

Sophie herself had been working late some evenings recently, and she had also gone out to visit Tony's family a few times as well, as seeing them somehow made her feel closer to him. Whilst she found them a tad loud and a little intrusive at times, she enjoyed listening to the silly stories that Mrs Shaw and her daughters loved to relate about Tony when they were all young. It was, she thought, a breath of fresh air compared to the formal, closed way her mother could be at times.

Things had thawed a little between her and her mother since the wedding. Although the situation about her father and the circumstances of her birth had faded somewhat in her mind, it could still catch her unexpectedly. She could be busy in the office at work when something with her father's handwriting would appear on her desk, and she would suddenly find herself in tears. She still missed him and his quiet, reassuring ways so much, and wished he had been alive to comfort her, and help her come to terms with the news that had completely shaken her.

Her mother, she acknowledged to Tony, was still trying to make things up to her. She had done everything possible to ensure the wedding went perfectly – which it undoubtedly had. Tony had advised her to try to forget about it, tactfully saying that her parents had obviously thought the way they had handled things was in her best interests. And, he gently pointed out, it was obvious that her father loved and adored her so much, that it was possible he just did not want to acknowledge – even to himself – that he was not her natural father. Perhaps he planned to do it, Tony suggested, but was never able to find the right words.

She had felt much better after the talk with Tony and had resolved to try her best to put it behind her. She would not drop it immediately because she wanted her mother to realise the seriousness of the situation, but she would gradually let things return to a more relaxed way. Tony, she realised, was wiser than she had imagined a young man of his age could be, and it was another quality about him that she loved.

The week before last, Tony had been sent to sort out phone lines over in Huddersfield, and Sophie had caught the train from

Manchester to go over to meet up with him, and they had stayed overnight in a small hotel. It had been wonderful seeing him again, and the night and following morning with him had left her feeling hopeful that she might become pregnant. The idea of starting her own family with Tony was something she found so exciting she hardly dared let herself imagine it.

Alice was ten minutes early to arrive, and Sophie was surprised to see that she had lost weight since she last saw her. 'You're looking very slim,' she said, as they hugged each other.

'Do you think so?' Alice said, vaguely surprised. 'It's probably being on my feet more often in the shop and then taking Bella out for regular trips to do her business.'

'You look as though you've lost about half a stone!'

Alice looked down at herself. 'I hadn't really noticed...'

'I'm just the opposite,' Sophie said. 'I've been eating too much since the wedding and I noticed that the waists of my skirts are getting tight. I think I'm eating anything sweet I can get because I'm missing Tony so much.' She shrugged. 'Some people go the opposite way and lose their appetite when things are difficult.'

Alice wrinkled her brow as though thinking, and then said, 'It's so lovely to see you, and thanks for organising the evening.'

Sophie was surprised that her friend had deliberately changed the subject. Alice was usually open and easy, and they often talked about the ups and downs of their weight. She suddenly felt a little flustered now as if she had said something wrong. 'Let's go down into the sitting room and we can have a drink while we're waiting for Emily.' She turned now and they walked down the hallway.

'How are things going?' Alice asked. 'Are you still busy at the factory?'

Sophie opened the sitting room door. 'It's actually slowed up a bit,' she said. 'Apart from military caps and hats, things are quiet. The ordinary hat orders are much smaller than before.'

Alice went and sat on one of the armchairs by the fire. 'Oh, I brought you a little gift,' she suddenly remembered. She went into her handbag and came out with a small box.

'You shouldn't have,' Sophie told her. 'I just thought it would be nice for the three of us to have a good old chat, without anyone at a table in a café or hotel lounge overhearing us. My mother went into Manchester to meet her friend.' She opened the box and there was a matching deep pink lipstick and nail varnish. 'Oh, how lovely of you!' she exclaimed. 'And just the perfect colour.'

'I'm glad you like it,' Alice said. 'I saw it yesterday, and thought the shade was the sort you like.'

Sophie took the lipstick out. 'I have to try it!' she said, going over to the gilt mirror on the wall. 'It's darker than the one I have on, so it will be fine on top.' She opened the gold tube and carefully outlined her lips. She pressed them together then stood back to view herself. 'Gorgeous!' she said, giving a delighted giggle. She went over and gave Alice a hug. 'Oh, it's so lovely to see you. We've all been so busy since the wedding that we've only met a couple of times. And of course, the last time Emily and I met up for the pictures, you couldn't make it.'

Alice nodded. 'I had no one to sit with the twins. It was just one of those nights when Maeve had to go somewhere and the Guernsey teacher who has been helping the children – Louis – was on Home Guard duty.'

'Well, I'm glad you made tonight.' She went over to the drinks cabinet. 'Sherry, port or gin?'

'I'd love a gin and orange, please.'

'I'll have the same,' Sophie said. She poured them and then gave one to Alice and sat down with hers in the chair opposite. 'Well, anything new or exciting?'

Alice shrugged. 'Nothing major,' she said. 'I was actually going to ask you how it went with Emily... you said you explained the situation with your mother to her.'

Sophie sucked in her breath. 'Yes, I did. I knew when I told you before the wedding that I would eventually have to tell Emily as well. It wouldn't be fair. The three of us have always been honest with each other.' There was a pause. 'Emily was very good about it, although it felt harder telling her. I think I must have accepted it and put it to the back of my mind, and it felt different dredging it all up again. When I told you, I desperately needed to talk it out with someone, and you were great that night. It really, really helped. I don't think I could have coped with the wedding and everything if I hadn't opened up to you and got it off my chest.'

'I'm glad you feel it helped,' Alice said. 'It might not change things, but sometimes saying it out loud to someone helps you to know it's not the end of the world.'

'Tony has been a great support, too,' Sophie said. 'Even though my mother was suspicious about him, he's been so good about all this.' She smiled. 'It didn't matter a bit to him.'

'Your mother did all this because she didn't want to hurt you, but at the end of the day, she absolutely adores you and that's what really counts.'

As Emily walked towards the shop, she could see Marco standing outside. He saw her and waved, then he came quickly towards her.

'You came,' he said. 'I'm glad...'

She hoped the fact she was there outside the shop as promised implied she was glad, too. 'I told you I would.' She smiled and said, 'I have a little while before I catch the bus to Stockport.'

'You look beautiful,' he said, his dark eyes warm and friendly, taking in her freshly curled dark hair and her red floral dress and white cardigan and sandals. 'Very, very nice.'

Emily blushed at the compliment. 'You look nice, too,' she said, smiling as she took in his blue shirt, dark trousers and blue sleeveless sweater. 'You look different from last time – not the concert, the last time I met you here at the shop. You're not wearing your uniform.'

'I'm happy you see me different.' He grinned at her. 'Also, I have very good news.'

'What is it?' she asked.

'This week, we have more freedom,' he told her, 'and I have a job with Mr Barlow in shop, now I am allowed.' He indicated his clothes. 'Mr and Mrs Barlow bought me these new clothes for work in shop and said I can keep other clothes in shop now. When we meet up, I don't need to wear camp uniform.' He rolled his eyes. 'I will change for going back later to camp, but I want for seeing you, nice clothes.'

'Thank you,' she said, laughing now. 'I am honoured you dressed so nice for me. And it is great news about you being able to wear your own clothes sometimes.'

'The clothes are not official,' he explained, 'and in camp we must wear Italian uniform, but some of the men in charge of camp don't mind so much when we are out with English people. They don't ask too many questions if you don't cause trouble.' He halted. 'The night of the fire I was very late – past curfew – but Father Dempsey explain and they were OK.'

'That is really good news,' Emily said.

'Most people very understanding, but I am still careful,' he told her. 'More good news is that we can also mix more, with local people, and go more places – up to five miles. I can go to cinema now.'

'That is a huge change.' Emily flushed now at the thought of them sitting close together watching a film, like a normal couple. Was it possible? she wondered.

He was serious again. 'But still not allowed to go on buses or trains, and not allowed in pubs.' He shrugged. 'I don't mind, I know there can be trouble with some English men, sometimes fight. I understand, Italy and Britain for first years against each other in war. It's good we can go out, but we have to be very careful.' He paused. 'If you would like, we could go to cinema? You go on bus, and I walk down and meet you.'

'I would like that, Marco,' she said. 'But maybe wait a while…'

'Of course,' he said. 'You will tell me when is good.'

Emily looked at her watch. 'We only have a short time now,' she said. 'I thought we could go to the park just down the road. It's only five minutes' walk and then maybe you could accompany me to the bus stop.'

'Anywhere!' he said, holding his hands out. 'I am happy to go anywhere with you, Emily.'

They walked along, every so often casting glances at each other, then Marco asked, 'How are your parents?'

'Fine,' she said. 'The kitchen is all clean and painted, and my mother has new curtains.'

'Good, good,' he said, nodding his head.

'It gave them a fright,' Alice said, 'and I don't think my father will ever cook at night again.'

'Very sad, what happened...'

'Father Dempsey called to the house the other day, and they asked him to find out about your suit and shirt – the smart one for the orchestra. He told them that your suit was OK after being dry-cleaned, and my father said they want to pay for that and buy you a new shirt.'

Marco waved his hands. 'No, no... it's OK. The shirt is under suit – not see too much.'

'We'll see,' Emily told him. 'Father Dempsey also said it would be nice if they asked you to come for Sunday dinner sometime.'

Marco's eyes widened. 'Really? To your house?'

'Yes, he explained that some of the other local people who have Italian men from the camp working for them, invite them to their homes.' She looked at him. 'He told them you have been to Barlow's house for meals and was invited to dinner at their daughter's farm.'

Marco's face became serious. 'Yes,' he said, 'I was helping at farm because daughter's husband away, still in war. I hope from now, only work in shop – not out on farm.'

'You like the shop better?' Emily asked.

'Yes,' he said, nodding eagerly, 'I like Mr Barlow's shop. Not serving people, just working out back, lifting boxes and stacking shelves. I like him and his wife very much, they are good people.'

'Father Dempsey said he would talk to my parents again,' Emily said. 'So, we will see if my mother feels OK about Sunday dinner.'

'OK by me,' Marco said, smiling. 'But it is more important that everything OK for you and your parents.'

Emily gave him a sidelong glance and thought she had never met anyone as good-looking as Marco, or who she felt so easy with. How strange she should feel that connection to someone she had spent so little time with, and from a foreign country that she didn't know much about. Even stranger was the fact that she knew little about his own life. She knew bits about how he lived in the prisoner of war camp, and she knew about his music, but she knew nothing about his family or what had happened to him during the war. He had obviously been captured somewhere and must have seen some awful things during that time.

He looked at her and smiled and she smiled back. They knew enough about each other to be going on with. For the time being that would have to do.

They came to the tall wrought-iron park gates and turned inside. It wasn't a huge park, but big enough for a ten-minute stroll around the perimeter. It had a square area with swings and a slide for children in the middle, surrounded by a well-kept garden with trees and colourful bushes and shrubs flanking either side of the path. There were only a few other people around, mainly mothers with children, and some older children playing on their own.

They talked as they went along, and Marco told her that Father Dempsey had arranged for the choir from the camp to come to the church to sing at Sunday Mass the following week.

'Will you come?' he asked.

'Of course,' she said.

'And maybe your mother and father?' he asked.

'I don't know.' Emily felt her throat tighten. She thought for a few moments, then she looked at him, her face serious now. 'I have to be honest, Marco. My parents don't know that we are friends. They think I met you at the concert for the first time. They don't know we met in the shop...'

Without saying anything, they both slowly drew to a halt.

'OK,' he said, nodding his head and looking down at the ground.

'I don't know what they will do about Sunday dinner. Before they met you, they were very unhappy about the Italian camp... They thought you were very good and kind about helping that night with the fire, but they might feel uncomfortable.' She gave a deep sigh. 'You see, my brother was killed in Dunkirk, and they are still very sad... still angry with Germany and Hitler.'

'Of course.' He nodded and put a hand to his head. 'And maybe still angry with Italy and Mussolini...'

Emily bit her lip, and she moved her gaze away from him. She looked over at the play area, where children were laughing and being pushed on the swings and helped to climb up the slide. 'It's difficult,' she said. 'I don't know how they will feel if they know we are friends.'

He reached out now and took her hand. 'Emily... maybe more than friends? I hope.'

She looked at him now and nodded. 'Yes, I hope, too.'

'I would like to kiss you again,' he said, 'but I know it's wrong place now.'

She nodded and smiled at him. 'It is the wrong place. There might be people here who know me and would talk. Not just because you are Italian – because you are a man. Any man.' She gave a little laugh. 'Although I have never walked here, in this park, before with any man. You are the only one.'

His hand tightened on hers. 'That makes me very happy.'

They walked a little further, their hands linked, then she checked her watch. 'I am so sorry, Marco,' she said, giving a little sigh. 'I have to go for the bus now. I'm late already.'

As they walked out of the park, Emily squeezed his hand before letting go of it. He looked at her and nodded in resignation, and she knew he understood. They crossed the road and then went down a small street that led out to the bus stop on Wellington Road. There were a few people already waiting, so they stood further down the road where they could see the bus approaching.

'When will I see you again?' Marco asked.

'I'll be there at mass on Sunday to hear the choir,' she replied, 'and I will find you afterwards. I don't think anyone would find it strange, after you helped out with the fire. We might not get a chance to talk much, but I will be there.'

'And the cinema? I am allowed English money now I am working in shop, and I can pay.' He rolled his eyes. 'As you say before – like any man.'

Emily smiled at his joke and then she felt a little dart of sadness at how small his life was compared to some of the other men she had been out with.

When she got off the bus near Sophie's house, Emily set off at a quick pace. She was three-quarters of an hour late, when normally she would have been on the early side. She wasn't overly concerned as she knew that it was just a casual night with her friends with nothing happening at a certain time, and Sophie wasn't the sort to mind.

As she walked towards the house, she went over in her mind the conversation she'd had with Marco about her parents. If they agreed to have him at the house to thank him properly – as the priest suggested – and present him with the new shirt, that would be a start. It would give them the chance to see him as an ordinary person. Seeing him for the first time in his orchestra suit, as opposed to his camp uniform, had been a stroke of luck she could not have anticipated. It had undoubtedly helped that they saw him as the person he was before the war.

The chip pan fire – she felt awful even admitting it to herself – was an even bigger stroke of luck as it had brought Marco and her parents together. Strangely enough, her mother had improved since the incident. Just recently, when she and her mother were alone having a cup of tea, her mother said that she felt guilty about the fire. She had been too tired to wait up for Emily coming home from the concert, but her father wouldn't go to bed without seeing she had arrived home safely.

'He then decided to make chips as a treat for you,' her mother had said, 'and that caused all the problems. I should have been up, keeping him company like I used to, chatting or listening to the radio. For the last few years, I've not been like a wife to him at all.' Her eyes had moved towards the window. 'We used to go dancing together and to the pictures, or out with friends on a Saturday night. We haven't done that since Jack died. I haven't had the heart.'

Emily had patted her mother's hand. 'Everybody understands that.'

'When Father Dempsey came the day after the fire, he said Jack wouldn't have wanted me to be like this. That if I carried on mourning, it would be like all our lives had ended when Jack went ... as if nobody else's life mattered.' She had taken a deep breath. 'He was right. We could have both been killed if your father hadn't woken up ...' Her voice had faltered. 'And you as well. When you arrived home, you ran straight upstairs to get me out.'

'What else would I have done?'

'You could have been burned or choked to death with smoke, and I was so dopey I didn't even know what was going on. If the priest and that musician lad hadn't been with you, God knows what would have happened.' Her mother had nodded slowly. 'It's made me realise that I need to give myself a good shake and get back to some kind of normal life.'

'Well, that's good to hear.'

'I thought I might get the kitchen papered instead of painted, what do you think? Maybe a nice floral print or something to cheer the place up. I thought me and you might run down to the shop one evening after school.'

Emily's heart had lifted. Her mother had not gone into Stockport recently unless it was a dire necessity. 'Tomorrow after school,' she had said. 'We'll go sooner rather than later, and get it started.'

'We might go into the Co-op and look for a white shirt for that young chap.' She had paused. 'Italian, is he?'

Emily caught her breath. 'Yes,' was all she said.

'I thought so.' Her mother had sighed. 'Your father thought

so, too. Well, whatever he is, the man did a decent thing. The least we owe him is a new shirt and the cost of cleaning his lovely suit. The priest had said about him coming to the house, but I'm not at all sure about that...'

Emily had said nothing. She had got up quietly and washed the cups and saucers then said she was going up to her room to sort out books for school in the morning. She had said nothing, but she had thought a lot. She would not interfere and try to influence her parents in any way. She would wait and see how things turned out.

'What happened to you?' Sophie said, when she answered the door. 'Alice and I were beginning to wonder if you were coming. It's not like you to be late.'

'Oh, I'm sorry,' Emily said. 'I got held up and then I missed a bus.' It was almost the truth, as she had let one go which arrived as she and Marco came onto the main road. 'You know I would have phoned if I wasn't coming.'

'We just thought you might have been sick or something and couldn't get out to the phone box,' Sophie said, as they walked down the hallway to the sitting room. 'It doesn't matter at all, as long as you are OK. Alice and I were busy chatting and catching up on things.' She opened the sitting room door. 'She's here!' she announced to Alice.

Sophie fixed a drink for Emily, and then the three of them sat down together. When Emily asked if either had any news about their husbands since she last saw them, Sophie told the girls about her visit to Huddersfield to spend the night with Tony, and how wonderful it was to see him again. 'It sounds awful, but there were times when I could hardly picture his face in my mind. I got up in the middle of the night once, to look at a wedding photo to remind myself exactly what his face was like – his eyes, his nose... everything.'

'That's an awful feeling,' Alice said quietly. 'I think lots of wives and girls feel that.'

They talked more about Tony and his very pressured work to

keep the telephone lines open in all the important government offices in the country.

'Greg mentioned in one of his letters that they had trouble with the phone lines out in Italy,' Alice said. 'He said local people cut them and steal the cable, and they have to constantly be replaced.'

'How is Greg?' Emily asked.

Alice told them about Greg's recent letter and how awful the situation in Naples was. 'He said lots of the people are starving, and half the time he doesn't know what he's eating in the cafes – it could be cats or anything.'

Sophie's hand flew to her mouth. 'Poor Greg!'

'Thankfully, he's billeted with an Italian family in a lovely, big old house,' Alice explained, 'and they often cook for the officers.' She raised her eyebrows. 'He seems very fond of the husband and wife and all their young children. I'm amazed how well he's taken to the Italian way of life – the food and music and even the wine. In one letter he wrote to me about an evening he had at the opera. He said when he comes home, he's going to start going to the opera in Manchester.'

'Who would have believed that?' Sophie said, shaking her blonde waves. 'I couldn't have imagined Greg Fairclough going to the opera.'

Alice shrugged. 'I'm his wife and I couldn't have imagined him being interested in anything like that.' She then told them about the parcel she had sent out to Greg in Naples. 'He asked for a large box of chocolates for one of the children's birthdays, but the man who delivers the confectionery said he couldn't get a box at short notice.' Her voice lowered. 'Of course, nobody has the ration allowance for boxes of chocolates now, but I have a few customers who will swap their sugar rations for tea or something else. I was going to try to do my best to juggle the ration coupons around to get him at least half a pound.' Alice's face lit up. 'You're not going to believe it,' she said, starting to laugh. 'I suddenly remembered that Betty told me she had hidden some chocolates in the loft when rationing came in, so I sent Freddy up on a ladder to check it out.'

'And?' Sophie prompted. 'Was there anything there?'

'He came back down with two half-pound boxes of Milk Tray and a full pound box of Cadbury's Contrast.'

Sophie's eyes widened. 'Are you serious?'

'Absolutely, Betty had them really carefully wrapped up. I know she had produced a box when Greg came home one time, and on another occasion, she took a box up to her friend's. I think it was a special occasion like a twenty-fifth wedding anniversary, and she thought it would be a great surprise for them.' Alice shrugged. 'I hadn't given any thought to them since Betty died, so I was delighted when I found them for Greg.'

'Did you send them all?' Emily asked.

Alice shook her head. 'Just the Contrast and one of the Milk Trays. I opened the other box for the children and Freddy,' she said. 'I thought it would have been awful for the poor twins to see the chocolates and not be allowed to taste them, and anyway, I needed to check they were still edible after all that time. I was worried they might have gone off – but thankfully they were fine.'

'The kids must have been thrilled getting chocolates,' Sophie said.

'Believe it or not,' Alice said, 'they all found the first one they tasted very sweet and so did I! We've all become used to the war-time blended chocolate, and it isn't half as sweet.' She laughed. 'It didn't put them off because they all had a second one and thought they were lovely.'

'What about you?' Emily said.

'I wasn't bothered,' Alice said. 'One was enough, so I left a few for Maeve.'

'One chocolate was enough?' Emily said incredulously. 'I would have wanted to scoff the whole box.' She looked at Alice now, as though studying her. 'I think you must be on a diet to refuse chocolate. When I came in, I was just thinking that you looked even slimmer than usual.'

'I said the very same when she arrived!' Sophie said triumphantly.

Alice shook her head and smiled in bemusement. 'Honestly, I'm not on any diet and I never have been. It must be because I'm on my feet all day, and maybe making the rations stretch further with the children and Freddy.' She laughed. 'He has an appetite like a horse.'

Emily held her hand up. 'We interrupted your story about sending the things to Greg – go on.'

'Just don't tell us about the chocolates,' Sophie laughed.

'Where was I?' Alice said. 'Ah, yes! I got a few more things for the children in Naples – ribbons and a couple of books of dressing dolls, some colouring books and pencils – and parcelled them all up and sent them out to Greg. Hopefully, they arrived safely and in time for the little girl's birthday.'

'The children will be delighted with those things,' Emily said, 'and it's so kind of Greg to think of them. From what we hear in the news, Italy is in an awful state.' She paused. 'As are Poland and France, and so many other countries. Hitler is an absolute maniac, and I hope he gets what he deserves when this is all over.'

'And what about our own country?' Sophie said sadly. 'Things have been bad enough in Manchester but look at what has happened down in London and over in Liverpool.' She shook her head. 'Tony said London is in an unbelievable state, and it's going to take years to rebuild it.'

They talked seriously for a while and then Sophie held her hands up. 'Enough about the war, it's too depressing! I invited you both here to cheer me up,' she said, 'because I'm missing my lovely new husband. We all need to hear some good news for a change.'

'I agree,' Emily said, looking over at Alice who was nodding her head and smiling.

'Finish your drinks,' Sophie instructed. 'I am going to get us another one and then we'll eat.'

'Just orange for me, please,' Alice said.

'Are you sure? It's only a little dash of gin because it's an occasion seeing you two.' She rolled her eyes. 'I've been ever so careful about alcohol since the Bluebell night.'

'The orange is fine for me, thanks.'

Sophie moved over to the two girls and collected their glasses. 'Remember – we want some good news!' she said. 'So, while I am pouring the drinks, I want you to come up with something. Anything at all – it can be weird or wonderful.'

There was a little silence then Emily said, 'I actually have some good news. I was going to wait a bit longer to tell you, but maybe this is as good a time as any...'

'What kind of news?' Sophie said.

'Something that will definitely please *you* and might stop you trying to match-make me with your friends' brothers.'

Alice's mouth opened in surprise. 'Have you met someone?'

'Maybe...'

'Tell us!' Sophie demanded.

Emily raised her eyebrows and said teasingly, 'Not until you've poured the drinks.'

'I don't believe it! You've finally met someone, and you've sat here all night without telling us.'

'Hurry up,' Alice said, laughing. 'The longer you take to sort the drinks, the longer we'll have to wait to hear it.'

'Argh!' Sophie threw her hands up and gave a theatrical sigh, then she rushed over to the cabinet where the drinks were kept.

Chapter Thirty

While Sophie was pouring orange into the tumblers, Emily ran over in her mind the explanation she would give, of how and where her new romance began. When they were all seated with their drinks, she took a deep breath. 'I bumped into a very handsome young man in our local shop a few months back. We got talking and I thought he was really nice, but I didn't give it much notice because I thought we would probably never meet up again...' She looked over and could see both Alice and Sophie were listening intently.

'And?' Sophie prompted.

'Then,' Emily said, 'I went to the concert in the town hall with Celia, who I teach with. It was a classical music concert – with an orchestra and solo performers – and it was absolutely wonderful.'

'What pieces did they play?' Alice asked.

'Never mind about the boring music!' Sophie said. 'We've waited long enough for her to find Mr Right, and we don't need a bloody list of all the boring classical music she had to listen to.'

'It wasn't boring!' Emily said, laughing. 'I really enjoyed it.'

'Ignore Sophie,' Alice said, laughing too. 'She is a total philistine at times.'

'The first half of the concert was all orchestra pieces. The second half started with the solo performers, and it was then I recognised him.'

'Where?' Sophie asked. 'Was he sitting near you?'

'He was up on the stage. He was one of the musicians.'

'He's a classical musician?' Alice asked.

Emily nodded. 'At first I didn't recognise him. He looked so different, all dressed up in a tuxedo suit with tails and a bowtie. I didn't catch his name when he was introduced, but when I got a proper look, I knew it was definitely him.' She halted, feeling herself blush now.

'You really like him, don't you?' Sophie said. 'I can tell by the look on your face just when you're talking about him. I've never seen you like this over a man before.' She turned to Alice. 'Have you?'

Alice smiled. 'I don't think I have.'

'Imagine you going out with a classical musician...' Sophie shook her head. 'Go on, tell us more.'

Emily rolled her eyes, then she recounted the story about having a drink in the bar and their journey in the taxi home.

'What did you say his name was?' Sophie asked. 'Mark?'

'No,' Emily said. 'It's *Marco*.'

Sophie's brow furrowed. 'Is he foreign?'

'He's Italian.'

'But I thought they were all gone,' Sophie said. 'I thought all the local Italian families were sent away to different countries until the war is over.'

Emily felt her stomach tighten. 'He's not from a local family,' she said. 'He's actually a prisoner of war in the camp in Gorton.'

'*What*?' Sophie said. 'You're going out with a prisoner of war?' She halted, as though trying to take it in. 'You're going out with one of the soldiers who fought against our country?'

Emily's heart lurched. She wasn't sure what sort of reception she would get from her friends, and this was worse than she imagined. 'He had no choice,' she said quietly. 'He's not a follower of Mussolini and he would have been killed if he didn't join up.'

There was a stunned silence, then Alice said, 'If Emily likes him, then I'm sure he must be very nice.'

'He *is* nice,' Emily said, her voice faltering a little, although she was heartened by Alice's support. 'And I really do like him.' She paused. 'But I do understand Sophie's feelings, and I know I'm going to get the same reaction from a lot of people. I actually felt the same myself until I got to know him. In fact, if it wasn't for Father Dempsey, I probably wouldn't have looked at Marco, or seen him as a person in his own right.' Thinking of him now – picturing his face – made her feel ashamed for the way she had been before. She tilted her head. 'He was forced into the army in Italy, he had no choice at all. He's a musician and a teacher, he's not a soldier and never wanted to be one. But most importantly, he's the nicest, kindest and most intelligent man I have ever met.'

Sophie's shoulders slumped. 'Oh God, Emily,' she said. 'I don't know what to say. You're so lovely and could pick any man. You don't have to go with a foreigner – if you just waited a bit longer, you would meet someone English. Someone more like yourself.'

'That's the problem,' Emily said. 'I've never met anyone like myself before. Marco is the only man I've met who I feel is anything like me.'

'It's because all the men our age are away in foreign places fighting our country, like Greg,' Sophie said, 'or like Tony, working to support the military and the government.' She clasped her hands together. 'If you just wait a bit longer – until the war is over – you'll meet lots of English musicians who play in orchestras or anywhere you want. The war is nearly over, and they will all be back home soon.' She shook her head. 'Emily, don't be angry with me for saying this. You and Alice are my oldest and best friends, and I'm saying this because I care about you. Please don't get involved with a foreigner – especially a prisoner of war – it will be so difficult for you. It will change your life forever. Wait and you'll meet one of our own nice Englishmen.'

Emily looked directly at Sophie. 'It's not about me being impatient or not wanting to wait, and it's not about being

English. It's about meeting someone and knowing they might be the right person.'

Sophie bit her lip. 'But where will that lead?' she asked in a low, anxious voice. 'What kind of life could you have with someone like him?'

'I have no idea,' Emily said. 'We'll just have to wait and see. It might not even work out between us; it's early days and we've only managed to meet a few times. The rules have just changed, and Italian people are now allowed to travel further, and are being treated the same as ordinary workers. He's working full-time in the shop we met in now, and the family are very fond of him.'

'Well, that's a good recommendation,' Alice said. 'They're local people, and they've obviously decided he's a decent and trustworthy person.'

'That's what I thought,' Emily smiled. 'We're going to the cinema together soon and planning a day out somewhere, to give us time to get to know each other properly like any other couple.'

'But what about your family?' Sophie probed. 'How do they feel?'

'They feel the same as you do about Italians, but they had cause to thank him recently, so I'm hoping that things might change.' She went on to explain about the chip pan fire, and how Marco managed to get it under control.

'Oh my goodness!' Alice said. 'Was anyone hurt?'

'Marco's face got splashed with the hot fat in the chip pan. Thankfully, when I saw him earlier this evening, the blisters had almost healed up.'

'Oh, Emily…' Alice said. 'I had no idea all this had happened.'

'I phoned to tell you both about the fire the following day,' Emily said, 'but there was no answer at Sophie's house and the shop phone was engaged. I wanted to tell you about Marco as well, but I knew it would be difficult to explain over the phone, so I was glad when I knew we were meeting tonight.'

'What will you do if your father and mother are against it?' Sophie asked.

'I'll have to cross that bridge when it comes. I know they were grateful for all he did that night, and they felt bad about his face and his lovely outfit almost being destroyed. They've bought him a new shirt and they offered to pay for his suit to be dry-cleaned, so that's a good start.' She paused. 'Father Dempsey said it might be nice to invite him to the house for Sunday dinner. Apparently quite a few local families do.'

Alice looked over at Sophie. 'You had a hard time when your mother was opposed to you getting married to Tony, didn't you?'

Sophie's mouth opened in shock. 'You can't compare that...' she said. 'That was totally different. It was because it was all so quick, and she didn't really know him. We didn't have any of the big differences that Emily and... that Emily has with an Italian man.'

'Well, it's good it all worked out for you, isn't it?' Alice said calmly. 'And if this relationship is meant to be for Emily and Marco, let's hope it all works out for them, too.'

'I would love to say that I hope it works out...' She looked over at Emily now, her hands spread out in an almost helpless manner. 'But being involved with a prisoner of war – an Italian who fought against British soldiers – is not something that a lot of people will be happy about. I feel terrible, Emily, but I'm only saying the truth... and I feel I have to say it because I don't want you getting hurt. I really don't.'

There was a silence and then Alice said, 'I'm sure Emily understands that you're genuinely concerned about her, but at the end of the day, she must follow her own heart.'

Sophie slowly stood up. 'I didn't notice the time,' she said. 'I'd better go and put the kettle on, and then we'll have the sandwiches.'

When she went off down the hallway to the kitchen, Emily looked over at Alice. 'Thank you,' she said, her voice flat. 'I appreciate all the things you said.'

'I mean it,' Alice said, giving her a bright smile. 'I do hope it works out for you. Marco sounds a lovely, talented man.'

Emily's face lit up. 'He's really handsome, too,' she said, 'although I know that's not the main thing.'

'It's not the main thing, but it's a nice addition.' Alice lowered her voice. 'You were very good taking all that from Sophie – it can't have been easy seeing her reaction.'

'No, but I was sort of prepared for it,' Emily said resignedly. 'I know a lot of people feel strongly about the Italian and German prisoners being over here in England. To be honest, I wasn't even sure how you would react.'

Alice smiled. 'Well, people in glass houses can't afford to throw stones.'

Emily's brow wrinkled. 'What do you mean?'

'You know things aren't perfect with me and Greg, so I'm not going to sit in judgement over anyone else.'

'Things are OK now... aren't they?'

'Well, I suppose they will have to be.'

Sophie's footsteps sounded along the corridor, and she came in carrying the crystal sugar bowl and milk jug.

'You're just in time,' Alice said, looking up at her.

Sophie looked surprised. 'In time for what?' She put the things down on the side table beside the cups and saucers and the plates of sandwiches and cakes.

'To hear my news.' She looked at her two friends. 'I've just had it confirmed that I'm pregnant. Greg and I are expecting a baby after Christmas.'

Emily caught her breath at the news, knowing that things had not been well between Alice and Greg. And something about Alice did not seem quite as normal, but she was smiling and appeared to be happy with her news.

When Sophie moved towards Alice, Emily moved, too, and then they both hugged her with whoops of congratulations. Things between Alice and Greg, Emily thought, must have sorted themselves out, as they often do.

'You lucky devil!' Sophie said. 'I keep hoping that I'll be pregnant one of these days. It would be great if we could both have babies around the same time.'

'I'm sure it will happen soon,' Alice said.

'You did well, considering that Greg's only had a couple of leaves.'

Alice raised her eyes and smiled. 'I suppose we did.'

'How far on are you?'

'Just over three months,' she said. 'You know my periods are often a bit wonky, so I wasn't sure. Then a few weeks ago I started feeling queasy and just a bit different somehow, so I guessed. I went to the doctor last week and had it confirmed the other day.' A light came in her eyes. 'I can hardly believe it, it's something so lovely to look forward to.'

'And you'll make a lovely mother,' Emily said, smiling at her. She stood up now. 'I'm just going to pop to the bathroom, if that's OK, Sophie?'

'Of course,' Sophie said, moving towards the door to see her out. 'You know where it is.'

She came back in and went to the table again, to take the cover off the sandwiches. 'I know you think I've been hard on Emily,' she said over her shoulder. 'But I'm really worried about her. I'm afraid of what lies ahead for her if she continues with this Marco.'

'I think Emily is intelligent enough to know what she's letting herself in for,' Alice replied, 'and strong enough to deal with it all. She seems to have thought it all through, and she understands and accepts that others have a different view on it.' She shrugged. 'The alternative might mean she stops seeing him, and then has to live knowing and regretting that she let the love of her life go.'

'But he might not be the love of her life.'

Alice sighed. 'We both saw how she was when she talked about him – how her whole face lit up.'

'She might find someone a lot more suitable who lights up her face,' Sophie said. 'Someone who everyone else will be happy to accept.'

'Emily can't live for other people,' Alice said. 'And it would be awful for her, looking back in years to come, and thinking that she let other people dictate how her life worked out.'

Emily came along the hallway now, and hearing the raised voices her stomach began to churn. She stopped in the doorway, just in time to hear what the biggest argument her two friends had ever had. Not even when they were all in school together had they clashed like this.

'I'm surprised at you, Alice,' Sophie said, her voice brittle. 'I'm surprised that you are actively encouraging Emily to keep up a romance with a foreign prisoner.'

'And I'm surprised at you, Sophie,' Alice retorted. 'I'm surprised that you can be so judging of Emily, just because she's fallen in love with somebody who doesn't come up to your standards. Someone you haven't even met.'

Emily walked into the room. 'Please stop,' she said, her voice wavering. 'Things are bad enough without this causing a horrible argument between my two best friends.' She went over to her chair and lifted her handbag. 'I've spoiled the night by telling you about Marco, and I wish now I had never mentioned it.' She looked at Sophie. 'I'm sorry this has happened – I know you went to a lot of trouble with the lovely food and drinks – but I think it would be best if I just go home now.'

'But Emily,' Alice said, 'we're your friends. We've always been able to talk about things before. Just give it time ... this will all sort itself out.'

'That's what I keep telling myself.' Tears started to trickle down Emily's face. 'I knew it wouldn't be easy for people to accept, but I never imagined that all this would happen tonight. I never imagined that telling you both would cause a rift in our friendship.' She turned towards the door.

Sophie suddenly moved. 'Don't go, Emily,' she said, 'please don't go ...' She looked from one to the other. 'Why don't we forget about it all just for tonight? Pretend we never mentioned it. As Alice said, maybe, given time, it will all sort itself out.'

Alice looked directly at her. 'How can we sit here with Emily all upset, and pretend that nothing has happened? When have we ever done that?' She lifted her bag now and stood up. 'Wait for me, Emily,' she said. 'I'm coming with you.'

Chapter Thirty-One

There was a stunned silence as Alice and Emily went towards the sitting room door.

Alice hated doing this to Sophie, but she knew that Sophie needed to think hard about what she had said to Emily. Only a jolt like this would make it happen.

'Why?' Sophie's eyes were wide and shocked. 'Why are you letting this Marco come between us? Doesn't our long friendship matter more?'

Alice looked back at her. 'It's not Marco who has come between us.'

'What do you mean?'

'Before, nothing would have come between us. You have changed the rules of our friendship, Sophie. You wanted Emily to find someone, but you've now made it clear that it has to be someone you approve of.' Alice was suddenly aware that her heart was racing, with this rare confrontation between the three good friends. And yet, uncomfortable as she was, she knew she had to stand her ground on Emily's behalf. 'She came here tonight thinking we would be the old friends she could open her heart to, the ones who would understand.'

'I did think you would understand,' Emily said. 'I knew you might point out the obvious problems to me, but I thought you would trust me to pick someone decent and good, in spite of his differences. I thought you would at least wait until you met Marco before making up your mind. Before saying all those things...'

Sophie's shoulders slumped. 'The last thing I want to do is hurt you.' She folded her arms and looked down at the patterned carpet.

Emily took a few steps back inside the room. 'I felt anxious coming here tonight,' she said, 'wondering how to explain it. I thought if I told you about Marco's music career first, and how distinguished he looked on the stage in his orchestra outfit, and how everyone reacted to his playing, that you would see him as you would have seen an English musician. And then when I told you about how brave he had been rushing into a house fire to help people he had never met, that it would let you see the kind individual he is.' She took a shuddering breath. 'There's no point in me saying anymore, I feel stupid now ... I don't even know why I'm explaining myself. I feel as though I'm talking to a total stranger who has already made up their mind, and nothing I can say or do will change it.'

'You know me,' Sophie said. 'You know I'm not like that ... please let's try to sort it.'

Alice could see that Sophie didn't want this dispute and found herself feeling sorry for her. She had got herself into a corner now, and only time would get her out of it again. Their friendship meant too much to allow this small crack to grow into something more. Something that might never be repaired.

She looked at Emily. 'Let's sit back down.'

Emily held her gaze for a few moments, and then she nodded. They both went back to their seats and Sophie came to sit beside them as before. 'I'm so sorry,' she said, looking at Emily. 'I really never meant to offend or hurt you.'

Alice felt it was too soon for the other two to go back to discussing Marco and decided everyone needed a change of conversation. She had been waiting for the right time to explain her situation to her friends, and the way things were going tonight, she reckoned she had nothing to lose. If she carried on, pretending all was well, she would be living a lie. That, Alice thought, was not what real friendship was about. 'Since we are staying a bit longer,' she said quietly, 'I thought I should also tell you more news about myself. Not about the baby – some not-so-good news that I have been keeping to myself.'

Sophie's brow creased. 'Is there something wrong?'

'Yes, there is something wrong.' Alice's throat suddenly felt dry, and she swallowed hard. 'I didn't want to tell you before because I didn't want to put a dampener on your wedding. Greg and I haven't been getting along too well.' Her heart was pounding again, but this time she felt an overwhelming sense of sadness. 'Well, that's putting it mildly.' She gave a small wry smile. 'The truth is that I discovered some time back that Greg had an affair.'

Sophie's hand came up to her mouth. 'Oh God, Alice...'

'I didn't tell anyone apart from Greg's mother – who already knew. But the night of the Bluebell, when you were asleep on the sofa, I broke down and told Emily. I told her because the woman he had an affair with was the singer in the bar.'

Sophie's eyes narrowed as she tried to think back. 'I was in a bad state that night, so I can barely remember,' she confessed. 'But I do remember there was a glamorous singer.'

'That was her.'

Sophie shook her head. 'I can't believe Greg would do such a thing...'

Alice nodded. 'Since then, he's tried to do everything he can to make it up to me,' she said, 'and I have done everything I can to forgive him, but it's been the hardest thing I have done in my life.'

Emily looked at her. 'At the wedding you said things were a bit better between you, so I thought you were OK again.'

'I wanted things to be better,' Alice said. 'I kept trying and trying to make myself believe things were better. When he came home on his last leave, I felt I had to do the right thing and be a wife to him in every way, even though my feelings towards him have changed. The result of that leave is that I'm pregnant, something I've dreamed of for a while – us starting a family – but that was before I discovered that he had been cheating on

298

me. I never imagined that when my dream came true, it would happen under these circumstances.'

'So, what will you do?' Emily asked.

Alice took a deep breath. 'Whether I like it or not, I'm having Greg's baby, and I've just got to get on with it. I am completely tied to him now.'

Sophie asked, 'If you hadn't got pregnant, what would you have done?'

'I would have waited until the war was over, and Greg was safely back. I would give him time to recover and reacclimatise to being home again, and then I would explain my feelings to him and say I think we should go our separate ways.' She shrugged. 'Of course, now I don't have any option, I have the baby to think about. The decision has been taken out of my hands and I have to make a go of things.'

'This must be awful for you, Alice,' Sophie said. 'And I'm grateful you didn't tell me before the wedding, I wouldn't have been able to stop thinking about it.'

Alice lowered her eyes. 'You had enough on your plate, and I wanted you to have a wonderful day – which you did.' She looked now at Emily. 'It's ironic that we're both in opposite positions. You feel pressurised by other people to walk away from somebody who might be the greatest love of your life, while I feel pressurised to stay with Greg, who sadly is not the greatest love of mine.'

Emily suddenly looked as though she could cry. 'Surely you loved him when you got married?'

'I did love Greg when we first got married,' Alice said, 'but I was young and didn't really know what to expect of life and marriage. As time went on, I felt things had faded a bit between us and that we seemed to drifting apart, but I just thought that was the way all marriages were. I could tell that Greg was bored at home and wanted to be out and about, and living a more exciting life. Probably the life of a single man. Of course, war intervened, and all the danger and drama that came with it gave him more than enough to be going on with. I was busy with school and the shop, and I remember thinking that as soon as everything was back to normal, if we could have a baby, it would give us something to focus on. That it would give Greg a reason to be at home more, to occupy his time and stop him from being so bored and restless. Then later, when I discovered he had been unfaithful to me, I realised any feelings I had for him were suddenly gone.'

Sophie's face was pale with shock. 'How did he react when you found out?'

'He has apologised over and over again,' Alice said. 'And I do believe he was sorry, and there was a definite improvement in him last time he was home.'

'In what way?' Emily asked.

'Well, he seemed more concerned about me, and he talked about how he felt bad about me giving up teaching to work in the shop. He said he didn't want me feeling trapped there and that when the war was over and things were settled, that he wants to get a manager for the shop so I can go back to school.'

'Maybe he's learned his lesson,' Sophie said. 'Maybe being away from you has made him realise how important you are to him, and now he wants to do everything to make things right.'

Alice gave a wry smile. 'Maybe.' She looked at them both. 'I'm sorry for having to tell you both such a depressing story.'

'No,' Sophie said, 'I'm glad you did because I would have had no idea what you were going through. In my head I would be picturing you content and settled in the shop.'

'I must be hopeless at understanding relationships,' Emily said, 'because recently I thought you seemed very happy.'

'I have been much happier lately,' Alice said, 'but it's nothing to do with Greg. Having Philip and Gabriela staying with me has changed everything. They have brought light and life to the house, especially after the shop closes in the evenings.'

'That's lovely to hear,' Emily said. 'I was worried it might be too much for you.'

Alice gave a small chuckle. 'Only months ago, I thought taking on a dog was too much, then Freddy appeared with little Bella and shortly afterwards the twins arrived. I had envisaged it being a real drudge – looking after two noisy children I didn't know – but it has turned out to be so different. Philip is quiet and studious and sensitive, and Gabriela is kind, funny and great at knitting and sewing little things for her dolls. They keep me busy at weekends, too, we go to the museums in Manchester or get the bus up to Lyme Park or Bramhall Park. We play board games and do things I've never had the inclination to do. I'm beginning to wonder how I will feel when it's time for them to go home.'

'I know Louis was relieved when you took the twins on,' Emily said. 'Those poor kids were going from pillar to post after the old lady who looked after them got sick. Louis said they have really settled with you, and it's lifted a great weight off his shoulders, and he has more time for himself now. He's thanked me several times for helping to find them a new place, but I didn't do anything very much. It was him that did all the work, putting notices up in shops and post offices. It was such a stroke of luck that he met you at the right time.'

Alice did not smile or show any familiarity at the mention of Louis's name. Some time ago she had decided that she would not tell Emily about their close friendship as she thought it would only complicate things. When she said that to Louis, he had been surprised that it was something that Alice had even considered, as he never discussed his personal life in school. It was different with female friends, especially old ones, Alice had told him, as they tended to share confidences more. But her relationship with Louis was complicated, and for a myriad of reasons, she knew she should tell no one. Although their relationship had never gone beyond a few tender kisses, it meant more to Alice than she could scarcely admit to herself. Those hours and minutes spent with him were too precious to risk losing. And, like the children, she knew that this time would inevitably come to an end.

'He's a nice man,' Alice said, 'and he and the children are still close. He's busy most nights, but if I need to go out and Maeve isn't available, he'll always do his best to help out. He's actually at the house with them tonight. When I left, he was doing sums with Gabriela, and Philip was patiently waiting for him to play a game of chess.'

Sophie looked at her. 'How will you manage if the twins are still there when the baby comes?'

'I haven't thought that far ahead. With the war, like everybody else, I'm just taking it a day at a time.'

There was a silence, then Sophie said, 'If you want to sit over at the table, I'll bring in the tea.'

Emily stood up. 'Do you want me to help you with anything?' she asked. Her face was still serious, but her voice was not as dry and formal as before.

Sophie looked at her, her eyes still anxious. 'I think everything is out apart from the tea,' she said. 'I'll just go down to the kitchen and get it now, but thanks for offering.'

When they were sitting at the table, Alice put her hand over Emily's. 'Are you OK?' she asked quietly. 'I know that was very difficult for you.'

'It was,' Emily said, 'but I'm glad it's not been the huge fallout tonight I thought it was going to be. I would have felt terrible walking out on Sophie. It's something I could never have imagined happening to all of us.'

'Well, it wasn't your fault.'

'I think I'm going to have to get used to this sort of reaction from people.'

'Not from everyone.' Alice squeezed her hand. 'If it's any help,' she said, 'I would love to meet Marco, and you're welcome to bring him for Sunday dinner any time, or to join us all for tea any evening.'

Emily's eyes widened. 'Really?'

'Of course. Next time you see him, ask when it suits and then you can ring me and let me know.'

Tears came into Emily's eyes, and she pressed the back of her hand to her mouth. 'You have no idea what that means to me...' She shook her head. 'I'll never forget you doing this.'

Alice thought she heard Sophie coming back and leaned across the table to Emily. 'Will you do me a favour?' she whispered. 'When we're going home later, you walk on down the driveway a little, and leave me on my own with Sophie for a few minutes?'

Emily nodded.

Later, after they'd had two cups of tea each, eaten all the lovely sandwiches and Mrs Wilson's carrot cakes, Alice said she would have to go home soon, and Emily said they would catch the bus together.

When Sophie was seeing them off at the door, Emily went first. She was diplomatic and thanked Sophie for having them, and then started off down the drive as planned.

As she came to the door, Alice stopped and looked directly at her friend. 'I'm glad the night turned out OK.'

'And so am I,' Sophie said. 'I'm very relieved.'

'The row with Emily tonight could have easily ruined our friendship.'

Sophie bit her lip. 'I didn't mean to upset her, I'm just really worried for her...'

'You have to let Emily decide for herself,' Alice said. 'If you were in this situation, I think you would do the very same. You would not have let anyone come between you and Tony.'

Sophie's face tightened. 'I know you're thinking about my mother before the wedding,' she said, 'but this is different.'

'It's not,' Alice said. 'Judging people without getting to know them or not giving them a chance is prejudice. It doesn't matter whether it's because of their background or what nationality they are. It's the same thing.'

'I don't see it like that, but I don't want to argue over it – I really don't.'

'It's best we leave it for tonight,' Alice said. 'Thanks again, and I'll see you soon.'

'Thank you,' Sophie said. 'I'm thrilled about the baby, and I really hope things work out for you and Greg.' She halted. 'Is it OK to tell Mum about the baby or is it still a secret?'

Alice smiled. 'It's fine,' she said. 'I'll have to tell my own family and Maeve soon anyway.'

'I won't say anything about you and Greg. When the baby comes, I'm sure that it'll all work out.'

'That's what I'm hoping. I always think a baby brings love and joy into most situations.'

'I'll start knitting for you,' Sophie said, a touch of excitement in her tone. 'Just yellow or white, so it will work for a boy or a girl.'

'That's kind of you,' Alice said. She turned now to catch up with Emily.

As Emily chattered on about the baby, Alice kept a smile pinned on her face, but inside, her mind was far away, going over the situation and how it would impact on her life. How suddenly things had changed, she thought. Having told the girls about the baby tonight had made it seem very real to her. She was just over three months now, and she could feel it was beginning to show. She couldn't keep it a secret for much longer. She would have to tell Louis very soon, and that meant that things would change. Alice knew it would undoubtedly mean the end of this special time in her life.

The thought of it brought a claustrophobic feeling from her chest up into her throat. Emily turned back to wave to Sophie, and Alice found herself fighting back the tears that had welled up in her eyes. Louis had brought so much to her life, he was almost like a part of her now. How she wondered, would she manage without him?

Chapter Thirty-Two

After several days of rain, the Sunday morning that Marco's choir was singing in church brought late September sunshine. Emily woke early and lay in bed, wondering whether she should chance wearing a floral summer dress or whether she would be safer with a costume and a blouse. She had washed her long hair last night and set it in curlers with some sugared water. When she had her bath this morning, she would carefully brush it out, hopefully leaving her hair in the fashionable loose curls. She would wear her half-hat if it looked hopeful that the rain had gone.

She picked up her latest *Vogue* magazine from her side-table and started reading a feature about how to put outfits together that bridged the gap between summer and autumn. The gist of it was to wear a light dress with a heavier jacket rather than a light cardigan. After she finished reading the article, she lay back in bed thinking about the dresses and suits she had which might combine as suggested. Her mind moved back to thinking about Marco and her family. She had asked her mother again last night if she would come to mass with her, as Father Dempsey had suggested.

'I'll see how I feel in the morning,' had been her mother's most promising reply.

Emily hadn't bothered to ask her father. He had never subscribed to being a Catholic, and only accompanied them for very special occasions such as weddings or funerals. Any choir-singing would hold no interest for him, far less a choir made up of Italian prisoners. She had thought of asking Alice to come to church with her for support but decided against it. She knew her friend would agree, but she thought her mother would find it odd as she knew Alice was not a Catholic. It was best, she concluded, to just go to mass on her own as normal, and maybe get the chance of having a few words with Marco afterwards. If Celia was there, that would be fine, since they had been to the concert together, even though it wasn't her usual church.

She heard her mother go into the bathroom and then afterwards go downstairs. Alice waited a few more minutes, then she put on her dressing gown and went down to check if the water would be hot enough for her bath. Her mother would probably be cooking breakfast for her father, as she often saved certain rationed foods for the weekends, like eggs or bacon and sausages. Emily would have to wait until after mass for breakfast, as she wasn't allowed even a sip of tea before receiving communion.

Her mother was at the cooker, with a lump of white lard melting in the pan, which signalled she was not coming to mass. Emily decided she would not mention church to her again. 'Is the water hot enough for a bath?'

'I put it on for you last night so it should be fine,' her mother said, unwrapping four pork sausages. She put two in the frying pan. 'I'm just doing breakfast for your father. I'm not having anything, as I thought I would come to mass with you this morning.'

Emily hid her surprise. 'It's a nice morning for walking down.'

'Father Dempsey was so good to us when we had the fire, so I thought I should make the effort. It would have been a lot worse if they hadn't come at that very time.'

'Well, at least you have a freshly painted kitchen out of it and nice new curtains,' Emily said, smiling, 'and thankfully nobody was hurt.' She went to the door.

'There are clean bath towels in the airing cupboard,' her mother said, 'and I ironed a few blouses for you last night.'

'Thanks,' Emily said, and went upstairs to get ready.

At half past ten Emily and her mother left the house, Emily wearing a pink floral dress with a wine-coloured jacket from one of her suits, and a matching half-hat. Her mother, she noticed, had made an effort, putting on a nice navy suit with a pale blue blouse, and a navy hat and bag. As they walked down, there was no more mention of Father Dempsey or the fact that it had been a long time since her mother had been in the church. They talked instead about Alice having a baby and how good she had been taking in the Guernsey children.

The church was beginning to fill up, and Emily motioned to her mother that they should move down towards the front where there were empty seats. It was only when they got down there that they noticed the signs taped to the end of the front two pews on either side, saying that they were reserved for the choir.

A picture of Marco flashed into Emily's mind, and she felt something turn inside her. Whilst part of her couldn't wait to see him again, she was torn about seeing him in this strange setting. She was anxious as to how she would view him with the other Italian prisoners. Seeing him with the orchestra had been an experience she could never have imagined, and it had shown him in the most illuminating light. The prospect of seeing him now, as one of a group of camp inmates – literally reduced to being a number – filled her with trepidation. All the more, knowing she had her mother by her side, who was oblivious to the fact that he was anything other than a foreigner who Father Dempsey had taken under his wing.

'We had better move further back,' Emily whispered. They turned around, and as they looked along the rows of pews behind, a lady who lived near them smiled and indicated that there was room for them beside her. The woman slid along the pew and Emily's mother moved in beside her while Emily took the place at the end. They both then put their handbags on the floor beside them and knelt down, taking out their rosary beads from their jacket pockets. They said a few silent prayers and then Emily sat back up on the pew and her mother followed a few minutes later.

More worshippers came in from the main door behind them, with the odd person appearing in the door on the left-hand side of the altar. This was mainly used by the men who voluntarily helped the priest, and who came in and out setting up the table with collection baskets and the vessels that contained the wine and oil for the offertory ritual, a main part of the mass.

As they sat in silence, facing the altar, it struck Emily that her mother appeared to have just fallen back into the usual routine of kneeling and praying, and she wondered if it was something so ingrained in her that she did it automatically or whether her earlier religious convictions had been restored.

More and more people came in, some squeezing in at the end of already full rows, whilst others wandered more randomly, looking for a decent space to sit comfortably. As each person came into her peripheral view, Alice tensed, thinking it might be the choir coming in. She pushed the sleeve of her wine jacket back to check her little gold watch and saw that it was almost five to eleven, which meant the priest would appear on the altar soon. She had just slid her sleeve back when the side door at the altar opened and a tall man in a British military uniform came in. He held the door open, and a few moments later a stream of men with tanned skin appeared, wearing black trousers with white shirts and black bowties. They came in silently, their arms down, one hand over the other, moving in procession towards their designated pew. When they reached the entrance to the pew, each one turned to face the altar and quickly genuflected, before moving in to take their seat.

Alice watched them with her heart in her mouth, searching for Marco. It occurred to her as she observed the choir's entrance that this smooth procedure had been well rehearsed and also that the men were comfortable in the familiar surroundings of the Catholic church. The door at the altar had been chosen, she realised, as it allowed them to come in with the least disruption, and without encountering other members of the congregation. It was also, she presumed, to avoid causing a spectacle by marching the men down the main aisle of the church.

She could tell that each man knew exactly where his place in the pew was, and how much space to allow for the next person to sit with reasonable comfort beside him. She watched intently as each one came in and was heartened that that they did not seem to be cowed or overly self-conscious about their status.

A little knot formed in her stomach as each man passed by, and there was still no sign of Marco. A few times she imagined she saw him, but it was another dark-haired Italian man of the same height and build or even a similar shape of head. The final man in the line came in and Emily sat back in her chair in shock and disappointment. Marco was not there.

And then suddenly, he appeared through the door in his pristine white shirt and bowtie, carrying his conductor's baton in one hand and a violin in the other. As she watched him walk to the end of the front pew, with a thumping heart, Emily wondered how she could possibly have thought any of the other men looked in the slightest bit like him. Marco, she thought – with his handsome, open face and friendly eyes – was uniquely Marco.

Her mother nudged her. 'Is that him? The fellow that was with Father Dempsey?'

Emily nodded. 'Yes,' she whispered back. There were several things she could have said to elaborate, but she decided again that the best policy was to say nothing.

There was a few more minutes' silence, during which the only sound was of the pews creaking and the footsteps of late worshippers, looking for any space in the pews that they might discreetly slip into. Several people came down towards the front only to turn – eyes cast downwards – and walk back up the aisle, to join the crowd gathered at the back of the church, who would have to remain standing throughout the service.

Emily checked her watch again to see the hands just on eleven o'clock. When she lifted her head, it was to see Marco come out of his seat carrying his baton. Her heart quickening again, she watched intently as he went to stand with his back to the altar, positioned several feet away from the first row, so he could be seen clearly by the members of the choir.

He straightened his back and then he gestured with his hands and all the men stood up, shoulders back and hands crossed in front of them. Father Dempsey, followed by four altar boys, emerged from the sacristy through a door on the left-hand side at the back of the altar. On seeing him, the congregation automatically got to their feet. Simultaneously, the organ up in the gallery filled the church with the introductory chords of 'Hail Queen of Heaven'. Marco lifted his arms and the choir started to sing in low, clear voices:

> Hail, Queen of Heaven, the ocean Star,
> Guide of the wanderer here below,
> Thrown on life's surge, we claim thy care:
> Save us from peril and from woe.
> Mother of Christ, star of the sea,
> Pray for the wanderer, pray for me.

As the choir sang, the priest and his little entourage performed the opening mass ritual of bowing in front of the altar, and then the congregation sat back down again as Father Dempsey went to his chair at the side.

As they moved on to the second verse, Emily thought she had never seen the congregation pay such rapt attention before. Everyone around her was sitting up straight in their seats, eyes glued to the choir, particularly the only man who was actually facing them, the conductor.

As she watched Marco, she could see his full attention was given to the other men, apart from occasional upward glances towards the organ in the gallery. Everything was operated with such meticulous timing that Alice could only assume the choir and the organist had obviously rehearsed the whole proceedings here in the church. There were now so many things that Emily wanted to ask Marco about the musical side of his life, and about his day-to-day life in the camp, and about his work in the shop.

Seeing him with the other smartly dressed men – some of them handsome, too, but none, she thought, as handsome as Marco – made her wonder about them as well. She looked at the backs of the dark heads and thought about their lives before the war, about their families back in Italy and what they might have worked at before they were conscripted to fight for their country.

The hymn came to an end and the choir, including Marco, all sat down in their places. Father Dempsey got up from his chair and as he went back towards the altar, he gave the men a small bow and mouthed 'Thank you' to them. He then walked to the front of the altar to begin the mass, conducted, as usual, in Latin.

Most Sundays Emily went through the routine of the service listening and responding where appropriate, and then at other times sinking into a reverie of her own thoughts. The rituals, so ingrained since she was a young child, meant that she found herself answering the priest with automatic responses or standing up and sitting down at the required times, with little awareness of doing so. This had happened each Sunday since she had met Marco again at the town hall, as he filled every little gap in her thoughts.

When the time approached for the priest to distribute Holy Communion, Emily felt her heart skip a beat as she saw Marco move out of his seat, this time carrying his violin. He genuflected as he passed the altar and went over to the end of the first pew on the left-hand side, where the choir had entered. His position was almost hidden, and well away from the aisle, where the people receiving communion would be coming down to kneel at the altar.

The organ started first and just as Emily was trying to work out which hymn it was, the violin came in with the unmistakeable, haunting strain of 'Panis Angelicus'. She caught her breath at the sound. She had only heard this hymn performed by a

311

choir or a solo singer, and had always loved it, but hearing the voice replaced by a violin was very different and more beautiful than anything she could have imagined. She looked down at Marco, almost hidden from view, the violin under his chin and his eyes closed in pure concentration as the bow moved up and down the strings.

As she watched him, a little catch came to her throat, and she suddenly felt she might cry. She took a gulp of air to steady herself before her mother noticed. She sat back in the pew, and as she did so, she noticed her mother lifting her handbag and discreetly opening it to retrieve a handkerchief from inside. She then saw her mother dab the hanky to her eyes, and Emily wondered what had caused the tears. Jack, she guessed. When he came into her thoughts, tears were never far behind. Emily kept her gaze fixed towards the front.

She watched now as Father Dempsey motioned to the rows of Italian men to come to the altar first. Emily glanced around and could see all the eyes around her transfixed on the dark-haired men in their sober black and white attire, who followed each other in a fluid movement towards the altar rails, to then kneel with their heads bent respectfully, and their hands joined in prayer. It was all done so naturally, she thought, that there could be no doubt in the local worshippers' minds that these men – like themselves – had grown up in families who lived by the same commandments preached by the church in every country. Following those same religious guidelines in their daily lives meant they had more in common with the Catholic Italian prisoners than some of their own neighbours and friends.

Marco's violin music, and the organ above, continued to fill the church as the men went back to their seats and people came out from the other pews to the aisle to join the queue for communion. Only weeks ago, Emily could never have imagined that her life would be so changed by their chance encounter in Barlow's shop. Before she realised any of his accomplishments, Marco had initially drawn her in with his open, friendly manner. And of course, there had undoubtedly been his Latin good looks.

Back then, she had only judged him superficially, and had decided that their differences were so great that nothing could possibly bridge the gap. She was a teacher, and although she knew there were other women who had attained higher qualifications in other fields, it was still a highly respected profession and, to most people, counted for something.

As she watched him now, playing the ending to the hymn, a thought suddenly occurred to her. Could someone so talented and cultured, she now wondered, really be interested in someone so ordinary as herself? There was nothing remarkable about her, and she was sure he would easily attract a more artistic, intelligent and studious girl. She wondered now whether if Marco wasn't in the vulnerable position of being in a prisoner of war camp, would he have even looked at her?

A little chill of realisation ran through her. Emily wasn't sure.

She saw Marco lay his violin down on a small table that had been left for the purpose, and then walk to the end of the altar nearest the door. As soon as there was a space between the worshippers, he knelt and waited until the priest reached him. After he received the white host, he then went back to where he had played and knelt again on the church floor, head bent and hands joined in prayer.

After a few minutes, he stood up once more and lifted his violin. The organ struck up, and Emily felt a lump in her throat as he began to play 'Ave Maria'. When it was time for their pew to go down the aisle for communion, Emily went out and then politely stepped aside to let her mother join the queue before her. She was so distracted by Marco that it was only as they were nearing the altar that it dawned on her that her mother was taking part in the whole mass by receiving the Eucharist. It had crossed Emily's mind this morning that she might avoid Communion – the core and most important part of the mass – if she had only come to hear the choir and to please the priest. People didn't go to communion for various reasons – having inadvertently broken their abstinence, feeling too ill to abstain from food or drink, or if they had committed some sin that made them feel unworthy until they had been to confession and received absolution. The fact that her mother seemed to be fully participating in the mass signalled to Emily that some sort of change had taken place.

When they reached the pews in front of the altar, Emily gave a sidelong glance to where Marco was playing. His eyes were closed in total concentration again as he played, so she moved her gaze to the altar, ready to take her place kneeling. She had a few moments waiting, during which she could not help but look over at him again, and this time his eyes were open, and he was looking directly at her. He made only the slightest movement to raise his eyebrows and smile, but it was without any embarrassment, and it let her know that he had seen her, and that he was happy she was there.

That small, silent link between them made her heart soar. It told her that whatever it was he saw in her mattered very much to him, and she was instantly reassured that their feelings were both on the same level. It struck her as she turned her gaze away from him that her mother was directly in front of her, and she wondered if she had seen Marco looking over at her.

She moved forward now to the altar, trying to conceal the relieved smile that had spread across her face. She lifted her skirt slightly as she went down on her knees and then she laid her elbows on the marble altar and clasped her hands. With her eyes directed at the cross hanging above the tabernacle, she said a voiceless prayer, asking Jesus to help her find a way to make people accept her choice and allow her and Marco to be together like a normal, courting couple. She was not asking for anything serious to happen – such as them being married or anything drastic like that – just to give them enough time and room to get to know each other. She closed her eyes, and then various images began to creep into her mind – her mother and father's angry faces as they talked about the Italians in the camp, then memories of the night at Sophie's house, making her chest and throat tighten.

She heard someone clear their throat and when she opened her eyes, Father Dempsey was standing in front of her, holding the white circle of holy bread in his hand. A flush came over her face and she quickly opened her mouth to receive it, and then blessed herself and turned to follow her mother back to her seat.

The rest of the mass passed, along with two more hymns sung by the full choir, which again held the church congregation in full, rapt attention. Father Dempsey came to the front of the altar to give his final, Latin blessing, and as he finished, he held his hand aloft to signal that he had something of importance to impart to his flock before they dispersed. Usually, it was to share news of a church fete or sale of work to raise funds for the maintenance of the church roof, or it could be to say that tickets were going on sale for a forthcoming dance in the parochial hall. On this occasion, the subject was the Italian choir.

The priest started with an unusual request in church – the sort that the more traditional priests would say was more suited to a concert hall – by asking everyone to give a clap to the choir for their singing, and to the church organist and Marco Benetti for their solo performance. His request was followed by an unusual ripple of conversation, which was rarely heard in church, accompanied by clapping from a reasonable portion of the congregation.

'It was a rare pleasure to hear such a professional performance here in church,' he intoned, 'and I just wanted to give a quick acknowledgement to all the men here present from the Mellands Camp, which I am sure most of you have heard of. The men are all – like us – devoted Catholics, who have grown up in the same faith in Italy. I am not going to talk about the war and the rights and wrongs of the different countries, I am just going to say that Italy is no longer regarded as our enemy.' He paused. 'This means that the men are allowed a little more leeway to mix with the local people, and I would ask you all to do your best to welcome them into our church and community – at the very least, to be civil to them.'

He then turned back to the choir, and said to them, 'Thank you again, gentlemen, for your excellent performance.'

As the people stood up to leave, there was a rumbling of conversation and Emily guessed that not all of it was positive. She looked to the choir again to see where Marco was, but the men were now gathered in a circle around Father Dempsey, who was talking to them, and it was hard to pick one identically dressed man from another.

Emily gave a small sigh and leaned forward to pick up her handbag at the same time as her mother reached for hers.

'It's hard to know what to make of it all,' her mother said quietly. 'The priest seems to think they are decent enough...'

'The music was lovely,' Emily replied, 'and the singing.'

'They're certainly talented, there's no doubt about that.'

They walked up the aisle now towards the main door, and as they did, several people acknowledged or spoke to them, and no one referred to the fact that they had not seen Mrs Browne at mass for a very long time. Emily thought her mother seemed to be the same as she would have been on any Sunday before she stopped attending, but wondered how she actually felt inside on her first attendance in such a long time. As the crowd moved slowly out of the church, Emily was tempted on several occasions to look back, but she fought the urge as she knew people, including her mother, would notice her interest in the choir.

When they got outside into the fresh air, she felt a pang of disappointment as she knew it was unlikely now that she would get to see Marco before they went home. She knew she couldn't speak to him properly in such a public place, but it would have been nice to see him one more time, even from a distance.

As they approached the church gates, Emily heard her name being called, and there was Celia coming towards her. She introduced her teaching colleague to her mother.

'I just wanted to say I'm so glad I came to hear Marco again. He is absolutely brilliant, isn't he?' She looked at Emily's mother. 'Did you enjoy it, Mrs Browne?'

'It was lovely,' she said.

'If we had music like that at mass every Sunday, the church

would be overflowing, wouldn't it?' Celia touched Emily's arm. 'If you are speaking to Marco or Father Dempsey, do say I came to church and how much I enjoyed it.'

'I will,' Emily promised.

As they walked along, her mother asked quietly, 'What are we going to do? We still have the shirt at home for that man . . .'

Emily suddenly felt a flatness descend on her at the thought of how even the most basic gesture was now deemed to be a big problem. 'We can give it to Father Dempsey,' she replied.

Then, as though saying his name had somehow conjured him up, they both looked up to see the priest striding towards them. 'Emily, Mrs Browne,' he said, breathless from rushing. 'Have you both got a minute?'

Emily looked at her mother and nodded. 'Yes,' she said.

He looked directly at her mother. 'The young man who helped you the night of the fire – our wonderful violin player – recognised you in the church, and he was asking how you and Tom were afterwards.' He indicated to the church. 'He's there at the back of the church now, and I thought you might like to have a quick word with him before you go . . .'

Emily looked at her mother and shrugged as though to say 'Why not?'

Before her mother got a chance to reply, a smartly dressed man with glasses, who they knew to be a solicitor in Stockport, touched Father Dempsey on the sleeve. 'I hope you don't mind me interrupting . . .' He tipped his hat at Emily and her mother in acknowledgement. 'I just had to say that this morning was wonderful, Father,' he said, 'the most uplifting thing I've heard in church in a long time. The choir, and especially the musician, were top class.'

The priest beamed at him. 'Ah, thank you, Eric,' he said. 'It's good to hear they got a positive reception.'

'I heard the violinist at a concert in Stockport Town Hall,' he said, 'but he was playing the piano that night. I couldn't believe he was there this morning leading the choir and then playing on the violin.' He shook his head. 'That rendition of "Panis

Angelicus" was nothing short of amazing. What a talented young man. I would love to shake his hand.'

Father Dempsey's face lit up, and he stepped back in a little movement that was something akin to a bow. 'Come on then,' he said, 'Marco is just inside the church. We were heading back to him now. He will be delighted to hear your glowing opinion of the choir.'

Emily looked at her mother, her heart racing. She wanted to be there to hear all the praise that she knew the man would shower on Marco. She wanted her mother to hear it, and more than anything, she wanted to be there with Marco to see his reaction. 'Shall we go in?'

'I suppose so,' her mother said, looking flustered. 'It would look very bad now if we didn't.'

They followed the others through the main doors and in through the porch to the second doors, which led to the main body of the church. When the doors were opened Emily could hear the sound of animated talk, and as she and her mother went in, there was Marco standing between the priest and the other man, smiling and nodding. As he spoke, his eyes moved just a fraction in Emily's direction; again, not enough for anyone else to notice but enough to let her know that he had seen her.

She heard voices and looked behind them to see the other men from the choir sitting in a relaxed, easy manner on the pews at the front, talking between themselves.

'We have very good Italian friends in Manchester,' she heard the solicitor say, 'and we're looking forward to seeing them again when this war is finally over.' They spoke a short while longer, and then the man shook Marco's hand and excused himself to everyone else. 'I'll just go down and have a few words with the other chaps in the choir before I head for home.'

Father Dempsey turned towards Emily's mother. 'Now, Hannah,' he said. 'As I told you, Marco was asking after you, and I thought it would be nice for you to have a few words with him in person.'

Emily looked at her mother and she saw the frozen look

on her face and her heart plummeted. Then, just as she felt an embarrassed heat rise to her face, Marco stepped forward with his hand out.

'Hello, Mrs Browne,' he said, 'it is very nice to see you again.' He held his hand towards her.

Emily saw he was smiling but she could see there was a careful look in his eye.

Her mother hesitated and then she reached her hand out to meet his.

'I am glad to see you are well,' Marco said, shaking her hand, 'and I hope your husband, he is well, too?'

'He is,' she said.

Alice watched as her mother withdrew her hand, and for a few moments she seemed to study him. Then, she lifted her head a fraction higher. 'I wanted to say thank you for everything that you did the night we had the fire. I was in bed asleep, and when Emily brought me down, I wasn't too sure what was happening. I know that you and Father Dempsey helped to sort it all out, and I'm very grateful.'

Marco's hands came up in a little waving action. 'I was very happy to help.'

'You're a wonderful musician,' she said, 'and it did my heart good to listen to you.' She gestured towards the choir. 'The other lads were great, too. They're all brilliant singers.'

'Thank you, Mrs Browne,' he said, beaming at her. 'I will explain your good wishes to them. They will be very happy.'

'We got the new shirt for you,' she said. 'It's back at the house.'

Marco shook his head. 'No need for shirt,' he said. He gave a little tug at the collar of the shirt he was wearing. 'I am OK.'

'Well, another white shirt will never go wrong,' she said, suddenly smiling at him. She narrowed her eyes. 'Would you be able to come to our house for dinner next Sunday? You could take the shirt home with you afterwards.'

Emily felt the blood rush to her face on hearing her mother's unexpected invitation. She turned her head away so she would not have to look at Marco or the priest, in case it would appear to them that she had somehow engineered this.

'Yes,' Marco said, 'that is very kind. I would very much like to come.'

'Three o'clock then,' her mother said. 'You already know where the house is.'

Chapter Thirty-Three

Alice knew on Monday morning that she was going to have to tell Louis about the baby the next time she saw him. She had awoken at six o'clock feeling nauseous and generally uncomfortable. The queasy feelings she had been having for a few weeks had gradually built up until the episodes were now leaving her on the verge of actually vomiting. She went downstairs and after having half a cup of tea and a few bites of toast, she had to rush up to the bathroom when she suddenly felt she was going to be sick. She brought very little up, but the sound of her retching woke Gabriela, who then rushed from her bedroom to the bathroom door to check she was OK.

She reassured Gabriela she was fine, that something must have upset her stomach, and told her to go back to bed for a little longer. She then went into her own bedroom and lay down until the feeling passed. She had felt queasy the night before when they had tea with Louis, but it wasn't so bad, and she had been able to cover it up, although she knew she couldn't go on concealing this more intense sickness.

She had imagined that it would go after three or four months, but the doctor had said that it was only in the majority of cases. In others, it could last longer and with certain women, the sickness could continue for the whole pregnancy. Alice had been startled by the news, and just kept hoping that every day it would get better and suddenly cease altogether.

Another factor that had decided her about telling Louis was that she had noticed Maeve giving her concerned glances when, on two occasions, she had to leave customers to rush to the toilet. She had made excuses, but she knew that her assistant wasn't stupid and would soon put two and two together when she started to show any further signs of her pregnancy. So far, her condition had caused her to lose her appetite and therefore lose weight, as Sophie and Emily had noticed on their last night together. Even so, Alice had realised that there was a definite swell to her stomach that had not been there before, which would only grow bigger with each coming week.

It was after the twins had gone to bed that Alice went to the cupboard and took out a bottle of brandy. She poured a small measure in a glass for her and a much larger measure for Louis. The doctor had suggested that a small brandy at night might help her to sleep, along with the odd glass of Guinness during the day to keep up her iron levels. She topped both brandy glasses up with dry ginger. Louis was like her, he could take or leave alcohol, but enjoyed a glass of wine with special meals and on other occasions would politely drink whatever was on offer. Tonight, Alice decided, was not an event to celebrate, but she thought they would both need something a little more comforting than the tea they usually had.

He had been coming to the house more often recently, as his Home Guard duties had been winding down and were expected to officially end very soon. The news that came in about the war in Europe was encouraging, and there was less need for the army back at home. Rationing was still as strict as ever, but fewer people carried gas masks and there was a general air of things returning to normal. This was the 'end in sight' that many people had prayed for, but it would bring about some unwelcome changes for others, and Alice now realised she was one of them.

She had hoped to postpone the end of her relationship with Louis for as long as possible. When she looked back, it had only been a few months, but they had spent a lot of time quietly talking together and getting to know one another. She now felt she knew Louis better than Greg. Better than anyone else she knew. She felt as if she had known him forever.

She was not surprised when Louis looked at the glass of brandy she had just given him, and quietly asked, 'What is it?'

Alice sat down in the chair opposite the sofa where he was sitting. 'I need to tell you something.' She took the tiniest sip of her brandy, which made her throat immediately constrict. She heaved a little breath and then set the glass back down on the coffee table between them. So much for the medicinal quality of brandy, she thought, because she could immediately feel her body rejecting it.

'I've just discovered that I'm pregnant.'

There was a stunned silence – louder than she had expected. He looked at her for a long time with narrowed, serious eyes. Then, without even taking a sip from it, he put his glass on the table.

'I know this changes everything for us,' she said, 'and it's the last thing I expected.' She stopped to pick the right words. 'It was on Greg's last leave ... the weekend of my friend's wedding.' She shrugged. 'It was before you and I got to know each other.'

Louis slowly nodded his head, as though still trying to digest what she had said. His hand came to his mouth, and he looked as though he was going to speak, and then it fell back down again.

'I guessed I was, but I only had it confirmed last week,' she told him, 'and whilst I have hoped for a baby for some time, I never imagined that it would happen now. I should have done, because when Greg was home, I was trying to be a proper wife to him and ...' her voice faltered, 'and that includes marital relations.'

'Of course,' he said. 'You are, after all, husband and wife, and we knew that from the beginning.' He gave a little shrug. 'It's the reason that you and I have kept things on a friendship basis, and I have always understood that.' He lifted his glass now and took a long drink.

Alice looked at him. 'I need you to know something important,

Louis,' she said. 'If I had not become pregnant, I had planned to separate from Greg.'

Louis's eyes met hers, level and clear, but he said nothing.

'I was going to wait until he came home, then I was going to tell him. I was not going to do it immediately; I was going to give him time to settle back home and recover properly from all he had gone through during the war. But I had made up my mind, I was definitely going to separate from him.' She took a deep breath. 'Having met you, and realising that there can be a different – and a much better – type of relationship, I know that staying with Greg is settling for second best.' Her voice dropped. 'Do you understand that?'

'Yes, I do,' he said, 'because I feel exactly the same. No one I met before you comes even close to those feelings, and I just know that there won't be anyone like you in the future.'

They stared at each other for what seemed a very long time. The feeling of loss was so painful that Alice had to bow her head and look away from him.

'It seems life has played a trick on us,' Louis said, his voice choked. 'Letting us find each other, and then, when we might have negotiated a way through this – however difficult or long – suddenly putting this huge obstacle between us.'

Alice could hardly speak. 'I have wanted a baby very much,' she said, tears in her eyes. 'Before we met, I prayed for it – and now my prayers have been answered. The price I have to pay for it is to stay with Greg. I have to try and make my marriage work for the sake of the baby.'

'What,' Louis said, 'if there was another option?'

'There is no other option, Louis. I have to do the right and decent thing. Greg is abroad and is still in danger every day. Whatever has happened between me and him in the past, I have to put it behind me now. I know the war has turned life upside down, put people in situations they never imagined.' Alice looked at him through lowered eyes, unable to meet his gaze directly. 'I never imagined being in this situation with you, and I don't regret a moment of the time we've spent together – but the baby changes everything. When Greg comes back, I have to at least give things a go. I have to stay with my husband and the father of my child.'

He slowly nodded. 'I understand. I guess I always knew this time would come, one way or another.'

'We can still be friends,' she said, hearing a hollow note in her own voice. 'It doesn't change anything with the twins or ...'

'But things must change between us.' Louis finished his drink then he stood up. 'It's best if I go now.' There was deep resignation in his voice. 'I don't think I should come here anymore. It would be too hard, knowing there is absolutely no hope of a future for us.'

'But we knew that,' Alice said sadly. 'That's why our relationship stayed so ... well, so innocent. We always avoided talking about it because I think we were hoping that something would happen. Some kind of miracle that would change the fact that I'm married and you have another life in Guernsey. A life you have to go back to when the war finally ends.'

Alice watched him now as he lifted his jacket from the back of the chair and put it on. He turned and looked at her and their eyes locked. There was nothing more to say, so they just stared at each other in silence for a few long moments. Then he turned away, going out into the hall towards the back door.

Alice stood there, frozen by her duty to do the right thing, listening until she heard the back door close behind him.

When she knew he had gone out into the darkness, she went back to sit at the table, slightly stumbling as she moved into the chair. She sat with her head in her hands, tears trickling down her face. At some point she felt something touch her leg, and when she looked down, Bella was there, staring up at her with anxious eyes. She bent down and lifted the little dog up, cradling her, tears falling on the warm white fur.

Chapter Thirty-Four

'Have you anything not in a brown envelope?' Dorothy asked as her housekeeper came into the sitting room with the post.

It was a Friday morning and she had taken the day off. She had woken several times during the night, aware of a familiar ache in the centre of her forehead which came down into her face. She rarely got headaches, but when she did, it usually went straight to her sinuses and left her feeling foggy and tired.

When she heard Sophie coming out of the bathroom, she called out to her, and said she was taking the day off as her sinuses had flared up, and she didn't feel up to going into work. Things were quiet in the factory now, the quietest they had ever been, and there was nothing that Sophie and the manager could not handle without her. The biggest task was sorting the wages, and that would be easily done.

'One white envelope,' Mrs Wilson said, giving a wry smile. She handed over three business envelopes and a long white one. 'I've stripped Sophie's bed and put the washing on. I'm going to go back upstairs and put the fresh linen on her bed now. You'll know where I am if you need me.'

Dorothy thanked her then set her coffee cup down on the table, and put the three brown envelopes down beside it. She cast a casual glance at the writing on the front of the white one and turned it over to open it. Then something stopped her in her tracks, and she flipped it back over again to study it further. She looked at the London postmark. A cold shiver ran through her.

'Surely not...' she whispered to herself. Shaking now, she ran her nail along the top of the envelope, then slid the letter out. She opened the page of white paper and her eyes moved straight to the signature at the bottom. 'Dear God.'

How could this happen now? When she and Sophie had made some kind of peace between themselves, how could this happen? She had hoped for a decent length of time to work this out. To find the right way to approach it with her. She looked at the clock. It was half past eleven. She went over to the phone and dialled Frances's number. After a few rings her friend picked it up.

'Frances?' Dorothy said. 'Have you a few minutes to talk?'

'Is there something wrong?'

'I've just received a letter from London – from the last person I want to hear from, especially now.'

'Do you mean...'

'From David – Sophie's real father.'

'Oh God,' Frances said. 'What are you going to do?'

'I had hoped to let things settle down with Sophie.' She paused. 'I had hoped that I might get Tony on side, to have him there to comfort her and reason with her, but since hearing of his plans for the factory and the whole Shaw family, there's little point in that...' She took a deep breath. 'I can't protect Sophie from this now. David seems determined to make himself known as soon as it can be arranged.'

'Is there anything I can do to help? I know this is really important to you.'

'You have been such a great support, but I have to do this on my own.'

'Ring me anytime, and if you want me to be with you when you speak to Sophie, you only have to ask. I could even wait in the Grosvenor, to be there afterwards.'

'I don't know what I've done to deserve such a good and loyal friend...'

'Nonsense,' Frances said. 'Don't forget the times I have cried on the phone to you with my problems. We all need a sympathetic ear.'

'Thanks again,' Dorothy said. She hung up, wishing something – anything – could make her feel better. Her past mistakes were all suddenly catching up with her, and the only person who could have shielded her from this current, much worse, situation was George. How she wished he had let her tackle this with Sophie years ago, but as always, he had held back. He had always wanted to wait until Sophie was older and to choose the perfect time.

Dorothy gave a deep, shuddering sigh. The perfect time had never come. Instead, the patient, guarded George had suddenly died. He had gone, leaving her to deal with the increasingly impatient David, all on her own.

But that was not all she had to deal with. As she opened each of the brown envelopes, Dorothy could see another problem that was demanding decisions. One that had been emerging for some time – in fact, it had started just before George died, and she knew had given him considerable worry. The factory was no longer operating at the same level as before. The military hat and cap orders had shrunk as bigger factories undercut their prices, recently growing even more aggressive. In recent months Morley's salespeople had heard rumours that plans were afoot to disband the Home Guard soon, and this was one of their major outlets. The news had also filtered through that many military units had stockpiled uniforms and military accessories like hats, belts and bags, and were placing no more orders until these had been used up.

All in all, Dorothy thought, it painted a dismal picture for the future of the factory, and, in a recent meeting with her manager, they had discussed having to let some of the staff go. It was something she was going to have to discuss with Sophie soon, but until now she had been hopeful that things would improve. The latest blow, of the Home Guard disbanding, drove home the point that the factory had become solely dependent on the need for military uniforms. With the possibility of war ending in the foreseeable future, Morley's main source of income was likely to dry up in the next financial year.

Dorothy suddenly felt an ache in her head again, and she closed her eyes. She moved her hand to the ridge at the top of her nose and pressed her fingers firmly on it. Codeine, she thought, was the only thing that would help. She had taken a couple of aspirins that morning, which helped a bit, but the codeine was stronger, and although it made her tired, it would completely shift it for a while.

She met Edna Wilson on the stairs and told her the headache was worse, and that she was going to take some painkillers and lie down for an hour.

'I'm finished upstairs anyway,' Mrs Wilson said, 'so I won't be making any noise to disturb you. Do you want me to make you a hot lemon with honey and bring it up?'

'No, thanks,' Dorothy said. 'I think a couple of tablets and a lie down is the only thing that will work.'

After taking the medication, she lay back on the bed, staring up at the ceiling. Thoughts about the factory intermingled with those about the letter. A feeling of dread suddenly came over her. Something was going to happen, she thought. Something was going to change, but she had no idea what. She had not had this feeling so intensely since she discovered she was pregnant with Sophie and entirely on her own, not knowing where she would go or how she would live.

She had felt it again when George died, but not to the same extent. She had been devastated at his loss, and while she still missed him every single day, she knew she had Sophie and their lovely home, and she had the security and routine of the factory.

Two major things had hit her today, and both were going to force changes on her that she did not want. She didn't want to think about them anymore. Dorothy felt a small wave of tiredness from the codeine, and was grateful as she drifted away from the ache in her head and the bigger ache in her heart.

Sophie walked towards the house, a lightness in her step as she thought about seeing Tony that night. He had phoned the office to tell her that he had received an emergency call to go out to an air base just outside Manchester, as there was a problem with their telephone lines.

'How long?' Sophie asked excitedly. 'Can you stay the weekend?'

'Yes,' Tony confirmed. 'I can stretch it out until Monday morning, but I'll have to leave on the first train back to London.'

She had managed to get away after lunch, using her mother as an excuse. It was partly true, as she was concerned that her mother had taken the day off because she wasn't feeling well. When she looked in on her mother's room that morning, she had a little jolt when she saw that Dorothy hadn't looked at all like her normal self. Although relations were still strained between them, Sophie was surprised at how concerned she had felt at the thought of anything being wrong with her mother. She knew she was a strong, healthy woman, but she had felt concerned when she saw her drawn, red-tinged face and her heavy eyes.

Sophie let herself into the house, and as she went down the hallway, she glanced into the sitting room and the dining room, and then she went straight on down to the kitchen where she found Edna Wilson.

'She's been up in bed for a while now,' the housekeeper said.

'Do you think she's awake?' Sophie asked. 'I don't want to go upstairs and disturb her if she's asleep.'

'I heard the phone ring a few minutes ago, and then it stopped, so I think she might have picked the one up in the bedroom.' She shrugged. 'Either that, or they hung up quick.'

Sophie nodded. 'I'll go and check.' As she walked towards the door, she suddenly turned around. 'I got a surprise phone call,' she said, smiling. 'Tony is coming up to Manchester tonight. He's staying the weekend.'

'Ah, that's lovely,' the housekeeper said. 'And I've just changed your bed this morning, so it will be lovely and fresh for you.'

A pink tinge came to Sophie's cheeks at the mention of her and Tony sharing a bed. 'Thanks, Mrs Wilson,' she said, suddenly brighter again at the thought of seeing him.

She went back along the hallway, stopping to take off her

cream, woollen coat and hang it up on the stand at the front door. She then kicked off her black stilettos and left them at the bottom of the stairs before tiptoeing up in her stocking feet.

As she neared the top of the stairs, she hesitated when she heard her mother's voice. She wondered if she should go back downstairs now, or whether she should go into her bedroom to sort out what outfit she would wear for Tony's arrival. She decided to go back downstairs and have a cup of tea, then come back when her mother had finished her call. She had just turned around when she heard a sound that stopped her. Her brow furrowed as she listened for a few moments, then was startled when she realised that it was the sound of her mother crying.

She stood still, not quite knowing what to do. Her mother rarely cried, and when she did, it was in a quiet and controlled way. The only times she had seen her mother absolutely distraught, and on the point of collapse, had been at the hospital when her father died and then at his funeral. She couldn't imagine what had brought her mother to such a state of upset today.

She froze when she heard her mother speaking again. She couldn't quite hear so she silently moved up a few more steps – just to check she was OK.

'She will never forgive me, Frances,' her mother said. 'Sophie will never forgive me for not telling her the whole truth.' There was another sob. 'And she will never believe me that it was all George's decision. The number of times I suggested that we tell her, and then each time he would find a reason not to. I practically begged him to tell her when she was sixteen and then again when she was eighteen, but he kept finding excuses. It was so difficult to be angry with him because he was so easy-going and would do almost anything he could to please me – apart from this. He simply did not want her to know who her real father is.' Her voice cracked again. 'What could I do? When I told Sophie that we always planned to explain things to her, it was the absolute truth. I love her with all my heart, but I loved

George, too – and I felt that I had to abide by his decision not to tell her.'

There was a silence during which Sophie gathered that Frances was speaking, and then her mother started again. 'I've been afraid to bring the subject up again since the wedding,' she said. 'I'm afraid of everything... afraid that if I tell Sophie about the letter, she will turn her back on me forever.'

Sophie's mouth opened in shock. She had never heard her mother so upset and so vulnerable. She always seemed supremely self-confident. Vulnerable was a word she would never have applied to her mother before.

Dorothy started to cry again, then there was another silence after which she cleared her throat. 'No, I didn't tell her what we overheard Mrs Shaw saying at the wedding. I would not risk upsetting her again. Even though her best friend, Alice, heard it and can vouch for every word that was said, I'm still too afraid to say anything. Besides, I wouldn't want to drag poor Alice into our problems.'

Sophie couldn't imagine what her mother was referring to. And why had Alice decided to keep something from her?

'Sophie is very happy with Tony's family, and I am not going to interfere. I have enough difficulties that I am actually responsible for, without raising other issues that will be seen as criticism. I've decided that from now on what Sophie and Tony decide to do is none of my business.' There was another pause. 'No, I'm afraid that Sophie won't value my opinion at all. Everything I do and say is an irritation to her. I'm sure she is counting every day until Tony comes home for good, so they can buy their own place and get as far away from me as possible.'

Sophie closed her eyes as her mother started crying again – a softer, more muted weeping now.

'No, no...' Dorothy said, beginning to speak again, 'please don't think for one minute that you are interfering, Frances. I am grateful to you for taking the time to ring and check how I am. It's nice to know someone cares... I've missed that so much since George has gone. And yes, I count myself lucky I had such a kind, caring man – but I do miss him.' Another little pause. 'You're right, I'm still not feeling too good, so I will probably go back to bed for another hour. I want to be bright for Sophie coming home later, I hate to worry her in any way.' Her voice lowered. 'Thank you again for your kindness... I won't forget it.'

There was a short silence then Sophie recognised the sound of the phone receiver being laid back in the cradle. She hovered at the top of the stairs, uncertain what to do and then she heard the muffled noise of her mother crying again. Sophie sank down to sit on the top step, a sense of panic building up inside her. Her mind was racing with all the things she had heard, and she tried to go over them, one by one, attempting to make sense of it. But there were too many aspects to think about and she felt overwhelmed.

Sophie suddenly found herself trembling and then she began to cry. Tears trickled down her face, and she moved her hands over her eyes. As she sat there, she became aware of a feeling building up inside her – something akin to alarm – overriding everything else. Then, it hit her with force as she recognised the feeling was *guilt*.

All the things she had overheard her mother telling Frances were tinged with fear as to how Sophie would react. Her mother, it now dawned on her, was not wholly the person she had recently painted her as – the woman who was so self-contained and impenetrable that she was above criticism and the opinions of anyone else. The phone call highlighted the other side of her mother, the side that demonstrated the caring person, who was willing to do anything to make her daughter happy.

Sophie knew that side had always been there. Unfailingly, always there. The loving side that Sophie had recently lost sight of, choosing to view her only through a small, critical lens. Sophie now felt a pang of guilt that her mother had shouldered the blame for almost everything surrounding her birth circumstances, rather than taint her father's memory. And Sophie had wanted that, rather than listen to even the smallest detail that might make her father seem less than the saint-like figure she wanted to believe he was.

A greater realisation slowly descended on her – that she had never let go of her anger at her mother's early reaction to the wedding. Even when her mother had come around to the idea and then done everything to help – organising and paying for flowers, buying Sophie's dress, sorting the Grosvenor – Sophie had still nursed that anger. Then, when it had all come out about her father not being her real father, Sophie had heaped another grievance, which was immeasurably bigger, on top of all that simmering emotion. And, in the weeks following the wedding, she had not let go of one little piece of that resentment, instead basking in the fact that she now held the upper hand. But did she? What, Sophie wondered now, did that even mean? Her mother was her mother, and if their relationship was to become much less because of her resentment – or entirely lost – what good would it do her? She was just realising what that loss would mean.

Listening to her mother – upset and broken – pouring her heart out to her good and caring friend made Sophie feel somehow diminished. The thought that her mother was so afraid of her reactions shocked her. By the sound of it, her mother had been feeling that for some time. This was not what she wanted. When she took up the cold, unforgiving stand against her mother – what she regarded as having the upper hand – she had not imagined the consequences that it might have. The effect the continuous distancing would have on her mother, and the fact that the coldness might lead to a permanent estrangement.

She was her daughter – the closest person to her – and if her mother was suffering, she should be the first person to comfort and care for her. Regardless of their differences, which was not uncommon when it came to mothers and daughters, there should still be an unbroken bond between them.

There was no denying that finding out about her origins was a shock, but she now knew that at the end of the day, nothing had changed hugely. In the grand plan of things, it was not anything that was going to matter to many people, and no one would know unless she chose to tell them. Tony had not minded, nor had Alice or Emily, and they had not changed one iota towards her. Anyone who did mind would not be a person she needed in her life.

It was time to move on and forgive her mother. Time to forget all these grievances. Sophie took a deep breath, wondering whether to go into her mother's room or whether to go quietly downstairs and leave her to sleep. She was still deciding when she heard movement in the room, and she automatically got to her feet. She would do it now, she decided. She would approach her mother, saying that she overhead some of the phone call, and that she wanted to sort things out and put an end to the cold war between them.

She moved across the hallway, and it was just as she placed her hand on the porcelain doorknob and went to knock on the door that she heard the dull, heavy thud. She shouted, 'Mummy? Mummy, are you all right?'

When there was no answer, she threw the door open to find her mother lying unconscious on the floor beside the fireplace. She stood, rooted to the spot, watching as blood started to trickle down from the gash on the side of her mother's head, which she had hit on the iron fender.

Chapter Thirty-Five

Sophie heaved the greatest sigh of relief as Tony, still in his uniform, came rushing down the hospital corridor towards her. 'Thank God,' she said, 'thank God you were coming home tonight.'

'How is she?' he asked, sitting down on the wooden bench beside her. 'Mrs Wilson explained as soon as I arrived, and I rang a taxi to bring me straight down.'

'Hopefully, OK. She's just been taken to a ward down there.' Sophie pointed along the corridor. 'She was asleep when they took her along on the trolley. They have stitched her head and taken an X-ray. The doctor said that hopefully there isn't any serious damage, but they don't know yet, until they have the results.'

Tony nodded, taking it all in. 'They'll probably have to keep her in tonight,' he said, 'until they know more. They'll want to keep her under observation.' He gave a deep sigh, as though he had been holding his breath. 'How are you, darling?' He drew her into his arms. 'You must have had a terrible shock finding her like that on the floor.'

Sophie put her arms around him and buried her face in his chest. 'I got such a fright,' she said. 'I thought Mummy was dead.' She started to cry, softly first then growing into sobs. He let her cry for a few minutes, and then when the sobs had subsided, she looked up at him. 'Oh, Tony, I was so frightened, especially since I've been so mean to her ... I've not been nice to her at all since the wedding...'

Tony patted her back. 'I'm sure you haven't.' His voice was quiet and reassuring. 'You don't have it in you to be like that.'

'I didn't think so either,' she said, 'but I was so angry with her about not being happy with our quick wedding and then when I found out about Daddy...'

'I've told you before, Sophie,' he said, cuddling her into him again, 'her reaction was normal. My own family were all against it. I didn't make a big issue about it because I didn't want it to put you off them. It's only normal – quick weddings make everyone nervous, especially during this bloody war.' He shrugged. 'They make people worry that the couple don't know each other well enough, and when the war is over, they'll get to know each other properly and find out all their little faults. They will find out that the person isn't as perfect as they thought, and then they'll regret it.'

Sophie froze. 'You don't think that will happen to us, do you? You don't think that we'll regret it?'

Tony looked at her in amazement. 'Don't be daft, I wasn't thinking about *us*. I couldn't wait to get back home to see you. You're the best thing that's ever happened to me – how could I regret that?' He lifted her hand and kissed it. 'The thing is, they don't know how we feel about each other. They don't realise that we've found our other halves – the person that makes us complete. But we don't need to care, because as time goes by, they'll realise. When we have half a dozen kids then they'll find out that we knew what we were doing all along.'

'Oh, Tony...' Sophie said. 'You've made everything better already, just by being here.'

They sat talking for a while and then a doctor appeared in the corridor, having come out of a ward.

'That's him,' Sophie whispered. 'That's the one who's dealing with Mummy.' She got to her feet. 'I'll just go and check, see if he has any more news.'

'I'll come with you,' Tony said, standing up. 'I'll leave you to talk, I'll just stand to the side and wait.'

Sophie went quickly down the corridor, her husband following behind. When the doctor saw her, he came over and stood talking for a few minutes. His face was very serious, and at one point, something he said made her shake her head, and then she had to search in her coat pocket for a hanky. When the doctor turned to go back to the ward, Tony moved quickly to check how things were.

'The X-ray seemed clear, but they are concerned that she hasn't come round properly,' Sophie said, her eyes filling up with tears. 'The doctor said they have to keep her in, just in case. They suspect she has concussion.'

'That makes sense,' Tony said. 'They have to keep her in for observation after a bang to the head, especially if they're worried about concussion.' He put his arms around her. 'This will be fine, Sophie. If it was something serious it would have shown up on the X-ray.'

The following morning – after a fitful night's sleep – Sophie woke at eight o'clock and went into her mother's room. She rang the hospital to be told that Dorothy had woken and so far seemed to be doing OK. She had eaten a slice of toast and drunk a cup of tea. The ward sister said the doctor would be around in the next hour or so, and asked her to ring again after lunch to give them more time to further evaluate the situation.

Sophie hung up the phone and went back to bed, grateful to have Tony to slide in beside and cuddle up to.

He turned towards her, propping himself up on one elbow. 'What did they say?' he asked concernedly. When she explained all that she had been told, he pulled her into his arms and said, 'She'll be fine, I promise.' He put his hands either side of her face and kissed her.

Sophie pulled away, tears in her eyes. 'I have to tell you something,' she said. 'I am so worried about my mother because I feel it was all my fault.' She started to cry.

'Tell me,' he said gently. 'Just tell me, you'll feel better for it.'

She then related the whole story from when she went upstairs and heard her mother upset and weeping on the phone to Frances and talking about Sophie's father. She told Tony everything, except for the bit about her mother saying her and Alice had overheard Tony's family talking. That, she thought, was something she would ask her mother about later. Before, she would have tackled her mother headlong about it – glad of another opportunity to put her in her place – but now she knew she would wait until the time was right and ask her quietly.

Tony was right; afterwards she did feel much better talking to him, and she felt even better again when he kissed her passionately and they spent the rest of the morning making love. When they went downstairs later to get breakfast, she felt much steadier and stronger, and ready to face whatever came.

The news was good from the hospital. The nurse who Sophie spoke to said that all the major tests were clear, although they were still concerned about concussion. If there was someone to look after her at home for the next few days, they thought that Dorothy was fit enough to leave. Later that afternoon they went to collect a tired and pale-faced Dorothy. She sat on the end of her bed, while Sophie and Tony perched on chairs, waiting for the ward sister to come with her discharge papers.

Sophie felt her mother was unusually quiet. She glanced over at Tony, and when she caught his eye, she indicated towards her mother then raised her eyebrows in question. Tony discreetly looked at Dorothy and back to Sophie and raised his eyebrows, too.

Sister Molloy came into the room and introduced herself to them. She was a small, Irish, matronly-looking woman in her forties, with an air about her that brooked no nonsense. She talked to everyone, including Dorothy, as though they were pupils in a classroom.

'Now,' she said, turning in a circle and looking all three in the eye, while holding up a warning finger. 'This lady needs to take it easy. She's had a nasty knock to her head and had to have an anaesthetic for stitches to be put in, and she still has a bit of concussion.' She paused. 'You'll all have to keep an eye on her for any changes in her condition – dizziness, seeing double or suddenly being sick – or if she becomes confused, anything like that. If she has any of those symptoms, you have to bring her back to the casualty department immediately.'

'We will,' Sophie said. 'And we'll make sure she doesn't do anything too strenuous.'

'Exactly,' Sister Molloy said. She gestured towards Dorothy. 'And while she's a fine-looking woman for her age, she needs to realise she's not getting any younger. I believe she's still working, running a factory?'

Sophie looked over at her mother, knowing she would not like the reference to her age. 'Yes, and she does a very good job. It has never seemed too much for her before . . .'

'Thank you, Sophie,' her mother said, rolling her eyes in the nurse's direction.

'Well, she might need to slow down a bit,' Sister Molloy said, as though Dorothy wasn't present. 'The doctor thought she was a bit highly-strung – agitated – when she became conscious again. She was talking as though things had been getting on top of her. Sometimes the anaesthetic can affect people like that – and so can concussion.' She paused. 'And age catches up with us all, so she might have been doing too much before the accident.'

Dorothy straightened her back. 'I wasn't well with a sinus infection,' she said, 'and the doctor has put me on antibiotics for it. I think that was the main problem, and nothing to do with my age.'

Sister Molloy raised her eyebrows. 'Be that as it may,' she said, 'but you now have stitches in your head and symptoms of concussion on top of that.' She sucked in her breath. 'I wouldn't be rushing back to work if I was you. I would take it easy for the next week or two.'

'Thank you for the advice,' Dorothy said.

There was a silence then the nurse handed over the discharge papers and said, 'There's a prescription there for your tablets. You have enough to keep you going until Monday.'

As her mother went to the locker to get her handbag and the bag with the clothes she had arrived in, the nurse beckoned to Sophie to go into the corridor with her. 'Keep a close eye on her – with concussion, she might be confused or just act a little different.'

'I'll make sure we are with her all the time,' Sophie promised. They had arranged to go to visit Tony's family, but he could easily go by himself, as she often visited on her own when he was away.

Sophie had arranged a taxi, and she took her mother's arm as they walked down the hospital corridor and then outside to where they would be picked up. 'How do you feel now you are out in the fresh air?' she asked.

'OK,' Dorothy said, 'just a bit light-headed.'

Again, Sophie looked over her mother's head at Tony and he just shrugged. There was no doubt that the accident had taken it out of her. When they arrived back at the house, Mrs Wilson was waiting for them, and after checking how her employer was – and echoing Sister Molloy's words about taking things easier – she went off to make them all tea and sandwiches.

Sophie and her mother and Tony sat chatting for a while, although Dorothy had the least to say. The other two kept the conversation up, with Sophie offering to help her mother – trying to be kind to her in any way that would indicate that she was back to her old, softer ways. It was, Sophie knew, not the time for more serious conversation with her mother, so she talked about things such as an article she had read on women's hats, and how they would be a huge fashion statement when the war was finally over.

When things went quiet, Tony talked about his work in the various telephone exchanges and then gave his opinion on how things were moving with the war abroad. At one point Sophie saw her mother's eyelids flicker and she motioned to him and said, 'I've just remembered, Tony, there was something I wanted to show you. A letter I got through from a life insurance company.'

When Tony looked at her with a confused look on his face, she stood up and pointed to the hallway. When they were out of earshot, she explained, 'I just said that as an excuse, as I didn't want Mummy hearing. I think you should visit your mother on your own this afternoon. I'm sorry, but you heard what the nurse said, someone has to stay with Mummy, so we can't both go.'

'I'll stay here, too,' Tony said. 'My mother will understand.'

Sophie shook her head. 'You haven't seen your family for a while, and they're really looking forward to seeing you. You need to go, even for a couple of hours.'

'I'm sure they'd prefer if the two of us were going,' he said. 'My mother loves you being there, she's never happier than when there's a crowd of women together.'

'She will still want to see you.'

Eventually, Tony agreed to go and see his family for a few hours and come home to have dinner with Sophie later that evening.

After he left to catch the bus, Sophie noticed her mother starting to doze again, and suggested she might go up to bed for a rest, to which her mother agreed. Sophie walked upstairs with her and saw her safely into the bedroom. She waited until Dorothy was lying down, and then she went around drawing the curtains.

She came back into the middle of the darkened room and was just going to quietly leave, when on an impulse she went over to the bed and bent down to kiss her mother on the cheek. When her mother looked up at her, she said, 'I hope you feel better soon, Mummy. It's awful you had that accident.'

'You've been so very good,' Dorothy whispered. 'Thank you.'

She looked and sounded so vulnerable that tears suddenly came to Sophie's eyes. 'I'm sorry for not being kinder to you before – all the arguments about Daddy . . .'

Her mother gave a deep sigh. 'You don't need to apologise; it was very hard for you. That's what we always worried about. Your reaction was natural, especially at the time of your wedding.'

'It doesn't matter anymore,' Sophie said. 'I can see that nothing has really changed. Daddy will always be my father, and . . . well,

I'm just so grateful to still have you.' As her mother reached her hand out, Sophie took it and sat down on the end of the bed. 'I want you to know that from now on, you can tell me anything. I'm a grown woman and I've recently realised that life doesn't always turn out the way you think it will. I've learned that we have to make the most of it.' Her hand tightened on her mother's. 'Later, when you're feeling better, we can talk more openly about things. I don't want you to feel there's anything you can't tell me.' She paused. 'Just before your accident, I was coming up to your room and I heard you upset on the phone to Frances. I know that you've been frightened to tell me about my real father . . . and I want you to know that it's OK. You don't need to worry. Whatever you tell me, I will be fine about it.'

'Did you hear me mention the letter I received?'

Sophie paused, trying to remember. Her mother had said something about a letter, but with everything that had happened since, the memory was vague. She was sure it wasn't anything important. 'Yes,' she said, 'but don't worry about anything like that.'

'It's about your father,' Dorothy said, indicating towards her dressing table. 'It's over there if you want to read it now.'

'It doesn't matter. We can talk about it all later – when you're feeling better. There's nothing now that you need to be concerned about.'

There was a silence, during which Dorothy clasped Sophie's hand tighter. 'Do you really mean that?' she whispered.

'Absolutely,' Sophie said. 'But you need to rest now. We can talk about all these things when we have more time. When Tony has gone back.'

'No,' her mother said, her voice definite. 'Tony is your husband, and if you need someone else to talk to about it afterwards – apart from me – then I would rather we do it while he is home.'

'Mummy,' Sophie said, 'we can do whatever you want. But you need to relax now and have a little sleep.'

'Yes,' Dorothy said, lying back on her pillow. 'I'm glad we talked. I'll sleep easier now...'

Sophie went out of the room quietly and headed downstairs. She had just walked into the sitting room when the phone rang, so she went quickly over to the table to get it before it disturbed her mother. She picked it up, reciting the number as usual.

'Sophie?' Frances said. 'Hello, dear. Sorry to disturb you, but I tried ringing your mother last night and got no answer, and then I've been ringing and ringing all morning...'

'Oh, Frances,' Sophie said, 'my apologies, I should have rung you.' She went on to explain about her mother's accident and her being in the hospital overnight.

'Oh no!' Frances exclaimed. 'I'm so sorry to hear about poor Dorothy. Is there anything I can do?'

'I'm sure she would love to see you when she is a bit brighter. In the meantime, I think we're doing everything we can – everything the hospital suggested.'

'I'm sure you are, dear.'

Sophie automatically went to make a pleasantry before hanging up, and then she suddenly thought. 'Frances, would you mind me speaking privately? I know Mummy confided in you about the recent difficulties we've had about my birth circumstances...' There was a pause, so she rushed on. 'And to be honest, I overheard your last conversation – you know, when Mummy was very upset about the way I had reacted, and about how I blamed her for everything. It really shook me up, as I hadn't realised the effect it all had on her. I suppose I was so shocked finding out about things that I never thought how Mummy would feel.'

'Oh, Sophie,' Frances said, 'it's not been an easy situation for either of you, dear.'

'It hasn't, but in many ways, I've got over it, and Mummy's accident has made me realise how I would feel if anything happened to her – and how I just want to get back to the way things were before all this happened.'

'I'm so happy to hear that. I know your mother adores you, Sophie, and so did George.'

Sophie took a deep breath. 'What's happened in the past is gone now and sadly, Daddy's gone. I only wish they had told me while he was living, but nothing can change that, and I know it wasn't all Mummy's fault. She wanted Daddy to tell me the truth.' She paused. 'I've told Mummy that it's time to put the past behind us, and that whatever...' The line suddenly crackled, and she halted until it cleared. '...I hear about my real father in the future,' she continued, 'I will deal with it. Whatever comes up, we will deal with it.'

'How does your mother feel about this change?' Frances asked, sounding slightly breathless. 'She must be very relieved to have got everything off her chest at long last.'

'She was,' Sophie said. 'It's great for us both to have everything out in the open, to have no more secrets.'

'Absolutely. I think the letter was a shock to her, but in many ways, it's come at the right time, after the wedding, when you have time to take it all in.'

Sophie's brow furrowed, and then she realised she had missed some of her mother's phone call, and that Frances obviously knew more than she did. 'Yes,' she said, 'you're probably right.'

'When your mother is fully recovered, you'll be able to talk it out properly. It's not an easy decision to make, and I'm sure you'll need a bit more time before deciding whether you're ready to take such a big step.'

Sophie picked her words carefully. 'What do you think Mummy wants me to do?'

'That's a difficult question to answer,' Frances said. 'Especially after her accident. I think she doesn't want to make any more mistakes, so she will probably leave it up to you. Although, from what you said earlier – about whenever you see him – I think you've already made up your mind.'

'About what?' Sophie said, holding her breath.

'About meeting him – about meeting up with your real father.'

Chapter Thirty-Six

After she came off the phone, Sophie walked over to the sitting room window. As she stared out over the garden, her thoughts turned towards her father, the man who had brought her up – George Morley. Pictures of him flashed through her mind, at various stages in their lives, and she felt a pang of sorrow again at his loss. Without a single doubt, she knew he had been a good father to her. She also knew she had been a good daughter to him, and had, in many ways, favoured him over her mother – but only slightly. On the whole, they had been happy – all three of them. Happier than Alice's family, who were probably as happy as the average, large family. Happier than Emily's, whose mother had been very religious and then seriously depressed when Emily's brother was killed. All in all, they had been happier than most.

All of it now, she thought, was in the past and was something she could look back on with happiness and love. But she now realised that the present mattered more, and how she dealt with it would affect what was to come in the days and years ahead.

She checked her watch and turned away from the window, then went to the kitchen. Mrs Wilson was there, draining the water from the vegetables before she left to go home.

'The dinner is all ready,' she told Sophie. 'Easy enough, since your mother won't be up to doing much. There is a cottage pie in the oven, which I made this morning, and it just needs warming up.' She held the pan out. 'The carrots and peas are cooked already, so if you just put them on the cooker with a knob of butter and some salt and pepper and warm them through,' she smiled. 'And I've made nice bread and butter pudding with custard for afterwards. Tony told me it was his favourite last time I made it.'

'That's very kind of you,' Sophie said, 'he'll be delighted.' She did not tell her that Tony's mother had planned on making his favourite pudding for him, too.

'Tell your mother I hope she's feeling better and that I'll be in tomorrow as usual to sort the Sunday dinner.' She paused. 'She's not herself at the moment, so we'll have to look after her. It can be hard for some women when they get to a certain age, and she's not had it easy lately.'

Sophie assured the housekeeper that her mother would be looked after, and said it in such a way that it emphasised the coolness between them was gone. She went back out into the hallway, stopping beside the sitting room door for a brief moment, and then she went straight upstairs.

She paused outside her mother's bedroom, and then she opened the door gently. The only sound was that of her mother's heavy breathing, signalling that she was in a sound sleep. Sophie slipped off her shoes and went silently across the floor to the dressing table, where she found the long white envelope with her mother's name on it. She retreated as quietly as she came in, then she went downstairs.

She waited until Mrs Wilson had called in to say goodbye and then, when she was entirely alone, she lifted the letter. After what Frances had said, she decided that she would rather read it when she was on her own, before talking about it with anyone.

She went over to the small table by the window and sat down, then slid the letter out of the envelope and started to read:

Dear Dorothy,

I do hope you and Sophie are well.

I know you don't want to hear from me, and I am so sorry for any distress my contacting you again may cause

- but I'm afraid I can't go any longer without meeting my daughter properly.

I have done everything that you and George asked of me all these years. After you and he got married, I did as he asked, and I did not contact either of you during all the years I was in America.

After my wife died and I returned to London, I contacted George, and again, he asked me to keep away, to give you time to explain the situation to Sophie. More time passed, during which I wrote to him several times, with no reply – and then I heard the sad and shocking news of his death.

I have to admit to feeling terribly hurt that you didn't think fit to contact me about it, and that I had to hear it through other family members. Regardless, I made no issue about it at his funeral, and had to meet Sophie for the first time without being introduced to her as her father. I had to observe her from a distance, as a total stranger might.

Afterwards, I asked you again, when the time was right, and when you had both recovered from George's death, to tell her the truth. Over a year has passed without any contact from you. You can never imagine my upset when I then heard that Sophie has married – without me ever being introduced to her. One of the biggest landmarks in her life, and she is, all these years later, still unaware of my existence.

It breaks my heart to think that my daughter was married without a father to give her away, when she has one alive and well – and only living a few hours away in London.

I could go on and on about how hurt I feel that I have missed out on Sophie's life. I do understand – and always have – that the mistake I made in leaving you cost me that opportunity. In my defence, I did explain it to George after you were married that I had always intended coming back to you and Sophie. Too late, I know, but fate unfortunately decided otherwise.

I am contacting you again to ask, once more, that I be given the chance to meet my daughter before any further time passes. The war is still on, and anything could happen to any one of us.

Dorothy, please find it in your heart to tell Sophie the truth and let her decide if she wants to meet me.

I will leave it up to you whether you tell her about our real relationship or leave me to do that. Either way, she needs to know. At this stage in all our lives, it probably does not make a huge difference now.

Yours respectfully,

David.

Sophie read down the letter, stopping at each paragraph to take it in, or to read it again. When she came to the end, she laid it down on the table. It was only then she realised her whole body was trembling.

'*Oh my God...*' she whispered to herself. The story of her life was laid out in front of her in three sheets of paper, answering questions she had wondered about – and leaving her asking even more questions about a situation she could never have envisaged. Her real father – this David, who she believed had disappeared into the mists of America long ago, never to return – was not only still alive, but living in England.

This, she realised, was what Frances thought she already knew, and what her mother thought she had overheard. This is what they both thought she had already digested and come to accept in a matter of hours. After all that had happened, Sophie desperately wanted to accept it all – but it was not what she had thought. It was much bigger and more overwhelming than anything she could have imagined.

Sophie leant her elbows on the table and lowered her head into her hands. She sat there, taking deep breaths to steady herself, and then she got up from the table to pour herself a brandy, before coming back to read it again.

She was still sitting there, having pored over the letter numerous times, when the doorbell jolted her. She went to the door to find Tony there. He looked startled when he saw her grey, drawn face and red-rimmed eyes, immediately realising something was wrong.

'Is your mother OK?' he asked anxiously as they went inside.

'She's still asleep,' Sophie told him.

'You don't seem yourself,' he said. 'What's happened?' He put his arms around her and held her close.

She buried her face in his chest for a while, then, when she felt the huge wave of emotion rising in her, she pulled away from him and went over to the table. 'Read this,' she said, 'and tell me what I should do.'

Tony was just at the last page of the letter when the sitting room door opened, and Dorothy came in. They both whirled around to see her standing, rather unsteadily, in the doorframe. She looked from one to the other.

'You found the letter then,' she said quietly. 'So you know everything now ...'

Instinctively, Sophie rushed over to take her arm to guide her to one of the armchairs by the fireside. 'You shouldn't have come downstairs on your own,' she said. 'How are you? Are you feeling any better?'

'A little,' her mother answered. 'The dizziness has eased a bit.'

There was a silence, then Sophie said, 'Mummy, I had no idea what was going to be in this letter. I didn't overhear anything about this.'

Dorothy gave a deep sigh. 'I can't remember half of what has been said over the last few days,' she said. 'And it doesn't matter anymore. However you found out, it was never going to be easy. It has hung over my head for years, and I'm glad it's out in the open. It's only right that you should know the truth – the whole truth.'

'Are you sure you both feel up to this now?' Tony said, looking from mother to daughter, clearly concerned.

Dorothy slowly nodded. 'Yes,' she said. 'We might as well finish it.'

Tony moved towards the door. 'I'll leave you to talk between yourselves. I'll go down to the kitchen and make everyone a cup of tea.'

'No, please stay, Tony – you should both know.' Dorothy took a deep breath. 'You've both read the letter now, so I won't waste time beating around the bush. You know Sophie's real father is called David.' She looked directly at her daughter. 'You also know that he mentioned something about his "real relationship" to you ...'

Sophie looked over at her mother, confused. 'About him being my father?'

'Yes, but it's also about his relationship to your father.'

'Were they friends or something?'

'They were more than friends,' Dorothy said, with a heave of her shoulders. 'They were brothers ... David is George's younger brother.'

Chapter Thirty-Seven

After dinner, Sophie cleared away the dishes and went down to the kitchen to wash them, leaving her mother and Tony in the sitting room.

Dorothy looked at her son-in-law. 'I'm so sorry your weekend leave has been spoiled,' she said. 'I know you and Sophie had plans, and you've had to stay in looking after me.'

'There's no problem,' he told her. 'We're just glad you're feeling better.'

'Physically I do feel a bit better, although my head is still fuzzy, and I can't really remember what happened last night and even this morning.' She sighed. 'Do you think Sophie will ever forgive me?'

'Of course,' Tony said, smiling reassuringly. 'She just needs time to take it in – this last bit.'

'You mean discovering that her estranged uncle is actually her father,' Dorothy said. 'It's all a bit of a mess, isn't it? Sometimes we do things because we feel they are in the other person's best interests, and sometimes these things backfire. The last thing George would have wanted was to upset Sophie.'

'I know that...'

They both turned around to see Sophie at the door.

'I wasn't eavesdropping this time.' She gave a weary smile. 'I've finished in the kitchen.' She came into the room to sit in a chair facing her mother. 'I promised you whatever you told me I would cope with – and I will. Tony is only here for a short while, and you're still not well, Mummy, so going over all this will only put a strain on everyone. I'm going to put it to the back of my mind with all the other things and decide what to do about it later.'

'OK,' Tony said, 'but you won't bottle it all up and not tell us, will you?'

Sophie felt a surge of gratitude towards him that he cared so much. 'No, I promise.'

Her mother looked at her now. 'Did I dream it, or did I tell you we're going to have to let people go in the factory? The orders are just dwindling away.'

Sophie's eyebrows shot up. 'No, you didn't tell me,' she said, 'but I know from the recent accounts. I was trying to work out how I would bring it up with you. I actually mentioned it to Tony in the hospital.'

Dorothy nodded her head. 'I don't want to have to let staff go, but with the drop in orders...' She stopped. 'I wondered if we should just go down to the very basic staff until after the war. When things return to normal, we could go back to manufacturing our usual men's hats. That's what our business was built on.'

Sophie shot an anxious glance at her husband. 'We were talking about that, too,' she said. 'Maybe Tony might explain...'

'You might not feel up to discussing this tonight,' Tony said. 'And it's only an outside opinion – I haven't a clue about the factory and orders or anything like that.'

Dorothy had a sudden sinking feeling, but she made herself sit upright. 'I'd like to hear anything you have to say.' She wondered if Tony was going to show his hand now; if he was already starting to inveigle his way into the factory business as she had initially feared. The thought saddened her, because since he had been around the house, she found there was something pleasant and easy about him, and she felt he had a soothing effect on Sophie. He had also been very kind and understanding about her illness, and the business with Sophie's father.

'While I've been travelling around the big cities,' Tony said, 'I've noticed that a lot of the younger men aren't wearing hats these days.' He shrugged. 'I rarely wear one myself, apart from my uniform cap or a formal hat for funerals and that sort of occasion. The other thing is, I've heard the lads I meet through work saying that they're sick of wearing uniform hats, and that when the war is over, they're never going to put on any kind of hat again.' He held his hands out. 'I know this is something you and Sophie probably don't want to hear, with Morley's being such a well-established, and well-thought-of factory. And of course, I have no experience in the world of hats – but I'm sure you'll know people who can advise you the best way to go forward after the war.'

Dorothy was surprised that Tony could speak with such certainty, but she also recognised the note of deference in his voice. She looked from him to Sophie. 'Do you really think dress hats have had their day?'

Sophie nodded. 'After I spoke to Tony about it, I noticed when I was in Stockport that a lot of men don't wear them anymore. Caps are still popular for working men, but the dress hats are definitely not as popular as they were even a few years ago.'

'That doesn't give us a lot of hope,' Dorothy said. 'We might need to think of selling out to one of the bigger firms. I agree with Tony, I think we'll have to take advice very soon.'

'What about women's hats?' Sophie said. 'They're still very popular, and when rationing is over, I'm sure the bigger, fancier ones will come back into fashion.'

Dorothy raised her eyebrows. 'That might be something worth considering. What do you think, Tony?'

'Sorry, Mrs Morley, but you're asking the wrong one now – I wouldn't have a clue.'

'Well, I mentioned it to your mother and sisters before the wedding,' Sophie said, 'and they felt that women's hats will always be in fashion. They said that a lot of women have been decorating their own hats for big occasions because they can't get new ones with rationing,' she smiled. 'In fact, they said if we started making women's hats, they would love jobs in the factory.'

354

'You've got to be joking!' Tony said, laughing incredulously. 'You'd have to be mad to take my mother and sisters on. They were rabbiting on about something to do with the factory yesterday, and I told them straight that families and business don't mix.' He smiled and pointed an accusing finger at Sophie. 'You're too soft, and they would become far too familiar and start to take liberties. Do not encourage them or you'll be sorry, for you're the one that would have to deal with them. The factory has nothing to do with me.'

Dorothy said nothing, but inside she felt almost giddy with relief, knowing that it was Sophie who had put the idea in the women's heads, and not Tony.

Sophie started to laugh now. 'It was only idle chat,' she said. 'And hearing them talking so enthusiastically about the women's hats gave me a bit of a boost for the future of the factory.'

'Just as long as they're not part of it,' Tony said, shaking his head. 'You don't want to give your poor mother a heart attack trying to manage them. She has enough on her plate.'

Later, when Tony went upstairs, Sophie looked over at her mother. 'How do you feel now?'

'I'm improving,' Dorothy said, 'and I'm trying not to worry about things. I still feel upset that you found out about your father the way you did.'

'Is he nice? Is he like Daddy?'

'Oh, gosh ... I don't know what to say. They're brothers, so there are some similarities, but they are very different people.' She shrugged. 'It's all such a long time ago.'

'Did you love David?'

'Yes,' Dorothy said, 'but he abandoned us, for reasons too complicated to go into now. I promise I will explain it all later.' She took a deep breath. 'In the long run, he did us a favour because I actually grew to love your father more. He was so good to us both, and he adored us. That's what counts.'

'In a funny way,' Sophie said, 'I feel better knowing that David is my father. I feel better knowing I am actually a Morley. It makes me feel closer to my dad.'

'Do you?' her mother said. 'I had never thought of it like that. You've made me feel happier now, too, that something good has come out of it.' She paused. 'I will do my very best to make all this up to you, Sophie – all the hurt you've gone through these last few months. I've also realised I was very wrong about something else ...'

'What?' Sophie asked.

'Tony. Now that I've got to know him, I can see what made you choose him. He is both kind and sensible, and you are very lucky.'

Sophie's face lit up. 'He likes you, too, and he's helped me to deal with everything. See it from your point of view.'

'Well, that makes me lucky, having him as a son-in-law.' She paused. 'And after hearing all he said about the factory tonight, I'm sorry that I doubted him. I think his opinions are definitely worth listening to.'

'Good,' Sophie said, 'because he has our best interests at heart.' She suddenly started to laugh. 'Although he is awful about his mother and sisters, isn't he?'

'I don't feel it's my place to comment, but I think he has the measure of them ...'

'They're nice in their own way, and they have been very welcoming to me, but I think Tony might be right about not mixing family and work.' Sophie suddenly remembered something. 'What did you and Alice overhear them saying at the wedding?'

Dorothy caught her breath. 'I wasn't going to tell you,' she said. 'I didn't want to cause any more friction between us.' She raised her eyes to the ceiling, and then, for the first time in ages, she started to laugh. 'Tony would go mad if he knew because they were acting exactly as he described. They were saying that Tony would take over the factory now you were married, because you would be off having babies, and once he was in charge, the whole Shaw family would get jobs in it.'

'Good God!' Sophie said. 'Apart from Tony having no interest in the factory, did it not occur to them that *you* would have a say in it?'

'According to the ladies, I will be retiring soon, since – as they repeatedly said – I am definitely no spring chicken.'

Sophie looked aghast. 'What an absolute cheek! You look fantastic for your age.'

'Give them their due,' Dorothy said, laughing again, 'they did say I looked well, but at the end of the day – I was no spring chicken!'

Sophie began to giggle. 'How embarrassing, and imagine Alice hearing them saying all that, too, and knowing they are my in-laws. She was very kind, she never mentioned it to me.'

Dorothy's face became more serious. 'Poor Tony,' she said. 'He has his hands full. Apart from his own family, he's had to deal with all the trouble that's gone on in our family, too.' She touched her hand to her sore head. 'And then all this happening.'

'How does your head feel now?'

'Clearer, the foggy feeling is more or less gone. When I look back, I think I must have had some sort of concussion. I wasn't myself at all. But I was lucky, it could have been a lot worse.'

'As long as you're OK, that's all that matters.' Sophie reached over and took her mother's hand. 'We'll get through all this,' she said. 'And we'll sort out the factory. It's what Daddy would have wanted.'

Chapter Thirty-Eight

Emily checked each of the silver knives and forks as she took them from the polished oak box, and then laid them down on the white linen tablecloth. Over the last few years, the ivory-handled cutlery had only been used at Christmas, since the Browne's no longer had family parties or invited friends to the house. Every so often she glanced at the clock or her wristwatch, checking how much longer it would be until Marco Benetti appeared at their door.

Her mother had been unusually busy in the days leading up to this Sunday meal. On Friday she had been down at the shops and had secured a chicken, which they only had on special occasions, and she had accompanied Emily's father to the allotment to pick carrots, turnips and onions, and collect apples to make some sort of pudding. She had further surprised Emily when she came back holding a large bunch of mixed roses wrapped in newspaper. One of Tom's friends, she explained, grew them for competitions, and he said she was welcome to take as many of the late blooms as she wanted, as he was due to prune the bushes the following week.

On the Saturday, Hannah Browne had risen early to start washing the windows and the skirting boards in the rarely used dining room, and to polish the wooden floor that surrounded the large, fringed rug she had vacuumed. When the room was spotless, she had then brought in the freshly starched and ironed tablecloth, and when it was sitting perfectly, she carried in her crystal vase filled with dark red roses to sit in the middle of the table. A smaller vase was then filled with the rest of the yellow, red, orange and white roses, and placed on the windowsill.

Emily put the dessert spoons at the four places, then put out a linen napkin by each setting, a little elegant touch only usually added at Christmas. She then went over to switch on the standard lamp in the corner, and another smaller lamp by the fireplace, which she thought gave a nicer glow to the room than the main light.

She had lain awake during the night, trying to picture how this meal would go between Marco and her parents. At one point, she had taken the rosary beads he had made for her from under her pillow, and said a prayer to Our Lady, asking that the visit go well and to make her parents like him.

She had kept her stance of saying nothing about Marco, letting them think their main link was Father Dempsey, and that she had not known him until the night of the fire. She had explained this to Marco when she met him earlier in the week, and he had understood how delicate the situation was. Apart from her parents' thoughts about the Italians being enemies of their country, they were aware that their romantic relationship still had to be kept very private. Whilst people like the Barlows and Father Dempsey, and other more liberal people, had got to know the Italians as individuals, there were others who considered relationships with the prisoners to be against the rules.

The Barlows now saw Marco almost as part of their family, and the customers in the shop had got used to seeing his cheery face around the place. Some now stopped to have a few words with him as they did the shopkeeper, talking about ordinary things like the weather and football matches. When they last met up, Marco told her that Mr Barlow had asked him about his friendship with her. Marco had told the shopkeeper about meeting Emily in the town hall, and about the fire at the house afterwards. After the choir had sung in church, he then told the Barlows that Mrs Browne had asked him for Sunday dinner. The perceptive shopkeeper had remembered the first time they met in the shop – and noticed the look on Marco's face anytime he mentioned Emily – and put two and two together. Shortly afterwards, when the shop was quiet, Mr Barlow told Marco that the next time Emily was in the shop, that his wife said they were welcome to go into their front parlour and sit together with a cup of tea.

Emily was delighted at the offer, but having thought it over, decided that for the time being, it was safer to meet in the park as usual. If they were seen together outside and someone mentioned it to her parents, she could say they had bumped into each other on the street. As she put the silver salt and pepper set on the table, she thought how wonderful things would be if she and Marco were free to go to the cinema together or even for a walk into Stockport. She pictured them together, her taking Marco's arm, and just doing the normal things that other young couples did.

Marco arrived on his bicycle dead on three o'clock, and Emily's mother – who had been back and forth to the window, watching for him – asked her to answer the front door and bring him in. When Emily went out, he was at the side of the house taking off his bicycle clips. He was dressed in his smart black trousers, a blue shirt and a navy tie with a small white polka dot. He grinned at her, and just the sight of him sent a warm, happy feeling through her.

'You look beautiful,' he whispered.

'Thank you,' she said. 'And you look very good, too.'

'Mrs Barlow gave me the tie – nice, isn't it? She say I must look well today.' He went to the saddlebag on his bike. 'One more minute.' He took out an unusual, cone-shaped container wrapped in colourful paper, and another square-shaped package wrapped in plain brown paper. He put them under one arm and with the other hand he put his bicycle clips in the bag and closed it over. 'OK,' he said, taking a deep breath. 'I am ready now.'

Emily brought him into the sitting room where her father and mother were waiting. He smiled and shook hands with them both and then he handed the colourful cone to Emily's mother, saying, 'A small gift from our garden.'

Emily watched as her mother opened the wrapping to reveal a white cyclamen plant and saw her face light up.

'Oh, that is lovely,' Hannah Browne said, a little catch in her voice. 'It's not one of the plants I've had before.' She turned to show it to her husband, who just nodded his head without saying anything. 'And the paper is lovely, too, with the tiny flowers and birds.'

'Franco, my friend, he is an artist,' Marco explained. 'He painted this paper for me.'

Marco handed the brown package to Emily. 'And these, I made. A small gift for each person here.'

There was a silence while Emily opened the package, which had three smaller packages inside wrapped in the painted paper. She handed her father the one with a tag that said Mr Browne and gave her mother one with her name on it. She then lifted the one for her.

'You shouldn't have done this,' Emily's mother protested. 'We were supposed to thank you for what you did…'

'My family custom,' Marco said, smiling at her. 'My mother always takes small gifts when visiting.'

There was another silence now as all three unwrapped their gifts – a round ashtray for Tom Browne, carved from polished mahogany wood, with a circle of beaten metal in the middle. 'Thank you,' he said, 'that will come in very useful.'

Emily's mother gasped when she opened hers to reveal a small heart-shaped jewellery box made from the same wood but carefully inlaid with tiny pieces of walnut wood in the shape of a butterfly. She opened it to reveal a lining made from handcrafted, marbled paper. 'This is beautiful,' she said. 'And you made this yourself?'

'Yes,' Marco confirmed, his face becoming more solemn, 'we have time in evenings.'

Hannah looked over at her husband. 'There's not many musicians who could make these, are there, Tom?'

'Indeed,' was all her father said.

Emily's gift was identical to her mother's but instead of a

butterfly in the walnut wood, he had made a delicate star design. The paper lining was a hand-painted music score with little notes and bars, and the words of a song in Italian. Emily thanked him, and then held her box out to her mother, who took it to examine and compare to her own. As she handed it back, Emily thought she saw tears glistening in the corner of her mother's eyes and suddenly felt concerned when her mother stood up.

'I'll go and check on the vegetables,' she said. 'We should be ready to eat in another quarter of an hour.'

There was a silence and then Emily's father looked over at Marco. 'Will you have a glass of beer while we're waiting?'

Emily caught her breath, as Marco had told her Mr Barlow had given him beer for the first time, and they had all laughed when he found the taste very bitter. Something told her that her father would not laugh, and she wished she had known he might offer it, and would have warned him. She hid her relief when Marco said, 'That would be very nice, Mr Browne, thank you.'

When her father left the room, Emily looked over at Marco, and her shoulders slumped as though a huge weight had been lifted from them. 'Are you OK?' she asked.

'Yes,' he said, 'your parents are very nice, and I am happy they liked my gifts.'

'They are all beautiful,' she said, 'and very thoughtful.'

He glanced towards the door. 'The heart box I make for you some time ago,' he said quietly, 'but I worried you have problem to explain where it come from. So, I thought if I make gift for your mother, same as yours, there is no problem.'

Emily raised her eyebrows, then pointed a finger in mock-accusation, and whispered, 'You are far too clever, Mr Marco.'

'So now,' he whispered back, 'you have my heart with you every day.'

Emily smiled and lifted her jewellery box up and held it to her heart.

Tom Browne came back in with two glasses of beer. He gave Marco one, then, when he sat down, he asked him about the tools he had used to stipple the metal on the ashtray, and the stain on the wood. Emily knew this would involve a long and detailed conversation, so she excused herself and said she was going to help her mother.

When Emily came back in carrying a bottle of lemonade and glasses for her and her mother, she heard Marco explaining that his grandfather had made musical instruments, and had taught him the basics of wood-carving. 'Very basic,' Marco had said, making a little movement with his hand, 'but some men in the camp are much more talented, and they teach me.'

'Those little boxes are as good as anything I've seen in the shops,' her father said, 'and I'd say you spent hours sanding and polishing them alone.'

Her mother came in to tell the men to sit at the table, and then Emily helped her to carry in the warmed plates. As the four of them sat around the table eating the chicken and roast potatoes, and the carrots from the allotment, Emily wished that she and Marco were just an ordinary couple, and that he had been invited to her house as her boyfriend. If that had been the case, she knew that he would have passed all the normal tests with flying colours. He had acquitted himself in every way. He had been mannerly and respectful, which showed a good upbringing from a decent family background, and had been able to talk to her parents on any subject they brought up. Everything about him was better than any other fellow she had ever met or could hope to meet.

But Emily knew none of that mattered because Marco was still a prisoner of war.

After they had finished the apple crumble and custard her mother had made, Emily's mother asked her to bring in the cups and saucers for tea. 'Put the sugar in the small crystal bowl,' her mother said. 'It will make the small amount we've left from the ration look more. I used the rest in the apple crumble.' She paused. 'He's a nice lad, Marco, isn't he? And very clever and talented.'

'Yes,' Emily said, turning away so her mother couldn't see her face.

'He seems very nice ... I think your father seems to be getting on with him, too.' There was a pause and then she said, 'Was it him who gave you the rosary beads?'

Emily's face flushed red, as she tried to think of an answer.

'I wasn't looking around your room or anything like that. I went in to change your bed recently, and I found them under your pillow. I left them back where they were. I knew you would tell me if you wanted me to know.' She paused. 'I've never seen anything like them before, and I knew they had to be made by someone who was good with their hands. It was just when I saw the lovely things he had made for us, and it made me wonder. Then, one of the times Father Dempsey was in, he said that you had met Marco in Barlow's shop a while back. When you didn't mention it, I thought it was best to say nothing.'

Emily briefly closed her eyes then she turned towards her mother. 'Yes,' she said, 'he did give me the rosary beads.' She went on to explain about her knocking over his box with all the things he'd made. 'He gave me the beads and I felt he would have been upset if I'd refused ...' She paused, picking her words. 'But I never saw him after that, and I purposely avoided going into the shop if I thought he might be there. I never saw him again until the night I was in the town hall, and I got the shock of my life when he appeared on the stage.' She shook her head. 'When he started playing the piano, I couldn't believe it.'

'You like him, don't you?' Her mother's voice was quiet and even. 'And he likes you. I know you've both been trying to hide it, but I can tell.'

Emily's heart was thumping, but she met her mother's gaze. 'Yes,' she replied. 'I do like him ... very much.'

Hannah Browne raised her eyebrows and then she suddenly smiled. The first proper smile Emily had seen in a long time. 'I'm not surprised,' she said. 'Apart from being nice and friendly, he's like a film star.'

'It's not just his looks,' Emily said. 'He's just so kind and good – and we can talk about anything.'

'His English is very good, too, you would hardly know he was a foreigner, apart from having a bit of a tan.'

Emily nodded and did not say that he had been studying hard to improve his English ever since they had met.

'It's not going to be easy for you... some people might not agree with it.'

Emily thought about Sophie's reaction. 'The only ones I care about are you and Dad. I know how you felt about it that time Father Dempsey mentioned the Italians from the camp – that's why I didn't have anything to do with him.' She halted. 'Well, I had my own reservations about it as well, until I got to know him.' She shrugged. 'Anybody can see that Marco's not a soldier – he's a musician.'

'He's too refined for fighting,' her mother said. 'That's what I always thought about Jack. That's what used to worry me all the time.' She sighed. 'I often think what he would have done with his life if the war hadn't happened...'

Emily suddenly felt the same raw pain as her mother – as though she had been punched in the stomach. She thought about Jack every single day, but after the first year, she had learned to keep the pain at a distance. It was only at times like this that it caught her unawares.

'After leaving school he got a good start in that architect's place in Manchester,' her mother remembered. 'He was doing so well the bosses were encouraging him to train as an architect himself. One of the last things he told me was that when he came back, he was going to design his own house one day.' She shook her head. 'Ah well – nothing we can do will ever bring him back.'

Emily moved and put her arms around her mother. 'I wish we could,' she said. 'I wish we could bring him back...' Usually, when she embraced her mother, she just stood there rigid. This time, Hannah let her body loosen, and then she put her arms around Emily. They stood there for a little while, before her mother moved back. She took her hanky out of her cardigan pocket and wiped her eyes. 'We better pour the tea, or it will be like treacle, and we can't afford to waste it.'

Emily rubbed the back of her hand to her own damp eyes, and then she sorted out the cups and saucers. Her mother poured more boiling water into the teapot and stirred it. 'He reminds me a bit of Jack, you know,' her mother said. 'I know it might sound daft with him being Italian, but he does. He doesn't feel like a stranger, he's got that friendly way about him. I read in the paper recently that the Italians are regarded as being our allies now, and they're allowed to mix with the local people.'

'They're allowed to go to places like the cinema, as well.'

'As far as I'm concerned, he can call in here any time he likes.' She looked directly at Emily now.

Emily's heart quickened at the thought of all the possibilities.

'You have to spend some time together to talk on your own – to get to know each other properly – in case he's sent back to Italy at the end of the war.'

'We haven't thought that far ahead.' She bit her lip. 'What about Dad?'

'Don't worry about your father. When I get him at the right time, I'll talk to him.'

Chapter Thirty-Nine

Alice was first to arrive at the Plaza tearoom.

The waitress, dressed in a frilled white apron and cap, showed her to the table. It was a cold, late November Saturday afternoon, and Alice was wearing a swing-style camel coat, with a green velvet beret and green floral scarf that Betty had bought her a few Christmases ago. The waitress took her coat, and Alice picked a seat where she could see people arriving at the tearoom, having climbed the stairs.

She lifted the menu and had a look at the sandwiches on the afternoon tea, but after a while she put it back down again, her mind drifting back to the few minutes she spent in Mersey Square with Louis, as she handed over Philip and Gabriela. He was taking them around the market to spend pocket money they had saved, and afterwards they were going to walk up to the art gallery, opposite the town hall. He told Alice he would drop them back at the shop around five o'clock. Maeve and Freddy would still be working, so would be there to keep an eye on the twins until Alice came home.

Not seeing Louis on his own had been one of the many changes in her life over the last few months – it had also been the hardest. At almost six months pregnant, her condition was now obvious to all her customers, and she could feel the physical difference as she moved around the shop. Maeve and Freddy anticipated any heavy lifting to be done, and the twins were both excited, looking forward to the new addition to the household. Greg had seemed happy when she wrote and told him their news, although concerned that she was on her own.

Your family will help out, I'm sure, he had written, *and of course your good friends. The evacuee children will be able to help you with little jobs around the house. You are a strong girl, Alice, and I know you will cope, whatever the future brings. I had some wonderful news which will make a difference to our circumstances. My Uncle Charles left me his house and bicycle business and whatever he has saved! I don't know all the details yet, and I can still hardly believe it. Apparently, his niece's family, who I thought would inherit the lot, had been swindling him out of money for years. They were caught out by his accountant, who informed my uncle, and he immediately changed his will and left everything to me. This means I can afford for you to take someone else on full-time in the shop, so that will let you spend all your time with the baby. Also, as I mentioned before, I want you to go back to teaching when the time is right for you. I don't want you buried away in the shop.*

He had thanked her for the gifts she had sent and asked if she might find some little things as Christmas presents for the family. He suggested silk scarves for the mother and two eldest daughters, and woollen scarves for the men and younger children. Alice thought that after they finished their afternoon tea, she might walk down to the market and pick them up. The post was slow, and she wanted to make sure the poor family received them in time for Christmas Day, as she knew they would probably be cooking for Greg and the other men. She thought she would also send more chocolates and whatever sweets she could find for the children. It was the least she could do to make life a little brighter for Greg and the family who were so good to him.

In his recent letters he had told her more of his colourful life in Naples – a trip to the Italian opera, a new pasta dish the family had cooked for him, the name of a wine he liked, an old and valuable book the father of the family had given him, which had the history of Naples and the surrounding towns and villages. His Italian had improved, he said, and the children had great fun laughing at his pronunciations. He also wrote about how desperate life still was for most people in Naples, with many starving, and how people would resort to anything – black marketing, prostitution, theft – anything that kept their families alive. *You have to actually live here to understand the place and the people,* Greg wrote, *and that experience changes the way you look at life forever.*

At times, the way he wrote, Alice felt she hardly recognised the Greg she had married. She wondered at how he had become so acclimatised to the Italian way of life and managed to find so many good things in a city so decimated by war. But then she reminded herself that Louis had settled well in Stockport, as had the twins. She often thought about the poor souls around the world who had been killed or taken by the Nazis from their homes, and people like Marco, who were interred in camps in foreign countries. The war had showed that human beings could adapt and survive even the most horrendous things.

Emily arrived next into the tearoom, smiling and looking around for Alice. She was wearing a red coat and hat, which set off her long dark hair. Her face lit up when she saw her friend and she came rushing over to the table to kiss and hug her, telling her how she was blooming.

Alice smiled and said, 'My stomach might be blooming, but I don't think my face looks quite as radiant as yours. Can I guess that it's something to do with Marco?'

Before Emily could reply, a waitress came to take her coat, then she sat down opposite Alice. 'Things have moved on an-other little bit,' she said, 'since we were over visiting you and the twins. My father asked Marco to help him fix something in the shed in his allotment this week, and afterwards he gave him a pair of cufflinks – black with mother of pearl – which he said were too fancy for him. He thought Marco could wear them when he's playing in the orchestra. They were my grandfather's, and Dad had kept them for Jack.' Her voice cracked a little. 'You have no idea how much that means to me, and to Marco.' She gave a teary smile. 'He was crying when he showed them to me, he's so typically Italian – all emotional!'

'I feel all emotional myself, just listening to that story,' she said. 'Oh, Emily, I am so pleased for you that things are going well.'

'It's lovely that we see each other regularly now. I drop into the shop, or he comes to the house in the evenings. He does little jobs for Mum, and he sits talking to my father about football. And the other night my father brought in an atlas with a map of Italy and got Marco to show him where his family were from, and all the places he knew.' Her face became solemn. 'That was a bit emotional, too, because he told Mum and Dad about his older brother being shot by the local Italian fascists at the start of the war because he spoke up against them at a big meeting. Then he was explaining how his mother and father and younger sister had lost their fine big city home during the bombing in Florence and had to leave with nothing, to live on a tiny farm with relatives. My mother was crying when she heard that.'

'That's so sad,' Alice said. 'It sounds similar to what Greg writes about in his letters about Naples.'

'And what happened here during the Blitz in London and places like Liverpool,' Emily said, sighing. 'It's all over the world. We can only hope and pray it will all be over soon, and that people's lives can start getting back to normal.'

'Have you any idea what might happen to Marco when it's all over?'

'We've talked about it,' Emily said, 'and he's hoping to stay here, if he's allowed. He's desperate to go back to see his family, especially his mother, and he'll do that as soon as possible. His family home was bombed, so even if he wanted to go back there to live, there's no room at his sister's house. There's also nothing professional for him back in Italy. He's involved with several orchestras and musical groups here, he's very popular, and has got to know so many people...'

'Especially *you*,' Alice said, grinning at her. 'I'm so happy for you, he's such a lovely chap, and just perfect for you.' They talked a bit more about Marco and how things were going in school. Then, at one point, Alice reached over and touched her friend's hand. 'Are you OK about seeing Sophie? I know it's been a long time and that you had to think about it...'

Emily took a deep breath. 'I'm not sure how I feel. We've been such good friends since school and it's not something you throw away easily. I thought I would at least give it another chance.'

'I'm glad,' Alice said, 'and I have a feeling...' She halted as Sophie came into the tearoom, wearing a navy coat and hat, but what caught Alice's eye was the anxious look on her unusually pale face. She was carrying a large brown paper bag in one hand, and her handbag was over her shoulder.

She waved when she spotted her friends and came across the floor to the table. 'So sorry I'm late,' she said, 'I had to pick something up.' She gave them both a kiss and when she was settled and her coat taken away, she lifted the brown bag. She took out a large bunch of white roses and baby's breath and handed them to Emily. 'Before we start, this is to say I'm sorry for what happened the last time we met.'

Emily's face stiffened at the memory. 'You didn't have to...'

'Yes, I did,' Sophie said quietly. 'I was rude and stupid, and I should have had more faith in you. I should have known anyone you picked was going to be a good and decent person.'

Emily looked at the flowers and gave a weak smile. 'Thanks, that's nice of you.'

'I really mean what I said... I shouldn't have spoken out until I'd met Marco.' She looked over at Alice, her eyes still anxious.

'I've heard lovely things about him, and I had a long talk with Tony, and he reminded me of how my mother was when she was opposed to me and him.'

'Forget it,' Emily said, 'it's something I've got to get used to, until people get to know Marco properly.' She held the bouquet to her nose. 'They're lovely, thanks.'

'I will make it up to you,' Sophie said quietly. She paused and then went to the bag again and brought out a smaller, mixed bunch of anemones and gave them to Alice, who thanked her.

'And how are you and baby?'

Alice patted her tummy. 'Good, the sickness has gone, and we now have lots of activity, especially at night. I think he or she must have long legs like their father; I told him that in my last letter.' There was a silence, and she knew the girls were not sure what to say. 'We're doing fine, and Greg is looking forward to getting home and meeting the new addition.' She saw the relieved look on their faces. 'It's the right thing, and I know he will make a great daddy. Things will work out when he comes home.' She looked over at Emily and smiled. 'Greg sounds fluent in Italian now, so when he comes home, he will be delighted to meet Marco. They can have great chats together about music and Italian food and wine.'

'Tony is home next weekend,' Sophie suddenly said, 'and I would love it if you and Marco came to the house one evening – and you as well, Alice. I'll ask Mrs Wilson if she can find an Italian recipe to surprise him.'

There was a silence then Emily smiled. 'I'll check with Marco what night suits him, and I'll give you a ring tomorrow.'

'Any night suits me,' Alice said. 'I'll check with Maeve when she's free to sit with the twins.'

Emily looked over at her. 'What about Louis?' she asked. 'Does he still help out as much?'

Alice lowered her eyes. 'He takes them out when he has time,' she said. 'He's actually taken them into Stockport this afternoon.' She did not want to think about Louis, so she looked at

Sophie and asked, 'How is your mother now? Did she have any after-effects from the concussion?'

Sophie went on to tell them that her mother had taken a few weeks to fully recover, but that she was fine now and back at work. She also told them both the story about her mother and Alice overhearing Mrs Shaw and her daughters talking in the bathroom at the wedding, and how it had all been her fault. She told it in a funny way, so they all ended up laughing.

Alice gave a little embarrassed sigh. 'I thought it was best to say nothing about it, and in fairness, so did your mother. She said she didn't want anything to spoil your day.'

'I was really happy to hear it was all my fault,' Sophie said, 'and Tony said worse about his mother and sisters than Mummy would have dared to.' They all giggled as she elaborated further on the story. She became more serious when she brought Emily up to date, about her estranged uncle who had been revealed as her birth father. Alice already knew about it, as Sophie had visited her just after Tony had gone back to London.

'Oh, Sophie,' Emily said, shaking her head. 'You must have found all that very difficult.'

'It was,' Sophie said, 'but I've realised you just have to get over these things. It was much more difficult for Mummy ... and then poor Daddy was only trying his best, and really, I couldn't have had a better, more loving father. Everybody has difficult times.'

'I'm so sorry about all you've gone through recently with your father,' Emily said, 'and about your mother's accident.'

'It has been hard,' Sophie said, 'and I'm not making excuses, but I think with all that anger at Mummy whirling around in my head and missing Tony and everything, that I wasn't thinking straight.' Tears glistened in the corner of her eyes. 'I honestly never meant to hurt you ...'

'We've all had a difficult time.' Emily leaned over and took her hand. 'Things will get better,' she said, 'and what matters is that we're all here for each other.'

Three waitresses came towards the table now, one carrying a large teapot, and the other two carrying silver cake stands filled with finger sandwiches, scones and tiny cakes.

When they had eaten everything on the cake stands and finished three cups of tea each, Alice told the girls she was going to walk to the market, and they immediately said they would accompany her. She found the scarf stalls and, after much discussion, picked three lovely silk squares and four warm woollen scarves. They walked around the other stalls in the beautiful wrought-iron and glass-covered indoor market, and Emily got some Chorley cakes to take home, while Sophie bought a bottle of bath salts for her mother. Afterwards they walked back into the town centre.

Alice and Sophie waited with Emily at the bus stop near Mersey Square, and after waving her off, they both walked up Wellington Road together. They stopped when they reached the town hall, before separating to go off in different directions.

'I'm so relieved that things are better between me and Emily,' Sophie said, 'and I've got my fingers crossed that she's going to bring Marco up next weekend. I've asked her if he'll bring along his violin, as my mother adores classical music, and she would love to hear him play. Tony and I want to hear him, too.' She made a little face. 'Although neither of us know anything about violins.'

Alice gave her a knowing look, and they both started to giggle. 'I haven't a clue about classical music either,' she admitted, 'but Marco is a lovely chap and it's something different to look forward to.'

'It's such a pity Greg isn't here,' Sophie said. 'He would have been the expert on music, but we can have lots of lovely nights when he comes home.' She gave a little shiver and drew her blue coat around her. 'We just have to get over this last winter and get that bloody Hitler to surrender, and then things will return to normal.' She shrugged. 'Well, at least, that's what the newspapers are saying.'

'When that happens,' Alice said, 'things will certainly have changed for me. We'll have the new baby and then Philip and Gabriela will be going home.' She paused. 'I don't even want to think about it yet.'

It would also be time for Louis to go away, too – and that was something that Alice couldn't begin to imagine.

Chapter Forty

When she reached the shop, after walking up the hill, Alice felt hot and out of breath. She was also uncomfortable because she had eaten too many sandwiches and cakes, and knew she would undoubtedly suffer heartburn later.

Maeve was serving a customer, so she just smiled at Alice and nodded her head towards the house and said, 'The twins are in through the back, and Freddy has just taken Bella down to the park.'

Alice could hear music playing and then Gabriela laughing, and she guessed they were playing the music hall record again. She went down the hallway past the empty kitchen to the sitting room. 'What's all the noise about?' she called, pretending to be annoyed.

When she reached the door, she went to say something funny again, but suddenly stopped in her tracks when she saw Louis sitting at the table, playing dominoes with the twins. He lifted his head, looking over at her and smiling.

'Hello,' she said, her heart quickening. 'Is everything OK?'

'Yes,' Louis said. 'I'm afraid I was dragged in by these two.' He put his dominoes down on the table and went to stand up.

Alice waved her hand. 'Finish your game, I'm just going upstairs to change my shoes.'

'Louis took us into a cafe in Stockport, and we had fish and chips,' Philip said. 'It was lovely.'

'Good for you,' she said. 'I had lovely sandwiches and cakes with my friends, so we've all been spoiled.'

She went upstairs, wondering what had made Louis stay with the children this evening. Since they had the conversation about the baby, he hadn't come into the house unless one of the children wasn't well, or if he had to pass a message on from school or the Guernsey groups. He had still been friendly towards her, and always enquired as to how things were going with the baby, but everything about his manner was careful.

She sat down on the edge of the bed and kicked off her heeled shoes. Seeing Louis again in the house brought back memories of all the nights they had sat up late, chatting together, relaxed and happy in each other's company. Then her mind flitted to the days they had spent with the children in places like Lyme Park and Chester Zoo.

She closed her eyes and shook her head, then she made herself move to go over to the side of the wardrobe to get her comfortable, flat-heeled shoes.

When she went back downstairs, Freddy was there with the dog, chatting away to Louis about a recent football match his school had won. When he caught sight of Alice, he grinned and said, 'I'm not skiving, honestly! I was only bringing Bella back. The shop's quiet, too, there's only old Mr Baxter in chatting to Maeve.'

'I believe you, though thousands wouldn't,' Alice said lightly. She looked at Louis. 'Did you have a cup of tea?'

'No,' he said, 'but if you're making one, I'll have it before I go.'

Alice went into the kitchen and put the kettle on, and a few minutes later Freddy went past her, whistling and heading back into the shop. He had stretched in height recently and had also matured in his manner in the last six months. Things had settled at home, he had told Alice, after his father had been sent to a clinic down in Devon, which specialised in treating servicemen who were traumatised by their war experiences. He had spent six weeks there, in the rambling and tranquil grounds of the clinic, where he received various treatments and therapies to help him understand how his brain and body were reacting to all the horrors he had witnessed and experienced. He had also been given medication which relaxed him and let him sleep at night.

The specialist in the clinic had suggested that Freddy's father should take up gardening, and, with the help of his local doctor, he had been offered a share in a large allotment set up for wounded ex-servicemen who had been through similar experiences, and were understanding of his condition.

This, Freddy said, had given his father new friends, new gardening skills and a new lease of life. He also told Alice that the positive change in his father had, in turn, changed everything at home. His mother was relieved now Freddy's father was more like his old self, and she had taken a part-time job in the canteen in the local fire station, which she loved.

'Dad has said I can bring Bella back home now, if I like,' Freddy had said, 'but I think she's happier here and I can still see her every day.'

'If you're sure?'

'Definitely sure. Mam said to give Dad a bit more time, then we might even get one of Bella's pups back from the farmer.'

Alice was relieved. She loved the little dog, and, at the back of her mind, there was a fear of how quiet things would be when the twins had gone back to Guernsey, and there was only her and the baby until Greg returned.

Freddy had learned to work the till and was now serving when the shop was at its busiest on Thursday and Friday evenings and all day Saturday. He was quicker than Maeve, and he was also popular with the customers, especially the elderly ones, with whom he showed great patience, and would offer to deliver their groceries when it was quiet. At almost fourteen, he would be ready to leave school at the beginning of the next year. After Greg's letter suggesting she take on another assistant, she now wondered if Freddy would be interested in working full-time with Maeve.

Alice thought that the experience of working in a general shop – learning about orders and accounts – would be a good grounding for him if he wanted to move to one of the bigger retailers in the future. It would also be a great help to her, rather than taking on someone they didn't know. Freddy might, she knew, have his own ideas, but she would catch him soon, at some quiet moment, and put the proposition to him.

She poured the boiling water into the teapot, and got two mugs, then she stood with her back against the cooker, trying to think of anything but Louis. She sliced up a Madeira cake and put it on a plate, before pouring the tea into the mugs. She had just put the milk away when he appeared in the kitchen.

He had a serious look on his face. 'Can we talk?'

'Yes, of course,' she said. 'Is there something wrong?' She picked up one of the mugs and held it in both her hands.

'I just want to speak privately to you.' He quietly closed the door and then came to stand opposite her. 'Since I saw you this afternoon, I've been thinking about our situation. What if there was another option?'

Alice took a deep breath.

'What if you were to separate from Greg – after a decent length of time, as you had planned – and I waited for you until you were free? I could go back to Guernsey to help the children settle in at home again, and then – when you felt you were ready – I could come back to Stockport. I won't have any trouble getting a job, and I could help you to bring up the baby.' He shrugged. 'It's been done before, and I would love it the same as if it were our own.'

'Oh, Louis . . . I wish I could do that . . . I wish it were as easy as it sounds.' She put the mug down on the worktop now, as her hands were shaking.

He opened his hands. 'We could work it out,' he said. 'We would make sure Greg saw the child whenever he wanted.'

Her mind was racing now, trying to take in what he was saying and the implications his suggestions would have. 'But what about Guernsey?' she said. 'After you go back, you might decide you want to stay there.'

'I do want to go back for a while, to spend some time with

my parents and the rest of the family, but after that I'm happy to come back to Stockport. I've got used to life here, and when things are settled, you and me and the baby could go over regularly, to visit my family and the twins.'

'That's a huge step for you... a lot to ask of you.'

'I'm not the only Guernsey person thinking about staying – there are other people who are not going back,' he told her. 'One of our female teachers recently married a doctor from Manchester. Things can work out, and people do get divorced and make new lives. We could do the same.'

She looked at him. 'I don't know what to say, Louis. I just feel this vast weight on me... a huge guilt. I don't want to be one of those women who betrayed her husband while he was in a foreign place defending our country. That's not the sort of woman I want to be.'

'You've never betrayed him, Alice, we've only had one kiss. That's all.' His eyes shifted away from her. 'I never imagined that I would be one of those men who would look at another man's wife. I never imagined that I would go to bed thinking of you every night, then wake the next morning thinking of you again. That I would lie there, wondering what it would be like to run my hands through your hair or to touch your skin – to feel your body in the bed next to me.' He shook his head. 'I never imagined that I would be the sort of man who would be willing to wait all this time for the woman he loves. The only woman he's ever loved.'

An intense sensation ran through her now, as she imagined what he had just described. She pictured them kissing and caressing – entwined as physically close as a couple could be. He had now put words to all the feelings that had hung silently between them almost since the first day they met.

'If I've got this all wrong,' he said, 'assumed too much of you, then tell me now. But please be honest, Alice. You owe me that.'

Alice lifted her eyes. 'You know how I feel about you, Louis.'

'Do I?' he asked quietly.

A bittersweet feeling settled on her now because she had

imagined saying these words in different circumstance. 'I love you, too, Louis…' She paused briefly. 'But I've already explained how things are.'

'You don't need to decide tonight. Knowing you love me back is enough for now. You can take time to think about it.'

Alice shook her head sadly. 'I've taken weeks and weeks to think about it,' she said quietly, 'and I keep coming back to the same conclusion. I have to do the right thing by Greg and his baby. I won't be able to live with myself if I don't.'

Chapter Forty-One

Sophie rushed to the door, stopping for a brief moment to glance at her new hairstyle in the hall mirror as she went past. She was both excited and nervous about this night – the Friday before Christmas – as she would meet Marco for the first time. It had been postponed from November, as Tony's leave was unexpectedly cancelled on the previously planned weekend, and this was the first available weekend when all three friends were free. Alice was busy with Christmas orders in the shop, Emily was organising school concerts and carol services, and Marco was tied up with choir practice and events.

Sophie pulled back the blackout curtains and opened the door to find Alice there with Emily and Marco, all wrapped in coats and scarves against the frosty night. 'Did you all come on the same bus?' she asked.

Alice stepped in first, giving Sophie a hug, saying, 'Yes, I got on at the town hall and Emily and Marco were already on the bus.' Alice then moved down the dimly lit hallway to allow space for Emily to introduce Sophie and Marco.

Sophie closed the curtains to keep both the light and the cold air out, and then she took the coats and outdoor things to hang on the stand, placing Marco's violin case in a safe corner. She then led them down into the sitting room, which had a sparkling Christmas tree in one corner, and branches of holly and ivy decorating the mantelpiece and draped over the pictures.

Tony, Dorothy, and Frances and her husband Len were already there, so Sophie introduced everyone to Marco. Extra chairs had been brought in from the dining room to ensure everyone found a seat, and when they were all comfortable, a smart-looking Tony went around with glasses of sherry. Within minutes there was a hum of mixed conversations in the room. Tony went to sit beside Emily and Marco, curious as to which part of Italy Marco was from, while Dorothy brought Alice over to sit in one of the armchairs by the fire, next to Frances and Len.

Everyone was dressed up for the evening, the men in smart suits or sports jackets with ties and pocket handkerchiefs. Dorothy and Frances were wearing their long evening gowns, which they had bought in Manchester the Christmas before the war began, and had worn every year since with glittering necklaces and bracelets. Sophie was undoubtedly the most glamorous in a strapless, black with floral-print organza dress, which showed off her tall, willowy figure, and the women all complimented her hair. Her blonde curls had been straightened by the hairdresser that afternoon, then swept up in a glamorous style and held in place by a large pearl encrusted clasp.

Emily wore a more demure, mid-length turquoise dress with three-quarter sleeves, a winged collar and a thin belt cinching her tiny waist. When Sophie complimented the dress and the matching hairband, Emily explained that her mother had recently dug out her sewing machine and found bags of material which had been up in the attic for several years, and had started making things again. The turquoise satin had been a wonderful find, and her mother had spent a week making the dress, with Emily helping hand-stitch the hems.

Emily did not mention that her mother had also altered the smart dark suit that Marco was wearing, which had been a new one bought for Jack before he went away. He was also wearing the white shirt the Brownes had bought him, with a navy tie, and a navy handkerchief with yellow polka-dots in his top pocket, which Hannah Browne had also made for him.

Alice was wearing a pale blue and cream, maternity smock-style jacket with a soft bow at the neck over a plain blue dress.

'You look absolutely blooming,' Dorothy told her. 'Have we long to go now?'

'Early March,' Alice said. She patted her bulging tummy. 'It can't come soon enough. It's awful trying to find fancy maternity clothes, so I only have two decent outfits for Christmas. It's not so bad at home as I can cover everything with my shop overalls.' She laughed and shook her head. 'I've cut the zip out of some skirts and extended them with elastic, but they are now becoming too tight as well.'

After a while Sophie and her mother left the guests chatting, going down to the kitchen to put the trays of tiny sausage rolls and vol-au-vents, and other little canapes that Mrs Wilson had made that afternoon, into the oven to warm them again.

She had made several new dishes, which she had found in an Italian cookery book she borrowed from Stockport Library – small meatballs in a tomato paste, a flatbread she had baked with grated cheese and slices of tomato and mushroom, which had then been put under the grill and cut into bite-sized pieces. She had made a second similar flatbread, topped with tiny slices of olives and onions. Mrs Wilson had said how much she enjoyed experimenting with the canapes, and was delighted that most of the ingredients were easily found, and that she could stretch their cheese and egg rations to such great effect.

After placing the pastry items in the oven, they took the damp dishtowels off the trays of finger sandwiches and pinwheel sandwiches, which Mrs Wilson had created using the minimum of ingredients. Sophie carried the cold plates up to the dining room, where they had bottles of red and white wine on the table to accompany the meal.

When they went back down to the kitchen for the hot dishes, Dorothy turned to Sophie. 'Are you happy with the way things are going with your evening?'

'Yes, I think it's fine, so far,' Sophie said, with a hint of caution in her voice. 'Everyone seems relaxed and they're all mixing well.'

Dorothy put her hand on Sophie's shoulder. 'You've done very well for your first time as a proper hostess. Your father would have been proud of you.'

'Thank you.' There was a little pause. 'Talking of fathers, have you given any more thought to David's letter?'

Dorothy gave a sigh. 'I'm still not sure about meeting up with him in Manchester. I do think you should go, but I don't know if I could face it... I wouldn't know what to say to him after all these years.'

'We have a week before he comes up,' Sophie said, 'and if you decide not to, Tony will come with me.' She shrugged. 'I'm not as worried about it as I would have imagined. Since receiving his letters, I feel he's actually more anxious than me.'

'Did you mention about meeting him to Emily and Alice?'

'Yes,' Sophie said. 'They think if I feel OK about it, then I should go ahead. I'm just going to take things as they come. Besides, we have enough to think about with the future of the factory hanging over our heads.'

'We'll get through,' her mother said, 'and at least we've managed without cutting any staff before Christmas. You never know what's around the corner,' she smiled. 'We thought things were hopeless when the king made the official announcement about the stand-down of the Home Guard, and then within days we received the big order from the railway offices. That should keep us going for a few months, and hopefully, when things settle down after the war, your idea of moving into ladies' hats sounds worth exploring.'

Sophie's eyes lit up. 'I'm quite excited about it,' she said. 'It's something that you and I would really be able to throw ourselves into because we both love hats. I thought I would start a scrapbook over Christmas, collecting ideas from magazines, and I've already done a few sketches of new designs. The sort of styles I've seen in photographs but never see in the shops.'

'I was actually thinking that we might be able to use some of the leftover military materials for winter hats for ladies. We could just change the design a little and add some extra details to make them more feminine.'

'Sounds great,' Sophie said. 'It's something to look forward to for 1945.'

'That, and hopefully the end of the war.' Dorothy went over to the oven and took out the tray with Mrs Wilson's sausage rolls, setting it down on the worktop. 'We can put these straight onto the platters now and take them up to the dining room.' She lifted out the tray of meatballs and the flatbread. 'I do hope Marco likes these little canapes. Edna was very pleased with herself, finding an Italian cookery book.'

'I'm sure he will love them,' Sophie said. 'They look lovely.'

Her mother smiled and said, 'Marco is a real hit with everyone, isn't he? What a lovely, friendly man ... and very handsome, too, just perfect for Emily. They look such a striking couple together, don't they?'

'They really do,' Sophie said.

'He and Tony have really hit it off. I can imagine in normal times they would have been terrific friends.' She shook her head. 'It's just terrible to think the poor man has spent the last three or four years of his life locked up in a prison camp. Now we've heard a bit about him and his background, it makes you wonder about all the other souls who are there, who were forced into joining the army.'

Sophie bit her lip. 'I feel awful for saying all those things about Marco before meeting him. I had no idea what I was talking about, and I've learned a lesson, about waiting until I know all the facts before giving my opinion. I should have given Emily the benefit of the doubt. I should have known she would only pick someone who was nice and thoroughly decent.'

'Hopefully, it will work out for them,' Dorothy said. 'If they get through this difficult time, then when the war ends, things should be easier for them.' She rubbed Sophie's arm. 'You did the right thing inviting them here tonight, and Emily seems to have got over it.'

When the platters of food were all laid out on a buffet table to the side of the room, Sophie invited everyone into the dining room to pick up plates and take whatever they wanted from the selection. Tony filled glasses with red and white wine, and the guests chose which they preferred then took their plates and glasses to sit at a place at the dining table. As she had hoped, Marco was surprised and delighted to see the familiar food.

'Pizza!' he said, lifting a slice of the baked flattened bread and cheese. 'Bella pizza! Beautiful pizza!' He thanked Dorothy and Sophie profusely, giving them a little bow, and then went on to explain the origins of the bread, and how the one Mrs Wilson had baked with cheese, tomatoes and basil was called a Margherita pizza, named after a queen who had visited Naples. The monarch had been presented with a variety of pizzas, and that particular one had been her favourite. He was just launching into an enthusiastic discussion about the meatballs when Emily laughingly nudged him, and suggested they should sit down and actually eat them.

Afterwards, everyone went back into the sitting room and after glasses were refilled, Sophie asked Marco if it was a good time for him to play a little music. He went out to the hallway, and spent a few minutes tuning his violin, and then he came back into the room and started to play.

The next half an hour passed in total silence as everyone sat riveted listening, then afterwards the room was filled with excited chatter as Marco was both praised and inundated with requests for music that the guests wanted him to play. He performed for another half an hour, and then Dorothy suggested to the others that Marco should have a rest, and Sophie and Tony went to put some lively music on the radiogram. After several drinks, everyone was in high spirits and the chairs were pushed back, then Frances led Len into the middle of the floor to dance to 'Don't Sit Under the Apple Tree', and was followed by Tony and Sophie, then Marco and Emily. By the end of the night, both Dorothy and Alice had taken their turn dancing with the men to The Ink Spots and Glenn Miller.

It was around half past ten when Emily drew Sophie aside to say that she was sorry, but she and Marco had to go. 'He usually has to be back at the camp for ten o'clock,' she explained, 'but the guards are more easy-going since it is Christmas. His bike is at Barlow's shop, so when we get off the bus, he'll collect it and walk me home, then he'll cycle back to the camp.' She then hugged Sophie and said they'd had a lovely night, and that Marco thought they were all wonderful people. 'It was so kind of you and your mother to have made such an effort with the Italian food for Marco. It meant the world to him, and I won't forget it either.'

Tears came to Sophie's eyes. 'I'm so sorry for the way I was before...'

Emily smiled and put her arms around her friend. 'It's long forgotten,' she said. 'We're still best friends, and that's all that matters.'

Chapter Forty-Two

Just after New Year, Sophie arranged to visit Alice on her way back from Manchester, and Alice suggested that she have tea with her and the twins.

'I'll send Philip and Gabriela out for fish and chips when you arrive,' Alice said. 'It's always a great treat for them, and it will give us a chance to catch up while they're gone.'

Like everyone else in the area, the first thing they talked about was the awful bombing that had happened in Manchester on Christmas Eve. Around fifteen bombs had hit parts of Greater Manchester, and one had landed closer to home in the Stockport area. Oldham had been hit severely, with twenty-seven people killed as they slept, and almost fifty people injured.

'One of my regular customers lost her brother in the Oldham bombing,' Alice said, 'and it's had a terrible effect on their whole family.'

'That's so sad,' Sophie said, shaking her head. 'We're both lucky that the bomb that dropped in Stockport wasn't near our homes. It was near Davenport golf club, and it killed one of the poor people in the nearby houses.'

'It certainly was a bad one and did a lot of damage to the area. The blast was so strong that some of the shops in Edgeley had their windows blown in.' She sighed. 'It's unbelievable that Manchester would get hit for the second time at Christmas. Thankfully it's not as bad as the 1940 blitz, but bad enough for anyone involved.'

Sophie then went on to tell Alice that the meeting with her real father in Manchester that afternoon had gone well. She had immediately liked David Morley, and after all the initial talk about their current lives, she had listened to his side of how things had happened between him and her mother.

'It was actually very sad,' she explained. 'When he went back down to London to break his engagement off, he discovered that his fiancée was very sick, and had just been diagnosed with a serious kidney disorder – so he decided to wait until she recovered to tell her. Then, her uncle in New York found out that there was a new treatment out there, and he offered to pay for everything for her. Before David realised, the family had organised a quick wedding for them so he could go with her. The uncle was very generous, and he set up an apartment for them, where they could stay indefinitely. From what he had gleaned from the doctors, the treatment was not a cure, and would only prolong his wife's life for a while longer. There was no one else to go to America with her, and he felt he couldn't let her down.'

Sophie then explained how her mother had moved away and David no longer had her address. While he was in America and still trying to contact her, he discovered from a family member that George had got married and was shocked to discover it was to Dorothy.

'My father, George, then refused to answer any letters David sent, and apparently never told my mother about them.'

'How do you feel about it all now?' Alice asked.

'I have thought about it over and over – and recently Mummy and I spent a whole night talking about it again. The truth is, after he heard David's wife had died in America, Daddy was terrified that his brother would come back to Manchester and take Mummy and me away from him.' Sophie gave a little sigh. 'It's sad to think he was so insecure, and Mummy said that would never have happened because she wouldn't have trusted David again, and she had grown to love Daddy very much, so would never have left him. The way it turned out was just meant to be.'

'It does sound like that...'

'I wouldn't change my childhood,' Sophie said emphatically. 'I loved Daddy with all my heart, and nothing will ever change that. As far as I'm concerned, he was my true father.'

'Of course he was,' Alice said gently. She paused then asked, 'Do you think you will see David again?'

'Probably in a few months' time,' Sophie told her. 'I'm hoping Mummy will come with me. I think if she met him, it would help her to understand what happened all those years ago.' She paused. 'You won't believe this, but David told me he never forgot Mummy, and that he's never loved anyone the way he loved her. He never remarried because of that.'

Alice caught her breath. 'It's hard to imagine that, after all these years.'

'It was strange hearing it – but I could tell that he meant every word.' She raised her eyebrows. 'I've no idea what Mummy feels about him deep down, and it's not my business, but she will never know if she doesn't meet him again.'

After Sophie left, Alice thought over what her friend had said, and wondered at all those years having passed and David Morley's feelings still remaining the same.

She wondered then what things would be like when Greg came home. She found it hard to imagine them together again – and with the baby. He felt like a distant stranger to her now.

Louis called to the shop around eleven o'clock on a Saturday in the middle of January – the first day that snow lay deep on the cobbled streets. The vicar had loaned him two wooden sledges, which he had dragged all the way down to Edgeley, to take Philip and Gabriela to the nearby park which had small hills, perfect for sleighing.

Alice had seen little of him over Christmas, as she and the twins had gone over to Altrincham to stay with her parents, from Christmas Eve until the day after Boxing Day, while Louis had spent the main festive days at the vicarage. She had received an Italian Christmas card and a letter from Greg saying that the scarves and presents she had sent were perfect. The family had also sent their thanks and warm wishes for the festive season to her.

Since then, things had settled back into a routine, and the children were now back at school. Freddy had been delighted with her offer of full-time work, and had been allowed to leave school after Christmas as it was only a matter of weeks until his fourteenth birthday.

He took over all the early shifts in the morning, wearing his new, slightly too big, brown shop coat, which had two sharpened pencils in the top pocket, so he never wasted time if one broke when he was serving a customer. He also encouraged the heavily pregnant Alice to lie in each morning, and only come down when she felt up to it.

'You won't get too many lie-ins when the baby comes,' he said, as though an expert on the subject. When she did come down, he had everything displayed outside, newspapers organised, and all the morning deliveries stacked on shelves by the time she arrived.

Alice felt that things were going well, so long as she didn't look too far into the future. The twins were settled and happy, and both doing well in school, and the shop was doing as fine as any local business considering the wartime conditions.

Louis waited in the shop, chatting to Freddy, until the twins came out in wellington boots and well wrapped up in scarves and hats and gloves, and then they set off to the park. When Freddy went in to serve a customer, Alice spoke to Louis for a few minutes, sticking to light, general subjects and avoiding any real eye contact with him. Then she stood at the shop doorway and watched as the twins ran on ahead of him, pulling the sledges behind them.

The sun was bright, making the snowy ground and the white trees sparkle – and Alice thought it was the sort of scene you would see in a painting. As they disappeared down the hill which led to the park, it suddenly struck her that this would probably be the one and only time she would see them in this wintry setting. If the war ended in the summer – as everyone predicted – all three would have gone back to Guernsey to their old lives. She could not imagine a reason that would bring them back any time in the foreseeable future.

The thought of all that loss brought an ache to her chest.

A blue van came slowly down the cobbled street, with a delivery of tins of corned beef and ham, and various tinned vegetables, and she went inside to let Freddy know, so they could make room on the shelves for them. A short while later, as Alice was stacking butter beans and peas, the postman arrived with two letters – one in a brown envelope and the other in a white one, which she immediately recognised was from Greg.

She put them to the side, and then when it was time to make tea, she slid them into her apron pocket and went down to the kitchen. She put the kettle on the gas ring and got out the mugs and milk and sugar.

When she took Freddy's tea through to him, he said, 'I don't mean to be cheeky, like, but you look a bit tired this morning. Why don't you go into the house and put your feet up while it's quiet?' He then puffed his chest out a little. 'There's nothing here that I can't handle, and Maeve will be in this afternoon to give me a hand.'

Alice went off with her letters, trying to hide the amused smile.

She sat down on the sofa and put her tea and two digestive biscuits on the coffee table, then she opened the brown envelope to find it was an appointment at the antenatal clinic for the following week. After the first few months of morning sickness, she'd had a very good pregnancy and so far, everything was on track for a normal birth. It was now just a matter of getting through the next couple of months until the baby arrived.

She took a drink of her tea and ate one of the biscuits, and then she lifted the letter with the Italian postmark and slid her thumb under the sealed part at the back, taking out two thin sheets of paper.

She took another mouthful of tea and then unfolded the paper and started to read.

My Dearest Alice,

This is the most difficult letter I have ever had to write.

I will start off by saying that I hope all is well with you and the child. Whatever happens, believe me, I care deeply about you now, and will always care about you in the future.

The time has come, and I realise I now must be honest with you. I have been forced to make the biggest decision of my life - one which has cost me much thought and pain - but it is the right and decent thing to do.

The truth is that during my time in Italy, I have fallen in love with another woman. It is not something I wanted to happen and believe me, I fought very hard against it. But it has happened, and the circumstances mean that I need to commit to this person - Mariagrazia - and to her family.

This is the family who I have been billeted with, and they have been more than kind to me. Mariagrazia is their oldest daughter, and although she is some years younger than me, we have grown to be very close. Whilst I was sick, she tended to me, and helped me learn the Italian language, and during that time we discovered we had feelings for each other, which have since turned to love.

I have to stress that this is not a casual fling (unlike the silly and regretful mistake I made earlier in our marriage). I know the difference now and would never have put you through that again.

The position now is that Mariagrazia is due to have a child in May, and I intend to stay on in Italy when the war is eventually over. Not only does she need me, but her whole family do. You have no idea what these people have been through, and I feel if I can help them in any way, then it is the right thing to do. It may sound strange, but something about the country and the people has drawn me in, and I feel as if destiny brought me here to do something worthwhile.

I am so sorry as I know this news will probably shock and upset you very much, Alice, but in truth, my relationship with Maria had already been formed by the time I received your letter telling me about the child you are expecting.

I realise this is an awful, awful mess and I take full responsibility for it, but I know that my heart and soul are now here in Italy. If I came back to Stockport, I would be unhappy and unsettled – which would be grossly unfair to you and the child.

In order to compensate in some way for the effect all this will have on you, I intend to sign over the deeds to my mother's house for you and the child, and also the business. It's no less than you deserve and what my mother would have wanted for you and her grandchild. I can manage on what I have received from my uncle's estate, and it will go further here in Naples than it would in England.

You must do what you see fit with the shop – continue to run it or sell it. Do what your heart tells you and think only of yourself. I do hope you will go back to teaching as I always felt guilt that you had to sacrifice your career for the shop when my mother died.

I will finish off by stating again, I never wanted to hurt you, and that I do care deeply about you, and always will.

With great respect and care,

Greg

Alice put the letter down on the sofa beside her. She took several deep, shuddering breaths and then she looked over towards the window where she could see the glistening white rooftop of the houses opposite. She stared out for a while, attempting to take in the details of everything that Greg had written, and then she picked the pages up and this time she read it through again, much more slowly.

This was the last thing she expected to hear from Greg. It was a situation she could never have envisaged, especially at this time. And yet, when she thought about it, when was the right time? He had waited until Christmas was over to write, not to spoil the festive celebrations. Should he have waited until the baby was born? Or until the war was over? Alice realised now that the ever-movable feast of *the end of the war* could carry on infinitely. They had been waiting for it to end for almost five years now, with many people putting their lives on hold until it was all over.

There was, of course, another date, which had obviously made Greg move quicker. The date that his child with this Mariagrazia would be born. She realised now that he wanted to have everything sorted out and above board by the time his Italian baby came. This was the reason, she now knew, why he had been so reticent in his letters, the reason he had been vague about the older children, in order not to arouse any questions about him living in the same house as a young woman. Alice now ran over the scant information about the girl and realised that she was probably the one who was the talented pianist, and the one who he had been teaching English. Probably seated under a tree in a sunny spot, in the rambling garden of the big old house he had described, a glass of Italian wine in his hand. She could picture the romantic scene clearly in her mind, and could now see where everything fell into place, like one of the jigsaw puzzles the twins enjoyed so much. This relationship – with the exotically named Mariagrazia – had obviously been the root of the euphoria that Greg now felt for all things Italian. So much so, he was going to make this foreign, war-damaged country his new home.

While she had been preparing to invest her future into making a good family life for her and the baby and Greg, she realised now that he was already settled and had made his own plans for when the war ended. And in that new sunny, Italian future of his, there was no place for her and their baby.

Whilst she was undoubtedly shocked by his letter – and was still working out all the ramifications – a new feeling began to settle over her. A feeling she recognised as relief. A feeling that her world was opening up again. Alice realised that she was free. She had choices that she alone could make, without considering Greg anymore.

And as those realisations settled on her – and new hopes began to rise – they were suddenly tinged with a cold fear. What if she had left it too late?

She walked over to the window and looked out on the street, where the hardened snow was now showing signs of being trampled down by footprints. There was no sign of a thaw coming, and the weather reports were predicting another heavy snowfall that night. She stood for a while, gazing ahead at nothing in particular, when out of the corner of her eye, she saw the three figures coming up the hill, pulling the sledges behind them.

She watched until they disappeared out of sight, and then she smiled and walked out into the hallway and down towards the shop door. The twins were already inside, laughing and telling Freddy all about their tobogganing adventures, whilst he was joking with them and telling them not to dirty his clean floor.

Philip rushed over to Alice and said, 'Can me and Gabriela

397

go down to Smith's garden for a while? James and Sally have asked us to help them build a snowman.'

'Go on,' she said, smiling. 'I'll have some tomato soup ready for you when you come back.' She was glad that the twins – Philip especially – had recently made friends with some of the local children. He still loved his books and board games, but she liked to see him out and about in the fresh air.

As they rushed out of the door, Louis said, 'Is it OK if I leave the sledges in the shed? The vicar said they can have them for a few more days, and they can take them out whenever they want without waiting for me.'

'Of course,' Alice said, smiling at him. 'You can bring them through the back entry now. I'll get the key from the kitchen and meet you.' She looked over at Freddy. 'Are you OK here on your own for a little while?'

'No problem,' Freddy said. 'I'm just going to get a dry mop and wipe over the marks on the floor.'

When Alice came out the back door with the key, Louis was waiting with the sledges. He smiled at her and said, 'Freddy seems to be doing well in the shop – he looked very officious there wielding the mop.'

Alice laughed and shook her head. 'He's marvellous,' she said. 'Taking him on is the best thing I ever did.' She stood while he sorted the sledges, and then she looked at him. 'Will you come inside for a few minutes? I have something to show you.'

'Is there something wrong?' he asked.

'No, I don't think anything is wrong. In fact, it might well be the opposite.'

They went into the sitting room and Alice gave Louis the letter while she moved towards the kitchen to make fresh tea. She had only gone a few steps when she stopped in her tracks, and went into the dining room instead, to the cupboard that held the drinks, and took out the brandy bottle and two glasses. She poured out a good measure for Louis and a tiny one for herself, which she topped up with lemonade.

When she went back into the sitting room he was still staring down at the pages. 'It came after you left to go to the park,' Alice said.

Louis eventually lifted his head and looked over at her. 'What does it mean?' he said quietly.

'It means that I am free,' Alice said. 'It means that if the offer you made still stands, that I am now free to take you up on it.'

Louis's eyes widened. 'But you've only just found out about Greg...' His voice was hesitant. 'Don't you need time to think this all through?'

Alice noticed the look on his face and her heart began to sink. She suddenly had the awful feeling that she had misjudged things. That in her determination to do the right thing by Greg, she had made Louis feel that he did not feature in any of her plans. 'Have I got this horribly wrong?' she said in a fearful whisper.

He took a deep breath. 'I'm afraid you are jumping the gun,' he said, 'just because Greg has found someone else for now. What if that changed? He's still the baby's father...' His voice tailed off now, as though he couldn't find the right words.

She heard the uncertainty in his tone, and she realised that she had put him through even more than she had imagined. What if he could not trust her feelings again? The fear of losing him now propelled her on. 'I don't need to think about it.' Her voice was strong and clear. 'Being with you is exactly what I want. It's what I've dreamed of for a long time, but there didn't seem any way to make it happen. Greg's letter is like a miracle to me. It absolves me of any obligations to him or our marriage.' She shook her head. 'You have no idea how relieved cutting all ties with him makes me feel. And believe me, if I did not love you as much as I do, the last thing I would want is to jump the gun with another man. If I had not met you, the chances are I would be on my own for the rest of my life.' She reached out and touched his hand. 'I would never meet another man like you again, and I'm not going to let you slip away.'

His hand came to cover hers. 'Are you really, really sure?'

'Absolutely,' Alice said. 'Are you?'

He took a deep breath. 'If you are a hundred per cent sure, then I'll be there with you, every minute of the way.' He drew her into him now and kissed the top of her head.

'Thank you,' Alice said, her voice muffled with emotion. 'I know it's not going to be easy, and we will have a lot of things to work out. The baby is due in a few months, and that is going to bring a massive change in my life, then I'm going to have to go through all the legal proceedings for a divorce.'

'We'll do it together.'

'Thank you,' Alice said. 'It's lovely to hear that, but I won't lean too heavily on you. If we hadn't met, I would've had to face this on my own, and surprisingly, I know I would manage – that I would be OK.'

'You are the strongest and most capable woman I've ever met,' Louis said, 'and it's one of the many things I love about you. Look how easily you coped with having the twins at a moment's notice.'

'And Bella,' Alice said, smiling and rolling her eyes.

'And Bella,' he said, smiling as well. 'And how you so easily switched from teaching to running a shop. How many people could do that?'

Alice became serious again. 'It will be a big change for you,' she said quietly. 'Your plans about going back to Guernsey...'

'It's not a million miles away,' he said. 'And we can visit regularly. Stockport is my home now.'

'There will be some people who may not approve of us,' she said. 'Who won't like the idea of me getting divorced, and think that Greg and I should have stuck things out, for the sake of the baby...'

'People can think what they want, it's our business.'

Alice thought about the opposition that Emily faced with Marco, and how upset Sophie had been when her mother didn't approve of Tony. And yet, in both circumstances, things had settled down, and life was just carrying on.

'I wonder how Emily will react when she realises there was more than friendship between us?' she said. 'She will be more than a little surprised, as I have never mentioned it to her or Sophie.'

'I don't know Sophie,' Louis said, 'but I am sure Emily will understand. She's your friend and will only want you to be happy.'

'You're right,' Alice said. 'Emily and Sophie will be happy for me. The people who matter will understand.'

Louis got to his feet and took her in his arms. 'I can't believe it,' he said, drawing her close to him. 'I can't believe this is actually happening.' He kissed her hair and then her face, and then he kissed her lips. 'I love you so much, Alice,' he said, 'and I had almost given up on us. I thought it had all come to an end.'

'I love you, too,' she whispered, 'and thankfully there is no ending. Today is only the start – the beginning of the rest of our lives together.'

Acknowledgements

A warm thank you to all the staff at Orion Publishers who were involved in the editing and publishing of *The Stockport Girls*.

I would also like to acknowledge the kind help received from Lewis and Jean Wilkinson, regarding life during WW2, and especially the link with Italy which sparked the setting in Naples.

Thanks also to their lovely daughter, Clare Dunne, for introducing me to her parents.

Thanks also to Rupert Battersby for corresponding with me, with regards to information about the history of the Battersby family hat-making business in Stockport.

Thanks to the staff at the Tyrone Guthrie Centre in Monaghan, for looking after me so well on my frequent visits.

Loving thanks to Mum and Dad for all their encouragement of my writing, and I miss Mum's proof-reading of my books which she did up until she no longer able to.

As always, thanks to my beloved Chris and Clare for all their support in my writing.

And a final acknowledgement with much love to my other half, Mike Brosnahan, who makes all this possible by being there with me when ever needed.

Credits

Orion Fiction would like to thank everyone at Orion who worked on the publication of *The Stockport Girls* in the UK.

Editorial
Rhea Kurien
Sanah Ahmed

Copyeditor
Amanda Rutter

Proofreader
Clare Wallis

Contracts
Anne Goddard
Humayra Ahmed
Ellie Bowker

Marketing
Lucy Cameron

Design
Debbie Holmes
Joanna Ridley
Nick May

Editorial Management
Charlie Panayiotou
Jane Hughes
Bartley Shaw
Tamara Morriss

Finance
Jasdip Nandra
Afeera Ahmed
Elizabeth Beaumont
Sue Baker

Sales
Jen Wilson
Esther Waters
Victoria Laws
Rachael Hum
Anna Egelstaff
Frances Doyle
Georgina Cutler

Don't miss Lilly Robbins' heartwarming world war II saga of friendship and hope in the face of adversity...

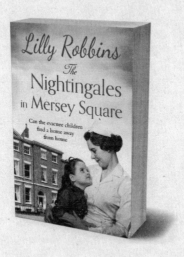

Can friendship save them in their time of need?

1940: When trainee nurses Clare and Gaye, alongside their new friend Diana discover that the war is forcing the mothers and children of Guernsey to seek safety in Stockport they immediately volunteer.

Yet, they each has their own troubles to face: Clare misses her family in Ireland, while Diana struggles to find her place in the parachute factory. And Gaye must hide a secret that could tear her family apart...

With the danger of war coming ever closer, it is their friendship and determination that will see them and the children in their care through. But can the girls and the evacuee families make a home in Mersey Square?